Praise for Michelle Willingham

"Two wounded souls find hope and redemption in *Surrender to an Irish Warrior*, a richly detailed and emotionally intense medieval romance."

—*Chicago Tribune*

"Using lots of emotion, *Seduced by Her Highland Warrior* is sure to touch your heart and soul with the tenderness and love that shines from the pages. Michelle Willingham has penned another winner."

—4.5 stars, CataRomance.com

"Michelle Willingham writes characters that feel all too real to me. The tortured soul that is Kieran really pulled at my heartstrings. And Iseult's unfailing search for her lost child made this book a truly emotional read."

—*Publishers Weekly* on *Her Warrior Slave*

"Willingham successfully draws readers into an emotional and atmospheric new tale of the Clan MacKinloch. Allowing a gentle heroine to tame a hero who has lost his ability to speak draws readers into the story and keeps them enthralled to the very end. Well-crafted, brimming with historical details and romantic from beginning to end, this is Willingham at her best."

—4 stars, *RT Book Reviews* on *Tempted by the Highland Warrior*

"Willingham neatly folds equal measures of danger and desire into her latest historical, and the snippets from Emily's cookbook that open each chapter add an extra dash of culinary spice to her well-crafted romance."

— *Booklist* on *The Accidental Countess*

Also by Michelle Willingham

Undone
by the
Duke

A SECRETS IN SILK NOVEL

MICHELLE
WILLINGHAM

Montlake
Romance

Published by Montlake Romance
P.O. Box 400818
Las Vegas, NV 89140

ISBN-13: 9781611098839
ISBN-10: 1611098831

To Charlie, for being such a wonderful father-in-law. You read all of my books, encouraged me, and I was truly blessed to have you in my life. I'll always remember your kindness and love. Rest in peace, Dad.

Prologue

BALLALOCH, SCOTLAND

DECEMBER 1810

Jonathan Nottoway, the fourth Duke of Worthingstone, was staring down the barrel of a gun.

He supposed he ought to be feeling fear or even a sense of impending doom. Instead, Fate had a way of mocking him. His attacker wasn't a seasoned killer or a disgruntled tenant. No, he had the damnably bad luck to be threatened by a boy who wasn't even old enough to shave.

"Put the weapon down," he ordered. "You don't want to shoot me."

"Yes, I do." Anguish lined the boy's face, along with a single-minded purpose. "It's your fault. All of it."

The boy's hands started shaking, and Jonathan tried to take a step back. The gun would go off if his finger tightened even a fraction.

"And what, precisely, am I accused of?" He spoke softly, as if soothing a wounded animal. Glancing around, he saw none of his servants nearby. Not his groom or even a blessed footman. He supposed it was his own fault for snarling at them this morning to leave him the hell alone. They'd done just that.

The outside temperature was growing colder, and a few fat snowflakes fluttered from the sky. Jonathan had tethered his horse back near the frozen stream, so he didn't even have the option of riding away.

"You know what you've done," the boy spat. "Burned our homes and murdered the others."

Though Jonathan was aware of the Highland evictions, with landowners forcing the Scots out of their homes, he'd had nothing to do with that. His reasons for being in Scotland were purely financial. After acquiring this land a year ago, he'd come to inspect the crumbling house that went with it.

Now it was perfectly clear why land stewards were meant to handle such details.

"I'm not the one who set your home on fire," Jonathan said. "And I've killed no one."

"Your men did," the boy insisted. He raised the gun to Jonathan's chest. "When you're dead, the burnings will stop."

"I'm not certain who you think I am," he said to the boy, "but I can assure you, you have the wrong man."

"You're the Earl of Strathland," the boy said, his eyes brimming up with tears. "And because of you, my mother was burned."

"I am not the earl," Jonathan began. "You've made a mistake. I only came to—"

His words broke off when the gun fired.

Chapter One

THREE DAYS EARLIER

Victoria Andrews knelt at her sister's feet, her mouth full of pins. With a careful eye, she judged that the hem was exactly the right length.

"Is it finished yet?" Amelia complained. "I've been standing here for *years*."

Victoria pulled another pin from her mouth, ignoring her sister's theatrics. "Hold still. Just a few more stitches."

The morning gown had belonged to their sister Margaret once, but with the help of some new fabric, Victoria had completely remade the skirt and bodice. She'd stitched delicate strips of blue silk to yards of white muslin, so as to give the illusion of a striped fabric. The fitted waist emphasized the girlish lines of Amelia's figure in the latest style.

"Should we lower the neckline?" Amelia suggested. "It seems a bit prim."

"It's a day dress, not an evening gown." The curved neckline exposed a good portion of Amelia's throat, and the long sleeves with vandyked cuffs provided an air of modesty. As a last touch, Victoria had made pink roses from a tired pair of satin gloves and fastened the flowers to the waist.

Her sister preened in front of the dressing mirror, scooping her brown curls into a more formal arrangement on her head. "Toria, it's wonderful. I can't believe how lovely it is." With a delighted smile, Amelia threw her arms around her.

Victoria basked in the warm hug. "Happy Birthday."

"I'll wear it when I pay calls with Mother." Amelia brimmed with excitement, twirling around. Her sister was more than eager to leave Scotland for London, even if it was only to visit Aunt Charlotte for Christmas.

"And perhaps when I arrive, I'll become best friends with the sister of a handsome earl or . . . even a duke! He might see me at a distance . . . and fall in love."

Her voice grew hushed, and Victoria hid her amusement at Amelia's dramatics. "You're sixteen and not old enough to marry."

"Oh, I know *that*." Amelia shrugged. "But he can pine for a few years." Her face brightened with a sudden thought. "You might find a husband, too."

When Victoria didn't respond, her sister's face fell. "You *are* coming to London, aren't you?" To Amelia, the idea of remaining secluded at home was like cutting off all her hair— unthinkable.

Truthfully, Victoria was perfectly content to remain within these four walls. Although they had lived in England for most of her life, the last five years had been spent in the western Highlands. Scotland had become her new home, although every time she looked out the window, the gnarled mountains reminded her of how stark and isolated this land was. In the distance, the snowcapped peak of Ben Nevis towered over the hills like a benevolent grandfather.

"I can't go with you," she told Amelia. "But you'll give Aunt Charlotte my best, won't you?"

"Toria." Amelia held on to her, not bothering to hide her dismay. "You can't stay inside this house forever. It's not right."

"You needn't worry about me." She smoothed an invisible wrinkle on Amelia's gown. "Mrs. Larson and Mr. MacKinloch will keep me company while you're away."

Her sister stepped back to look at her, a worried expression on her face. "Don't you . . . want to find a husband?" she asked softly. "Or have children one day?"

Victoria said nothing. The unbidden tears heated her eyelids, and she stared down at the floor. Of course she wanted that. She wanted a normal life, more than anything. But after so many years of living with fear, the possibility had stretched into an unreachable dream.

"You never leave this house," Amelia continued, "and I don't know what you're afraid of."

"I can't explain it. But it's impossible for me." Each time she drew close to the front door, her insides twisted into knots. She couldn't stop shaking, and the air choked off in her lungs until she couldn't breathe.

"I wish I could go," Victoria whispered. "But it's better if you travel without me." She couldn't stop the physical overreaction, no matter how many times she'd tried to walk out into the garden.

Their hundred-year-old house had cozy rooms and polished oak floors that creaked. Made of stone, it sat atop a small hillside, overlooking fields of gorse and heather. The road leading from the house curved down toward rows of makeshift tents erected by the Highland refugees. Dozens of men and women had been evicted a few weeks ago, and her mother had allowed them to take shelter here. Victoria often watched the people, wondering about how they lived and whether they were all right. But not once had she spoken with them. Though she loved her home, it was also her prison.

For she hadn't gone outside in five years.

Victoria helped her sister out of the gown, and Amelia pleaded, "Will you unlace me, just a little? It itches dreadfully."

Her sister's stays were drawn tight, and the chemise was made of a rough cotton that wasn't entirely pleasant against the skin. Victoria loosened the laces, all the while studying the construction of the corset. It was functional, with no embroidery, and made from little more than whalebone, buckram, and a steel busk.

Amelia sighed with relief as she scratched her skin. "I've heard there are women in London who don't wear stays at all. Can you imagine?"

"No, I can't." Though her own figure was slender enough that she could wear short stays instead of the longer ones, the idea of wearing only a draped gown with nothing beneath the bodice was scandalizing. "Our mother would never allow it."

"No, but I would happily burn this torturous garment, if I could."

Victoria hid her smile. "It's not so bad, really, when you're used to it." Yet, as she laced the corset again, a strange thought occurred to her. *I wonder if I could make something like this. Only something softer, more comfortable to wear.*

If the chemise were created out of a delicate material like satin or velvet, the fabric would cling to a woman's skin. Even the corset itself could be lined with silk.

Her hands stilled upon Amelia's back, the idea evolving and taking shape. Already she'd seen patterns for embroidered petticoats, made of fine lawn or muslin. Yet, she'd never seen a corset made out of anything except unyielding, coarse material. All of them were white, as if proclaiming a woman's purity.

Slowly, Victoria began to pull the laces tight, unable to stop turning the idea over in her mind. Was it possible to construct a corset out of silk or satin, or would it tear under pressure? Perhaps it could be made of buckram but covered in silk, with a double lining next to the skin.

The idea intrigued her with a challenge she'd never before attempted. She had no idea how long it would take to make such a complicated garment . . . and yet, she found herself wanting to try it.

There was an older set of stays she could take apart to study for a pattern, and she knew there were gowns belonging to her grandmother in the bottom of a trunk. If she took one of them apart tonight, she could—

"Victoria?" her sister prompted. "Aren't you going to help me get dressed again?"

"Of course. I'm sorry." She lifted her sister's woolen dress over the undergarment, but her mind was still caught up in the vision. As Victoria buttoned her sister up, Amelia wouldn't let go of their argument. "Toria, you can't stay in Scotland. It's too dangerous for a woman alone. We heard gunshots yesterday when we were visiting the crofters."

"They're fighting again?"

Amelia nodded. "There's not enough space and barely enough food to feed them all. Some have talked of taking back the land and killing the Earl of Strathland."

Victoria moved to the window. In the distance, she could see the smoke curling from their campfires. A child wandered outside in the snow, her hair covered with a plaid, her clothing hardly more than rags. It bothered Victoria to see them suffering in this way. She wished her family had more to give away, but there were simply too many of the crofters. Worse, with the food shortages, it wasn't surprising that some would turn to stealing from each other, if it meant feeding their children. The winter was always difficult, and Victoria's mother had sent for more supplies from London, simply for their own survival.

"You can't stay here alone. Not while we're gone." Amelia's face tightened. "What if they attack the house?"

"We've given the crofters sanctuary," Victoria reminded her. "There's no reason for them to turn against us. And it's only temporary until they find a new place to live." She wanted to believe that, praying that the MacKinlochs would leave before the fighting worsened.

"It isn't safe," her sister argued. "Without Father here . . ." Her words broke off, her eyes filling up with tears. Their father, Colonel Henry Andrews, now Baron Lanfordshire, had been fighting in Spain for the past three years. There was no way of knowing when he would return.

Or *if* he would return.

Victoria took her sister's hand in reassurance. "Most of the crofters don't even know I'm here. And the ones who do, know that I never leave the house. I'm no threat to anyone."

Her sister fell silent, and she took it to mean that Amelia had finally given up. Good. There was no sense in entertaining ideas that would never happen. Victoria took the white and blue gown and picked up her thimble, intending to start sewing the hem.

Instead, Amelia walked over and took the gown from her hands. "I want to see this gown on you."

"Amelia, no. Really, I—"

"We're nearly the same size. Let's see what it looks like." Before she could protest, her sister started unbuttoning the gray merino gown Victoria was wearing. With great reluctance, she forced herself to stand still while Amelia helped her into the muslin dress. "Careful, or you'll tear the sleeves."

She stood before the mirror while Amelia fastened the four buttons lining the back of the gown and tied the sash. Although the waistline fit well enough, her bust was too small, and the bodice gaped slightly. She needed an extra layer of padding to fill out the areas that were too flat. It was rather dismaying that, despite Victoria's being six years older, her sixteen-year-old sister was better endowed than herself in the bosom.

Victoria's thoughts drifted back to her idea for undergarments made of silk. With a few strategic tucks and a bit of quilting to add support, there was a way to make a woman's breasts look bigger. The idea was scandalous, but she couldn't quite let go of it. Surely she wasn't the only woman with less-than-desirable curves.

The more she thought of it, the more she longed to attempt it. If she sewed quickly, she could send one corset to be sold along with the gown she'd made earlier.

But women might not want a corset made of silk, the voice of reason interjected. It might be an utter waste of time. And yet, she couldn't dismiss the idea.

"There. Now look at yourself." Her sister turned her to face the mirror, and Victoria stared at her reflection. It felt foreign, seeing herself dressed like this. The stripes of blue were too pretty, the roses too feminine. In the mirror, she saw a woman with pale skin, and a flush of embarrassment upon her cheeks. Her gray eyes were accentuated by the stripes of blue, and the waistline curved inward before the skirt draped in graceful folds. The gown transformed her into someone else—the woman she was afraid of becoming.

"I should take this off. It fits you better," she started to say.

"You're pretty, Victoria. Don't hide yourself away." Amelia rested her hands upon her shoulders, offering, "Let me do your hair."

Though both of them knew that she'd never attended any sort of ball and never would, Victoria surrendered to Amelia's whims. Her sister ruthlessly twisted and pinned the locks of dark blond hair until all of it rested upon her head in a coronet.

"You look perfect," her sister pronounced, "and when we get to London, we're going to order more gowns for you."

"Amelia, no." Clearly, her sister was ignoring her decision to stay.

She helped Victoria with the rest of the buttons while chattering on. "We could visit Madame Benedict's shop."

"I'd rather not." The very idea sent a ripple of dread through Victoria. She'd kept her identity hidden over the past year, sewing ball gowns for Madame Benedict in London. Each of her creations had been unique, but Victoria had resorted to using the services of their neighbor Cain Sinclair to deliver the gowns and bring back the money. He'd also been her source of fabric during the war, and she didn't doubt that Mr. Sinclair had engaged in illegal smuggling to acquire her supplies.

Thus far, her mother hadn't questioned the unexpected funds, for Beatrice had never been good with numbers and didn't understand where the money was coming from. It was a secret Victoria wanted to withhold for as long as possible, for no doubt her mother would be furious. A baron's daughter was not supposed to sew for money.

"Don't you think Madame Benedict will want to meet you?" Amelia continued. "You earned a good deal from the last gowns you sent to her. And you deserve some new clothes of your own."

Victoria ignored the question, for her younger sister didn't understand the need for secrecy. "The gowns I have suit me well enough." She had many that hung untouched in her wardrobe. "I don't need anything, for I'm going nowhere."

Her sister helped her to undress, her mood growing somber. "Christmas won't be the same if you're not there."

She braved a smile she didn't feel. "We'll celebrate again when you return. Now, I need to fix this hem."

Amelia cast her a disappointed look. "Do you want me to help you back into your old gown?"

Since it was already dark and they'd finished their dinner, she shook her head. "Help me out of my stays, and I'll get ready for bed."

Her sister obeyed, and Victoria put on a cotton nightgown that fell to her ankles. Then she sat in a rocking chair and picked up her needle and thread. It was easy to fall into the rhythm of sewing, making each stitch neat and even. In time, Amelia left her alone.

Victoria pushed the needle with her thimble, reminding herself that it would be all right. Yes, it would be lonely without her family on Christmas, but she would manage.

She would fill her days with sewing, letting the activity push away her loneliness. And this time, she had a new challenge to attempt. There was still the problem of finding the right fabric, however.

Victoria set aside her sewing and went to open the trunk on the far side of the room. It was filled with old gowns that she and her sisters had played in as children. They had pretended to be grand ladies, hosting parties for their dolls.

She rummaged around the trunk, looking for a bit of silk. Near the bottom, she found a crimson satin gown that had once belonged to her grandmother. Her mother had loathed the color, believing it was far too garish.

But it was irresistibly soft. She ran her hands over the surface, wondering if it would be too delicate for an undergarment. Frowning, she eyed the door. Downstairs, she heard the sound of her sisters talking, and the low voice of her mother.

There wasn't a great deal of time, but she went to the door and locked it. Then she brought over the stays she'd worn earlier, examining the construction. The boning tended to mash a woman's rib cage, making it hard to breathe. But it was the stiff, unyielding buckram that made it itch.

Victoria stripped off her nightgown until she stood naked in her room. It was cold, and she shivered as she reached for the crimson satin. Gathering it into a length, she molded it against her breasts, experimenting as she lifted them up to create cleavage.

In the mirror, she stared at herself. The soft fabric enveloped her nipples in a sensual way, making the tips erect. The candlelight cast a golden glow over her skin, and the red satin appeared scandalous.

She looked like a courtesan, a woman about to be undressed.

What would it be like to have a man standing before her? Would he want to caress the satin? Would it allure him, making him desire her as a woman?

Though she'd never touched herself in that way before, Victoria moved her palms over the fabric. Her breasts ached, and a sensual warmth bloomed between her thighs. She knew, from talks with her mother, that within a marriage, a husband would touch his wife intimately. And that she would enjoy sharing his bed.

She let the satin fall away, baring her nudity before the mirror. For as long as she buried herself within the house, no man would ever touch her. No man would ever want her.

The thought made bitter tears spring up in her eyes, for she simply didn't know how to overcome her fear.

Beatrice Andrews did not consider herself a meddling sort. Yet, as the mother of four daughters, it was her duty to see them married off to good men. Despite her husband's long absence, she had remained steadfast in that goal. Though she couldn't afford a Season for any of them, her sister Charlotte was investigating marital prospects in London for the girls. Their December visit would give them the chance to meet men who would make good husbands. If all went according to plan, she might be celebrating a wedding for one of them as early as next summer.

She smiled at the thought while she carried the basket of wet garments outside to the clothesline. The housekeeper, Mrs. Larson, would scold her for taking on the duty again, but Beatrice found it easier to think while she kept her hands occupied.

The problem of Victoria was getting worse, and she didn't know what to do about it. How could she leave one of her daughters behind, much less during Christmas? She shuddered at the thought of the last time she'd forced her daughter outside. It had taken two men to physically bring her into the garden, and once she was there, Victoria had shut her eyes, her cheeks wet with tears. She'd been white, trembling so hard until at last she'd fainted.

If Beatrice tried to force her into society, would the effect be the same? Would Victoria humiliate herself in public, making a spectacle?

And what would everyone say about her other daughters? Amelia, Juliette, and Margaret shouldn't have their own marital hopes dashed simply because their older sister was a recluse. At the ages of twenty and nineteen, Margaret and Juliette were both old enough to be wives. Almost too old, if the truth be known. Beatrice herself had been wed at eighteen.

She lifted a petticoat to the line and fastened it, the disappointment shadowing her hopes. Victoria hadn't always been this way. Once, she had merely been shy, remaining silent instead of talking to other girls her age. Then, after their disastrous journey here, nearly five years ago, her eldest daughter had been forever changed. It was a wonder Victoria hadn't gone mad, after being lost for several days in the Highlands with no food or shelter.

Ballaloch was a property that Henry's brother had purchased nearly twenty years ago. It was meant to be a summer retreat, a country residence her husband had preferred, instead of living in London with his brother. Never her daughter's permanent home.

Beatrice picked up a damp muslin gown and hung it upon the line with wooden clothespins. As she added each garment, it struck her suddenly that in almost three years, she hadn't hung up anything belonging to her husband. Only gowns and petticoats rippled in the morning breeze.

She rested her hand upon the frayed rope, the guilt filling up inside her. Not once had she admitted to her daughters that she was glad to have her husband gone off to war.

Even when Henry had been home, they had never revealed any of their troubles to society. To an outsider, theirs was a strong marriage: quiet, respectable. Ever polite and virtuous. And completely devoid of the love they'd once shared.

The December wind whipped the sheets and petticoats, while the morning sun did little to allay the chill. As Beatrice hung up the remaining pieces of clothing, she wondered when their marriage had begun to fade into habit.

Was it after Amelia was born? She hadn't shared his bed more than twice that year. Between Amelia's sleeplessness and their own exhaustion, there was never time. And gradually the good-night kisses had stopped, too.

Oh, they were cordial to each other. The girls never suspected what was happening. But now, after twenty-three years, their marriage was dying as surely as any wounded soldier on a battlefield.

The empty ache magnified when she thought of Henry. An unexpected rush of tears filled her eyes, grief over what had happened to them. He'd stopped loving her, somehow, and she didn't know why. After they'd come to Scotland, their few conversations had rarely ventured past the girls or the weather. He was careful to sleep on the far side of the bed, so that he would not inadvertently brush against her. And then he'd gone off to war.

Beatrice touched one of the bedsheets, feeling the cold linen against her palm. With a heavy sigh, she jammed another clothespin onto the line. She'd gotten old, when she wasn't looking. Perhaps it was natural for a husband's affections to dim. Better to give her love to her daughters, doing whatever was necessary to help them find what she had lost.

Glancing up at the house, she saw Victoria sitting beside the window. Sewing, no doubt. Her daughter had a miraculous talent with her needle, and Beatrice couldn't imagine how she dreamed up such creations. When she'd glimpsed Amelia's birthday gift, she'd marveled at the way Victoria had remade the old gown.

She only wished it weren't necessary for Amelia to always wear her sisters' clothing. A girl ought to have a wardrobe of her own, not one passed down over the years. But their slow descent toward poverty had worsened, ever since Henry had inherited his brother's debt-ridden estates. Though her husband had sent them money often, Beatrice had been forced to spend it on taxes for the London house or repairs to the Norfolk estate. The property was so far away, in the eastern corner of England, that she'd not been able to visit it or even meet with the land steward.

Sometimes she wondered if he was trying to take advantage of her . . . if the house was truly that bad. But then, she was hopeless at understanding the expenses. All she could do was send money and pray that he was using it to keep the property in good condition. She intended to meet with Henry's solicitor in London, to better understand the situation.

Then, too, the Earl of Strathland had offered to buy this house and the land on several occasions. Though the property was not entailed and Strathland had offered a handsome price, she couldn't consider selling it without Henry's permission. Until her husband returned, nothing could be done.

An uneasiness clenched Beatrice's stomach. For the time being, she had to put it out of her mind and hope that they could manage a little longer. She returned to the house, walking upstairs until she found Victoria seated by the window.

Her daughter wore a fawn-colored morning gown, and the muted color brought out the darker colors in her blond hair. Beatrice wished that she could somehow help Victoria overcome her fears, for there was no reason why she couldn't find a decent husband, especially with her pretty face.

A blue-striped muslin gown rested on her daughter's lap. She was busy threading a needle, and Beatrice sat down across from her. "Is it nearly finished?" she inquired, pointing to the muslin. "Amelia told me how much she loved her gift."

Victoria nodded, never ceasing her work. When long moments passed, Beatrice struggled to find the right words. She had planned this visit to London for months, and the last thing she wanted was to leave Victoria behind again. Each time she'd gone to visit family during the past three years, she'd pleaded with Victoria to come along. And every time, her daughter had refused.

She felt certain that if she left her behind once more, any hope of finding a good marriage for Victoria would be forever lost.

"I know why you're here," Victoria said at last, setting the sewing down. "You want me to go to London with you."

"We're a family. And this means so much to your sisters." Beatrice reached for her hand. "If you won't go for yourself, do it for them. They want you there with them. And it's Christmas."

Victoria's expression turned sad, "I wish I could."

"You can," her mother insisted. "You simply have to make up your mind to walk out the door. I promise you, you won't be separated from us ever again. I swear to you." She touched a hand to her heart, remembering how terrifying it had been when they couldn't find Victoria on that day five years ago. She'd lost a year of her life for each day her daughter had been missing.

"When I go to the doorway," her daughter continued, "my heart starts to beat faster. I can't breathe. And no matter how much I despise myself, I can't stop it from happening."

Beatrice squeezed her hand. "Let me help you. We can see a doctor in London. We could—"

"They would put me in an asylum, and you know it." Victoria turned back to her sewing. "Or give me medicines to make me sleep all the time. That's not how I want to live."

"But you're not living now," Beatrice argued. "You've chosen to shut yourself away from the world."

"It's not my choice!" Victoria shot back. Then she gathered her composure, her eyes brimming with tears. "How can you think it is?"

Beatrice lowered her head to Victoria's, gathering her in an embrace. "What do you want me to do?"

"I'm not ready to leave. And the more you try to force me, the worse it gets." She let out a breath and tried to smile. "Another year, perhaps. But for now, don't spoil the holiday for the others. They would resent me if they had to stay, simply because of my problem. Just go without me, as you've always done."

It was an impossible situation, one a mother shouldn't have to face. She started to refuse, but Victoria stopped her with an embrace. "I know you don't want to. But you must."

Beatrice caressed Victoria's hair, then pulled back to study her. "You're getting too old to remain behind with only Mrs. Larson and Mr. MacKinloch. Whom shall I send to look after you?"

"I will be fine with our servants."

Beatrice shook her head at her daughter's naiveté. "There are dozens of MacKinloch crofters on the land. You cannot remain here without a chaperone." She said nothing of the danger, not wanting to alarm Victoria. But tempers were rising, and she needed someone else who could watch over her daughter.

"I would feel better if we had a family member to stay with you," she said. "What if I sent for my cousin Pauline and her husband?" The idea eased her worries somewhat. Pauline's husband was a strong bear of a man who could defend himself and the women against any threat. Though they lived a few days' journey away in Northumberland, certainly it was better than leaving Victoria alone.

"If that would make you feel better." Victoria picked up her sewing again and began to embroider a blue petal chain stitch along the hem of the gown.

"I'll write to her today and have Mr. MacKinloch post the letter." She braved a smile, feeling better that her daughter wouldn't be alone. With a squeeze to Victoria's hand, she stood and departed the room.

Downstairs, Beatrice entered the small sitting room. The space was cozy, although the blue drapes and the carpet showed signs of fading. The wallpaper also needed to be replaced, for it was peeling off in the area near the window. With a sigh, she reached for paper and a pen. As she began her letter, her gaze fell upon the account books she'd left open, her spirits sinking lower.

She didn't understand the numbers, and a sick feeling permeated her stomach at the thought of all the money they'd lost.

Worse, the numbers never added up. Whenever she tried to account for it, it seemed that there was inconsistent income from another source.

It will be all right when Henry returns, she reassured herself. *He'll straighten matters out.*

She touched her bare wrist, remembering the sapphire bracelet he'd bought her fifteen years ago. He'd surprised her with the stunning jewelry, catching her in his arms. She'd given him a warm kiss of thanks, delighted with the gift.

Last Christmas, she'd sent it to her sister Charlotte, to be sold. And although the sacrifice had been necessary, her wrist felt empty, like a part of her had gone missing. Beatrice sent up another prayer to God, that her daughters would find husbands to marry soon.

Before she no longer had a dowry to give them.

Chapter Two

THREE DAYS LATER

THE HOUSE seemed empty without her mother and sisters, but Victoria was thankful Beatrice had allowed her to stay behind. Her mother had given Mr. MacKinloch a stack of letters to post, but Victoria had intercepted the letter meant for Cousin Pauline. Though she understood her mother's intent, the last thing she wanted was to be smothered by relatives she hardly knew. When they returned, she'd simply tell her mother that the letter must have been lost.

Lost in the fireplace where Victoria had cast it, but Beatrice didn't need to know that.

She glanced outside the window. The weather had turned colder, and snow had begun to drift against the house. Though it was still mid-morning, she suspected the snow would keep on throughout the day.

All around her room lay undergarments. Over the past three days, she'd used an older set of stays to create a pattern, and she'd made a matching chemise and corset lined with the red satin. Using bits of silk as padding, she'd sewn them into the corset so that it had the effect of lifting a woman's breasts upward and pressing them together.

Even her own too-small breasts looked more interesting. Without telling her sister what was in the parcel, she'd wrapped the garments in brown paper and ordered Margaret to give them to Mr. Sinclair to be sold, along with the other gown she'd made a few weeks ago.

Yet, she worried about the dressmaker's reaction. What if Madame Benedict hated the garments? What if she refused to buy any more ball gowns?

It had been such a risk sending the corset and chemise. She didn't know at all if anyone would want to buy them. Women were supposed to wear chaste, plain undergarments. Certainly not crimson satin that molded to their bodies and emphasized their breasts.

But it was too late now to take back her impulsive decision.

Today, using an old silk mourning gown, she'd begun creating a second corset, made of buckram but covered entirely with black silk and lace. The color was awful, but she had no other fabric to use. She could only hope that a woman in mourning might want to buy it.

This time, she was intent upon making the garment as lovely as she could. It was one of the most difficult challenges she'd ever attempted—not only constructing a second corset, but somehow finding a way to make the dark color beautiful. Even if it came to nothing, she welcomed the work. Perhaps it would bring in additional money for their family.

Although her mother was trying to find wealthy husbands for her sisters, Victoria was practical enough to understand that rich men didn't usually marry women without respectable dowries. They would want heiresses to add to the family fortunes. And even if Margaret and Juliette married, there were still the financial problems their family had inherited upon the death of their uncle last year.

What they needed was money and a great deal of it. Since she wasn't likely to ever find a husband, Victoria intended to make the most of her sewing talent. Someone had to take care of her mother, now that Father was off fighting in Spain. A painful knot tightened within her at the thought of him never returning. But war was a capricious master, one who could sever lives with a single bullet. If the worst happened and her father died, she could help her family survive with the profits from her garments.

The sudden thought of living within these four walls for the rest of her life made her heart clench. Always alone . . . with no man to ever see beyond her crippling shyness.

You should have gone with them, her conscience taunted. *You should have tried to face your fears.*

Her family cared about her. They'd wanted her to come with them, to enjoy the holidays with Aunt Charlotte and their cousins. What harm was there in that? But now it was too late, and she would spend Christmas alone.

Victoria cleaned up the remaining scraps of fabric, saving them in the trunk for future bits of trim. As she worked, she wondered when they would arrive in London. Her mother had promised to write letters, with all the news about the parties the girls attended and accounts of any young men who showed interest in courting them. Perhaps Margaret and Juliette could stay with Aunt Charlotte through the spring and have their first Season. She would miss them terribly, even if her mother and Amelia returned early.

A queer ache caught in her stomach, her eyes burning at the thought of her sisters entering the glittering world of the ton. She wanted them to be happy, she truly did. But even more, she wished she could be there to listen to their stories late at night. To hear them whisper of which gentlemen they favored or which gentlemen they loathed.

When they were girls, Mother had allowed Margaret and her to attend their uncle's supper party for an hour, before they were escorted back to their governess. Victoria had been enchanted by the sight of the men and women dressed in silks and finery. Both of them had been awestruck by the gaiety and wonder of it all. She'd never forgotten the vivid colors of the gowns or the exquisite embroidery, and that very night, she had stayed up late to sketch images of the dresses.

"We'll be just like them one day," Margaret had whispered. "I'll wear rose, and you'll wear blue. We'll have pearls in our hair and ostrich feathers."

A wistful smile crossed her lips, for now, her sister would have that chance. She hoped Margaret would dance and flirt until she won a gentleman's heart. With a heavy sigh, Victoria rose from her seat, just as a loud cracking sound caught her attention from outside.

A gunshot. And it was far closer to the house than it should be.

She glanced at the window, unsure of what had happened. In her mind, she formed explanations that would make sense. It was probably a crofter, hunting food for his dinner. He'd wandered off the boundaries, perhaps getting lost in the woods. Nothing more than that.

Even so, her nerves grew taut with uneasiness. She left her room and walked downstairs, only to find Mr. MacKinloch, their footman, donning a heavy coat. He reached for a rifle and checked to ensure it was loaded.

"What's happened?" Victoria demanded.

"I don't ken, Miss Andrews. But I'll be finding out." He wound a scarf around his neck. "Stay here with Mrs. Larson, and I'll return in a wee bit."

Victoria's hands clenched as he opened the door. Snow swirled inside, and she stood at the doorway for a moment, afraid of what he would find.

🏃

Pain. Indescribable pain burned through him until Jonathan craved death. He wanted so badly to push past the wall of misery and reach the haven of emptiness. There would be no glimpse of heaven for him, no Elysium.

Many had damned him, and rightfully so.

The bitter snow was trying to bury him alive, and his body trembled with the cold. His leg was an agonizing fire that rivaled Hell's flames.

He clenched his fists and tried to calm himself. How long had it been since the boy had shot him? He didn't know, but at least he'd regained consciousness before freezing to death. When he reached down to touch his leg, the slickness of blood nearly made him pass out again. Jonathan supposed he ought to be thankful that the boy's aim had been bad. He might have died from the bullet or lost part of his leg. As it was, it seemed the bullet had gone through the outer part of his thigh.

He gritted his teeth, enduring one minute at a time. This journey to Scotland had been the worst idea he'd ever had. He doubted if his family even knew he'd left England, as often as he traveled to the different estates. They saw him so infrequently, he could die tonight, and it might take half a year for them to realize it.

But he refused to die without a fight. His first priority was to keep from freezing to death.

Jonathan heard the sound of a man shouting, but his vision blurred. He felt someone lifting him up. Who had found him and where were they taking him? Not that he had any strength to protest. He could barely lift his head, much less escape whatever fate awaited him. Anywhere was better than lying in a snowdrift.

But soon enough the darkness swallowed him whole.

Mrs. Larson hurried into the parlor, her face stricken. "Miss Andrews, I'm sorry, but Mr. MacKinloch found a body outside where we heard the gunshots. The puir man's bleedin' right bad."

All the air seemed to evaporate from Victoria's lungs. "Who's bleeding?"

The housekeeper shook her head and shrugged. "We don't ken. He's got a bullet wound in his leg and he's had his brains knocked in a bit. He may no' . . . live." She muttered in Gaelic beneath her breath, as if to ward off evil spirits.

Her mother, Beatrice, would wring her hands and worry, if she were here. Perhaps even cry. But a strange calm descended over Victoria, and she took a deep breath. "Can you and Mr. MacKinloch set up a bed here in the parlor?"

Mrs. Larson nodded. "Aye. And I'll send for Dr. Fraser as well."

Victoria ignored the trembling fear that began to undermine her courage. A man's life depended on her. She couldn't turn cowardly and let him bleed to death, no matter how much she wanted to run upstairs and bury her face in a pillow.

Instead, she took another deep breath to steady herself. Mrs. Larson would need fresh linens and blankets. She could fetch those, as well as strips of leftover muslin that she'd cut from the hem of Amelia's gown. They might serve well enough as bandages. She grabbed them, racing back downstairs, her mind spinning off in a thousand directions.

What did she know about tending a man's wounds? Nothing whatsoever.

Victoria hurried upstairs into her mother's sitting room, where she searched the bookcase for something that would help. There was a book about animal breeding, but that was all. She flipped through the pages, hoping to find some information about tending wounds, but it was useless.

You're stalling, she warned herself. *While he's bleeding.*

She counted silently to ten and walked back downstairs. Mrs. Larson and Mr. MacKinloch had indeed made up a bed for the stranger in the parlor, elevating the mattress upon two low tables. He was lying there unconscious.

Panic boiled inside her throat, but she forced herself to take one step forward. Then another. She realized she was still holding the animal book and the muslin. When she neared the man's left side, she placed the volume upon a nearby table.

The stranger had blond hair the color of tarnished gold and a strong jaw. He was older than her, possibly in his late twenties. The light prickle of a beard covered his cheeks, and she wondered what it would feel like to touch it. Would it be sharp and scratchy? Or smooth and silken?

It was the first time she'd taken the time to study a man so closely. At any moment, she expected him to open his eyes. A tremor caught her just thinking of it.

"Will he live?" Victoria asked, embarrassed that her voice came out with a quaver.

"He's wearin' his grave clothes," Mrs. Larson pointed out. She studied Victoria, her mouth tightening. "Aye, 'tis possible. But then, ye're standing at his left. I can nae be certain."

"What do you mean?" She knew the housekeeper was inordinately superstitious, but she'd never heard anything like this before.

Mrs. Larson only shrugged. "I'll go to the kitchen and do what I can to drive off the spirits."

Mr. MacKinloch glanced back where the housekeeper had gone. "I'll fetch Dr. Fraser." Within moments, both of them had fled.

Victoria held her ground, suddenly realizing that they'd left her to handle him alone. She gripped the muslin in her hands and went to his side. Beneath the coverlet, a reddish stain rose, near his leg.

Had they done anything at all to help him?

She glanced behind her, but she could hear only the clang of a copper pot from the kitchen. With shaking hands, she pulled back the sheet Mr. MacKinloch had used to cover the man. Snowflakes had dampened the man's clothing, a few white crystals dotting his topcoat.

Her gaze passed down his neck to the rumpled linen neck-cloth. Beneath the long coat, he wore expensive riding clothes with a matching waistcoat, turned-back cuffs upon his sleeves, and box pleats on his brown tailcoat. Such detailed work she'd never seen before. She practically itched to take the coat apart, to study the way it was made.

But one thing was clear—this man possessed a great deal of money, to wear such fine clothes.

When she pulled back the rest of the coverlet, she saw that Mr. MacKinloch had tied a bandage to the man's leg. It was covered in blood, and the very sight made her ill.

He's going to die, she realized. And she didn't know if there was anything she could do to save him.

Jonathan smelled lemons. Not an acidic aroma, but a fresh citrus scent, like tropical flowers. Against his skin, he felt the softness of cool cotton sheets with a mattress beneath him.

He thought he remembered voices speaking about what was to be done with him, but pain radiated through his thigh, wracking him with agony. The bullet wound felt hot to the touch, his skin tight. He wasn't sure who was looking after him, but it had to be a woman, from the scent.

Why wasn't she chattering? Women always talked, flittering around like infernal butterflies. They drove him to madness, which was why he avoided them.

Rude, they'd called him. Insufferably arrogant. He didn't give a damn. He had better things to do than patronize the matrimonial-minded misses, who wanted nothing more than to capture a duke.

The silence within the room was beginning to make him uncomfortable. He heard the whisper of skirts, and then he opened his eyes. The woman had her back to him, and he couldn't tell much of what she looked like. She wore a soft blue gown, and her hair was blond with hints of brown in it.

Turn around. But she didn't. She rested her right hand upon the wallpaper, the left poised at her waist. Reminiscent of a small bird, her figure was petite and delicate.

Like his mother.

Tight anger and frustration knotted inside him at the unwelcome thought. It was over and done with. *Don't think of her,* he warned himself. He couldn't change the past, though he would bear the guilt forever.

Thank God his father was dead. He hadn't mourned the bastard for a single minute. His fists gripped the sheets, to strangle the memory.

The woman kept her back to him, as though she didn't want to be seen. She moved toward the piano that rested against the adjacent wall, its surface covered with a white fringed shawl. And then he saw her pick up a bottle of brandy.

Was that for him? God, what he wouldn't give for a drink. He wanted to sink into a drunken oblivion where he wouldn't feel any pain.

Her gaze remained downcast, as if she were afraid. Jonathan closed his eyes, wondering when she would come back to tend him. The feather mattress enfolded him like an embrace, and he silently pleaded for her to help. But instinct stopped him from opening his eyes again. He suspected he'd scare the hell out of her if he confronted the woman.

After several minutes, the scent of lemon returned. When her hand covered his brow, he forced himself to remain still. *Tread carefully,* he thought. He was completely at her mercy, and he didn't know this woman at all.

But then, her hand moved down his cheek, stroking the unshaved bristle. She touched him with the innocence of a young girl, curious in her exploration. Her palms were smooth, and the scent of lemons caught him again. The gentle caress distracted him from the vicious pain of his leg. This woman did something to him, with nothing more than a simple touch. For a moment, he kept his eyes closed, imagining the face of an angel.

She adjusted the sheet, baring his wounded thigh. From the cool air, he guessed that she'd cut away part of his breeches.

"Who are you, I wonder? You're not one of the crofters." Her voice was like velvet, rich and lush. He held himself motionless, listening to her speak.

"My name is Victoria Andrews," she murmured.

Jonathan opened his eyes to see her face. Gray eyes widened with shock, and she stumbled away from him. Terror invaded her expression, as though she'd never expected him to awaken.

"I'm not going to harm you," he told her, his voice rough from lack of use. "You needn't be afraid of me. I can't even move with this leg."

His reassurance did little to ease her nervousness, for she kept twisting her hands together.

"Mr. MacKinloch went to fetch Dr. Fraser," she told him, "but I don't know how long it'll take for him to get here."

Jonathan tried to sit up, to have a better look at his injury. A linen bandage was tied around his thigh, but it did little to absorb the blood. "Did the bullet go through?"

She nodded. He was grateful for small mercies. The last thing he wanted was for someone to go digging through his leg for a ball of lead. The throbbing pain wasn't abating, and he suspected he was slowly bleeding out.

"How bad is it?"

Her long lashes lowered with solemnity, her lips tightening when she shrugged. He felt the first stirrings of fear. He'd thought the bullet wound was an inconvenience, not a life-threatening wound.

"Pour me a drink," he said. "It seems I'll need it."

She clutched the bottle of brandy, and glanced down at his leg. "That isn't why I brought the spirits. I thought I should"—her words broke off, and she looked embarrassed—"pour it on your wound. To clean it."

"And where did you get that idea?"

"From a . . . book I read once."

He'd heard of such things, too, but the idea of anything touching his leg made him wince. He preferred to wait for the doctor to arrive.

"It's expensive French brandy," he noted. "It would be criminal to waste it on my leg. Your husband would be furious."

"My father," she corrected in a low voice. "And he's fighting in Spain."

"All the more reason not to steal his brandy." He studied her, wondering aloud, "Where is the rest of your family?"

She didn't answer, but lifted the stopper from the brandy. He realized, with some alarm, that she truly intended to use it. "Don't you think we should wait a little longer?"

"There's a bad snowstorm. I don't know how long it will take Dr. Fraser to get here, and you're bleeding badly." Her face showed her discomfort, and she looked as though she were about to be sick. "I wouldn't want you to die while we're waiting for him."

"Even so, I wouldn't—" His voice broke off, and he let out a yell as an unholy fire burned through him.

Chapter Three

THE BRANDY soaked through his wound and into the sheets beneath him. Victoria hadn't realized it would hurt him that badly, and she wished she'd taken a bit more care.

"Are you *trying* to kill me?" he demanded, before letting off a string of curses. "Don't you know anything about tending wounds?"

"No. I don't." She handed him the clean linen, and crossed the room to stand by the piano. Yes, she'd made a terrible mistake. But he didn't have to bite her head off for it. Heated tears burned at her eyes, but she would not cry in front of him. Weeping wouldn't do either of them any good.

"Come here," he ordered. Victoria ignored him, huddling beside the piano against the wall, as though she could melt through it.

"I don't want to." The idea of taking even a single step near this man was impossible. "I'll just wait here for the doctor."

"I might be dead by the time he arrives. And I need you to properly bandage my leg."

She glared back at him. "I didn't mean to hurt you. I was only trying to help."

The corner of his mouth turned up. "Were you?" He rolled to his side, propping his head up on one hand. The white sheet slid down his torso, and though he was fully clothed, he reminded her of a man who had just awakened from sleep. Her gaze was caught by the rumpled neckcloth. It exposed a hint of male skin, and she wondered what the rest of him looked like.

"Come here, Miss Andrews," he repeated. The use of her name made her swallow hard. The resonant tone of his voice was like a siren, beckoning her toward something forbidden.

"I'd rather stay here. You can hold the bandage to your wound yourself."

"You'd make a wounded man suffer by forcing him to wrap his own wound?" he queried. "When he could have a beautiful woman tending him instead?" Though she recognized he was teasing her, she didn't miss the edge of pain within his voice. But she shied away from him, embarrassed by his words.

"I'm not beautiful. And I shouldn't be touching you . . . there."

A wicked glint came into his eyes for a moment, making her blush. Then he closed his eyes, as if trying to block out the pain. "I'm bleeding," he reminded her, "and I really do need your help."

"I don't make a habit of touching strangers," she hedged, stalling for the doctor. Where was he? Or Mrs. Larson? She couldn't understand what was taking them so long.

The man hesitated, as though he didn't want to tell her his name. There was something in his expression that held a world of distrust, as though a simple name would give her power over him. But then he offered, "You may call me Jonathan."

The idea of using his first name was completely inappropriate. She suspected he was hiding something from her about his identity. Was he one of the Strathlands? She prayed it wasn't true. The last thing she wanted was to be harboring an enemy.

Keeping her voice brisk, she said, "I cannot call you by your first name."

"I think we can dispense with formalities. You've already seen me without my breeches."

"Not all of you."

Dear God, had she actually said that out loud?

A slight smile pulled at his mouth, though his lips were tight with pain. "I suppose that would offend your maidenly sensibilities."

"Indeed." Right now, she wanted to go upstairs and pretend none of this was happening. But that wasn't possible, was it? "I would prefer your family name, please." She wanted the distance, needed it. Somehow, she had to assert herself and make him understand this. "I will call you Mr. Smith, if I must," she continued, "but I will not call you Jonathan."

Even with her threat, he didn't offer his name. Instead, he crooked his finger, beckoning to her. "I need you to fix the bandage."

She knew it. But a vain hope kept her in place, with the silent prayer that Dr. Fraser would walk through the door.

His green eyes locked with hers in a silent battle. Then he gritted out, "Please."

There was no humility in his voice, but he was right. Likely he needed stitches to stop the bleeding.

Victoria eased away from the wall and took a step toward him. Then another. Every inch forward was a mile, and she dared not take her eyes off him. It wasn't right to watch him suffer, not if something could be done.

He wasn't at all courteous or refined, like the men she'd read about in stories. Strong-willed and forceful, this was a man accustomed to getting his own way. But he was also handsome, beneath the stubble of his beard. Something in the way he stared at her made her heart pound faster. He eyed her as though he wanted to touch her in a way that he shouldn't.

I don't like him.

The intensity of her reaction was like a kick in the stomach. Beneath her dress, her skin grew sensitive, and her cheeks were blushing. For Mr. Smith, despite his handsome appearance, was a threat. It didn't matter that he hadn't laid a finger upon her. His words were enough.

She reached his side and realized that he'd fallen silent. And when she finally looked at him, she saw the crimson stain widening upon the sheets.

Jonathan was losing his sense of awareness. The dull ache in his thigh drew all of his focus. Each breath merged with the next, while he fought to keep his body from shutting down.

"Oh, dear God." Victoria's hand touched his sweaty forehead.

Through the glaze of pain, he wanted to tell her not to be afraid, that he wouldn't threaten her. But survival seemed more important than conversation just now. Instead, he took her hand and gripped it, as if he could hold on to life by touching her.

With her other hand, Victoria pulled back the sheet, evoking a slight chill against his skin. Her complexion turned gray, and she stared at him, as if frozen. Then abruptly, she extricated her hand from his and jerked into action.

He couldn't see how bad the bleeding was, but he knew the linen she'd pressed against the injury wouldn't stanch the flow. Beneath her breath, she murmured the Lord's Prayer.

Wouldn't do a damned bit of good. His soul was already lost.

Abruptly, she stood up. There was an odd expression on her face, one he didn't like.

"What are you—"

"Just a moment." She held up a hand, her gaze suddenly searching the room. "I think I know how to help you."

In the meantime, he was losing more blood. The clouded veil of consciousness was about to drop. A ringing noise resounded in his ears.

He faded out for a moment, not knowing how long. Then something stabbed his wound. "Jesus Christ!"

"Don't blaspheme. Hold still while I sew this wound closed."

"I am not a damned embroidery hoop," he argued. "And you can't sew me back together."

"You're going to bleed to death if I don't!" she snapped.

So. The waif had a backbone after all. He hadn't expected it. "See that you do a proper job of it, then."

Her reply to his gibe was to pierce his skin. Over and over, he endured her needle. First on one side of his thigh and then through the exit wound. He must have passed out at another interval, for when he awakened, she was sitting on the other side of room. The sheet rested at his waist.

"Is it done?"

"It's done."

Jonathan pulled back the edge of the sheet and the linen bandage. "What the hell did you do?"

She glared at him. "You're welcome."

His wound now had a series of tiny, even stitches to keep it closed. And she'd used bright pink thread.

Never in her life had Victoria imagined she would have to ply her needle to a man's flesh. She shuddered. There were no words to voice what she felt right now. No, Mr. Smith hadn't overtly threatened her. But his green eyes had stared at her in a way that made her skin sensitive beneath her gown. She didn't understand why she was so aware of every move he made, every breath he inhaled. He'd gripped her hand before he'd lost consciousness, and she'd held on to him, letting him take comfort from her. The unexpected contact had seemed so forbidden.

Even now, she trembled to think of it. No man had ever touched her before, and her cheeks burned bright red at the memory.

She'd had to hold his thigh to stitch the wound closed. The hard, well-formed muscles were so different from her own leg. Worse, the sensation had awakened a dormant curiosity inside her. She'd found herself wanting to bring her hands over the hardened flesh, to explore his skin. Focusing on his wound had not helped alleviate the discomfort, nor the feelings rising up within her. It had shaken her deeply.

At that moment, the front door opened, and Victoria hurried toward it. Mr. MacKinloch stood before her, snow dusted upon his shoulders. His expression was grim, and there was no sign of Dr. Fraser. "He's no' coming."

"What do you mean, he's not coming?" Victoria demanded. "This man needs a doctor."

"He can't. There were more fires last night on Strathland's property. His factor, Mr. Melford, set the houses ablaze. Some of the crofters tried tae get their belongings out, and Dr. Fraser is tendin' half a dozen who were burned."

"What of your family?" Victoria dared to ask.

Her footman shrugged, his gaze stony. "My sister was nae among the burned." But nothing else would he say about her.

"Mr. MacKinloch, the doctor has to come," she insisted. "I can't do this alone."

The footman took off his hat and brushed off the snow. "It's nigh impossible to get through the roads, with all the snowdrifts. Even if he wanted tae come, he couldn't." With a grim look, he added, "I found a horse and the body of another man nearby. Might be a servant of the man we found, if I guessed rightly."

Her stomach sank with a desperate fear. She'd known of the rising anger of the crofters, but to be surrounded by murderers and fires . . . Amelia was right. It wasn't safe here any longer. Now, more than ever, she wished she'd found the courage to accompany them to London.

Mr. MacKinloch disappeared into the kitchen, and Victoria

realized that Mrs. Larson had been absent for nearly an hour. When she followed the footman, she found the housekeeper preparing a tray of food.

"I thought you were bringing hot water." Victoria kept her voice steady, wondering what had kept the housekeeper in the kitchen for so long.

"First, I walked around the house three times with a hot coal, driving the evil spirits off. I've done wha' I could to keep Death away. Whether he lives is up to the good doctor when he comes." Mrs. Larson folded a napkin upon the tray and ladled hot soup into a bowl.

"You left me alone with him while you—"

Indulged in your silly superstitions, she'd been about to say. But then, to Mrs. Larson, they were real. The Scottish housekeeper had been raised to believe in them, and no amount of reasoning would change her heart.

"—while you cooked him dinner?" Victoria amended.

Mrs. Larson turned embarrassed. "Now, Miss Andrews, he'll be needing to eat, won't he?"

"Not if he's dead." Her voice revealed her frustration, as she rested both hands upon the kitchen table. "I needed you. I know nothing about sewing up wounds."

The housekeeper's face fell. "I'm sorry, Miss Andrews, but I can nae abide blood."

Victoria sent her a look of utter disbelief. "And you thought it was appropriate to leave me alone with a strange man?"

The older woman lifted her chin in a stubborn tilt. "Wouldn't do ye much good if I was to bring my breakfast up for another look, all over Lady Lanfordshire's fine carpet, now would it? I'm a housekeeper, nae a nurse."

Victoria clenched her hands together. "Neither am I. But I'm doing the best I can."

"I'm sorry, Miss Andrews. Truly." With flushed cheeks, Mrs.

Larson took the tray of food and offered, "Is he . . . well enough to eat?"

"If he lives through the next few hours, I suppose he'll be hungry."

The housekeeper had the grace to look guilty. "I'll say prayers for him, that I'll promise. And . . . if ye want me t'look after him, I'll try my best no' to be sick." She brought the tray into the parlor and set it down, her complexion turning waxen as she eyed their patient. Without another word, she went to the far side of the room and removed the only hanging mirror.

Victoria sent her a curious look, and Mrs. Larson explained, "If a mirror falls off the wall, death isna far away. Best to take precautions."

It was clear that the older woman and her superstitions would be of little use. "Please, just send Mr. MacKinloch," Victoria insisted. "In the meantime, our guest will need some new clothing. Will you bring something of my father's? I'll alter it to fit."

The housekeeper bobbed her head. "I'll see to it." Casting her a sympathetic gaze, Mrs. Larson added, "Dr. Fraser still might come tomorrow."

But that wouldn't help her now. As the housekeeper departed, leaving the door ajar, Victoria brought the bowl of soup over to Mr. Smith. His face was pale, but at least he didn't seem to be bleeding quite as badly.

Her stomach twisted, for she'd had to sew up muscle, as well as skin. She'd never gone through anything so horrifying in all her life. But he was resting quietly, and he was still alive. The question was, what should she do with him now?

❧

The scent of roasted chicken broth drew him back into awareness once more. Jonathan's stomach felt like razors had shredded the insides, and hunger roared inside him. Right now, he'd offer up a king's ransom for beef. Or hot yeast rolls, dripping with butter. He struggled to open his eyes, but the lids felt too heavy.

A spoon touched his mouth, coaxing him to eat. Warm broth slid against his tongue, only arousing his hunger more. He drank until the spoon stopped coming. "I think I could marry whoever made this soup."

"She's sixty-two and is widowed."

Jonathan forced his eyes open and saw Victoria seated beside him. There was a tray of more food, and he wondered what he'd have to do to get the rest of it.

She broke off a piece of toast slathered with strawberry jam and lifted it to his mouth. He caught her wrist, guiding it forward. The jam was sweet, but he found himself studying her hand. Her palms were soft, but her fingers were rough and callused.

"Are you really a member of this family," he asked, "or are you a servant here?"

She pulled her hand back. "I'm not a servant. My hands are this way because I sew. I prefer to spend my time in useful pursuits."

He watched her, noticing the soft blue of her gown, the sweep of her honey-brown hair. She wore no jewelry, but there was a natural beauty about her. Gray eyes eyed him with distrust, but it didn't diminish the haunting quality of her face. Her cheekbones were flushed with embarrassment, and she nibbled the edge of her lip. He could imagine claiming that mouth, unraveling her proud sensibilities, until she stopped being so practical and kissed him back.

The innocence of her entranced him, and he couldn't understand why this creature had captivated him in such a way. Perhaps it was because she didn't know of his rank. To her, he was an ordinary man.

The idea appealed to him in so many ways. With her, he could be anyone. And she would never know differently.

"I should go," she murmured. "You can finish feeding yourself, I suppose."

He could, but he didn't want to be alone. It made it too easy to concentrate on the throbbing pain. "Stay with me."

She handed him the last fragment of toast. "I shouldn't."

"Probably not." He let out a sigh and closed his eyes. "I'll just lie here and die, shall I?" When there came no reply, he risked opening one eye. Miss Andrews had a faint smile upon her lips.

Then he nodded toward a book he'd spied on the table. "Why don't you read to me? Something tedious that will put me to sleep."

She picked up the book and reddened. "No, this one wouldn't interest you. It's *The Breeding Habits of Animals*."

"I can assure you, I'm quite interested in breeding."

She rolled her eyes and set it aside. "I should read to you from the Bible. Perhaps you'd learn something."

"'Let him kiss me with the kisses of his mouth. For thy love is better than wine,'" he quoted.

She stood and walked over to the family Bible, bringing it close. "I won't be reading to you from Song of Solomon."

"What about Samson and Delilah?"

She opened the Bible near the beginning, and he settled on his side. A tendril of hair had fallen from her topknot, sliding over her cheek. He decided that if a man had to suffer being shot, it wasn't so bad to have a nursemaid who resembled Miss Andrews.

"Adam and Eve?" he suggested.

She shook her head. "You asked for something tedious. I believe I have something that would suit." The look in her eyes held a stubborn glint. "And unto Enoch was born Irad: and Irad begat Mehujael: and Mehujael begat Methusael: and Methusael begat Lamech."

As she continued reeling off names from the book of Genesis, he interrupted, "Where is your family?"

She ignored his question and continued, "Lamech took to

himself two wives: the name of the one was Adah, and the name of the other, Zillah."

"You're alone here, aren't you? It's just you and the servants."

Miss Andrews closed the book. "Do you want me to read to you or not?"

"I want to know why they left you behind." He couldn't understand it. "Aren't they afraid something would happen to you?"

She placed the book upon a table. "I refused to go. I've no wish to be dressed up like a paper doll and paraded about in front of everyone." Her cheeks reddened, and she added, "My cousins will be coming soon. Perhaps tomorrow."

He recognized a lie when he saw it, but he ignored it for now. "I thought every woman's goal in life was to find a rich husband."

"Not everyone's." She tucked the sheet around him, and he caught her hand again. Once more, the fresh scent of lemons seemed to emanate from her. He saw her lips open slightly, her eyes widening with a hint of fear. And he realized, she meant it. She truly didn't want to marry.

It intrigued him. Like a challenge, he wanted to understand why. "Is there a reason?"

She gave a shrug that meant nothing. "I never met anyone I wanted to marry."

Jonathan detected a note of sadness in her voice and a hint of secrecy. He probed a little further. "You've never had any suitors, have you? I'd wager that you haven't been kissed either."

His gaze traveled to her mouth, and he imagined again what it would be like to take her lips, to teach her what it was to kiss a man. Would she taste sweeter than her temperament?

"Whether I have or haven't is none of your affair." Miss Andrews tried to pull away, but he wouldn't relinquish her hand.

The pain of the wound on his leg was worsening, and he struggled to think of other things. Any distraction that would transport his mind away from the agony. The last thing he wanted was to reveal any weakness or the pain he was enduring.

Better to let her believe that her stitching had worked, that he was in no discomfort now.

He held her fingertips, bringing them to his cheek while he fought to steady his breathing. Watching Miss Andrews's reaction was a diversion, in and of itself. Her face transformed with his touch. She didn't speak, but a flush came over her cheeks. He held her hand so lightly, she could have pulled it back any time she wanted to. But she remained frozen in place.

"What are you—what are you doing?" she managed at last.

"Distracting myself from the pain." His mouth drifted down to her palm, the barest kiss against her flesh. It was softer here, a lady's hand.

When he moved his mouth to the pulse point at her wrist, he stole a glance at her face. Her gray eyes looked stricken, as if torn between experiencing his touch and pulling away. He kept his mouth there, his breath warming her soft skin. Her fingers trembled, and at last, he released her hand.

Miss Andrews clenched her fingers together, taking slow steps away from him. "I think it would be best if you went to sleep n-now." Without waiting for a reply, she fled the parlor.

࿊

Inside her room, Victoria curled up on the window seat, staring outside as the snowflakes poured from the sky. Her hand was cold, though she still felt the phantom memory of the man's lips upon her skin.

Why had he done such a thing? They were strangers. He didn't know anything about her, nor did she have the faintest idea who he was.

He'd kissed her fingers, treating her as though she were someone he wanted to touch. She rested her forehead against the wall, wanting to die of humiliation. In a matter of hours, nearly every rule of propriety she'd ever learned had been broken.

She'd been alone with a man, with no chaperone.

She'd removed part of his breeches, and she'd touched his bare thigh.

He'd kissed her fingertips in the manner of a lover.

If her mother knew of this, she'd be demanding a betrothal within the hour. Thankfully, no one knew that he'd acted in such a way. Only her guilty conscience chided her, and she was having trouble silencing it. Mr. Smith was a terrible man, not at all a gentleman. He'd taken far too many liberties, and she didn't want to return to the parlor.

A knock sounded upon her door, and Mrs. Larson entered. She held a tray containing supper, and Victoria told her to set it down on the table.

"I shouldna have left ye alone, Miss Andrews." The housekeeper cleared her throat. "It's sorry I am, that I did. I sent Mr. MacKinloch to give our guest some chamomile tea. It should help him sleep well enough."

Victoria thanked the housekeeper, and before Mrs. Larson could go, she asked, "Could you help me to undress? I'm tired, and I intend to go to sleep after I eat."

Mrs. Larson helped her with her gown and corset before she returned downstairs. Once she was ready for bed, Victoria sat down beside the tray and picked at the food.

Her mind was tangled up with distraction over Jonathan. It was as if she'd taken a bite from the apple of sin, tasting the sweetness of a man's touch. There was so much confusion, between the desire to avoid him . . . and the temptation to be near him.

He'd been honest with her—the kiss on her hand was a distraction for him, nothing else. Likely he'd gone to sleep, forgetting all about it.

She reclined upon the chaise longue, imagining his mouth upon her fingertips. Then she let the vision spin away, wondering what it would be like if his kiss had traveled up her arm, to her shoulders . . . down to her breasts.

With her palms, she touched the soft swell of her nipples, and she imagined him kissing her there. Shuddering, she rubbed the tips with her thumbs, her breath starting to tremble.

Her eyes flew open when she found herself clenching her legs, imagining other sensual things. There was a restlessness brewing inside, one she couldn't explain. She thought of the night she'd stood naked before her mirror, wearing nothing but crimson satin. A man like Mr. Smith would, no doubt, be fascinated by scandalous undergarments. She imagined his hands unlacing her, his fingers caressing her skin.

Victoria stood and walked to the door, pressing her palm against the wood. Her heart was racing, and she couldn't understand why she was thinking of such things.

He doesn't know about your fears, a voice inside whispered. *He believes you chose to stay behind.*

With his injury, he could be stranded here for days before his servants or family came to claim him. He might . . . become her friend. Or something more.

Her hand rested upon the doorknob. A sensible woman would return to her chair, finish her supper, and go to sleep. Mr. MacKinloch and Mrs. Larson would look after Mr. Smith. There was no need for her to sit with the stranger. He didn't need her.

But something drew her to open the door. And though it might end up being the greatest mistake of her life, Victoria couldn't stop herself from walking down the stairs.

Chapter Four

T HE CLOCK chimed ten o'clock. Jonathan could feel his leg
tightening, swelling up with blood. His fever had worsened,
and when he reached up to touch his forehead, he found it damp
with perspiration.

Every second that ticked by was another moment of torture.
He stared up at the ceiling, wondering what to do if he did somehow survive the next few days. He'd overheard the servants talking about the other body they'd found. Though he couldn't be
certain who the dead man was, it was likely his groom or his
footman. If either had lived, they would have found him by now.
But no one had come.

For the first time, he allowed himself to consider the danger.
He was the Duke of Worthingstone, and if he let that be known,
others might seek to ransom him. It was best to keep quiet over
his identity for now and let them believe he'd been lost.

Though he'd acquired his land from the Earl of Strathland,
after the man owed him a gambling debt, he saw no reason to
associate himself with the man. Particularly if the residents
wanted the earl dead.

And although Jonathan had no quarrel with the crofters, neither did he want to live between the two warring sides. Of
course, it might not matter, if this fever killed him first.

He reached down to touch the hot skin, remembering how Victoria had sewn the wound shut. Her handiwork might have saved his life, but there were far too many questions about this woman. Why had she chosen to stay behind, in the midst of such danger? Was there a scandal she was avoiding?

At first glance, she appeared to be a lady with a modest upbringing. The room held elegant furnishings with mahogany carved chairs, a crimson velvet settee, and oil paintings of men he assumed were family relatives. But at a closer look, he saw that there were no silver candlesticks or touches of wealth.

Miss Andrews had claimed that her father was fighting in Spain. It was likely the man was an officer, given the size of this house and the surrounding land. But he doubted if any father would voluntarily allow his daughter to stay here with only two servants.

From the corner of his eye, Jonathan saw a movement near the door. Miss Andrews held a candle in one hand, and wore a blue wrapper over a prim white nightgown. Her hair was unbraided and fell to her waist in long honey-brown strands. In the candlelight, he saw the emotions pass over her face—uncertainty, nervousness, and curiosity.

"Have you come to finish me off?" he asked.

"I thought you would be asleep."

"I suppose I am a better companion when I'm unconscious. My family would agree with you on that point." He beckoned for her to draw closer. "I'm sorry to disappoint you."

She remained near the door, as if she were afraid of him. The candle flame flickered in the darkness, and when he said nothing further, she took a tentative step forward. "Are you feeling all right?"

"No. But I'll try not to die by morning."

His black humor didn't deter her, and she moved a little closer. He was disappointed in the opaque white garment. Though already she'd broken countless social rules by visiting him in a state of undress, already he knew that Miss Andrews was different from the other women he'd known.

The rest of them would have screamed and fainted at the sight of his blood. They most certainly wouldn't have taken the time to stitch him up.

In her other hand, he spied a swath of black lace. "Have you brought mourning garb in preparation for my funeral?"

"It's just some . . . sewing. I thought perhaps I shouldn't leave you alone through the night." She pulled up a chair and sat an arm's length away from him. He couldn't quite tell what the lace was for, but there appeared to be crape or some other fabric with it.

"You aren't concerned about being alone with me?" Or especially remaining near him in her nightclothes.

"I'm far more concerned about you bleeding to death, leaving me to explain your corpse to the authorities."

She had courage; he'd give her that. For the next few moments, he entertained himself by imagining her wearing a more revealing garment, perhaps one made entirely of black lace. From the shapeless form of her wrapper, he couldn't tell anything at all about her body. She had a slight figure, so no doubt it hid a slender waist and modest curves.

"What would your mother say if she knew you were downstairs with a stranger, wearing only your nightclothes?"

Victoria slid her needle into the black material, sewing quietly. "She would likely be thrilled and hope that I was terribly compromised so you'd have to marry me."

"If that was your intent, I'm sorry to disappoint you, but I'm not the sort to be trapped into marriage."

"And I'm not the sort of woman who ever plans to marry." She folded over a bit of fabric and continued stitching the seam. "So it would seem neither of us is in any danger."

It should have been a relief to know that she wouldn't try to ensnare him. But if her mother learned of this—especially if she discovered his rank—she would undoubtedly force the issue. Therefore, it was quite necessary for him to heal quickly and not reveal to anyone that he was a duke.

Jonathan watched her hands moving effortlessly with the needle. It was an extension of her hands, darting in and out of the silk with a fluid expertise. "I won't tell if you won't."

Her gray eyes held surprise for a moment, and a flicker of a smile tugged at her mouth before she dropped her gaze back to the fabric.

Jonathan propped up on one elbow to stare at her. "So tell me, why don't you plan to marry? Surely you could bring a country gentleman up to scratch."

"I am quite happy to remain a spinster."

"You've no wish for children?"

She set down the needle and regarded him. "I wouldn't make a good wife."

He didn't believe her. For the life of him, Jonathan couldn't imagine this woman without a husband. When he'd kissed her hand, he'd glimpsed the awareness rising in her eyes, and she hadn't been unaffected by his touch. Her mouth had drifted slightly open, while her cheeks turned crimson. And she hadn't pulled her hand away. His mind could easily imagine this angel naked with her hair falling around her shoulders, her eyes closed as she arched with pleasure.

The erotic vision made him clench the sheets. What the hell was the matter with him? Clearly, the wound had turned him delusional.

"I'm thirsty," he admitted, changing the subject.

"I'll bring you some water." She seemed grateful for the request and retreated to the kitchen to fetch it.

Jonathan gritted his teeth against the pain, wishing he'd asked for brandy instead. He could have drunk himself into oblivion. A tremor took hold of him, and he gripped the coverlet, trying to still his body's reaction. The pain and swelling from his leg was starting to conquer his willpower, for it was like nothing he'd ever experienced. Even breathing took an effort.

When she returned, Victoria sat beside him and helped him lift his head. As he drank, she murmured, "Your fever is worse. You should have told me."

"It's not surprising." But the greater fear was that the wound might slowly poison him. He'd seen countless soldiers returning from war without a leg, from a gunshot wound that had led to gangrene. "Will the doctor come tomorrow, do you think?"

"I hope so." She helped him lie back and asked, "Is there anything else I can get for you?" Her hand moved across his brow, and he closed his eyes, trying to fight back against the vicious pain.

"No." Not unless she had anything to dull the pain. But if she had, she'd have offered it by now. Victoria sat beside him and resumed sewing the black lace.

"You should go back to your own bed and sleep, Miss Andrews. We both know you shouldn't be here alone with me."

"Is that what you want?"

He said nothing, not about to admit that he wanted her to stay. With his eyes closed, he murmured, "Go on. I'll be fine."

"Close your eyes, then." She drew her hand over his forehead and down his eyelids until he obeyed. "I'll stay a few moments longer, until you're asleep."

The softness of her touch made him far too aware of her feminine scent. She distracted him with her presence, and he was glad to have her at his side, rather than the formidable Mrs. Larson. Even so, he would only be here until he was strong enough to leave Scotland. One of his men could inspect the land he'd acquired, along with the house.

He feigned sleep, but as the minutes passed, he began to notice something else. When he opened his eyes, Victoria hadn't left. She continued working by candlelight, seemingly unaware of the looming danger.

The acrid scent wove through the house, tainting the air with a distant smoke.

"Do you smell that?" He wrinkled his nose. "Is there a fire burning somewhere?"

"There are always fires," she answered. "Some of the refugees tried to return to their homes for their possessions. According to Mr. MacKinloch, the earl ordered the houses burned." Though her voice remained calm, her face was pale with fear.

Jonathan didn't like the thought of being surrounded by refugees. Men who had lost their homes rarely left without a thought of vengeance. And if they had taken shelter here, it would take only a small spark to ignite the fury of their anger.

Before he could ask more about the fires, he heard a pounding at the front door.

Victoria started to rise from her chair, but he ordered, "Don't answer that. The hour is too late for visitors."

"I was going to wake Mrs. Larson," she told him. "It might be the doctor."

He doubted it. And if they were indeed caught in the middle of an uprising against Strathland, the last thing he wanted was to be caught unarmed and helpless.

"Do you have a gun in the house?"

She stared at him and took a step backward. "My father has a set of dueling pistols. But that won't be necessary."

"Bring one of them to me."

Victoria shook her head. "I'm not bringing you a weapon. You might accidentally shoot one of our neighbors who needs help."

"I was *shot* by a boy who believed I was the Earl of Strathland."

At the mention of the man's name, she blanched. "It was a mistake, that's all."

"And one or more of my men are also dead." He struggled to sit up, while outside the pounding on the door grew louder. "The last thing I intend to do is sit quietly and let them finish me off. Now bring me the gun."

The look in his eyes was dangerous. Victoria bit her lower lip, taking another step backward. She didn't want to bring him any weapon at all, much less a dueling pistol that wasn't very accurate.

Quietly, she hurried from the room and found Mrs. Larson standing near the front door. "It's Dr. Fraser. Shall I let him in?"

Relief rushed through Victoria, and she nodded. Paul Fraser had been a family friend since they'd arrived in Scotland. He'd been particularly close to Juliette and had written to her all during the years he'd studied medicine in Edinburgh. Although Victoria had only spoken to him on a few occasions, she trusted him implicitly. And more important, she needed him to look at Mr. Smith's leg.

"Wait a moment," she murmured, searching for a cloak to cover her nightclothes. Only when she was covered from throat to ankle did she nod for the housekeeper to allow him in.

Dr. Fraser's dark blue eyes were bloodshot, his face darkened from soot, while his hair hung in a wild dark tangle. He looked like a man who'd come straight from a battlefield with blood covering his hands. He called out an order behind him. "Bring them in!"

"'Them'?" Victoria whispered.

"I have men needing shelter from the cold. I've put a few patients in your barn, but these are more critical. They won't be surviving the night in a tent. Will your mother mind, do you think?"

"She's in London with my sisters." Victoria hung back against the wall, pulling the cloak tighter around her. The idea of filling the house with wounded men bothered her, but neither did she want someone to die because of her cowardice.

"Good. We'll set up a space in the parlor, and—"

"No. Not there." Somehow, she managed to find her voice.

"I-I've another patient in there. Mr. MacKinloch brought him in earlier after he was shot. He's . . . English," she finished.

Dr. Fraser's face narrowed. "Aye, so your footman said. What do you ken of him?"

"Very little. I suppose he was a gentleman caught in the wrong place. He nearly bled to death after a boy shot him."

The furious look in the doctor's eyes made her retreat another step backward. Victoria wondered what she'd said, but it was clear he believed Mr. Smith was somehow involved in the burnings.

"He had nothing to do with what happened to the crofters," she insisted.

"Strathland hired Englishmen to burn the crofters' homes and drive them out," Dr. Fraser said coolly. "He might have been one o' them."

She wanted to protest no, but the words wouldn't come out. The anger in his eyes made her shrink away. In her heart, she didn't believe it. The wounded stranger had been blunt in his demeanor, but never once had he tried to harm her. Somehow, she felt the need to protect him.

"I want you to heal his leg," she said in a voice that belied her true fears. "Only then will I allow you to bring other patients into the house."

"You're nae understanding what's happening out there," Dr. Fraser argued. "These men are dying. Some of them with wives and bairns. You can't be expecting me to help a man who might have caused it."

"I expect you to tend a wounded man who caused none of their troubles. Or you will not use this house."

Without waiting for an answer, she ascended the staircase, beckoning for Mrs. Larson to follow her. And when she reached the sanctuary of her room, she buried her face in her hands, wishing that all of them would go. Go away and leave her in the solitude she needed. She couldn't bear to think of the hurt people surrounding her, invading the place she called home.

Asking her to be braver than she really was.

"Help me to get dressed," she ordered Mrs. Larson, choosing a simple gown. The gray high-waisted garment did not flatter her, but she wanted to remain as invisible as possible.

Only belatedly did she remember that she'd left the black lace corset on a chair beside the wounded Mr. Smith.

⚜

Dr. Paul Fraser wiped his hands on a damp linen cloth, studying the wounded man who lay still within Victoria Andrews's parlor. In the past three months, he'd treated so many burn victims, he never again wanted to smell the odor of charred flesh. The agony they'd suffered made him only more determined to bring down the Earl of Strathland. Hundreds of men, women, and bairns had been driven off their land, and countless others had died. All for a flock of damned sheep.

But this new patient wasn't a farmer or a fisherman. His clothing was unusually fine, though the colors were plain. The brown wool tailcoat fit the stranger's form as if it had been cut especially for him.

But who was he? Not one of the Strathland factors, nor a local landowner. Paul had never seen the man before.

English nobility. He'd stake his life on it.

"Where'd you find him?" he asked the footman, Mr. MacKinloch, who was lurking behind the door.

"Near Loch Monel," he answered. "His servant was dead, too."

From the tension in the patient's body, Paul suspected the man was listening to their words. He didn't for a moment believe that the stranger had been in the wrong place at the wrong time. Men didn't come to Scotland in the middle of winter for no reason.

"He's someone important," Paul observed, examining the gold ring upon the stranger's finger. "This is a signet ring."

"I asked my kinsmen, but they didna know him. He's no' a Sinclair, either."

Paul opened up his bag and chose a scalpel. "Send for Mrs. Larson."

The young footman did, and when he'd gone, Paul sensed a quiet presence behind him. With a glance, he spied Victoria standing at the door. "Planning to assist me, were you?"

She shook her head, retreating from them. It surprised Paul that she'd attempted to defend the man, as shy as she was. He didn't doubt for a moment that the stranger was somehow connected with the Earl of Strathland. The question was, how?

"MacKinloch told me the stranger was shot in the leg," he prompted, hoping she would reveal more.

"Y-yes. He was bleeding so badly, I sewed the wound shut. His name is Jonathan."

"And his surname?"

"He wouldn't tell me. I've been calling him Mr. Smith."

If the man had refused to give his true name, then he had something to hide. Paul kept his tone quiet as he examined the wound more closely. "Why is he here?"

"I don't know that either."

Of course the stranger would never admit the truth. Not if he was intending to drive more crofters off the land.

God above, he was so tired. If he closed his eyes for a second, he'd sleep for the next year. He'd spent hour after hour tending to the wounded, but so many had suffered and died. He'd rescued a four-year-old girl from one of the burning homes, only to have her die in his arms an hour later.

Men like Strathland deserved to burn in hell for what they'd done. And if this man was involved . . .

Paul's fist clenched as he struggled to gain control of his anger. As he stared at the wealthy man lying unconscious, he could almost smell the money. Men like this one knew naught of what it meant to go hungry.

But could he use the stranger to help the clansmen? Could he bargain with the Devil, demanding a ransom to feed the hungry survivors this winter? Fate had granted him an opportunity, and he'd not ignore the advantage. He'd fight for the weak, even if it meant facing the worst of consequences.

To begin with, he needed to gain the man's attention. And he knew of one definite way to bring the man out of his stupor, if the stranger was indeed feigning his unconscious state. "I might have to remove the leg," he lied. "Would your father have a saw I could use?"

The blood drained from Victoria's face. "You will not cut off his leg in my house. He-he's not that bad."

With that pronouncement, the stranger opened his eyes and glared at him. As Paul had suspected, the man had heard every word. "I would prefer that you leave my leg on, Doctor."

"Most men would." He eyed Victoria and opened up his bag. After choosing a pair of scissors and a scalpel, he handed over the tools and instructed, "Boil these and bring them in the pot of water. Don't be touching them. I also need strong soap and water for my own hands, if I'm to help this man." His mother, a fey wife, had claimed that dirt attracted evil spirits. She'd sworn that boiling water would drive them off. Though it might be superstitious blethering, Paul had lost fewer patients than his colleagues. He hardly cared whether dirt caused the faeries to snatch men's souls, but he'd clung to the homespun wisdom, in case there was a grain of truth in it.

He pulled back the dressing and studied the wound. "A bonny shade of pink thread," he remarked to his patient. "Did you pick that out yourself?"

The stranger glared at him. "I was hoping for purple."

Paul studied his patient. Intelligent green eyes stared back at him, as if assessing his character. "While she's away, there are some things we should be talking about."

"Like why you're invading her household with wounded men?"

The so-called Mr. Smith propped his head up with one hand and stared back at Paul. "How would her parents feel to know that you've taken possession of their home like this?"

"The same as they'd feel about their eldest daughter harboring a traitor," he countered.

"I'm not a traitor."

"You haven't given your full name to Miss Andrews. You were shot, and I don't doubt you have ties to Lord Strathland." He stared at the man, hoping for any reaction to the name. There was none.

"I own land here, not that it's any business of yours." The stranger stared up at the ceiling. "But if you'll fix my leg, it will be worth your time."

Paul recognized the promise of money, but it wasn't his own wealth he was interested in. There were dozens of families who needed it more than himself. Before he could voice a reply, Victoria returned with his instruments in a steaming pot of water. She set it down on the carpet beside the stranger, while Mrs. Larson followed with another basin and soap for him to wash. He scrubbed at his hands, keeping the shirtsleeves rolled up, while the two women retreated.

"How is your sister Juliette?" Paul asked Victoria while he snipped at the thread holding the wound closed. The young woman hadn't answered any of the last three letters he'd sent, and her silence bothered him. It was as if he'd offended her somehow, and he didn't know what he'd said.

"Juliette is in London with my mother and sisters," Victoria answered. Paul grimaced, wondering if Lady Lanfordshire was seeking husbands for her daughters. There was no need for that, not when he'd proposed to Juliette twice already. She hadn't said no . . . but neither had she given a reason for her reluctance. They'd been friends since he'd first laid eyes upon her . . . more than that, if he were honest.

If she didn't care for him, she would have refused, he reminded himself. Once she returned, he was all the more determined to win her heart.

Paul concentrated on the stranger's wound, opening it up. Thankfully, it was a small-caliber bullet and had missed the artery. It had only gone through the outside of the man's thigh, and likely he'd survive. Yet, from the tightness of the skin and inflammation, this man would have a painful night ahead of him.

"You decided to stay behind again, did you?" he remarked to Victoria, inspecting the wound for any stray bullet fragments. "I wouldn't say that was wise. I've warned the men to stay away from the house and leave your family alone, but I've no control over Strathland's men."

He knew Victoria had not left the house since the moment she'd arrived. Her shyness was different from most women, almost crippling in the way it kept her indoors. Though he'd heard of such conditions in his medical studies, he lacked the training to help her. The human mind was more complicated than any of them could have guessed. And if he attempted and failed, Juliette would blame him for it.

"I'll be fine," she answered. Paul made no reply, but he intended to ask more of the MacKinlochs to keep a close watch over her.

The stranger's face tightened with pain, and Paul extracted a bit of torn clothing from the wound. "I'll keep this open and let him bleed for a while to reduce the pus. When you sew it up too soon, it's harder for the wound to heal."

"I can't let him bleed to death," Victoria argued.

"Not all night," he agreed. "But for a short time it will help." With a sardonic glance toward his patient, he added, "I can give him sutures out of purple thread, if you have any."

Victoria moved to the far side of the room while he continued to let the wound drain. When she was out of earshot, Paul lowered his voice and spoke to the wounded man. "I have other men who need my help."

"Don't bring them in here," the stranger warned. He gritted his teeth as he sat up. "You might think nothing of taking over Miss Andrews's house, but there's no need to bully her further."

"These are men's lives."

"And she's an innocent." Fury darkened the man's face. "Use the other rooms for your field hospital. Not this one."

"You're no' in a position to be giving orders," Paul reminded him. Still, the icy tone to the man's voice spoke of one who was accustomed to obedience.

Nodding toward Victoria, the stranger dropped his voice to a low whisper. "Don't frighten her."

Paul glanced over and saw that Victoria had picked up a black scrap of fabric. She folded it and tucked it away into a sewing basket. Though she had spoken not a word, he studied her more carefully. Her cheeks were red with embarrassment, and her movements suggested that she didn't want to be noticed. When Paul glanced back at the stranger, he saw a man who was trying to shield her in the best way he could. Which made no sense at all, given that they'd only just met.

"There are some unpleasantries she has no need to witness," his patient said.

Paul's opinion of the man shifted, but he still didn't trust him. "I'll put them in the dining room this night." Though the stranger's wound was already inflamed and draining, the true test would come later, to determine whether the inflammation worsened. Turning back to Victoria, he said, "If he begins shivering, come and fetch me quick."

Her eyes widened, but she gave a nod. He didn't need to say more for her to understand what that meant.

"Do you have anything for his pain?" she asked.

Paul wanted to laugh. Though he'd acquired small quantities of medicinal herbs from the Royal Botanical Gardens on his last visit to Edinburgh, he didn't possess nearly enough. "It depends on what he's willing to pay for it."

"You should be ashamed of yourself, Dr. Fraser," Victoria chided. "If you have medicine that will take away a man's pain, then you should not be asking for money."

"I've a tincture of opium that cost me dearly," Paul admitted. "I had planned to use it for one of the crofters, but if he pays me for it, I can get more. Cain Sinclair can arrange it."

Mr. Smith revealed his waistcoat, offering, "These buttons are gold. Take them as payment." His face had gone paler, and Paul saw that the blood from his bullet wound was now running clear. He nodded to Victoria. "Bring me the thread now, and I'll stitch him back up."

"Please, Doctor," came a child's voice. Paul turned and saw a small boy standing at the doorway. "Could you come and help me mother? Sh-she's bad off." The child's eyes held fear and Paul nodded. It took every ounce of his physician's training to remain stoic, for he knew the woman was going to die. Her wounds were beyond help, and all he could do was attempt to make her passing more comfortable.

"I'll be there in a wee moment, lad." Paul took the threaded needle and began stitching up his patient's leg. Once he'd tied off the sutures, he changed the dressing on the wound. From his bag, he withdrew the tiny vial of opium and handed it to Victoria. "Put a few drops of this in his tea. Not too much, or he might never awaken."

After he'd given it over, he used the scissors to snip off the promised buttons. They weren't worth a great deal, but he might be able to get more opium or laudanum. With the war going on, it was getting more difficult to buy medicines.

He excused himself from the pair of them, but before he could go with the boy, the stranger asked, "Your mother was hurt?"

The boy's brown hair flopped as he nodded. "In the fire, sir. She was burned and . . . she's crying." Small fists clenched as if he were trying to hold back his own tears.

Mr. Smith caught his gaze, and Paul said nothing, letting him draw whatever conclusions he would. Then the stranger sighed and lay back upon his pillow. "Go to her. I'll manage on my own."

Feeling as if he'd been dismissed, Paul left both of them, still wondering who the stranger was.

Chapter Five

"Take the opium and follow the boy," Mr. Smith ordered, pointing to the medicine he'd just paid for.

"But it's yours," Victoria protested. "Dr. Fraser said—"

"I know what he said." As he steeled himself, his green eyes regarded her. "Give it to the woman."

A hard knot formed in her throat, and she understood then. He didn't want the young boy to watch his mother suffer. Victoria tightened her grasp around the vial and took an unsteady step forward. She wasn't at all eager to find out exactly how many wounded men, women, and children had occupied the house. The idea of facing the blood and burned flesh sickened her.

"Shall I bring the rest back?" she managed, swallowing hard.

Mr. Smith ignored the question and continued, "If there's any left, distribute it among the others. No doubt I'll regret this decision later tonight."

He closed his eyes and lay back upon the bed, his hands gripping the coverlet. In the dim light of the room, her form cast a shadow over him. His face held sharp angles, with bristled cheeks and the mask of pain tensing his features. In the brief moments she'd known him, he'd spoken with a sharp tongue, almost mocking in his demeanor.

But she'd never expected him to give away the medicine.

"I could put a few drops into your tea," she offered. "Before I take the rest to her."

"Don't bother. I suppose I'll live through the night."

Unlike the boy's mother, he didn't say.

Victoria stood at the door, the vial enclosed in her palm. His sacrifice shifted her opinion of him, making her wonder what sort of man he truly was. She stared back at him, remembering how he'd held her hand, drawing it to his warm mouth. There was something forbidden about him . . . and she couldn't quite pull herself away.

For so many years, she'd faded back in her sisters' shadows. No suitors had ever come to call upon her, much less look upon her with interest. She'd grown accustomed to living a life where she was unnoticed . . . and sometimes it was lonely.

But Mr. Smith appeared to see past her years of solitude to the woman beneath. And that was more dangerous than she'd ever guessed. If she stayed by his side, helping him endure the night ahead, it would bring them closer. It would also violate every rule her mother had dictated in Victoria's two-and-twenty years of existence.

And yet, she wanted to remain.

"Giving your medicine to the woman . . . ," she began, not knowing quite how to phrase her words. "It's a noble deed."

He emitted a sharp bark of laughter. "I'm not at all noble, Miss Andrews. I'm an ill-tempered tyrant with no patience at all."

She didn't believe that. A true tyrant wouldn't give his medicine to a stranger.

"I'll be back," she murmured, retreating toward the dining room.

With the precious vial of opium in her hands, she saw Dr. Fraser moving among the different patients. There were three men and one woman, all resting upon the floor while the dining room table and chairs were pushed back. The young boy she'd seen earlier was holding his mother's hand, tears streaming down his face. His older brother was standing beside the wall, tracing his finger over a pattern on the wallpaper.

"What is it?" Dr. Fraser gritted out. "I can't be leaving these patients right now."

"Mr. Smith asked me to give this to the woman," she said, averting her eyes from the patient. She held out the vial, but he didn't take it at first. "For her pain," she repeated.

Dr. Fraser leaned in close, dropping his voice low. "She's dying, Miss Andrews. 'Twould be a miracle if she lasted through the night."

"It was Mr. Smith's request. Her sons don't need to watch her suffer," she murmured. When she met his gaze, she saw the surprise in the doctor's eyes.

He took the vial from her, his expression turning thoughtful. "Aye, you're right." Reaching into his waistcoat pocket, he held out the buttons. "Return these to him."

"Keep them," Victoria advised. "And buy more medicine for the others when you can."

Upon his face, she saw a hint of relief. Before he turned back to his patients, he added, "Thank you, Miss Andrews, for letting us use your father's house. All of us are very grateful indeed."

She managed a faltering nod before she exited the room with more dignity than she felt. Her hands shook as she returned to the hallway where she rested her back against one wall. Though she'd tried to shield her eyes from their suffering, she'd seen enough to know that the strife was getting worse instead of better. They'd granted sanctuary to the nearby families, trying to help where they could.

But there were simply too many of them.

She went to sit upon the stairs, resting her face against the spindles. Her world was tearing apart at the seams, leaving frayed edges that she couldn't put back together. The familiar fears cloaked her mind, and her hands began shaking.

Coward.

If she were a woman with any fortitude at all, she'd offer her assistance to Dr. Fraser. Or she'd order Mrs. Larson to prepare food for the families of the wounded. She would have taken some of the tincture of opium for Mr. Smith and given him a good night's rest instead of passing it on to the others.

But then, that was what he'd wanted. He'd paid the doctor for the medicine and given it away, knowing that he would suffer for the rest of the night. Even he had more courage than she.

You must go back, her conscience reminded her. *You told him you would.*

It was easier to grant that promise before she'd glimpsed the man beneath the arrogance. She might distract herself with sewing, pretending not to look at him.

But the truth was, she *did* find him interesting. Handsome, too. Fate had delivered him to her doorstep, like a gauntlet thrown to the ground.

Cold truth spiraled within her, reminding her of what she was—an awkward spinster too frightened to leave the house. How could she even imagine that a man like him would be interested in her? And if he ever found out about her fears, he'd look upon her with disgust.

No. She didn't want that. It was easier to lock away her attraction, steeling herself with reality. Once he'd healed, he would leave Scotland, and she'd never see him again. It was better that way.

Each step was harder than the next, but Victoria forced herself to return to the parlor. It had grown so dark, she could no longer see Mr. Smith. She fumbled her way to the piano and lit an oil lamp, turning it down low.

His face held the grim reality of a man in terrible pain. His fists clenched upon the coverlet and unclenched, his mouth drawn in a tight line.

"You gave them the medicine?"

"I did." She drew up a chair and said, "I pray her suffering will end this night."

"I pray *my* suffering will end," he countered. "Perhaps you should fetch that pistol after all."

"You're stronger than that." Victoria reached for her earlier sewing to occupy her hands. She threaded her needle, holding the black lace across the padded corset. As she folded and stitched the seam, she felt her nerves growing calmer.

"Talk to me," Mr. Smith ordered. "Tell me about yourself or your family. Anything at all."

She fumbled for an appropriate conversation, uncertain what to say. "I have three sisters. Margaret, Amelia, and Juliette."

"I never had any brothers or sisters. Only cousins," he answered. He inhaled sharply, reaching toward his leg as if he could stifle the pain.

"Would you like some of my father's brandy to drink?" Victoria offered.

"An hour ago, I'd have said no. Now, I think I'd like to pass out, if you wouldn't mind assisting me." The rough timbre of his voice was laced with misery, and she found herself reaching for the crystal decanter and a glass. The bottle was only half-filled, and she had no idea how much brandy it took to make a man drunk. Or whether it was a good idea or not.

She filled up the glass and held it out to him.

"Sit beside me," he said. "I'll need you to help me raise my head while I drink."

Victoria hesitated, her heart quickening at his invitation. "I'll get you some pillows." Setting down the glass, she used two pillows from the sofa to help prop him up. All the while, his eyes were upon her, watching. He took the brandy and swallowed it quickly, but as he drank, he made no effort to avert his gaze.

"Afraid of me, are you?"

"There's no reason for me to be that close." She threaded her needle again, pretending as if she weren't at all nervous. Perhaps if she told herself that often enough, her heart would calm down.

"Pour me another."

She gave it to him, watching as his mouth curved over the glass. She imagined that firm mouth upon her skin, without knowing where the thoughts were coming from. Exhaustion had likely turned her head. And still, she wondered.

What would his kiss taste like, with brandy lingering upon his tongue? If his mouth were upon hers, would it be hard and demanding? Or softer, coaxing her to yield? Abruptly, she stabbed herself with a needle.

"What are you sewing?" Mr. Smith asked, draining the second glass. She poured a third and averted a direct answer.

"It's—it's a lady's garment."

"For mourning, I presume?" He took another sip of brandy and she felt his gaze fixed upon her.

"It . . . well, yes, of course." What else could she tell him? Until Mr. Sinclair returned from London with her supply of fabric, she'd had to use whatever material was available. She liked the way this one was transforming, and she'd begun attaching the lace just above the top of the bodice.

"I've always thought that black was a fine color, especially upon a woman's pale skin. It's beautiful."

His voice was casting a spell over her, leaving her frozen in place. A thousand warnings rose up in her mind, telling her why she shouldn't be here. Victoria moved a small end table beside him, hoping he could now pour his own brandy. "Are you drunk yet?" she asked hopefully.

His hand trembled as he took another sip. "Sadly, no. I've always been able to hold my liquor. No doubt I'll have an excruciating headache in the morning."

"Would you like me to bring back the medicine? Dr. Fraser won't mind."

Mr. Smith shook his head. "Let him use it on those who need

it more." He grew silent, setting down the brandy. Against the amber light, his skin held the sheen of perspiration, and she realized that his tailcoat was only making his fever worse. "Shall I help you remove your coat?"

"Please."

Almost as soon as she'd made the suggestion, she realized the error she'd made. Not only would she have to sit beside Mr. Smith, she would also have to touch him.

His green eyes held the color of summer grass, a dark hue blended with gray. When she helped him to sit up, he slid a hand around her waist for balance. She tried to slide his coat over his broad shoulders, but he had flexed them backward as if to prevent it. His face was dangerously close to hers, and the scent of brandy hung upon his breath.

"I like your hair down," he murmured. He reached out to touch it, and she was caught spellbound, his warm hands moving down the strands to rest upon her back. His touch burned through the thin layer of her gown to the skin beneath.

Her thoughts fractured into a thousand pieces, leaving her unable to grasp a single coherent idea. She was fully aware of him, and within her, he'd awakened a new yearning.

"I think you *are* drunk to say such things." She knew better than to believe them.

"Just in a great deal of pain," he corrected. "Any distraction is more welcome than this wound." His mouth was tight, his eyes glazed with the beginnings of fever, and she understood his need for conversation.

She pulled against his tailcoat, and he relaxed his shoulders, letting her aid him. At last, she jerked his arms free, revealing his waistcoat and a shirt of fine cambric.

"The waistcoat, too," he reminded her, and she unbuttoned it. Beneath her fingertips, the warmth of his feverish body radiated through the fabric. When he wore only his shirt, she eased him back down to the pillow.

"Do you want more brandy?"

"It's nearly empty, and I can't say it's done anything to ease the pain." He closed his eyes and said, "I don't mind it if you talk to me, though. It's a suitable distraction, so long as you're not reading Scripture."

An unexpected smile faltered at her lips. In the stillness that hung between them, she found herself unable to take her eyes from him. His clothes revealed him as a man of wealth, yet he clung to his anonymity.

"Who are you, really?" she asked.

He didn't look at her, but his voice broke through the silence. "No one of interest."

"Now then." Charlotte Larkspur, the Countess of Arnsbury, stared at her sister like an army general preparing for battle. "I've invited two dozen guests for a quiet gathering. Two baronets, a knight, and an earl were the best I could do. Without much of a dowry, the girls have no prayer of winning the earl—not to mention he's a widower and has shown little interest in remarrying. However, once we've seen to their wardrobe—"

"I can't afford new clothes for the girls," Beatrice admitted. The thought of it made her face burn with shame. She wished the house in Norfolk hadn't needed so many repairs and that they hadn't had so many bills piling up. Thankfully, their London town house was a small property in good condition. But every time she stared at the columns of figures, her stomach grew nauseous with worry. She was a failure at managing money, and her children were suffering from it.

"We'll have to make do with what they have," she told her sister.

Charlotte released a sigh. "You know they can't, Beatrice. It may be a pinch now, but in the end, you must secure a good marriage for them."

"I know," she admitted. "But I can't spin straw into gold. And Henry will be so angry with me when he learns how impoverished we've become since he went off to fight. I know he believes his officer's pay was more than enough to see us through. Mr. Gilderness sent another letter a week ago, explaining that the house in Norfolk needed a new roof."

"I'll help you," her sister insisted. "I will see if some of my gowns can't be altered. And we'll go to Madame Benedict's in the morning to measure the girls for new clothes. It will be my Christmas gift to them."

"You're too generous," Beatrice murmured, knowing she ought to refuse. But her pride was already in tatters. She didn't have enough money to buy presents for her own daughters. The clenching fears rose up again, taunting her. *You're useless. Without Henry, you can't do anything.*

Her sister's hand reached for hers. "It will be all right, Beatrice."

"But when Henry finds out—"

"He won't. By the time he's back from the war, all will be as right as rain."

She wanted to believe that. For the past year, she'd desperately clung to false hopes. But what could she do? She'd sold nearly everything of value to provide for them. And when that ran out . . .

"Mother," came the voice of Margaret. From the faint blush on her daughter's cheeks, she'd overheard part of their conversation.

"What is it?" Beatrice forced a smile. "Have you been enjoying yourself? Did you go out walking with your sisters?"

Margaret touched a hand to her light brown hair, smoothing an imaginary stray hair back. Even though it was early morning, she'd taken great pains with her appearance. At her waist, she'd tucked a sprig of holly, and Charlotte smiled upon her with approval.

"I beg your pardon, but I-I couldn't help but overhear—" Her face turned crimson. "I know it isn't polite to eavesdrop, but the door was open. And, well, I know the real reason you brought Juliette and me to London."

"It's no secret that we want you girls to make a good marriage," Charlotte agreed, beckoning for Margaret to join them. Beatrice's gaze narrowed upon a reticule Margaret was holding. It appeared that her daughter was trying to hide the contents.

"Yes." Margaret raised her chin. "It's something I want very badly. To make a good marriage, I mean. And I may not get another chance to meet a proper gentleman." She turned to Beatrice, still clutching the reticule. "I know you believe there isn't money for new gowns or for a Season."

Beatrice felt her own face warm with color. "No. There isn't."

"You're wrong," Margaret blurted out. "There is enough for new gowns. And there may be enough for a Season for one of us."

From her daughter's embarrassment, Beatrice understood that Margaret desperately wanted it to be her. And certainly, of all the girls, Margaret had the greatest marital ambitions. She was a cool, polished rose who deserved the chance.

"Darling, if there were any way to give you a Season, I would," her mother answered, shaking her head. "But Aunt Charlotte has arranged to have a few parties. She will introduce you to possible husbands, and it will be nearly as nice."

"One or two gatherings won't be enough," Margaret protested. "I want to stay longer. Please, Mother." She held out the reticule, and when Beatrice took it, she realized it was filled with money.

"This is for you Victoria and I have done some sewing, and we arranged to sell some . . . garments at Madame Benedict's. Here are the profits."

Charlotte let out a sigh and sank into a chair. "You didn't. Darling child, don't you know that if you—you *sell* things, it makes you no better than a common merchant?"

Margaret straightened as if her spine were made of steel. "Of course I know that. Which is why it was done through someone else. There will be no connection to us."

Beatrice opened the reticule and stared at the collection of guineas and pound notes. Though she ought to be overjoyed at the modest sum, it only served to remind her that her daughters had taken it upon themselves to earn wages. And all because of her failure to manage her husband's money. "You didn't sell your old clothing, did you?"

There was a slight hesitation before Margaret admitted, "No. It was a gown that Victoria made and"—her face turned scarlet—"another new garment." She clasped her hands together, straightening. "We weren't going to tell you, but . . . you sound as if we're only staying for a fortnight. I don't want to return to Scotland. And, well, this might help."

Though Beatrice hadn't counted the coins, she knew it wasn't enough. *Tread carefully,* she thought to herself. Margaret had already done something rash in order to improve their finances. She didn't want a family scandal upon their hands that would endanger their good name.

"You shouldn't have sold Amelia's gown," Beatrice chided. "As much as she loves clothing, didn't you know it would break her heart?"

"It wasn't Amelia's birthday gown," Margaret insisted. "It was a different one."

"How *did* you find someone to sell it for you?" Charlotte interrupted. "You didn't just hire someone off the street, did you?"

Margaret's mouth tightened into a thin line, and she was making a concerted effort not to glare at her aunt. "It was someone we could trust. An acquaintance of Mr. MacKinloch's named Mr. Cain Sinclair."

Beatrice knew of the man. Both of his parents were dead, and he'd taken it upon himself to care for his younger brother. Though Mr. Sinclair was undoubtedly a man of poor means, she hoped he possessed discretion.

"Absolutely not," Charlotte interjected. "Ladies do not engage in commerce. It is uncivilized."

"So is starving to death," Margaret countered coldly.

That such words could come out of her daughter's mouth was appalling. Beatrice stood up, moving between them. "It's not that bad, truly. Margaret, you should be ashamed of yourself for speaking in such a way."

A rise of color came over the girl's cheeks. "I apologize for speaking too plainly, then. But I promise you, we've done nothing to risk our family's reputation. I would never dream of it."

"It only takes one person's idle conversation to bring down a good name," Charlotte warned.

Beatrice agreed with her sister. The girls could not endanger their futures by taking such a risk. "I am grateful that you and Victoria were so resourceful, Margaret, but truly, I cannot condone this. You will not sell garments to Madame Benedict again."

Her daughter looked as if she wanted to argue, but when she caught sight of her aunt, she stifled the words. Beatrice pressed the bonnet back into her daughter's hands. "Hold on to this for now. And dearest"—she took Margaret's hands in hers—"thank you for trying. It was thoughtful of you."

Though she murmured the expected apology, Margaret didn't look at all satisfied when she left the room. After the door closed, Beatrice turned back to her sister, feeling small and slight. "I didn't realize they knew."

"They're your daughters. Of course they know." Charlotte folded her hands in her lap. "And although their actions were ill-advised, their hearts were in the right place."

She believed that. Though she might not have given her daughters a life of wealth and privilege, she'd always made it clear that she loved them.

Her sister was staring at her with a curious look. "When was the last time you had a letter from Henry?"

"I can't remember," she lied. It had been seventy-nine days, to be precise. He'd sent her a terse letter asking about the sheep. The *sheep,* for God's sake. Not about their daughters or about her. He'd wanted to know how the livestock were faring. And didn't that just speak volumes for their marriage?

"Beatrice, may I broach a delicate subject?"

Though she nodded, she wasn't at all certain this would be a good conversation.

"I'd like you to be measured for a new gown yourself," Charlotte said. "You may be married, but it's no excuse to ignore your own appearance."

Her cheeks burned brighter at the accusation. "But I haven't."

"How old is the dress you're wearing, then? I'll wager it's more than five years old."

"Ten," Beatrice admitted. "But it's good enough for me. It's not as if *I'm* trying to win a husband."

"You don't want to embarrass your daughters tomorrow, do you?" her sister chided. Beatrice glanced down at the green gown she was wearing. The color had once been as bright as an emerald, but it now resembled moss. The hem was peppered with tiny holes that were easily visible, but she'd never paid any heed to it, for how many people would actually stare at the hemline?

She was about to suggest that she borrow one of Charlotte's, but then, she'd grown thinner over the past three years until this gown hung upon her shoulders. Her sister had generous curves, and there was no chance that any of her clothing would fit.

Charlotte sent her a sympathetic look. "Let us go and talk with Madame Benedict, at least. She may have some suggestions. Or perhaps you should keep the funds that Margaret procured. Just this once."

Her cheeks were heated with embarrassment, for Beatrice knew her sister was right. It had been years since she'd ordered a gown for herself.

"You've grown so thin," her sister said. "Now that you're here, you should look after your own health. Try to put some flesh back on these bones. When he comes home, Henry will see how beautiful you are."

The thought took root within her mind. Henry had never seemed to notice anything about her appearance. She'd stopped making any effort, for it hardly mattered to him. But over those years, she'd lost herself. She no longer remembered what it was to feel pretty.

"Yes," she heard herself saying. "I'd like that very much."

✻

Margaret walked downstairs, her thoughts torn apart with elation and dread. So much money. She'd never dreamed of it, and yet it was appalling what they'd done. If anyone found out, it would ruin them.

And yet . . . the sale of the red corset had been more money than the last three gowns put together.

Her sister Amelia had penned a note, explaining to Madame Benedict that the undergarments were part of an exclusive collection, only to be sold at the highest price. She'd even invented the name: Aphrodite's Unmentionables.

Personally, Margaret thought the corset was the most wicked garment she'd ever seen. It made a woman's breasts bigger. And if that wasn't scandalous enough, it was a shade of red that a harlot might wear. Not that she'd ever met any harlots, but she imagined it would appeal to them.

She entered the drawing room, her posture straight as she sank into a chair to think. Covering her face with her hands, she wondered what on earth she was going to do about this. Amelia would be thrilled by the amount of money, as would Juliette. Given their financial state, she saw little choice but to continue their secret sales.

"Aren't you going to kiss me goodbye before I go?" came a low male voice.

Instantly, her spine stiffened, and Margaret stared over at the drapes. The nerve of that man. She thought he'd gone by now. There was no man she despised more than Cain Sinclair. If anyone was the Devil come down to Earth, it was he. He never seemed to *care* about manners and propriety. In fact, he appeared to enjoy making her blush. Sometimes she wished he would simply go away . . . but then, they needed him to deliver and sell the garments. He was a necessary evil.

"Mr. Sinclair, you have been most helpful in your services," she said calmly. "I must ask you to return to Ballaloch and deliver the fabric you acquired. Victoria will give you more garments to sell within a fortnight." She pointed to the reticule of coins, which she'd set upon a nearby table. "I presume you have collected your payment already."

He inclined his head. "You can count the sum if you don't believe me." He emerged from behind the drapes, leaning one hand against the wall, sending her a lazy smile.

His black hair hung down to the middle of his back, as if he didn't care enough to cut it. He was uncommonly tall, and though he wore clothes that were worn down and discolored from years of use, it did nothing to diminish his looks. The look on his face held the promise of sin, and she wasn't about to take a bite from that apple.

"You ken why I'm helping you, don't you?" he said, coming closer.

She gazed frantically behind her, wondering if anyone would see them. "B-because of the money. You're well paid for what you do."

"That's one reason. Can't you guess the other?" He took another step closer, resting his hands on the top of a chair.

Oh, she knew the reason well enough. Not that she wanted anything to do with him. Margaret lifted her chin. "You may keep your reasons to yourself, Mr. Sinclair. I have no need of them."

He was watching her intently, and her cheeks burned beneath his gaze. No matter that she'd told him, time and again, that she had no interest in a man like him . . . he kept returning. Watching her with those piercing blue eyes that seemed to see beneath her skin. His strong jaw and firm mouth caught her attention, along with the knowing smile. The room was closing in, and he moved in abruptly until she stood before him, her face directly in front of his chest.

"You're playing a dangerous game, lass," he said. "I saw the corset."

"It w-will only be the one garment," she stammered. "Mostly dresses."

"Not anymore." His hand came out to capture the back of her neck, and a liquid column of heat poured down her spine at his touch. She tried to pull back, but he held her captive. There was only a hand's distance between them, and the air tightened in her lungs. Like a wild Highlander, he towered over her. When he spoke, his breath warmed her skin. "Your sister caused a sensation. She'll have to make more of them, in many different colors."

"She never should have sewn such a garment. I-I'll speak with her about it and tell her so."

"Don't be spoiling her triumph with your prim ideas, Miss Andrews. You don't even ken what that corset was for, do you?"

She tried to move away from him, but his hand threaded into her hair, loosening her topknot. "You shouldn't speak of such things."

"It's for a man to look at. A lover or a husband." His voice dropped to a deep baritone. "A man who is wanting tae watch her take it off."

She moved far away from him, pointing toward the door. "Take your money and go, Mr. Sinclair. Our business here is finished."

But the cocky smile he sent her said that he was far from finished.

To Jonathan's great surprise, he wasn't dead.

He grimaced against the pounding headache, and his mouth tasted as if it were stuffed with cotton. Dying sounded like a marvelous escape at the moment. He struggled to open his eyes, and his hands brushed against something soft.

It was a Herculean effort to turn his head, but when he opened his eyes, he saw Victoria sleeping with her head beneath his hand. Her sewing had fallen to the floor, and it looked as if she'd laid her head down for a moment and dozed off.

From this close view, he glimpsed a delicate nose and high cheekbones. Her blond hair had darker streaks in it, almost as if her locks couldn't decide whether to be golden or brown and had settled on both.

But it was her mouth that fascinated him. The top lip was slightly smaller than the bottom, like a rosebud. He imagined taking command of that mouth, coaxing it to open for him. Victoria's innocent shyness allured him, making him wonder what secrets lay beneath. The scent of her skin and the warmth of her body were a far greater distraction than the bullet wound he'd suffered.

As if in answer to his daydream, she snuggled closer, her hand moving up to his chest as if she wanted him to protect her. His hand slid against her silken hair, caressing the side of her face. Her cheek was warm, her eyes closed like a dormant bloom.

The gown she'd worn was the color of London fog, a shade of gray unflattering on most women. But instead of dispelling his interest in Victoria, it only intrigued him more. She was nothing like the women he'd known, those who obsessed over the latest fashions and jewels. There were no pearls or rings upon these fingers. From his vantage point, he could see the work-roughened fingers that had labored with a needle. She was utterly unsuitable for a man like him.

Perhaps that was why he liked her.

She'd kept her promise to stay at his side, despite how improper it was. And knowing she was there had made the night more bearable.

Miss Andrews had a steadiness of nerve that defied all expectations. An intelligence he admired. And she'd weathered his bad temper with a sharp tongue of her own, sewing him up with pink thread.

His thumb grazed Victoria's temple, waiting for those gray eyes to open. It surprised him that she didn't move when he touched her. His hand stilled, for he realized just what he was doing— taking advantage of her during her sleep. If those gray eyes opened, he'd see her fear and embarrassment.

For whatever unknown reason, he didn't want her to be afraid of him. He removed his hand from her hair and coughed. She didn't move, and he realized that she was truly in a sound sleep.

"Miss Andrews," he said, nudging her head. He must've nudged too hard, for she slipped off the edge of the mattress and landed facedown on the carpet.

He winced at that, for he'd not intended to hurt her.

"Ouch," she groaned. She managed to stand up, rubbing her nose as she sat back down. "I must have fallen asleep and tumbled out of the chair."

Now was probably not the time to tell her that she'd slept beside him, her face burrowed against his chest. "Are you all right?" he asked.

She nodded with a sheepish smile. "Aside from my wounded pride." With a blush in her cheeks, she added, "How is your leg this morning?"

He decided to be honest. "It hurts. I'm wishing I had that pain medicine now, because it's worse today than yesterday."

"Are you still feverish?" Her hand came out to his forehead, but she stopped before she touched him.

In answer, he took her hand and brought it to his forehead.

The cool touch of her fingers on his skin was a relief, and he lay back, closing his eyes.

"The fever hasn't broken," she said, her hand moving across his forehead, inadvertently stroking his hair. "You need medicine and more rest."

"I can't sleep when my leg feels like it's been butchered." He eyed her.

"Do you want me to see if there's any laudanum?" She stood from the chair, seemingly grateful for a reason to leave. He didn't want her to. It was bad enough with his leg aching, but worse to be left alone with only four walls to stare at.

"Go and find out what happened to the woman," he bade her, not answering the question. His leg was killing him, but when he thought of the burned woman, he was haunted by his mother's face. It was his fault Catherine Nottoway had died. He'd been unable to save her, and no matter how he tried to atone for her death, the guilt plagued him still.

Nothing he did would bring her back. All he could do was continue to build his fortune, to somehow prove that he was worth more than his father had believed. Money meant everything to the ton. Once he'd built a fortune beyond all imaginings, it would eventually eradicate the shame upon his family's name. The power of wealth would drown out the whispers of scandal, silencing anyone who dared to point a finger at him.

It was all he had left.

Before Miss Andrews could depart, the housekeeper returned with a covered plate. Her face was grim, her eyes red-rimmed. Without a word, she took down all the portraits in the room and opened a window.

"It's freezing outside," he started to protest.

"And ye want to stay here with spirits of the dead lingering, do ye?" She moved to the other window and forced it open, letting snow blow inside.

But it was Miss Andrews's reaction that caught his attention.

She moved as far away from the windows as possible, blurting out, "I have to go." The sound of footsteps resounded upon the stairs as she fled.

Yet, the housekeeper didn't seem at all surprised. "We'll wait a few minutes and then when the spirits have gone, I'll close the windows. Miss Andrews will be comin' back then, sure enough. In the meantime, Dr. Fraser took the puir dead woman's body out to the barn for the laying out. Her family will be with her to grieve."

Despite the frigid air blowing inside, the housekeeper set down the food on a chair beside him and sprinkled the chair with droplets of water. "I've made porridge for ye, and some toast."

Jonathan lifted the cover and saw an iron nail embedded in the toast. "And what's this for? Were you hoping I might swallow it?"

"Don't be foolish, lad. It's to keep death from entering." The housekeeper walked over to the grandfather clock and stopped the pendulum. "There won't be any milk today, either, for I've poured it all out." She brushed her hands against her apron and then went back to close the windows.

"Do you truly believe in such nonsense?" he asked.

"Well, I'm not dead yet, am I? It's working, isn't it?"

Jonathan removed the nail from his toast and set it aside. "I suppose."

Lowering her voice to a whisper, the housekeeper added, "I put a wee dram of laudanum in that tea. The doctor won't miss it, nor will the others."

Gratefully, he reached for the tea and drank it, ignoring the bitter flavor. Mrs. Larson departed, and within a few minutes more, Miss Andrews returned. She wore a woolen shawl over her shoulders, and glanced at the windows as if to verify they were closed.

"Forgive me," she apologized. "I was . . . I was cold." From the way she averted her gaze, he suspected there was something else she hadn't told him, but he didn't press the issue. Changing the subject, he said, "Some of my belongings are at my house on Eiloch Hill. I would appreciate it if you could send someone to bring clothing for me. I'd also like to know if any of my staff are still there."

"I'll send Mr. MacKinloch," she agreed. Then she turned back, frowning. "Eiloch Hill, you said?"

There was a note of distress in her voice, and he wondered what else could be wrong with the house he'd acquired. "Yes. Why do you ask?"

"It used to belong to the Earl of Strathland. These crofters were evicted from that land before you arrived."

It annoyed him that Strathland would overstep his authority, when he'd already sold the land. As their new landlord, it should have fallen to Jonathan to determine the crofters' fate.

Instead, due to the earl's evictions, it meant that he was indirectly responsible for the suffering of these men and women. Remaining here was dangerous at best, fatal at worst.

"Will you not tell me who you are," she asked quietly, "and why you've come?"

"I'm just a landowner," he hedged. "I came to inspect the house and land, and then I'll move on again, as I always do." He attempted to sit up, but the moment he raised his torso, the room began to spin. From the unsteadiness in his head, he suspected the laudanum was beginning to take effect.

"Is your home in London?"

"I have many houses." He didn't consider any of the properties a home. They were piles of stone and brick, filled with people who would be glad to see him gone.

"But what of your family? Have you a wife and children?"

"Neither. Though I intend to marry and get an heir soon. I'll need someone to inherit my many houses."

A wry smile crossed her face. "You speak of a wife as if you're going to buy a horse and breed it."

"Is there a difference?" he remarked wryly. "I'd wed the next woman who walked through that door before I'd let my cousin inherit." He'd avoided marriage for years, especially after the death of his parents. The whispers of scandal were only fueled by his presence, and it was easier to concentrate on managing the estates. He'd buried himself in travel and adding to his holdings, blocking out the shadows of guilt. Word had spread of his increasing wealth, and most of the ton would have no trouble overlooking his darker past in the hopes of a gilded future.

Mrs. Larson chose that very moment to enter the parlor. "Would either of you care for more tea?"

Victoria burst into laughter. "The next woman?" she teased. The humor in her eyes transformed her. Without the haunted shyness on her face, her beauty took on a vivid quality that he'd never expected. Jonathan didn't share in her laugh, but instead locked his gaze upon her features. He let his imagination wander, remembering what it was like to see her golden brown hair falling over her shoulders, down to slender hips.

Her soft smile faded abruptly, as if she'd read his errant thoughts. She stood so quickly, she nearly tripped over her gray skirts. "Thank you," she said, accepting a steaming cup from Mrs. Larson. "Tea would be wonderful." She glanced down at him and added, "It's a weakness of mine, I know. It's impossible to get tea in the Highlands, so whenever Mr. Sinclair goes to London, he brings some to us."

Mrs. Larson brought out cream and sugar and refilled Jonathan's cup. Before she departed, Victoria reminded her, "Send Mr. MacKinloch to Eiloch Hill for Mr. Smith's belongings, if you would."

"Eiloch Hill?" The housekeeper paused at the door, muttering curses in a blend of Gaelic and English.

"It was not Mr. Smith who set fire to those houses, Mrs. Larson," Victoria reassured her. "It was under the earl's orders."

"Oh, I'll not be blaming him for what happened to those puir people. But strike a bargain with the Devil, and ye're like to sprout horns in unwanted places." With a huff, the housekeeper turned her back and moved on.

When she'd gone, Victoria sent him a regretful smile. "I fear, with the mention of that house, your hopes of wedding Mrs. Larson are sadly not meant to be." She reached for his cup and refilled it. "Do you take sugar?"

"Three lumps, if they're not too large."

She raised an eyebrow. "You must like it sweet."

His gaze settled upon her countenance, moving over the slim curves hidden beneath her gown. "Sometimes."

Her face flushed as she caught his meaning. When she stirred in the sugar and lifted the steaming cup to him, he didn't take it. "My hands aren't very steady. You'll have to help me drink," he said.

She blew upon the hot liquid, using one hand to support his head while he took a sip. After she took the cup away, he caught her hand. "Thank you for staying with me last night."

Her face flushed, but she gave a nod. Raising her gray eyes to his, she added, "The woman died without suffering. Her sons were beside her, and you gave them a gift when you gave up the medicine."

She made it sound as if he were a saint, when nothing could be further from the truth. It discomfited him to have her hold him in such esteem. "I fear others will speak ill of you for staying at my side last night."

Her countenance held a sad smile. "Your fear is misplaced, for I chose to stay." She folded her hands in her lap, casting a glance toward the dining room. "You own Eiloch Hill, the land where these people were evicted. If you want to repair damage, try helping them." She pointed to the dining room, her face sober. "They need it far more than I."

Chapter Six

"THERE'S SOMEONE tae see you, sir," Mrs. Larson said, as Jonathan attempted to sit up. "One of your servants, I believe. From Eiloch Hill." She muttered something about evil spirits and motioned for the man to enter.

He was relieved to see Giles Franklin, his footman. Franklin hurried forward, bowing low. Before the man could utter a word, Jonathan turned to the housekeeper. "That will be all, Mrs. Larson."

He motioned for Franklin to come closer, pressing a finger to his lips. Mrs. Larson looked disappointed, but disappeared into the hallway.

"Your Grace, I am terribly sorry about all of this," the footman apologized. "The snow made it difficult to track you, and after the burnings, I feared the worst. Carlson didn't . . . that is, he—"

"He's dead, isn't he?" Jonathan had suspected as much. "And what of the others?"

"Others?" Franklin appeared confused at the question.

"The remainder of the staff you were supposed to hire. Did they not arrive?"

His footman shook his head. "No, Your Gr—"

"Do not call me that here," he interrupted in a low voice. "Call me sir, if you must."

"Sir," Franklin amended. "But no, the staff did not arrive. It seems that, well, no one wants to work at Eiloch Hill. They claim it's a cursed house."

Ridiculous superstitions again. "Then hire Englishmen, if you must."

"Of course, sir. It's just that, with the snow, travel is difficult right now. But I have a horse, and if you should care to leave, I could arrange it."

"Not yet." His leg hadn't healed enough to travel, and with no staff awaiting him, it would be far more difficult to convalesce. "I'll remain here a little longer." He stared at Franklin. "When they sent Mr. MacKinloch to you, did you reveal my rank?"

His footman turned crimson. "Forgive me, sir. Perhaps I should have, but . . . it did not seem safe. After I found Carlson's body and learned that you were wounded and taken to this household . . . it seemed imprudent to trust a Scot." His gaze dropped to the floor, and he whispered, "These men are so poor, I feared they might try to hold you as a hostage if they knew who you really were. I told them you were the youngest son of a knight."

Jonathan breathed a little easier at his footman's confession, grateful that the man had kept his silence. "You were right to keep my identity a secret. I presume you brought the clothing I requested."

"Yes, sir. Is there anything else I can bring you?"

There was, but it meant sending his footman to London, which would take over a week. For now, he thought it best to remain here.

"Lock up the house and bring everything here," he added. "Then I want you to go to London and acquire an adequate staff to maintain the house." Reaching down toward his leg, he added, "And bring back laudanum." Though the medicine hadn't eradicated the pain, at least it had granted him a little sleep.

"Yes, sir."

The footman brought the clothing forward and added, "Would you like me to act as your valet, Your—that is, sir?"

"That won't be necessary." It wasn't likely that the new breeches would fit until the swelling had abated in his leg. "You may go now." He waved his hand in dismissal, and his footman departed.

A few minutes after the man had left, Victoria appeared in the doorway. "Will you be returning to Eiloch Hill, Mr. Smith?"

"Not yet. It seems there was some difficulty in acquiring a staff to maintain the property. Some superstitions, I believe."

Miss Andrews paled and nodded. "Several men were hanged upon Eiloch Hill, including Dr. Fraser's father. Their bodies were left as an example, and no one wants to go near the house."

Her explanation made sense. Still, Jonathan preferred keeping a local staff instead of bringing in outsiders. "I've sent Franklin to London, to bring back a land steward and a few others to begin restoring the property," he told her. "If you don't mind my staying here a little longer, that is." He didn't feel at all capable of traveling yet.

"You may stay as long as you wish." But she remained far away from him, her shoulders pressing against the doorway.

"It's not my intent to make you uncomfortable. But I am grateful that you're here. It's extremely tedious, being unable to walk or move," he admitted. "Except for the odd moment when Mrs. Larson comes in to open the windows, remove the mirrors, and cover the portraits. I half expect to find iron nails instead of silver spoons to stir my tea," he said. "In case any wayward faeries slip into the house."

"She means no harm." The faint smile at her lips gave him a slight hope, and she took a step closer. "Is your fever any better?"

It wasn't, but he wouldn't mind having her hands upon him again. She smelled good, and he liked having her near. "You may inspect me, if you wish."

Tentatively, she approached him, as if he were a wolf about to feast upon her. He remained still, waiting until her hand came to touch his forehead again. The cool touch of her fingers was merciful, and she admitted, "You're still hot, but it doesn't seem as bad as last night."

He caught her hand in his, searching for a reason to make her stay. The laudanum had begun to soften the edges of his pain, but he didn't want to succumb to sleep. Not yet.

"I need a distraction," he muttered.

"W-what do you mean?" Her mouth twisted with worry, and he drew her hand to his face, leaning back. He shouldn't be enjoying teasing her, but he'd come to like this woman. And watching her was far more interesting than staring at four walls.

"Have you a chessboard?"

She nodded, and the relief on her face nearly made him smile. "But I don't play. My father does."

"Bring it," he suggested. "I'll teach you how. It's easy enough to learn, but it takes years to master the strategies."

"Perhaps later. I really do have to finish my sewing," she protested.

Jonathan ignored her, continuing, "While you fetch the chessboard and pieces, I'll change my shirt. I wouldn't mind some water and a basin for washing."

"Should I send Mr. MacKinloch to help you?" she offered.

"I believe I'm capable of managing it myself." He'd only been wounded below the waist, so it should be simple enough.

Victoria retreated from the room while he reached for the bundle of clothing Franklin had left behind. When his hands untied the knot, a wave of dizziness made his head ache. It seemed he'd underestimated the power of the laudanum. He steeled himself against the discomfort while he undressed and chose a clean shirt. From his haggard appearance, he didn't doubt that he would frighten any woman at all, especially Miss Andrews. He hadn't shaved in days.

A slight motion drew his attention, but he didn't turn around. *She* was standing there, watching him. He knew it from the rustle of skirts. When she didn't speak, a wicked urge came over him.

So, she wanted to have a look at him, did she?

It was terribly wrong to spy upon a half-naked man. Victoria held the wooden box containing her father's game board and chess pieces, but Mr. Smith was not yet clothed. He was holding his shirt in his hands, while his bare back faced her.

The color of his skin was golden, contrasting against the white sheets. His broad back revealed strong shoulders with carved ridges, tapering down to his ribs. She imagined touching those shoulders, running her hands down his back.

Her gaze drifted upon Mr. Smith as he pulled on his shirt and cast a glance behind him. In the shadows, she was certain he couldn't see her watching. But her heartbeat quickened, nonetheless.

You'll never have a man like him, her fears taunted her. *Especially once he knows the truth about you.*

The brittle edges of her courage crumbled a little further. Of course he would never want a woman too afraid to venture outside. It was foolish to even dream of it.

She glanced behind her at the front door. Though it was only wood and brass, it might as well have been made of steel. Behind it lay hills and glens covered in glistening snow. She wondered if she would ever step outside again or feel the warmth of sun upon her face. Would she ever feel the kiss of rain on her skin or walk barefoot in the grass?

She wanted to, so desperately. But more than that, she wanted to seize control of her life, to push back the fear and be the girl she'd once been before.

Victoria clenched the boxed chess set, gathering her courage to step back inside the room. Mrs. Larson followed behind her, bringing a kettle of warmed water, soap, and a towel. With a sharp look toward her, the housekeeper chided, "Miss Andrews, ye should nae be here while he washes."

Before she could answer, Mr. Smith interrupted, "I quite agree. I'd never forgive myself if the sight of my wet face sent her into maidenly shock."

"Ye are a wicked man, sir. Teasing a lady so." The housekeeper huffed and set down the basin, pouring the hot water and handing him the soap. "Someone ought tae be washing out yer mouth, I'd say."

"I presume you're volunteering for the task?"

Before the pair of them could start a war, Victoria stepped between them. "Mrs. Larson, that will be all."

"If ye had any decency at all, ye'd send for Mr. MacKinloch to be your valet," Mrs. Larson informed him. "Lady Lanfordshire will be hearing about this."

And Victoria could just imagine what her mother would say. Even so, it seemed ridiculous to leave the room while Mr. Smith did nothing more than wash his face and hands.

"I like your housekeeper," he remarked. "She's not afraid to speak her mind. Even if she does put nails in my food."

Victoria turned her back to allow him privacy while she opened up the chessboard set, placing the black and white pieces upon the board. He gave her detailed instructions on how to line up the pieces, but she hardly detected a word of it.

She heard the light splash of water and imagined the scent of male skin and soap. Her mind conjured up the vision of what it would be like to watch a husband perform such intimacies in the morning. And it was nicer than she'd thought it would be.

Her conscience warned her against these thoughts. With every moment she spent at this man's side, her proximity to temptation increased. He made her want all the things she believed she'd never have.

When the pieces were ready, Victoria turned back to him, unable to resist the urge. His face was damp, his cheeks smooth. A droplet of water rolled down from his temple, over one cheek. Her hands itched to touch his skin, and she prayed he could not read her thoughts.

"When you look at me like that, I don't want to play chess anymore," he said quietly. His voice allured her, the deep tones sliding past her inhibitions, guiding her closer.

"What do you mean?" She placed the chessboard on a table between them.

His hand reached out to cup her cheek. Against her skin, she felt the warm moisture of his hand, and she caught her breath. "You know precisely what I mean, Miss Andrews."

She could give no answer to that.

"I won't give you any idle promises," he admitted. "Nor will I try to win you over with meaningless words." His thumb touched her mouth in the softest gesture. "But I'd be lying if I didn't admit that you fascinate me."

She jerked back from him and knocked over the queen. "Don't say such things. You don't mean them."

"How do you know?"

"Because a man like you has no cause to be interested in a woman like me. I'm a nobody." She righted the fallen queen and took a deep breath. "Let us continue our game and then I must attend to my sewing."

He propped himself up with one arm, sending her an intense look. "Be assured, I'm not a man who has pursued a great deal of women."

"You've drunk too much laudanum," she argued. "You're only looking at me because you're ill. If my sisters were here, you'd—"

"Stop belittling yourself," he ordered. "Let us play our game."

He gave her the basic rules, but few of them made sense. She decided to mirror his actions instead, watching as he moved a pawn two spaces forward. "I like looking at you," he said. "Your eyes and your face are quite pleasing."

Instead of being flattered by his words, she felt dismayed by them. She knew what she was—passably attractive, but certainly not beautiful. "You're trying to distract me to win the game," she said.

"I don't have to distract you. I'm already winning," he said, as he captured another piece.

"I'm not a woman you can ensnare with words. I know full well that you'll be leaving," she countered, moving a pawn on the board.

His hand paused upon a black rook. "I will, yes."

"And I'll only be hurt if I allow myself to feel things I shouldn't." She made another move, seeking an escape from his attack. "Therefore, it seems best if I remain only your caretaker."

"That's not a good move," he informed her, touching the knight she'd just placed. "Check."

They played for a while longer before he won the game at last. Victoria was about to remove the pieces when he caught her hand again, threading his fingers with hers. "Do you find my attention offensive?"

"N-no. Not at all." Quite the contrary. She was fascinated by his sunburnt hair and the green eyes that burned into hers. The very touch of his hand sent her heart racing, but she couldn't understand what he wanted from her.

"Good." He rubbed the soft part of her hand, still staring at her. "I'm going to kiss you one day soon, Miss Andrews. When you least expect it."

"Juliette," Beatrice called from the doorway. "We're leaving for Madame Benedict's. Aren't you coming with us?"

Her daughter sat upon the floor of the nursery, watching as her youngest cousin shook a rattle with one hand. Charlotte's seven-month-old son had been an unexpected blessing, one they'd never believed would happen, since she'd been barren after years of marriage. With his dark hair and gray eyes, he resembled his father. His sunny personality had captivated everyone—especially Juliette. She'd spent every waking moment playing with the boy.

"One day, you'll have a son like him," Beatrice promised. "But only if you find a husband first." She smiled warmly and held out her hand. "Perhaps you'll meet someone while we're here in London."

"Perhaps." When her daughter rose from the floor, her eyes were reddened as if she'd been crying. It startled Beatrice to see her tears, for she couldn't guess what had upset her.

"What is it, darling?" Beatrice asked. "Are you not well?"

"No, I'm fine." Juliette sniffled, wiping at her eyes. Nodding toward the window, she shrugged. "I made the mistake of touching my eyes after I petted the cat. It's nothing to worry about." She dabbed them with a handkerchief, but her gaze lingered upon the boy as she rose.

"We're attending a dinner party tonight," Beatrice said. "It will be your first chance to meet some of the men Charlotte has selected. Promise me you'll give them a chance." She smoothed back Juliette's light brown hair, pinning a wayward lock back into the updo.

The enigmatic look on her daughter's face revealed none of her thoughts. "I won't embarrass you, Mother."

When Beatrice took her hand, Juliette asked, "There's something I've been wondering. Has the . . . Earl of Strathland been troubling you about the house at all?"

She shrugged. "He still wants me to sell it, but you know I can't. Not without your father's approval. Besides, Victoria would never leave." A frisson of dismay rose up inside her at the thought.

"I wouldn't mind leaving Scotland," Juliette admitted. "It's so isolated and I don't like what's been happening with the crofters. I'm worried about Victoria being there."

Beatrice's smile faltered, for she worried about Victoria as well. She hadn't wanted to leave until she was certain their cousin Pauline could come and stay, but her daughter had been adamant.

"It's only for a few weeks," she reassured Juliette. "And in the meantime, if you find a man to marry tomorrow night, then you *can* leave Scotland," Beatrice informed her. Pasting on her smile again, she tried to bring their conversation back to happier thoughts. "Shall we go and have you measured for some new gowns?"

Juliette's expression grew uncertain. "The money Margaret brought back . . . you aren't using that to buy gowns for us, are you? Not when there are debts to be paid."

"The new gowns are a gift from Charlotte," Beatrice admitted, unable to hide the flush that came over her. It was wrong to accept so much from her sister, but she saw no alternative. "You needn't worry. Our debts will all be paid, in due time."

"If Victoria continues to sew," her daughter pointed out. "Have you gone to speak with Mr. Gilderness?"

"Of course," Beatrice lied. She hadn't met with the solicitor at all, not wanting to spoil Christmas with more bad news. "Everything is in order. You've nothing to worry about." Putting on a bright smile, she took Juliette's hand in hers. "What color do you think you'll choose?"

"Spend the money on Margaret," the young woman advised. "She's the best hope any of us could have of getting married."

"You have the same chance as your sister," Beatrice chided. "You're nineteen years old, and you have your entire life ahead of you." Glancing back at Charlotte's infant son, she added, "Before you know it, you could have a child like this one."

Juliette's face softened. "I hope so." As the baby's nursemaid came to take him, she blew him a kiss and he gurgled at her.

Beatrice guided her daughter away. "We'll measure all three of you for new gowns and if you would rather stay behind when I return to Scotland, perhaps Charlotte wouldn't mind."

Juliette gave a nod. "I would prefer to stay here."

They were joined by Amelia and Margaret while Charlotte sent for their carriage. Beatrice gripped her reticule, trying to decide what to do about the money the girls had earned. It shamed her to think that they had taken it upon themselves to try and solve the financial difficulties . . . but by the same token, they needed a new wardrobe. She ought to gather up her courage and write to Henry, asking him for advice. Yet the idea of admitting her failure was even more humiliating.

No, it was better to solve their financial problems on her own. She would arrange a meeting with the solicitor in two days, and find a way to make everything right.

One week later

The last crofter had gone, and Victoria breathed a sigh of relief. It had been a grueling seven days, with her hours spent tending the wounded crofters, as well as Mr. Smith. In so many ways, the time she'd spent in the man's company had been a welcome respite from the injured people in the dining room. She'd shied away from the strangers, though she'd allowed Dr. Fraser anything he needed to treat his patients.

The doctor had arranged for one of the MacKinlochs to build a set of crutches for Mr. Smith, and he'd begun using them a day ago. Though his leg had improved, he could not yet walk unaided.

"The patients are gone, I see," he remarked, leaning against the crutches. "You must be glad to have your house back again."

"Yes. I won't deny that. And I'm happy that most of the men have healed." She clasped her hands together, eyeing the dining room table that had been put back in place. The table was set for one, but the sight of the lonely plate deflated her spirits. She didn't want to sit in the empty room, missing her mother and sisters when there was an alternative.

"I'd rather not eat my meal alone," she blurted out. "Would you care to . . . join me?"

As soon as she voiced the request, she saw his expression grow guarded. "It depends on your reasons for wanting my company, Miss Andrews."

She didn't understand what he meant by that. "It's just a meal."

"Alone with me," he added. He moved a little closer, remaining at the entrance to the dining room. "I've already done a great deal of damage to your reputation, simply by being here."

"You were recovering from a bullet wound," she pointed out. "We've done nothing wrong."

"So far," he admitted, using the crutches to draw nearer. From the darker timbre of his voice, she wondered what he meant by that. "But the longer I stay here, the greater the risk to you."

"I don't care what people say about me," she insisted. It was the truth. She never left the house, so even if others did talk, she would not hear it spoken to her face.

"I wasn't talking about the risk of idle gossip." Mr. Smith stood directly in front of her, and his proximity made her skin warm with apprehension. "I was talking about this."

He smoothed a strand of hair off her nape, and a thousand warnings roared through her mind. But she didn't move away. His warm hand drew down her spine, pulling her closer while his deep green eyes held her captive. She was nearly in his arms before his hands moved up to frame her face. The forbidden pull tempted her with the promise of something more.

He'll leave you, her head warned, even as her heart whispered, *I don't care.*

He'd been the answer to her loneliness, and God help her, she didn't want him to go. The hunger for companionship had been awakened, and she'd grown accustomed to seeing his face each day. She'd spent every moment at his side, moments that she wanted to hold on to, no matter what else happened. She'd seen him awaken each morning, learned that he preferred his toast with jam but no butter, and had talked with him until she fell asleep in her chair, late at night.

"Nothing will happen between us," she lied, pulling out of his grasp.

Mr. Smith glanced over at the table and added, "Then we shall eat and continue this pretense. I'd rather dine here than alone in the parlor." He adjusted the crutches, following her into the smaller room. When they reached the table, he pulled out her chair for her.

"I should be the one doing that for you," she said, feeling ashamed that she'd forgotten to offer. "Especially with your wound." But she took her seat and scooted forward, waiting for him to join her. He sat at the head of the table, to her left.

"How are you feeling?" she asked.

"It doesn't hurt as badly as it did. But it will be a few months before I'm able to dance again." His mouth tilted with mockery.

"I can't imagine a man like you dancing," she confessed.

"I'm quite good at it. Or was, before my leg was nearly blown off." He eyed her. "I'll wager you've never danced before."

"I learned how, but it's not something I've done often. I can safely name myself the Queen of Wallflowers."

He reached for a pitcher and poured her a mug of ale. She was startled to see him take a sip from it, before passing it over. Then again, he had no mug of his own.

"You might be a wallflower," he agreed, "but there's more to you, isn't there?"

"Why would you say that?"

"In my experience, the quietest women tend to be the most adventurous. There's a wildness that they let no one see."

"I'm not at all wild." But she worried that he'd glimpsed the black corset she'd been sewing. When she'd fitted it to her body, the contrast between her skin and the dark color was vivid in a way she'd never expected. She'd cut it a little too low, and although she'd covered the silk with lace, it revealed the curve of her breasts.

Hastily, she took a sip of the ale. It wasn't her favorite beverage, but it was readily available in the Highlands. He reached for her mug, turning it so that his mouth touched the place where her lips had been.

He covered her hand with his and guided the mug to her lips in a silent invitation. Sharing the beverage had become intimate, and as she tasted the ale, she imagined the touch of his lips upon hers.

The soft candlelight cast a glow between them, and he remarked, "You're hiding something, aren't you?"

"So are you," she reminded him. "I still don't know who you are. You never once gave your true name."

Victoria hadn't pursued it because it had seemed far more important to save his life. But now, she wanted to know who he was and why he was reluctant to share more about himself.

"I gave you my first name," he said. "Isn't that enough?"

She shook her head. "You know it isn't." Passing him the ale, she tilted her head to the side. "I believe you're wealthy, but I doubt you're titled," she predicted. "Perhaps a baronet, at best."

"I could be a prince, for all you know."

"Heaven save us, no. Thank goodness for that." She studied him, trying to determine who he really was. "A knight?"

"Wrong again," he told her. "I'm far more important than that. All the society matrons would cast themselves in front of charging horses if I would spare their daughters a look."

She shook her head at his teasing. "I don't believe that." Eyeing him closer, she offered, "But you don't seem eager to return to London."

"Or perhaps I have a reason to stay."

The words softened her heart, but she couldn't bring herself to face him. He wasn't going to stay. These were just words, nothing more.

Now, she realized that it was probably best if she never knew who he was or why he'd been so secretive. None of it mattered. It would simply tear her feelings apart, leaving a ragged hole in her heart.

"Are you disappointed that I'm not a prince?" he asked.

"Relieved, actually." But then, if he were someone important, he wouldn't have wasted time speaking to someone like her.

Abruptly, he remarked, "Money isn't important to you, is it? I could be a penniless beggar and you'd treat me the same as a duke."

"It doesn't matter how much money a man has. It's what's here that matters." Gently, she reached out to touch his heart. But he didn't take her hand this time. Instead, he stared at her, as if making a decision.

Had she said too much? He was still a stranger to her, regardless that she'd taken care of him this past week the way a wife might have done.

In the end, it was nothing but a daydream, one that would fade away as soon as he walked out the door. He would return to his mysterious life, and she'd be left locked away in a house she was growing to hate. For it would be empty without him there.

"Nottoway," he said at last. "Jonathan Nottoway is my name." He stared back at her, and she realized it was the truth. For a time, he waited, as if he expected her to recognize it.

"I am pleased to make your acquaintance," she said, not knowing what else to say.

His green eyes held wariness, but he didn't press any further. At that moment, Mrs. Larson entered and brought a bowl of soup, setting it before Victoria. "I thought *he* would be in the parlor."

"*He* is going to eat in the dining room, like a civilized person," Mr. Nottoway countered. "And if it wouldn't be too much trouble, I would like silverware and dishes of my own. Unless you believe I should share utensils with Miss Andrews." He said nothing of the cup they'd already shared.

"Insolent rogue," came Mrs. Larson's muttered retort. At Victoria's silent reprimand, she corrected in a louder tone, "Yes, sir. That is, if Miss Andrews would desire your company."

"He is here at my invitation, Mrs. Larson," she remarked. When the housekeeper had gone, she apologized, "Don't be offended by her. She has a harsh tongue but a gentle heart."

He shrugged and stole another sip from her mug of ale. "How long has she been in the service of your household?"

"Five years. We lived in London with my uncle before this." Though she tried to keep her tone even, Victoria pulled her shawl tighter around her shoulders.

"I'm surprised you stayed that long. Scotland's an unforgiving sort of land."

"It's harsh, but beautiful." She glanced outside at the falling snow. Though it was dark already, the candles in the room illuminated the dusted windowpanes. "Sometimes I'll sit in my room and look out at the mountains."

"And do you go walking in the summertime?" he asked.

She gave no answer to that but stared back at the table. Though she ought to nod or lie about it, she couldn't bring herself to speak. Every time she imagined walking through the meadows, she remembered being lost in the forests and the glens. She'd been unable to find the main road, and after a day without food, she'd grown even more disoriented. The grassy hills had become a desert, the endless glens a labyrinth that were too vast for a seventeen-year-old girl to navigate.

He was still waiting for an answer, so she changed the direction of their conversation. "I know you'll be leaving. But . . . will you visit your house on Eiloch Hill, from time to time?" She tried to keep her words casual, as if they meant nothing.

Will I ever see you again?

He shook his head. "I never stay in one place for very long. I'm hiring a land steward to oversee Eiloch Hill."

She veiled her dismay, but at least he'd been honest with her. It was strange to think that he would enjoy moving from place to place so often. The very thought made her shudder. "I would hate traveling. I much prefer to remain at home."

"You would enjoy some of the places I've visited. The Amalfi Coast of Italy is lovely. The sun is warm, and the water is so blue it almost hurts your eyes." He continued describing it, and in his voice, she heard the longing. Although she could not imagine walking upon a sandy shore alone, with *him* it was a different image. She had no desire to explore foreign lands or leave her safe haven . . . but if Mr. Smith—no, Mr. Nottoway—wanted to show her the world, she would try it for his sake.

While he spoke, she found herself studying his features, as if she could forever capture them in her mind. His sun-darkened hair was cut short in a careless manner, and she'd watched his green eyes flash with anger and soften with intensity. Right now, he was looking at her as if awaiting a reply.

"Was that your favorite place?" she asked, passing the soup and spoon over to him.

"One of them." He tasted a spoonful of the soup and passed it back. His knee bumped hers beneath the table, and at his close proximity, goose bumps raised upon her skin.

Mrs. Larson returned with a second bowl of mock turtle soup and a spoon for Mr. Nottoway. Although the food was a distraction, she was intensely aware of his eyes upon her. They ate in silence for a time, before he ventured, "I haven't seen you working on the black gown. Did you finish it?"

She didn't correct him, but nodded. "I'll begin sewing another design soon."

"How do you get your materials? They must be scarce this far north."

"I've used older materials," she explained. "Sometimes Mr. Sinclair brings me fabric from London, though."

"You really do love the work, don't you?"

She brightened at the thought. "There's a sense of power in it . . . to make something beautiful out of something no one else wanted."

His gaze turned discerning, as if she were speaking of more than the fabric. "Indeed."

She fell silent for a time while Mrs. Larson cleared away the soup dishes and returned with a freshly baked cod pie. Steam rose from the crust as she cut into it, serving each of them a slice. Mr. Nottoway waited until the housekeeper had gone before he said, "You've helped me heal from this wound and given me your hospitality. I mean to repay you for it. Name your reward."

"Why would I need a reward for saving a man's life?" Victoria countered, startled by his offer. "Isn't the fact that you're breathing reward enough? And that you still have your leg?"

From the enigmatic look on his face, she wondered if she'd offended him. Shyness caught her, but she forced the words out. "I-I've enjoyed spending these past few days with you. Your companionship has been gift enough." Her face warmed with embarrassment, especially when his green eyes stared into hers, as if trying to read beneath her words.

"Surely you want something."

"You've been kind to me. And that's worth something." *Kind* wasn't the right word, but how could she explain to him that he was the first man who had paid any attention to her? The first man who had shown any interest at all, despite the futility of it.

"*Kind* is not a word most people would use to describe me," he countered. His tone turned dark, coated with bitterness.

"Perhaps they should."

Slowly, he rose from his chair, using his crutches to aid him toward the fireplace on the far end of the room. It was just over a week until Christmas and already Mrs. Larson had decorated the mantel with pine boughs and holly. Candles glowed around the room and near the windowsill. Victoria followed him, unsure of why he'd left the dinner table. His face was haloed against the firelight, but the expression was shielded. She didn't know whether he wanted to speak with her or whether she should return to the table.

"Why are you staring at me?" she whispered.

His green eyes held her captive. "Don't you know the answer to that?"

She couldn't bring herself to answer, for her heart was racing. She wanted to believe that he cared for her, but she was afraid of the true reason.

"I like what I see when I look at you," he told her. "And I've never been particularly good with obeying conventions."

The compliment slipped beneath the crevices of her heart, leaving her to feel awkward, not knowing how to respond to it. Snowflakes swirled against the windowpane, and he stared outside at them. "I've always enjoyed watching snow fall. Especially when it's warm inside, with a fire burning on the hearth."

"It's not as warm as it could be," she apologized. "The fire is dying down, and it's a little cold in this room because the house is old and drafty. I'm sorry, but—"

"I'm making you nervous, aren't I?"

"Very." She wanted desperately to return to the dinner table, to sit apart from him and gather up her muddled thoughts.

Mr. Nottoway moved away from her to stand beside the window, still watching the snow fall. "You've nothing to fear from me, Miss Andrews. After spending a week together, I think you'd know that."

For long minutes, she stood watching him. He was taller than her, but not so much that she had to lean back to look at his face. His hair was lighter than her own, and against the moonlit snow, it had a silvery gleam to it. But upon his face, there was a hardness, like a man who wanted no one to see inside him. Shuttered, leaving no trace of emotion.

She took a tentative step forward, but he didn't appear to notice. Invisible strings seemed to pull her closer, until she stood slightly behind him.

The darkness loomed through the glass, and her hands clenched at her sides as she pushed back the fear. Over the past week, she'd grown to be friends with this man, and Mr. Nottoway knew nothing of her seclusion. He never looked upon her as if she were a madwoman, and with him she felt . . . almost normal.

"The snow is lovely," she confessed. And despite the blackness of the night, the candlelight illuminated the fat flakes drifting downward.

This time, he turned toward her. "Yes. It is lovely."

But he wasn't looking at the snow at all. Instead, his eyes were fixed upon her, with a hunger she didn't understand. He set his crutches against the wall and slowly lifted his hand to her cheek. The unexpected touch of his palm froze her feet in place, and beneath her skin, a sudden tremor rose up.

"We've done this all wrong, haven't we?" he murmured. "I've ruined you, and I haven't even touched you."

"You haven't ruined me."

"Haven't I?" His voice was warm velvet, a caress in the dark. She covered his hand with her own, reveling in the contrast between her cool skin and his warm fingers. Never had she imagined that she could stand before a man who was looking at her in this way. As if he wanted her.

"Tell me if I should stop." He leaned in, his heated mouth stealing hers.

Chapter Seven

VICTORIA STOOD motionless, not knowing what to do. The shock of the kiss was a searing heat against her frozen senses. She accepted the firm pressure of his lips, uncertain of how to respond.

"Kiss me back," he ordered, framing her face with his hands. Color blazed in her cheeks, but she obeyed, hesitantly moving her mouth against his. She'd never kissed anyone before, but he was lazy about it, drawing her into a deeper temptation. Victoria opened her mouth, and his kiss intensified, pushing away any hesitations she might have felt. The fiery heat was spreading through her, tightening her breasts, and making her want . . . more. She was losing herself in him, and she didn't care.

Abruptly, she gripped his neck, pressing her body against his. A hard ridge pressed against her stomach, and she faltered, not knowing what was happening to them.

"Don't be afraid," he said against her lips, kissing them again. "I would never hurt you."

She believed him, but deep inside, she wanted to experience more of this temptation. Soon enough, he would be gone. And never again would she know what it was to be kissed by a man. The thought broke away another piece of her heart.

He ended the kiss, drawing her into a tight embrace. "I

shouldn't have done that. But I've wanted to kiss you since the first day I saw you."

He drew back and brushed a lock of her hair over one ear. "You're not the sort of woman I'm used to."

It wasn't clear whether or not that was a compliment. "What sort of women have you kissed in the past?"

A sardonic expression twisted his mouth. "Women who pretended to be someone they weren't. They acted as if they wanted my attentions, but I knew they didn't. It was always about money."

Though he behaved as if he didn't care, she sensed the ghost of pain behind his words. "Was there ever a woman you loved?"

He nodded, his gaze turning distant.

"What happened to her?"

"My father made a few bad investments and fell into debt. She ended our engagement because she believed I would become penniless."

"Then you were better off without her." It angered her that someone he loved would be so callous as to give greater importance to money than to him. Although she and her sisters had been brought up with the expectation of making an advantageous marriage, she couldn't imagine abandoning a man she cared about.

"Even though I told her I wasn't without funds of my own, she refused to believe it. I had some income my father never knew about." He reached out to rest his hands upon her shoulders, and she held herself motionless, drinking in his touch.

"You needn't worry about me now, Miss Andrews. I've repaid his debts, and money is no longer a problem for me. Rest assured, I'll repay you for any expenses incurred from my care."

"I wasn't worried about that." She didn't move when his hands moved up to her bare nape, skimming down the surface of her skin. A breath caught in her throat, and she closed her eyes at the sensation.

"You intrigue me," he murmured, lowering his mouth to her shoulder. "I find myself wanting to know your secrets."

"I have none worth telling."

"Liar." The word vibrated against her throat, sending a thousand shivers over her skin. Her thoughts were slipping away as her body responded to him. She touched his hair, feeling like a wanton woman. He rewarded her by pulling her flush against him. His hard strength contrasted against her softness, and he bent down, as if to kiss her again.

But this time, his mouth found the softness beneath her chin, and the dark heat sent a shuddering pulse between her legs. She ached for more, even as her conscience reminded her of how wrong this was.

"I will be leaving," he murmured against her throat. "But it doesn't mean we couldn't enjoy the last moments we have together." His hands moved from her waist to her rib cage, and her heart pounded faster. "If you're willing."

A river of ice slid through her veins at his implication. He was asking her to behave like a mistress, to allow him even more liberties. Was that what he thought of her? That she would welcome his seduction?

Why wouldn't he? her conscience chided. *He's already stolen a kiss. And you've done nothing to hold him at a distance. You've let him believe you desire him.*

With every moment she'd spent with this man, she'd allowed her loneliness to take command of her senses. He'd filled up the empty spaces in her heart, letting her imagine what it would be like to have a husband.

But he wasn't going to fall in love with her and marry her. And if she allowed him to touch her, to show her the face of desire, it would only hurt her more when he left.

Victoria grew still, pushing free of his embrace. Emotion caught in her throat, along with the wild need to escape. She needed to breathe, to think. "No," she whispered. "That's not the woman I am."

An indifferent mask slid over his face, and she moved away from him. Her corset was starting to cut off the air, making her feel faint. "I can't." She picked up her skirts, and tried to leave in a calm manner, but her hands were shaking. He would think the worst of her, but she didn't care.

In the foyer, her knees nearly buckled, as she took the stairs two at a time. Bursting through her bedroom door, she moved toward the window, lowering her head.

The tears were bottled up inside of her, locked away. Right now, she wanted to shatter the pane of glass that separated her from the outside world. Why had he said such a thing? She'd broken many rules in the past week, true enough, but it didn't make her a woman of loose virtue.

Victoria bit her lip, trying to quiet the storm of anger inside. His kiss had reached past the boundaries, awakening her to desires she'd only imagined. Even to think of it now sent a shudder of need pooling inside.

She'd responded to him, succumbing to temptation. She hadn't recognized herself, and when his mouth had moved over her throat, she'd imagined it upon her skin . . . lower, in more wicked places.

It terrified her to realize that it could have happened this night. If she had fallen into his seduction, he might be in her bedchamber this very moment.

But he'd not asked her to wed him . . . he'd wanted to enjoy her, like a woman he could use and cast aside. And she had never given him any reason to believe she would say no. Embarrassment flooded into her cheeks, and she wanted to hang her head in shame.

A quiet knock sounded at the door. "Miss Andrews, are ye all right?"

"Come in." She needed Mrs. Larson to help her get undressed.

Even better, she wanted to burrow under the covers and pretend that none of this had happened.

She didn't know how to explain to Mr. Nottoway that she'd allowed her imagination to wander down the wrong path. Her wayward heart had somehow hoped that he would come to love her, that he would unlock the prison of her fears. If she had a reason to leave the house, if he wanted to marry her . . . it might happen.

She moved to stand by the window, touching the frigid glass. Outside, the snow was battering the house, blanketing the ground with the frost of winter. Beyond the glass lay her deepest fears and the future she wanted. If ever she intended to be a man's wife, to be a mother, she would have to venture beyond it.

Mr. Nottoway knew nothing of her inability to go outside. And she didn't know if she could bring herself to reveal it. He might believe it was madness instead of fear. God help her, she never wanted to see him stare at her with revulsion instead of desire.

When the housekeeper entered, she took one look at Victoria and the sympathy on the matron's face was enough to break through the shield of pain. A single tear rolled down her face, a manifestation of the feelings she couldn't release.

"I'll be telling your mother about this," Mrs. Larson insisted. "And if that bampot needs to be struck across the nob, I'll be glad to do it for ye."

A raw laugh broke through the tears. "No, it doesn't matter. He'll be leaving, and I suppose that'll be the end of it." Though Victoria didn't want him to go. She gripped her arms, taking a slow, deep breath. She wanted so much more from her life, and she would never reach it if she didn't find the courage to try. "I'm not the sort of woman he'd want to marry anyway."

"Now what's the matter with a lady like yourself?" Mrs. Larson demanded. "You're a bonny lass, and if he can't see that, then he's got nae sense at all."

"He doesn't know about . . . the way I am."

"There, there, pet." Mrs. Larson came up behind her and began helping her undress. "You're as good as any other woman, despite your troubles. When the right man comes along, everything will be fine. You'll forget all about this one."

Victoria said nothing, but her gaze fell upon the brown paper package she'd prepared to send to London. It contained the black corset she'd finished. Though it had followed a similar design to her own undergarment, the silk was far softer, and she'd trimmed it with lace. All in all, it appeared expensive and luxurious—a garment that would please any woman, even if she had to suffer through a period of mourning.

But right now, it only reminded her of the feelings Mr. Nottoway had stirred. As Mrs. Larson unlaced her corset and drew the heavy garment off, Victoria touched her swollen lips. He had done this to her, offering her a glimpse of what it was to be touched by a man. Again and again, she replayed his words in her mind, trying to understand him.

He wanted her, and his proposition had bothered her deeply. He likely wanted her as a mistress . . . when she wanted to be a wife.

Her brain cried out that it wasn't possible, that he would never consider it. But he'd fired up feelings of need she'd never known. She needed to find her courage and confess the truth, no matter how great the risk.

Quickly, she drew on a wrapper over her nightdress. "Wait," she whispered to the housekeeper. "There's more that I need to say to him."

※

Jonathan sat in the parlor beside the hearth, his discarded crutches within reach. He should never have made such an offer without thinking of how it would sound. Victoria was nothing like the avaricious ladies who'd graced the London ballrooms, trying to ensnare a duke. She was completely unaware of his vast wealth.

He could gift her with a thousand pounds and never miss the sum. Yet, it would irrevocably change her life. Her earlier remark, that she saw no need to be rewarded for saving his life, confounded him. The house was old, in need of repairs. Her clothing was worn and outdated. Surely, her family would welcome the money.

But when she'd kissed him back, every reason why he needed to leave simply dissolved against the honey of her mouth. She fit beautifully against him, and when her arms had come around his neck, he'd wanted to take her upstairs. He wanted to know this woman, to touch her and watch her face transform into passion.

He wanted to keep her, though it was impossible. As an officer's daughter, she wouldn't survive the complex rules that governed the ladies of the ton. Bringing her there would be like throwing her to a pack of snarling wolves. She'd never belong.

But it was so different here. Her innocent kiss had crumbled away the years of loneliness, the horrifying images of the past. In her arms, he forgot about who he was.

He'd destroyed their emerging friendship with a few careless words, and he didn't know how to undo the damage he'd wrought. She . . . meant something to him, though he didn't know what name to give the protective emotion.

It was nothing like the feelings he'd felt for Lady Meredith Baldwin. Beautiful, elegant, and the daughter of a marquess, Lady Meredith had charmed him with her sweet disposition. She'd sent him secret smiles from across the ballroom, making him believe that she wanted no other man but him. He'd fallen hard for her, only to find that her promises were as empty as her words.

Yet, Miss Andrews had never once told him what he'd wanted to hear. She'd given him nothing but honesty, from the first.

"I should like to say a few things to you," came her voice from the far end of the room. "If you have a moment."

He turned and saw Victoria standing in the shadows. The creamy wrapper she wore made it appear that she was wearing moonlight. Her dark blond hair spilled over her shoulders, as if she hadn't had time to braid it yet. The locks rested upon her breasts, leading his irresponsible thoughts down the path to sin.

"I regret what I said," he began. "And while yes, you may say what you wish to me, I'll begin with my apology."

She tightened her grip on the dressing gown, as if to shield herself from him. "I don't know what kind of women you are accustomed to, Mr. Nottoway, but just because I kissed you didn't mean it was going to go any further than that."

"You're right. And it's been a long time since I've kissed a woman," he admitted. "I'm notably bad at it."

His dark attempt at humor made her frown. "It was my first kiss." The confession held a note of regret, as if she didn't intend to do it again. And didn't that make him feel even worse?

"I believe I have a solution," he said. "One that would suit both of us."

She frowned as if she'd already guessed his proposition. Jonathan didn't allow her to speak, not wanting her to protest until he'd had his say. "I know you'd prefer that I leave, but unfortunately I can't until my staff returns." He sent her an apologetic smile, adding, "Though I supposed you'd be glad to get rid of me. I tend to be a man who speaks his mind and doesn't care about the consequences. Few would call me good-natured."

She remained with her back pressed to the wall, but shook her head. "Any man would be ill-tempered after being shot."

He grimaced as he stood up, holding on to the furniture as he made his way back toward the bed. "I'm always this way. No woman in her right mind would want a man like me."

Lady Meredith had already proven that. She'd swiftly abandoned him, as soon as his father's debts were revealed. And when the ultimate scandal struck and his parents were found dead, she'd wanted nothing to do with him. If she'd cared, even a little, she might have stood by him. Instead, she hadn't spoken to him again.

"Why would you say that?" she asked. Her hand fell away from the dressing gown, giving him a view of her curves and the dip of her waist.

"Be frank, Miss Andrews. You never liked me when I arrived, and you certainly don't like me now. The kiss was something you now regret. My solution is to pretend as if it never happened. We'll continue as we were."

He didn't give her an opportunity to answer, but instead lay down upon the bed he'd used during his convalescence. Though he waited long moments for her to leave, he sensed she had not departed at all. Instead, he heard soft footsteps approaching, until she came to sit beside him.

Her quiet, steady presence made him turn toward her.

"It hurt, what you said to me." She folded her hands, her voice revealing an unsteadiness. "I know I've made choices that a proper lady would never make. Even now, I should not be here, sitting near your bed."

"Then go."

She leaned close to him, her gray eyes studying him as if she could see past his rough words. "If you wish to be my friend, then do. But don't treat me like a woman who wants to give her affections for money."

"I've apologized for what I said. But tell me this," he said, sitting up until he faced her. "If you only wanted to remain friends, why did you let me kiss you?"

She didn't answer at first, but then she confessed, "Because you're probably the only man who ever will. I wanted to know what it would be like."

She believed that; he could see it in her face. And he couldn't understand why she would say such a thing. "You're a beautiful woman, Miss Andrews. I highly doubt that I will be the only man to kiss you."

He lay back down, and while reclining, it felt more intimate to be across from her. It recalled the morning when he'd awakened with her face nestled against his chest.

A strange smile twisted at her mouth. "I highly doubt that another man will come along who will want to." She straightened in the chair. "Now that it's all settled, I'll bid you goodnight." Her form was silhouetted against the faint light in the hall as she started to leave.

"It was a good kiss," he added, when she stood. "Should you wish to practice again, I am willing."

In the faint light of the room, he saw the startled surprise upon her face. She didn't answer, but her silence made him wonder if she was thinking about it.

A pounding resounded upon the front door the next morning. From the intensity of the sound, Jonathan suspected it wasn't a welcome visitor. He used his crutches to make his way forward and opened the door before Mrs. Larson could get there.

Jonathan stared at the Scot standing before him. Tall, with long dark hair, the man wore a tartan of brown, red, and green. His coat was black, and from the murderous glare in the man's eyes, he hadn't been expecting to see a man dwelling at the Andrews residence.

"And just who the hell are you?" the Scot demanded.

"I might ask the same," Jonathan countered. The man gave no answer, but pushed his way through the door, dropping a covered bundle on the floor.

"Miss Andrews!" he bellowed. "Should I be killing this man for you?"

Before he got an answer, Mrs. Larson bustled into the room, closing the door. "Now then, Mr. Sinclair, you're letting the snow in. If you've brought us tea from London, I'll brew you a cup."

"I never drink tea. And who would that Sassenach be?" he demanded.

Jonathan barely had time to use his crutch as a shield against the dirk Sinclair had unsheathed. Though he couldn't fault the man for drawing incorrect conclusions, he wasn't about to let himself be skewered. He blocked the dirk, using all of his strength to hold the man away from his throat.

"Miss Andrews saved my life," he said. "Not that it's any business of yours."

The man's eyes gleamed. "I could end it for you and save her any more trouble."

Jonathan shoved the crutch toward the man's throat, pinning him against the wall. Though it took every last bit of his strength, he had no intention of being a victim. Or allowing this man to threaten Miss Andrews in any way.

From his strong reaction, Jonathan suspected he had a prior interest in Victoria. A primal rise of jealousy roared through him, an irrational response that he couldn't control. It made little sense, but the idea of another man touching her only heightened his anger.

"Gentlemen," came Victoria's quiet voice from the top of the stairs. Both of them stopped at her presence. "Mr. Sinclair, please leave the fabrics at the bottom of the stairs, if you please. I presume my sister paid you your share of the proceeds."

It was then that Jonathan remembered Victoria talking about a Mr. Sinclair, who went to London for them. Sinclair might have been a merchant or a messenger, but at the moment, he appeared more like a pirate. Jonathan released him, and a self-satisfied expression came over the man's face.

"She did pay me, aye." Sinclair brushed at his doublet, his gaze narrowing upon Jonathan. "It's getting harder tae find these materials, and I had tae buy some secondhand gowns. The price is dear."

Jonathan eyed the man, wondering where precisely he had "found" fabric during a war. And the veiled hint that he would be charging more for his services was sounding more and more like a way of swindling the Andrews family.

But Victoria didn't seem dismayed at all. "I'll make do with whatever you can bring to me. Did the dress sell?"

Sinclair cocked his head and eyed her for a moment before answering. "It was the . . . red garment that sold the best," he said. "Twenty pounds for it."

"Twenty?" Victoria whispered, sinking down to sit on the top step. "But . . . that's so much. For . . ." Her voice trailed off, flooding with color.

"Madame Benedict wants more of them in different colors," Sinclair added. "I took her orders and brought the fabric and materials."

Victoria touched her hand to her mouth, an awkward laugh escaping. "I hope you gave the money to my mother and sisters. Minus your own fee and the cost of materials, of course."

"I did, aye."

Her eyes brightened. "They'll have a merry Christmas after all." She imagined the look on Margaret's face when Mr. Sinclair gave over the money. They could buy gifts for one another, with more left over. A slight wistfulness came over her, as she wished she could be there with them.

"Did you have any other gowns you're wanting me to sell?" Mr. Sinclair prompted.

Victoria nodded, a blush coming over her cheeks. "I-I've made another garment . . . like the red one."

"What color?"

Her face twisted in an apologetic expression. "Unfortunately, black. I had nothing but an old silk mourning gown. I cut it up and tried to make it pretty with some lace."

"Black lace." Sinclair started cursing in Gaelic, shaking his head.

"You don't think it will do? I thought perhaps, for the women in mourning—"

"It will sell. And you should double the price."

"But black is not a good color," she protested. "I'm not certain . . ." Her face flushed, and from her embarrassed expression, Jonathan suspected they were no longer discussing gowns.

"Exactly what sort of garments are you making?" he inquired.

Sinclair gave no answer, but Victoria stood up from the stairs. "Just . . . items for ladies."

Her reluctance to give him more information sounded quite suspicious. When she drew closer, Sinclair withdrew a letter from his coat. "Your sister Amelia wrote to you."

Victoria started to take it, but the man stopped a moment. "Miss Andrews, has this man bothered you in any way?"

She shook her head, turning back to Jonathan. In her gray eyes, he saw embarrassment as she answered softly, "No. Mr. Nottoway has done nothing."

"Nottoway?" Sinclair repeated, a warning note in his voice.

Jonathan shook his head, and thankfully Victoria didn't see it. From the silent exchange with Sinclair, he'd likely have to line the man's pockets to keep his silence.

"Why don't you look through the fabrics and read your sister's letter in the parlor?" Sinclair suggested. "Mr. Nottoway and I can become better acquainted. Since you've become *friends*."

Victoria sobered at the implication. "Mr. Sinclair, please. You mustn't tell my family about this. Mr. Nottoway was wounded and I helped him. It was nothing more than that, and Mrs. Larson was here the entire time." She took the letter from him and walked toward the bundle.

Sinclair intercepted the fabric and carried it for her into the parlor. "As you say, Miss Andrews." Though his voice offered reassurance, the glare he sent was unmistakable. So be it.

Jonathan left the pair of them alone and returned to the dining room on the opposite end of the house with no doubt at all that Sinclair would find him. And as he'd predicted, within a few minutes more, the man appeared in the doorway.

His expression revealed a Scot who wasn't afraid to speak his mind. And one who posed a very real threat.

"I've heard of you," Sinclair began without preamble. "All of London knows about how your parents died."

"Miss Andrews has no need to learn of it."

"Doesn't she?" The man crossed his arms, staring at him. "What do you suppose she'd say if she knew Jonathan Nottoway, the Duke of Worthingstone, was standing in her house? You didna tell her, did you?"

"You're not going to tell her, either." He kept his voice low, in case the others were listening. "What's it worth for your silence?"

Cain Sinclair stared back with the eye of a predator. "I'll let you know." Without another word, he turned his back and left.

Chapter Eight

VICTORIA HAD READ Amelia's letter three times in disbelief. It seemed that Madame Benedict had adored the corset she'd sent and had raised the price so high that only affluent ladies could afford to look at it. She'd raved about the choice of fabric and how well made it was.

They wanted twenty-five more, in every color. *Twenty-five.* She couldn't believe it, and she didn't know how she could possibly make so many. It was impossible.

Mr. Sinclair had taken the black lace corset with him, and presumably it would fetch a similar price. When she'd opened the bundle of fabric he'd brought, she found not only satin, silk, and velvet . . . but also muslin, painted silk, and sarcenet. There were trims and laces, whalebone and strings—enough that she was torn between wanting to laugh with delight and panicking over all the work to be done.

Amelia's closing words sobered her mood. It seemed that she, Margaret, and Juliette had come up with a name for the new creations—Aphrodite's Unmentionables. The name Aphrodite conjured up the goddess of love. It suggested undergarments that were sensual and forbidden.

Garments a woman like her could never wear. For what did she know of love anyway? She'd been kissed for the first time, but it would never go beyond that. Her life was here. Mr. Nottoway's life would take him elsewhere.

"You shouldn't allow a man like Mr. Sinclair to act as your messenger." Mr. Nottoway used his crutches to return to the parlor, and he cast a glance back at the hallway.

"He's been useful to us," Victoria countered. "He may not be quite a gentleman, but we can trust him."

"How long have you known him?"

"A few years." She avoided a direct answer, not wanting him to hear the full story. Though she knew Cain Sinclair walked on the rougher side of life, her sister Juliette insisted that he was trustworthy. And he'd proven his worth, time and again. It was good enough for her.

Mr. Nottoway set aside his crutches and sat across from her. "And what if he's stealing the fabric?"

"Oh, he's not a thief. We pay for the materials and he keeps a portion of the money for himself." From the wary expression on his face, she could tell he believed Mr. Sinclair was little more than a common criminal.

"How do you know he doesn't steal the materials and keep the money? You have no reason to trust him."

"Do I have a reason to trust you?" Victoria countered. She folded the letter and set it back upon the sofa. "While I appreciate your concern, you needn't worry. Mr. Sinclair sells the garments I make and is discreet about it."

"He could be holding back most of the profit for himself."

"My sister verified the amount in her letter."

She saw the doubt on his face. Without asking, he picked up her father's chess set and lined up the pieces. Picking up a white pawn, he moved it two squares. "It's your choice, of course. But you weren't discussing gowns, were you?"

His voice held a knowing tone, and color rushed to her cheeks, afraid he would guess the truth. "What makes you say that?" To distract him, she studied the chessboard and moved her black pawn one square forward.

"You were embarrassed by whatever Sinclair said to you." He moved his knight into position, watching as her lips pursed while she considered how to respond.

"Some of the . . . gowns were daring. I wouldn't wear them myself."

Liar, her conscience chided. When she'd tried on the silk padded corset, it had been far more comfortable than her usual garments. She'd considered making one for her own use, though perhaps in a more demure color.

"You would look beautiful in crimson," he said, taking her pawn. "The color would be well-suited to you." Though he didn't look at her, his deep voice was low, intimate in tone. Almost as if he were imagining her wearing red silk and nothing else.

Her hand trembled as she moved another piece upon the board, not knowing what move either of them had made. "I prefer gray."

"Because you think no one will notice you in it?" he questioned.

"I have no need to be noticed." Nor any desire, truthfully. In her heart she quaked at the thought of wearing a color that brought her to the center of attention.

"It has been my experience that the women who do not desire notice are the ones most worthy of it. And vice versa." He captured another piece, adding, "Why would you have any need to make gowns in secret?"

"My father would not approve of it." She was losing the game already and couldn't see a way out of the mess she'd made. "He doesn't know how difficult things are at the moment. Mother hasn't told him, and as long as we can pay our debts with the money from our sewing, it's not necessary."

She moved her rook and offered, "Besides, our problems are nothing compared to what he's enduring in the war. When he returns, there will be no need for our sewing. Our arrangement with Mr. Sinclair will suffice until then." After he made his move, she captured one of his pawns, moving her piece into a different position.

A wry smile crossed his face. "Check."

She sent a dismayed look toward the board. "You might as well finish it now and say 'Checkmate.' I can't win. I'm terrible at this game, and I don't know why you want to play against me."

"It's better than listening to you read to me." But he pushed the chessboard aside in silent agreement. Candlelight shadowed the planes of his face, his green eyes staring into hers. His white shirt contrasted against the darker skin of his throat, while the top button of his waistcoat was unbuttoned. Though his cravat was tied in a simple manner, his face was bristled from not shaving. It gave him a dangerous look, like a highwayman.

"Was there something else you'd rather do to pass the time?" he asked. Although it was a natural enough question, her thoughts turned wayward.

"I should go," she said, standing up so quickly, she knocked over a few chess pieces. "I-I've sewing to do and . . . you can read if you wish."

Without waiting for an answer, she hurried from the parlor. Inwardly, she hoped that his servants would arrive soon. The longer Mr. Nottoway was stranded with her, the more her treacherous mind wished he would stay.

Jonathan heard the sound of voices in the middle of the night. He opened his eyes and caught the flare of torches outside the parlor window. From the arguing, it sounded as if a crowd was forming. He didn't know what their intentions were, but he had no plans on becoming a victim a second time.

He tore off the coverlet and slid his feet to the floor, reaching for his crutches. From the last threat they'd experienced, he knew Victoria's father had a pair of dueling pistols in the bottom drawer of a large secretary. He moved swiftly to locate them, though it was impossible to load one in the dark. They wouldn't know it wasn't loaded, however.

He cursed his swollen leg, knowing he wouldn't be much of a protector with his healing wound. With the pistol in one hand, he hobbled forward through the hall, moving toward the front door.

Victoria hurried down the stairs in a nightgown, a gray shawl around her shoulders. Her eyes held terror when she saw the pistol. "What are you doing?"

He pointed outside and raised a finger to his lips.

"You can't confront them," she insisted in a loud whisper. "Just . . . pretend no one is here. They might go away."

"They know we're here, and they have torches, Miss Andrews. I don't mean to let them set this house on fire." He set his crutches against the wall and reached for the doorknob.

"And you think shooting them will put an end to it?" She gripped the banister, looking horrified at what he was about to do.

"I'll do what I have to. If they try to burn the house, go out the back door and wait near the garden wall. I'll find you there and—"

"No." She shook her head, sinking down to sit upon the stairs. "No, I can't leave."

"If they set the damned house on fire, you will."

A bone-deep fear had settled into her, and he saw her hands shaking. "I can't."

The whisper held a terror that he didn't understand. But he didn't have time to ask her more, so he simply said, "Perhaps it won't come to that."

He reached for the doorknob, and the shouting had grown louder. Though he'd never faced an angry mob, he'd faced his father's fury often enough. He pushed back the doubts, letting in nothing but cold logic. Whatever the reason for this attack, he would find a way to dispel it.

When he opened the door, the bright flare of their torches gleamed against the fallen snow. There were nearly two dozen of them, men of all ages. Despite wearing the same tartan colors, the men were a blend of many clans forced to leave their land. Their rage at the injustice was palpable, and some wore ragged clothing hardly suited to such freezing weather.

Jonathan steeled himself against what was to come, knowing he had to protect Victoria. That need stretched beyond all else. Closing the door behind him, he ignored the winter chill and nodded to them.

"Gentlemen. Is something the matter that you would disturb Miss Andrews from her sleep?" He kept a firm grip upon the pistol at his side, letting them see it but not creating an overt threat.

"He's the one that drove us off the land he bought from Strath-land," one remarked, his face filled with fury.

Jonathan regarded the man with a calm look. "I only arrived here a short time ago. Your anger is misplaced."

"We canna keep living here," another said. "There's no' enough room, and it's far too cold for the bairns tae be living in tents."

Jonathan didn't argue but said, "I believe Miss Andrews gave shelter in the barn to several of the wounded men, not long ago. I doubt if she would mind if the children slept within that shelter."

"When she's got a fine house like this?" the first demanded. "I say we take the house. Or let it burn."

The wildness in the man's eyes did not suggest he was willing to listen to a reasonable discussion. Jonathan lifted the pistol, aiming it toward the man. "You should leave."

"You've only got one shot," the man reminded him. "And there are more of us."

"You would do this to her family, after she gave you a place to stay?" Jonathan said. He struggled to think of another argument, one that would make sense to them.

"A place to stay?" The man spat upon the ground. "There's naught here but crowded land where we haven't got a pot to piss in. What have they ever done for us?"

Jonathan stared back at the angry tenant, refusing to back down. Money wouldn't solve their problems, and if he attempted to bribe them, they would only demand more. His brain searched for a way of pacifying these people, and a flash of inspiration struck.

"Miss Andrews has work to offer your wives. She has been sewing gowns and there is a demand for more. I know she would welcome their help as seamstresses."

Doubt covered their faces, but he continued, "Mr. Sinclair has been selling them in London for a profit, and she can't manage the sewing by herself. Ask him if you don't believe me."

"Sinclair's already gone back south," one remarked.

"Then you know I speak the truth." Whether or not that was so, he added, "There would be a share in the profits for you."

"We can't eat coins," the man argued, but his anger had diffused somewhat. The crowd had shifted, and many were talking among themselves in Gaelic.

"No, but Sinclair has brought back food and supplies with those coins. It would feed your families through the winter. But if you'd rather burn down the house and see that opportunity disappear, it's your choice."

After a time, a tall man approached, one who seemed to speak for all of them. "I'll be sending my wife and several of the women to the house in the morning. If what you say is true, and Miss Andrews can provide work and money for our families—"

"It's true." Jonathan lowered his pistol. "Come back in the morning and speak with Miss Andrews yourself."

With that, several of the crowd members began to disperse. He watched as they left, but the first man didn't join them. "This isna finished," he said. "Ye'd best be watching your back, Sassenach."

When Mr. Nottoway walked back through the door, thankfulness and relief poured through Victoria. He was alive. And from the sounds growing fainter, he'd somehow made the men leave.

"Are they gone?" she whispered.

He nodded, reaching for his crutches. "They agreed to leave for now."

A slight noise from the hallway revealed the presence of Mr. MacKinloch and Mrs. Larson. Neither was armed, but after a look from Mr. Nottoway, they retreated back to the servants' quarters.

"Thank you," she whispered when they were alone.

Her heart was pounding so fast, she doubted if she would sleep at all this night. The mob of people could have set the house on fire, forcing her to leave or be burned alive. Dear God, she'd been so foolish to stay here. She'd not really understood the danger or the anger of these men. For the millionth time, she cursed herself for being too afraid to leave these four walls.

Mr. Nottoway acknowledged her thanks with a nod, moving steadily toward her with his crutches. Though he'd managed to undermine the threat, she didn't miss the concern on his face. "The women will be coming to pay a call on you in the morning. I told them you would need help with sewing. In return, you'll share your profits with those who assist you."

Victoria hadn't considered it before, but it might solve her problem. If she gave the women simple instructions, it was quite possible they could help her. The vision took shape and expanded within her mind. If the women were good at stitching, she could spend her time designing the garments instead of making them herself. It would be so much more than she'd hoped for.

And yet . . . they didn't know *what* she was sewing. Her cheeks brightened with the thought.

"They need the work and money," he said. "I said you could give that to them."

"It's possible," she hedged, not wanting to say too much.

He set the crutches against the stairs and held on to the banister, watching her. "I've a question for you."

When she waited, he continued, "Why did you say you couldn't leave the house? I told you they might burn it down . . . and you insisted you couldn't go."

Her skin went cold with the fear that he'd guessed her secret. She could give him no answer. He drew closer, until he sat a few stairs down from her. His shoulders were so close, she could reach out and touch him. "Was it the men who frightened you?"

She shook her head, not looking at him. The reason was poised at her lips, and she didn't know if she could hide this truth from him any longer.

"Is it me?" he asked softly.

"No." She drew up her knees beneath the dressing gown, feeling so vulnerable, she wanted to fade away into the wall. "It's my own cowardice."

He moved up a step, sitting just below her so that her face was even with his. "I wasn't going to let anyone hurt you, Victoria."

The use of her name unraveled the edges of her shielded fear. She took a breath and when she met his eyes, she saw no condemnation in them. So be it.

"Something happened to me . . . years ago," she began. "I'd prefer not to speak of it." The memory of being separated from her family, lost in the Highlands, was a terror she'd buried deep inside.

He made no remark, waiting for her to continue. As he leaned back against the wall, his face was shadowed in the darkness. She couldn't tell what he was thinking right now, but she forced herself to finish it.

"Since that day, I haven't left this house." Taking a deep breath, she lifted her face to look at him. "I haven't gone outside in five years. Whenever I try, it's as if my body won't move. I can't breathe, as if someone is crushing my lungs." Her mouth trembled, and she averted her face. "I wish I could force myself. But it's so hard for me, and I don't know how to overcome it."

In the darkness, his hand reached for hers. He spoke not a word, but simply held her palm in his. His thumb grazed the center, in a silent caress.

Her fingers threaded in his, and he brought her hand to his mouth. The warmth of his breath held her spellbound, and in the shadows, she felt no censure in his touch. Only understanding.

"You must think me foolish," she whispered. "Perhaps mad." The words dug into her confidence, and she braced herself for an answer she didn't want to hear.

"Fear is real. Not something to be ashamed of." There was a tightness in his voice, an edge she hadn't noticed before. "Someone made you afraid to leave your house. Was it your father?"

"No. I-It's nothing to do with him. But it's been this way for so long, I don't know how to live any differently."

"Then these walls are your prison." He drew her hand downward, releasing her fingers.

"I don't want it to be this way," she whispered. "But after all these years, it's getting worse. My mother and sisters don't understand why I can't walk outside, and they've tried to let it alone. As if it would . . . just go away."

She didn't know why she was confessing this to him, but in the darkness, it seemed less intrusive. Somehow easier to spill out the secrets she'd held back.

"Ignoring your fears won't make them disappear."

"I wish it would."

For a long moment, he didn't speak. Now that he knew, she supposed he would want to leave sooner rather than later. The thought bruised her spirits, and she desperately wished she could somehow change the way she was. Years of loneliness stretched out before her, and the spindles of the stairs suddenly did feel like iron bars.

Finally, he spoke. "You saved my life," he admitted, "and I am a man who pays his debts." He moved to sit beside her, with his knee touching hers. "I believe I could help you. But if I did, I suspect you'd dislike me even more than you do now."

"I don't dislike you," she argued. "But you do like getting your own way."

"Of course I do. Because I'm right."

The arrogance in his voice made her smile in the darkness for a moment. His knee nudged hers, and she allowed herself to enjoy his nearness, taking comfort from the slight touch. "You might believe that," she answered quietly. "But you cannot help me. I am the only one who can overcome this."

"I suppose your family was kind about it, weren't they? Nurturing you."

"They were, yes."

"I wouldn't be kind at all," he said. "Forceful, most likely."

She had a sudden vision of him dragging her outside, like a primitive barbarian. He did have a strongly ingrained sense of confidence, as if he expected his orders to be obeyed.

"And you think that would help me overcome my fear?" She didn't at all believe it.

His arm came around her waist, almost in an absent manner, as if he weren't aware of his actions. "Their methods didn't work, did they? What harm is there?"

She could think of no reply, except that it was probably best if he didn't get involved. But as she searched her excuses deeper, she realized another truth. It was vanity holding her back. She didn't want Mr. Nottoway to see her when she was afraid. She didn't want to show any weakness in front of him.

"If you'd like, we could make a wager," he offered. "I'll have you walking outside within a fortnight."

No, he couldn't. The urge to contradict him came to her lips, but she forced herself not to admit defeat so easily. "And if I can't?"

"Then I'll compensate you financially for the care you've given me, and go back to London."

His offer tempted her. She wanted so badly to leave this house, to overcome the invisible chains that bound her here.

"If you succeed, is that . . . all you want from me?" she whispered. "Just to repay your debt?"

In the shadows, his hands came up to frame her face. He leaned in so close, she could feel the warmth of his breath upon her skin. "There's a great deal more I want from you, Miss Andrews."

A shiver passed over her, his voice conjuring up images she'd never dared to dream of. "But whether or not you choose to take advantage of my interest is entirely up to you."

⚜

"Please. You have to leave," came his mother's voice. "If he finds you here—"

"I don't care if he does. You're the one I'm worried about." Jonathan hadn't missed the dark bruises upon Catherine Nottoway's face. His mother had received the brunt of her husband's fists on so many occasions, she'd stopped appearing in public.

"I'll be all right. He just has a terrible temper. I can manage him, just as I've always done.

"I don't believe that." He reached out to take her hand and turned it over, drawing up her sleeve. More bruises marred her forearm, where her husband had gripped it.

"It's only because I disobeyed him. I deserved to be punished for it." Her face held an apology, and only years of good breeding prevented him from cursing in front of her. How could she ever believe that?

Jonathan wanted her to leave his father, traveling to a place far away, where the duke would never find her. He had spent the last two years buying unentailed property in secret, never letting his father know of his assets. He intended to take his mother away, giving her a sanctuary where no man would ever raise his fists to her.

"You don't deserve to be treated like this," he said, holding her hand gently.

"I'll be a better wife to him," she insisted. "When I'm obedient, he truly is a good man, Jonathan."

"He's the Devil incarnate."

Her face filled up with dismay. "No, he's not. He loves me, Jonathan." She covered her bruised arm and tried to muster a smile. "You just don't understand him the way I do."

"He's a blackguard and a bully. You're better off without him." Lowering his voice, he added, "I've purchased land for you. If you ever wish to leave him . . ."

"No. Don't even suggest such a thing." The stubborn glint in her eyes revealed her determination not to abandon her marriage. "I am well enough where I am."

Though he'd tried, time and again, to convince her, in the end, she'd stayed with the bastard.

Jonathan opened his eyes, the heaviness weighing down upon him. He'd acquired the house in Scotland for his mother. He'd been glad of the remote location in the Highlands, hoping that it could give her the freedom she'd lacked in London. But Catherine had refused to leave the town house, never believing she could live apart from the duke.

If only he'd forced her to go, things might have turned out differently. He lived with the guilt each day, knowing that he'd held the power to protect her but had allowed her to remain in a place that was far too dangerous.

He'd respected his mother's wishes, and it had ended . . . badly. Jonathan closed his eyes, pushing back the dark memories. He hadn't been able to save his mother.

But he could save Victoria.

Her position was not at all safe. She was surrounded by rebels who were desperate enough to burn down the house rather than find new homes. It infuriated him that her family had left her here with nothing but a housekeeper and a footman. Were they so naïve about the danger? Or didn't they care? After last night, he wasn't about to leave Victoria alone. He wanted her out of this region, preferably in London where her family could take care of her.

Jonathan settled back to stare at the ceiling, wondering how he could help her overcome her fear. Dozens of strategies played out in his mind, one in particular taking precedence. He'd told her he wasn't going to be kind. Kindness clearly hadn't worked in the past. But neither did he want to become a bully like his father. He considered different tactics, making a list of each possibility.

The one clear advantage was that she *wanted* to overcome her fears. She didn't want to live like a recluse, and that was a point in her favor.

The answer lay in trust. She had to learn to trust him, to realize that the danger was from the risk of an uprising, not from the physical outdoors.

❧

"Lady Lanfordshire." Cain Sinclair tipped his hat and waited for the matron to acknowledge him. Beside her, Margaret Andrews glared. "Miss Andrews," he continued.

"What a surprise to see you, Mr. Sinclair. I never thought we would see you this close to Christmas, especially with your brother in Scotland."

Cain ignored the remark. He'd promised Jonah that he would

return before Christmas Eve, and so he would, even if he had to pay more precious coins for a coach ride home. Though his brother was fourteen and believed himself to be nearly a man, Cain didn't like leaving Jonah for long periods of time.

"I've brought you more money," he said, handing Margaret the purse of coins. "Another garment your sister made. Thirty pounds this time."

Margaret's eyes widened, and when she took the sum, his hand brushed against her gloved fingers. In his mind, Miss Margaret Andrews defined the word *prim*. Her brown hair was pulled back tightly as if a single strand didn't dare escape from her topknot. Every inch of her was pressed and perfect, from the toe of her polished shoes to the immaculate dress she wore. A woman like Margaret was off-limits, entirely unapproachable. Which was why he delighted in teasing her, watching a shocked expression transform her face.

"She made another gown so quickly?" Lady Lanfordshire gaped at the sum, and when he studied Margaret, she gave a slight shake of her head as if to say, *She doesn't know. Do not tell her, or I'll murder you where you stand.*

Interesting.

Cain gave a shrug. "It's all there. And I delivered the new fabrics to Miss Andrews, as you asked."

"Mr. Sinclair, it's very kind of you, but your services are no longer needed. My daughter cannot engage in commerce, or it will harm her chances of making a successful marriage."

Another warning look from Margaret. It seemed he was caught squarely in the middle of this.

Though Miss Andrews counted out the sum due to him, her hand tightened over his for a fraction of a second. Just long enough to let him know there was more she wanted to say.

He bid them farewell and departed, using the servants' entrance. Nearly five minutes passed while he waited outside. His breath misted in the morning air, and he leaned against the back of the house until Margaret emerged, glancing behind her to ensure that no one had followed.

Slipping behind an arborvitae tree, she beckoned for him to follow her. When he did, she whispered, "Thirty? Why on earth would anyone pay that much?"

"I raised the price," he informed her. "Your sister sent a black lace corset."

"Black?" Her face twisted with dismay. "But that's for mourning."

Her innocence amused him. "There is no' a man alive who wouldna love tae see a woman wearing black silk. Especially if the lace barely covers her—"

She clapped her hands over his mouth. "Don't say it." Her cheeks were bright red, but he couldn't resist nipping at her palm in a light kiss.

"Mr. Sinclair." She straightened her posture, lifting her chin. "We will no longer sell anything except the gowns Victoria creates."

"The corsets are selling better," he pointed out. "I used the name your sister gave me—Aphrodite's Unmentionables. Madame Benedict has been telling the ladies all about them."

"I cannot, in good conscience, permit my sister to continue selling such scandalous garments. It's—it's unladylike."

Cain couldn't stop his grin. "That's why all the women want them." He rested both hands on either side of her, trapping her against the house. "There's naught more arousing than a prim and proper woman on the outside . . . and a wicked, wanton woman beneath her clothes."

Margaret stared up at him, her blue-gray eyes holding worry. "I don't want this to hurt my family's good name. We do need the money, but if anyone finds out . . . my chances for a successful marriage will be over."

"Your secret is safe with me," he assured her.

"You?" Her mouth tightened, her gaze dropping to the ground.

"You're a man who doesn't care about anyone or anything. You wouldn't care if we were ruined."

"I care about my brother," he swore. Tipping her chin up, he demanded, "I do this work for him. Not for you or your sisters. I'll take the percentage we agreed upon, and keep your secret. But I'm no' your damned errand boy, and stop treating me like one."

Cain stepped away and regarded her. "And you might be letting your mother ken that your sister Victoria has a man abiding with her in the house. If you're worried about anyone being ruined, it's her."

With that, he tipped his hat and left.

Three days later

"Good morning."

Victoria walked into the dining room and saw Mr. Nottoway holding a bowl of snow.

She couldn't understand what on earth it was for. "You brought me snow?"

"When was the last time you touched it?" he asked, holding it out to her.

His gesture was so unexpected, she hardly knew what to do. "It's been a long time." But she crossed the room and dutifully touched the cold, fluffy snow. "It's as cold as I remember."

"We'll begin our wager today."

"I thought you'd forgotten." She hadn't pressed the issue after several days had passed, thinking he'd changed his mind.

"I wanted to wait until I could stop relying on crutches. It will be easier that way."

"You speak as if you believe it will be accomplished this morning."

"There's little point in pessimism." He leaned upon the

walking stick Victoria had loaned him and drew closer. "I've promised to stay a fortnight," he reminded her. "The sooner we begin, the better. And it's nearly Christmas. What better gift could you receive?" From his matter-of-fact tone, she supposed there was no harm in trying. She set down the bowl of snow, and he led her back into the hallway. "Do you trust me?"

It wasn't a matter of trusting him. It was her inability to trust herself. Every time she'd attempted to go outside, she'd been too afraid. But she kept those thoughts to herself. "What do you mean?"

"Show me how far you've gone outside," he directed.

"I told you, I haven't been out at all."

"Then walk toward the front door," he ordered. "Open it, if you can."

Victoria remained in place, studying him. Though his intentions seemed reasonable, she was uncomfortable with the way he was watching her. She hesitated, unwilling to walk away from him, because soon enough, he would see how weak she was.

Her nervousness welled up inside her, her skin growing colder as she took a few steps toward the door. One by one, she moved closer, until she stood two arms' length from it.

"Can you touch the door?" he asked.

She shook her head. Already her heart was racing, her body overreacting to the senseless fears. The only thing that kept her from retreating was his quiet stare.

He leaned upon the walking stick to move beside her. "Take my hand."

"I'm not going outside," she warned. "Not yet." At the thought of him forcing her into the cold, her hands began to shake. The fear spread out from deep within her, knowing that she would fail in this, as she always had.

"If you want to overcome your fear, you'll have to take the first step," he commanded. "Just one." Without waiting for her to comply, he took her hand.

She remained with her feet in place, even when he took the first step. "I want to, but I-I can't."

"Close your eyes."

"No, really, I—"

"Do it." He moved one hand over her forehead, brushing it down over her eyes until she obeyed. For a moment, he simply stood with her, his hand on hers. "Can you take a step forward with your eyes closed?"

She shook her head. Her feet were rooted into the floor, her fears rioting within her. "I'm sorry."

"Then you'll need a distraction."

She wasn't certain what he meant until, without warning, his mouth descended upon hers. Her eyes flew open, but he didn't stop kissing her.

Anyone could see them here, before the front door. Embarrassment flooded through her, only to be transformed into a shuddering response that she'd never anticipated. His heated mouth merged with hers, and she realized she'd underestimated this man. He wasn't going to accept her surrender or let her fall back into the shadows. The kiss continued on, demanding a response from her.

The last time had been nothing like this. Conquering, defying her fears until she had no choice but to let him take what he wanted. His tongue slid against the opening of her mouth, and when she gasped, he invaded the warmth in a sensual assault.

To avoid losing her balance, she reached for his shoulders. She closed her eyes again, fully aware of his hands moving down her back, pulling her close until her hips were against his.

"We shouldn't," she whispered against his mouth. "Someone will find us."

"Let them."

Before she could form another rational thought, he took her mouth again, kissing a path down her jaw and toward her sensitive earlobe. A thousand prickles of sensation poured over her, and instead of pushing him away, she pulled him closer. Against her body, she felt the hard evidence of his arousal, and her body ached.

"I never promised not to tempt you," he said, forcing her to come closer to him. His mouth plundered hers again, while his palms lowered to her hips. Her breathing quickened, and she could think of no reason at all why he should stop touching her.

Until there came a sudden invasion of cold. Frigid air blasted against her skin, and Victoria jerked away from him. She was standing before an open door. Outside, snow swirled in the air, moving toward her.

"Look," he murmured. "You've made it this far."

Instead of seeing it as a triumph, the urge to flee came over her. Her body was trembling violently, the cold air reminding her of those terrible nights when she'd been so alone. She couldn't breathe, and when she tried to pull away from him, he held her fast.

"It's all right, Victoria. Just another step."

"No," she breathed. It wasn't just another step. It was a pathway toward her recurring nightmare, a terror that held no measure. She tore herself free of him and ran away, returning upstairs as fast as she could. Leaving him to stare after her with the frozen air swirling behind.

Chapter Nine

BEATRICE STOOD behind the other dinner guests, feeling every last one of her forty-four years. Her sister Charlotte had arranged her hair, tucking strings of pearls in the upsweep, along with ostrich feathers. She'd worn a bishop's blue gown, appropriate for a woman of her age, with a lacy fichu to cover the square neckline. Matching pearls hung around her throat, and she felt as nervous as she had so many years ago, when she'd attended her first ball.

It was as if *she* were trying to catch a husband instead of her girls. Feeling embarrassed, Beatrice fanned herself, trying to remain on the outskirts of the ballroom.

"May I offer you a glass of lemonade, Lady Lanfordshire?" a male voice inquired.

She turned, blushing like a maid of sixteen, when she saw an older man standing nearby. Charlotte had introduced her to him earlier as a friend of the family, but for the life of her, she couldn't remember his name.

"I, well—I suppose," she stammered. A genuine smile spread over his face as he bowed and went off to get it.

Her mind stumbled through a thousand reasons why he'd suggested it. Maybe he'd taken pity on an older woman. Or perhaps it was merely to be polite.

But the horrifying question . . . of whether he was *interested* in her reared its head. Men never paid any attention to her. Her first and only Season would have been a disaster had it not been for the arrangement her father had made with Henry Andrews, the second son of a baron. She had been offered upon the sacrificial altar of marriage, when no one else had proposed.

Henry had been kind enough, and she'd accepted him, knowing that she could not have done any better. Eventually that kindness had grown into affection and love during their first few years together.

But right now, her heart was hammering with bewilderment, not knowing how to conduct herself. The gentleman was bringing her lemonade, nothing more. And yet, it rattled her comportment. He returned within moments, and Beatrice fanned herself, feeling her cheeks flame.

"From the look on your face, I suspect you don't remember me," he apologized. "I am Sir Alfred Harrow." His red hair was graying on his sideburns, and he had a mustache and beard that were rather distinguished. When he offered her the lemonade, he added, "I hope you don't mind my company."

"Not at all." Though she couldn't quite understand why he would single her out among the other matrons.

"I enjoy watching ballrooms," he admitted. "You can almost imagine the stories of each man and woman. That one there"— he pointed toward a young woman with ribbons in her hair—"I imagine she has her own ideas about which beau to choose for a husband. While her parents have chosen someone like him, instead." He nodded toward a stoic gentleman wearing a bottle green tailcoat. "He's the most titled gentleman in the room. The Earl of Castledon."

"He looks rather melancholy." Beatrice studied the man, whom she knew her sister had deliberately invited as a potential husband for one of the girls. He looked to be thirty or so, but from the world-weariness on his face, he might not suit any of them.

"His wife died years ago. He spends most of his time in Wales with his daughter, so I hear. I don't know why he's here now, except I suppose he wants a new wife. Perhaps a son."

Beatrice studied the earl again. The man was a veritable wall-flower, remaining away from the other guests. Title or not, she wasn't certain he was a good prospect.

"Do you have any daughters?" she asked Sir Alfred.

"Sadly, no. I never married." There was a slight flush on his face. "And I know none of these young girls would have any interest in an old man like me."

"You're not old at all," she protested.

His smile softened. "I thank you for your kindness, Lady Lanfordshire. But I know where I stand. I'm only grateful that I have someone with whom I may converse." His warm smile stirred the sympathy rising within her. He did seem like a nice gentleman, and she returned the smile.

"If I may, you look quite lovely this evening." He lifted his own glass of lemonade in a silent salute, causing her to blush again. Guilt flooded through her, for she was speaking to an unmarried gentleman. And he might get improper ideas the longer she stayed.

"Thank you," she replied. "But you'll have to forgive me. I must go and see about my youngest daughter." Though Amelia was perfectly safe with Aunt Charlotte, it was the best excuse she could think of.

"By all means." He bowed, leaving her to cross the ballroom alone. But even when she joined Charlotte and her daughter, her heart was beating a little faster.

"He's handsome, isn't he?" her sister remarked. "A little old for your girls, but not *too* old for some." Her smile held the traces of wickedness.

She didn't acknowledge her sister's comment. To Amelia, she asked, "Will you tell Margaret I would like to speak with her?"

Her daughter brightened and slipped away, leaving her alone with her sister.

"Charlotte, why ever would you say such a thing? I'm married," Beatrice hissed under her breath.

"You look beautiful this evening," her sister countered. "And it's been a long time since you've been to a party. Henry should have brought you to London far more often."

"He hates dancing, and he doesn't have many close friends in London," she admitted. "It's not his way."

"And what about you? Do you hate dancing?"

Beatrice had never really thought about it. "I can't say as I care, one way or the other. It doesn't matter whether I do or not."

"Dear sister, if I may say so, you've begun to fade away. You're behaving as if your life centers around the girls."

"It does."

"And what will you do when all of them are married? Will you be left alone with a husband who doesn't care anymore?"

Her eyes filled up with unexpected emotion, but she didn't let go of the tears. "He does care, a little."

"Then why hasn't he written to you?"

"Because he's fighting in the war. He's occupied with more important matters."

"More important than you?" Charlotte put her arm around her waist and guided her away from the wall. "He should be grateful to have a lovely, charming wife like you. And if he doesn't appreciate what he has, then you need to make him jealous."

"Make him—but why? There's no one who would be interested in me."

"Sir Alfred noticed you."

"Don't be ridiculous." She'd done nothing at all to attract his interest, and even if it were true, she wasn't about to be unfaithful to her husband.

"Enjoy yourself, Beatrice," Charlotte chided. "You have a freedom now that you didn't possess before. You can be the woman you want to be, without fear of your husband's disapproval."

She couldn't answer, for she had long ago given up on being

anything other than Baron Lanfordshire's wife and the mother of four daughters. It wasn't as if she could suddenly break open the cocoon and become someone else.

"It's not that easy," she admitted. "It doesn't feel right to enjoy myself. Not without Henry."

"Because of him, you've been shut away in Scotland for the past five years. I've only seen you a handful of times, and I haven't seen Victoria at all." Her sister's disapproval weighed upon her, but Beatrice could only shrug.

"Victoria won't leave the house anymore. Not since our journey to Scotland, you know that." With a sad smile, she added, "We tried to convince her to come."

She was saved from further discourse when Margaret arrived. Taking her daughter's hand in hers, she walked with her and lowered her voice. "Are you enjoying yourself? Have you met anyone of interest?"

Margaret nodded. "Possibly." A flush of guilt spread over her face. "But there's something I should have told you earlier. I've been quite selfish, for I-I wanted to attend this party." She squeezed Beatrice's hand, guiding her away from the others, into a corner. "I was wrong to keep it from you. But I've learned that Victoria isn't alone at the house."

"Well, of course, she isn't. Cousin Pauline and her husband came to stay with her."

Margaret shook her head. "No, they didn't come. Victoria has been there alone, with only Mrs. Larson and Mr. MacKinloch. And there's more. Apparently, a wounded man was brought to the house."

Beatrice covered her mouth with a gloved hand. She *knew* she shouldn't have left before ensuring that her cousins had arrived. Perhaps she shouldn't have come at all. The thought of Victoria alone with a wounded stranger was horrifying. "Did he . . . die?"

Margaret shook her head, lowering her voice to a whisper. "No.

He's been staying there with her, with only the servants to chaperone."

"If this is true, then we need to return home," Beatrice breathed. Were it possible, she'd have left this very minute. Her daughter needed her.

Margaret clenched her closed fan, lowering her head as she nodded her assent. "I only learned of it this afternoon, from Mr. Sinclair. I should have said something then, but I wanted to come to Aunt Charlotte's party." She let out a heavy breath. "I know you're disappointed in me."

"I'm too worried about Victoria for that." Her mind was racing with the knowledge. If her daughter had indeed lived with this man for the past week, then there would be consequences—none of them favorable.

But if the man were suitable . . . it might be the answer to her prayers. He'd compromised her reputation and should be made to marry her.

Please, dear God, let him be a gentleman of means. She didn't care whether he was English or a Scot, so long as he could take care of Victoria. Her daughter deserved a husband, like her sisters.

"I shall leave, first thing in the morning," Beatrice pronounced.

At her declaration, Margaret frowned. "But what about us?"

"I think it would be better if you remained with Aunt Charlotte through the holidays," Beatrice said. "I will find out what has happened to Victoria, and you may join us, after you've had the opportunity to meet all of the gentlemen my sister has arranged." She squeezed her daughter's hand in silent reassurance.

Margaret flushed. "I'm certain that there will be one who is suitable." She ventured a smile and took Beatrice's arm. "I shouldn't be too fastidious about possible matches."

"Of course you should. Marriage is not a choice to make lightly," Beatrice argued. "Just because a man may seem suitable does not make him the right husband for you." Although her marriage to Henry had grown into mutual respect and love, it was rare among arranged marriages. She didn't want Margaret to settle for less than she wanted.

When it was time for supper, Beatrice saw that her sister had paired Margaret up with the melancholy Earl of Castledon as her dinner guest. Although Amelia could have dined with them, Beatrice did not want her youngest daughter to entertain ideas of marriage since she'd only just turned sixteen. Better to wait a year or two, until she could mature and become a polished lady, instead of revealing her enthusiastic nature too soon. No doubt Amelia would be upset about having to take her meal upstairs, but then, she'd been fortunate to attend the party for a short interval.

Beatrice joined the procession of guests and found that Charlotte had given her Sir Alfred as her partner.

"Lady Lanfordshire," he greeted her. "I am so pleased that we will have the chance to talk further." His genuine smile was warm, and he offered her his arm.

She took it, but her thoughts were thoroughly distracted about Victoria and the wounded man. Beside Sir Alfred, she felt awkward and out of sorts. He guided her to her chair and pulled it out for her, making small conversation about the greenery and candles Charlotte had chosen for the dining room.

As the first course was served, Sir Alfred offered, "Forgive me, Lady Lanfordshire, but have I offended you in some way?"

She forced her attention back to him. "No, no. It's not you. I've received some worrisome news about my eldest daughter, and I fear I'll have to leave in the morning with all haste." With an apologetic smile, she said, "My mind is elsewhere at the moment while I must make unexpected travel arrangements back to Scotland. We hired a coach to bring us here."

"Then allow me to be of service to you. I would be glad to have my coachman bring you back home again."

"Truly, you are most kind, but I will find my own conveyance."

"So close to Christmas?" he pointed out. "It will be nearly impossible to find someone, and my coachman is a man with no family. He would appreciate the extra funds, and it would be my pleasure to be of service."

Her heart sank, for she couldn't accept his proposition. It was entirely improper. "Sir Alfred, I'm afraid I could not repay you."

His smile turned sad. "Lady Lanfordshire, I have a comfortable income and no family to spend it upon. Granting you this favor allows me to use my title of knight." He raised his glass of wine in a silent salute. "I have no expectation of anything in return. Except, perhaps, one dance from a lovely lady."

"One of my daughters, perhaps . . ." she suggested.

"From you," he corrected. "Allow a lonely, not-so-young gentleman a chance to enjoy the evening."

Although her conscience warned against it, Beatrice found herself nodding in agreement. "Very well. But only one dance."

※

"Are you all right?" Mr. Nottoway entered the parlor, leaning heavily on the walking stick. He paused a short distance away, his green eyes discerning.

Victoria had known her effort to walk outside would fail from the start. She supposed he'd thought to distract her with the kiss, hoping she wouldn't notice when he'd opened the door. Though she understood his methods, he didn't know what she had suffered. It wasn't a fear she could overcome in a matter of minutes.

Her fear had come from a moment of terror when there had been no one to help her. She'd faced her own death, and it had been like falling through the black sky into an endless void. No kiss could change that.

"I wasn't trying to hurt you," he said.

"You didn't. It's just that I was angry with myself. When I felt the snow, I—" She broke off and settled her hands in her lap. "I couldn't breathe. I had to go."

At the moment, she wished she could fade away into the wall so she wouldn't have to see annoyance on his face. A dark fist of anger gathered within her that she couldn't find the strength to overcome this.

He'll want nothing to do with you, now that he knows the truth. Exhausted tears welled up, but she refused to let them fall.

He moved to sit beside her, propping the crutches against the settee. "Was it because I kissed you again?"

"No," she whispered. "I know what you were trying to do." And though it had taken her by surprise, the distraction had made her feel desirable. She'd savored his mouth upon hers, wanting to cast off the brittle shell of cowardice that imprisoned her. Swallowing back the tears, she added, "I wasn't strong enough."

"We'll try again in the morning," he said.

Instead of making her feel better, his calm acceptance only spurred her temper. "Why?" she demanded. "What makes you believe we can change five years in a matter of days?"

"Because you said yourself, you don't want to live like this."

Her hands tightened into fists. "There are days when I loathe myself. If there was anything I could do to change it, believe me, I would." She lowered her head, caught between anger and frustration.

His hand came to touch her shoulder. The silent reassurance seemed to burn through the layers of her clothing, until she could almost sense his palm against her bare skin. Awareness made her want to lean against him, to drink in his touch.

"Why would you bother with a woman like me?" she whispered. She didn't want his pity, or his sympathy. When she turned to him, his hand moved from her shoulder to her throat. His green eyes were serious, staring at her with an unnamed emotion.

"I don't like to see a woman hurting. Not when it's in my power to change it." His hand dropped away, and she caught a trace of bitterness in his tone. "But if you want my help, you can't give up so easily."

"I'm not giving up. But I am well aware of my reality." She moved over to the window, where the snow was falling steadily. The crystalline fragments drifted upon the wind, mocking her against the glass pane that shielded her.

When he said nothing, she continued, "You're right that I don't want to remain imprisoned in this house. But we both know you aren't staying much longer. This *problem* of mine won't be solved in that time."

Using the walking stick, he came to stand behind her. She stiffened, sensing the heat of his body and the masculine scent of shaving soap. Gooseflesh broke over her, though he hadn't touched her at all.

"No, I won't be staying for long," he agreed. "I have other responsibilities I'm neglecting."

Casting a glance at the window, he added, "But it wouldn't surprise me if Sinclair informs your mother about us. He doesn't strike me as the most trustworthy of men."

"We need his help to sell our garments. And though you may be right about him telling my mother, it doesn't matter. Nothing's changed." She turned around, only to be startled when his hands moved to the glass, trapping her in place.

"Hasn't it?"

The dark look in his eyes reminded her of the demanding kiss and the way he'd broken through the fragile web of her loneliness. She couldn't take her eyes from his, and he watched her with an interest she didn't understand. There was sensuality in him, and Heaven help her, she wanted to touch the man before her. She wanted to feel his arms around her, pressing her body against his.

And she sensed her last and only chance for a different life slipping away.

"It won't be long before your family returns for you," he murmured, his voice tempting her with the promise of a forbidden attraction. "We'll have to make the most of the time we have left."

Her pulse beat like a hummingbird's wings, wondering what he meant by that. His strength was mesmerizing, drawing her so close, she didn't understand why such a man would fascinate her.

"I can't think when you're so near to me, Mr. Nottoway," she admitted. But he didn't move away. Instead, his hands moved into her hair, loosening it as he framed her face.

"Jonathan," he corrected, though it was entirely improper for her to use his first name. She wouldn't even consider it.

"I don't want you to concentrate on fear," he continued. "I want your attention elsewhere."

Oh, it was elsewhere all right. And that wasn't good at all. "It won't work," she protested.

"I have other methods." He leaned against the wall, letting his hand fall away. "I've already put Mrs. Larson to work."

"On what?" She couldn't imagine what he'd done, but she doubted it would be useful.

"An indoor picnic." He crossed his arms, a satisfied expression on his face. "Trust me."

She didn't. Not when he'd practically tossed her outside into the snow during a kiss. Victoria tried to bring order to her stormy thoughts, as he pulled a sheet from his bed.

"Bring this," he ordered, using his walking stick to move back into the hallway. When he spied the footman, he instructed, "Help me to spread this beside the door, if you would."

Mr. MacKinloch obeyed, but Victoria had no intention of eating so close to the entrance. "Why would you think I'd want to eat in front of the door?"

"Small steps, remember?"

It was ridiculous to even consider it. But Mrs. Larson seemed to approve and had begun setting out plates for both of them, along with roasted chicken, creamed spinach, bread, and a tureen of soup.

Victoria stood against the stairs in disbelief. Mr. Nottoway leaned against the walking stick as he eased himself down the wall into a seated position. His face tightened with pain as he positioned his leg, but he gave no word of complaint. "Will you join me for luncheon?"

"I'm not having a picnic in front of the door," she argued. "Someone could come in."

"Oh, I've locked it. You don't have to worry about getting knocked in the head if someone arrives." He patted the place across from him. "Come and eat."

"I'll eat in the dining room."

"Mrs. Larson is under strict orders not to serve luncheon any-where but on the floor."

"Now why would she obey you? She doesn't even like you," Victoria protested, after the servants were gone.

"No, but she agrees with me that this needs to be done. If I could walk better, I'd simply drag you outside and let you cry or faint as it pleases you."

His lack of sympathy annoyed her. "You make it sound as if I can control my responses."

"You can. While you cannot stop yourself from being afraid, you can choose the way you want to respond to it." He beckoned to her with a finger. "Come and sit down, Victoria."

The personal use of her name was too intimate, and she didn't want to leave the safety of the stairs.

He never took his eyes from her, and she shrank against the banister, unwilling to go any nearer. "This isn't going to work."

He beckoned again. "I won't open that door. I give you my word." When she hesitated, he added, "Don't make me try to get up again. It was difficult enough to sit on the floor." Holding up a silver fork, he waved it at her. "Come and join me."

"Why are you doing this?" she asked, feeling as if the entire household were watching them.

He leaned back against the wall. "You remind me of someone. Someone I wanted to help once."

"And what if I can't be helped? What if I'm never able to change?" She folded her arms and regarded him. The rush of frustration filled her up as her worst fears stripped away her courage.

"Then your life will go on, as it has for these past five years. Is that what you want?"

"No," she whispered. "I want this . . . but it's so hard."

"You really are going to make me get up, aren't you?" With a sigh, he leaned hard against his walking stick, easing back to his feet. Slowly, he walked past the food and stood in the middle of the room. "Meet me halfway."

There was no anger or frustration in his voice, only a calm command. Victoria took a step forward, then another. Slowly, she continued toward him and took his outstretched hand. His palm was warm, enveloping her freezing hand in the comfort of heat. "I'll stand at your side, until you're ready to take a step."

"You needn't hold my hand."

"It will keep you from running away," he countered. "And I like holding your hand. It's an interesting hand." His thumb rubbed the center of her palm, and a shiver broke over her. "It's soft here, at the heart." Then he moved his fingers higher, to touch the edges of her fingertips. "But these have known work. A needle has pricked these fingers over the years. I imagine that now, you feel nothing when something sharp pierces you."

"It's not so bad."

"And yet, you're soft beneath it all." His hand clasped hers. "You can be as afraid as you like, underneath the surface. But we must strengthen your exterior, so that no one knows your fear."

He eased her forward to take another step, and she found it

wasn't as difficult. The edge of the sheet lay only a short distance away.

"Can you manage to sit down?" he asked. "Or is that too much to ask?"

She raised her eyes to look at the front door. It stood tall, like a sentry guarding her. And although it bothered her to do so, she took one last step forward and sat down on the outer perimeter of the sheet. Jonathan smiled and took his place on the opposite side. "Now see? That wasn't too terrible." He passed her a plate of chicken with creamed spinach and a slice of bread. In turn, she poured him a cup of tea, breaking off three lumps of sugar with the tongs.

They ate for a time, and although she remained tense, it wasn't as bad as she'd thought it would be. She sat across from him, and when they had finished, he asked, "How are you?"

"Still nervous," she admitted. "But I made it this far."

He lifted his cup of tea in a silent salute. "So you have."

Their conversation was interrupted by a knocking at the door. Jonathan tried to rise up from his place on the floor but lost his balance. The walking stick clattered to the floor, and Victoria went to his side. She took his hands, helping him up.

Once he was standing, he held her there a brief moment longer. "Look at where you are." His arms held her captive, and she realized she was touching the front door. "Do you want to open it?"

"N-not with these dishes." She scrambled away from him and Mrs. Larson came forward, helping her to pull their picnic aside. Mr. MacKinloch opened the door, while the housekeeper removed the evidence of their food.

Victoria's heart was racing, but even as she retreated, she felt a slight sense of triumph. She'd touched the door without fear, while helping Jonathan. It hadn't occurred to her to be afraid.

It wasn't the greatest achievement—but it was a beginning. And she couldn't stop herself from smiling.

Mr. MacKinloch opened the door wider to reveal dozens of women standing beyond the doorway. All were looking at her anxiously.

Mr. Nottoway sent her a knowing look. "It seems, Miss Andrews, that your army of seamstresses has arrived."

$$\mathcal{R}$$

While the women gathered in the dining room, Jonathan retreated to the parlor. He didn't know if Victoria would want him to remain at her side, but what did he know about sewing? Nothing at all. It was better to stay out of her way.

His gaze settled upon the chessboard, the white and black figures neatly lined up. It was so easy to move the pieces in a precise, logical manner. Winning the game was a matter of strategy. When he lost, it was usually because of his opponent's skill.

But the wager he'd made with Victoria had nothing at all to do with skill or strategy. And though they had made good progress this morning, he didn't know if the success could continue. She'd barely managed to get close to the front door. How much longer would it take for her to move beyond that?

Or would she? Any day now, he expected Franklin to arrive with his staff. Given the harsh winter and the conditions here, Jonathan didn't intend to stay much longer. Victoria Andrews wasn't his responsibility, after all.

Yet, every time he saw the hurt in her gray eyes, he thought of his mother. He'd been unable to save the duchess from his monster of a father. It forever haunted him that he'd obeyed her, leaving her behind, after she'd asked him to go.

If only he'd stayed . . .

He reached for a white pawn, fingering the curves. He couldn't go back and undo the mistakes he'd made. Neither could he bring back his mother.

He set down the chess piece and saw the open letter that

Victoria had been reading the other day. Though he knew it was wrong to sneak a glimpse, the words *Aphrodite's Unmentionables* caught his eye. Now why would Victoria's sister mention something so improper in a letter? He read the note, startled when he came across a list of requested garments. Silk-lined corsets with padding, gowns to be worn upon a woman's wedding night. Scandalous colors of fabric, all luxurious, meant to caress a woman's skin.

And Victoria—quiet, reclusive *Victoria* was meant to sew all of this?

He stood up, leaning against the walking stick as he approached the hallway. Keeping out of sight, he watched as Victoria spoke quietly to the women, explaining what she needed. The bundle of fabric lay upon the dining room table, and he saw her holding up what appeared to be whalebone.

His gaze narrowed. By God, it was true.

She was now showing them the lengths of fabric that Cain Sinclair had brought. Silks, satin, and lace in every color for constructing the unmentionables. He recalled Victoria's earlier admission, that the garment she'd given to Mr. Sinclair was black with lace.

The image of her wearing such a corset, of black against her silky skin, her breasts veiled by a layer of lace, was deeply arousing. He'd never imagined she was the sort of woman who would make such garments, but clearly she had already done so. Was she that desperate for money that she'd resorted to something this scandalous?

Her father was likely an officer, and from the modest house in which they lived, he suspected they were upper middle class. They ought to have enough funds to live on, without lowering themselves in such a way.

And yet, she'd mentioned financial difficulties that she didn't want to reveal to her father. Surely there was another way of clearing their debts rather than indulging in such prurient methods.

If anyone found out, the scandal would ruin their family. Jonathan couldn't let that happen. He owed Victoria his life, and a large sum of money would eliminate the need to earn funds in this way. She could return to embroidery or sewing samplers, instead of working as a seamstress.

Laughter abruptly resounded from inside the dining room. Curiosity overcame him, and he used the walking stick to move in closer. He balanced against the wall beside the doorway, leaning in to eavesdrop on what the women were saying.

"It's nae good, making these out o' silk or satin, Miss Andrews. If ye wash it once, the lye soap will burn right through it," one remarked.

"But only a lady could afford them," another interjected. "The cost would be too dear for the rest of us. And if they don't use them more than a few times, it will nae matter. They'll have to buy more, won't they?"

A courtesan certainly would. Jonathan still couldn't grasp what he was hearing, and it was all he could do not to interrupt them.

"Miss Andrews, pardon me for saying so," the second woman continued. "Ye shouldna be afraid to take chances. If a woman's trying to get herself a wee bairn, then why put anything at all over her breasts? Make it out of lace or very thin nettle cloth. She'll have her man on his knees, beggin' for her."

Jonathan nearly choked at what he was hearing. Nettle cloth was almost entirely transparent when it was woven thinly—just as daring as lace.

His mind reeled at the discussion. He couldn't even conceive of Victoria creating seductive unmentionables. Not a woman who, until a few days ago, had never been kissed.

Why does it matter what she does? his mind demanded. *You'll be gone from here, soon enough.*

She was an innocent, completely unaware of the consequences of these actions. She knew nothing at all about the intimacies between a man and a woman, and he was torn between wanting to drag Victoria out of there . . . and wondering if she was as naïve as she seemed.

The taste of her lips haunted him still. He wanted to conquer her mouth again, driving her mad with desire. He wanted to share her bed and awaken in the morning beside her body.

She was an unfulfilled desire—that was all. Why, then, couldn't he convince himself to let her go?

Chapter Ten

OVER THE PAST few days, the women had spent their time cutting up silk, sewing in various rooms throughout the house. Jonathan had glimpsed bold colors and unmentionables that would make any man uncomfortable. Though the women had raised curious eyes at his presence, they'd kept their distance. And true to her promise, Victoria had paid them wages, though he didn't know where she'd found the money. Possibly from her own saved coins.

Today, thankfully, was Christmas morning, and they were all gone. Even the servants, whom Victoria had granted a few days off for their holiday.

Using his walking stick, Jonathan hobbled toward the kitchen in search of food. He made up a plate of cold goose and sliced a chunk of clootie dumpling that Mrs. Larson had made last night. It was simple fare, but enough to keep them from starving.

He balanced the plate while struggling to return to the dining room. Victoria sat at the long mahogany table, with piles of fabric surrounding her. She was busy stitching whalebone into a panel. When she saw him, her face flushed, and she gathered up a pile of material to hide her work.

"Good morning," she greeted him. "I didn't expect you to be up and about this early."

"Merry Christmas," he countered, setting down the plate. "I thought you might be hungry."

"Christmas." She set down her needle, an embarrassed smile coming over her. "I'd completely forgotten."

"I suppose you didn't buy me a gift, did you?" he ventured.

"I'm afraid I couldn't go out to buy one." But she'd recognized his teasing and answered it with a soft smile of her own. Her hair was tucked up in a hurried arrangement, and a long blond strand curled across her neck. He wanted to touch it, to pull the pins from her hair and see it spilling out over her shoulders.

Although he'd come to know her as a demure lady, he'd glimpsed another side to her that he'd never suspected. Knowing that she was spending her hours creating seductive unmentionables only intrigued him more. He imagined her slender body clad in red silk and lace, the chemise following the lines of her curves before flaring out again.

Being with her now was weakening his sense of honor. He wanted to entice this woman, to awaken her into desire until he could taste the sweetness of her skin, watching her come apart.

She was a forbidden temptation, entirely too innocent to be sewing such garments.

"What are you making?" he asked, knowing full well what it was. He wanted to hear whatever explanation she could come up with.

"It's a-a ladies' garment."

"With whalebone," he added. "I suppose you're making a corset."

A red flush came over her cheeks. "What would make you believe it's something like that?"

"Your sister's letter. And I overheard what you said to the crofters' wives the other day."

"Now why would you read my sister's letter? It was never meant for you." She rested her hands upon the table, dismay in her eyes.

"You left it open." He leaned against the table not denying his guilt. "But even if I hadn't, it's not difficult to guess what you're making."

Victoria stiffened, as if not knowing what to say. When at last she raised her gray eyes to his, she remarked, "I suppose you're appalled."

Jonathan reached for the hidden pieces and saw that the newest corset was made of a deep violet satin. He ran his fingers over the material and noticed a bit of padding sewn into the bottom of the bodice. The effect would make a woman's breasts appear larger than they were. He didn't know whether to be amused or indignant.

"You're selling lies, Miss Andrews."

"Not lies." She bit her lip, snatching the garment back again. "Just a bit of help. To those less fortunate."

Jonathan bit back his laughter. "And what happens when her unfortunate lover discovers that the lady's curves are not her own?" She gave a shrug, and he knew he'd cornered her. "Lies," he repeated.

"All right. So they are. But I've earned more from these unmentionables than any of the gowns I've made." She picked up her needle again and pulled out the purple satin. Her needle moved in and out of the fabric in tiny stitches as she attached the boning. "This may be shameful to you, but it provides money for my family. And for those women."

"What will you do when your secret is discovered? How do you think your father will react when he learns what you've done?"

"He won't learn of it. Mr. Sinclair is quite discreet."

"All of London is not discreet, Miss Andrews," he pointed out. "If no one knows who is making Aphrodite's Unmentionables, the secrecy will drive the gossips into a frenzy. It could harm your father's military career."

"We don't have a choice," she countered. "My mother spent

most of my father's income on repairs to the Norfolk estate and on taxes. Unless we come up with enough money to pay our debts, it may be inevitable that we'll have to sell this house."

"And you're not ready to leave."

She shook her head, reaching for her needle and continuing her work. Her mood had grown somber, as if she questioned her ability to get past the front door.

Jonathan crossed the room, leaning on his walking stick, until he reached the fireplace. He tossed a few more peat bricks on the fire and asked, "What work did you give to the crofters' wives?"

"We've already cut out the pieces, and I showed them some samples. They'll stitch them together, and I'll teach some of the other women to add the whalebone."

"You're enjoying this, aren't you?" He could hear it in her voice, in the bright tone of interest.

Her needle moved in a rhythmic pattern, and she nodded. "I'm giving them a way of helping their families. And it helps my sisters and me, for when Mr. Sinclair returns, we can give him dozens of garments to sell." She added another strip of whalebone and admitted, "It's a sort of work I've never done before. I like the challenge of it."

He stood by the fire, warming his hands. She didn't truly understand the purpose of the unmentionables—to tantalize a lover. And though he recognized her desire to make a profit, her innocence would hold her back.

"Will you come and join me for a moment?" he asked quietly.

She finished sewing a seam and set it aside. "Of course. Is something bothering you? Your leg, or—"

"It's not my leg." He stared into the bright coals, and she came to stand beside him.

"What is it?"

He faced her, but when he looked at her face, he saw a woman who allured him like no other. A woman without guile, who had never once asked for his money. Instead, she'd begun creating her own business. Despite the way she lived like a recluse, he respected her intelligence and her willingness to solve her family's debts.

He liked her. And he admitted to himself that he'd enjoyed these days spent within her house. It had been such a relief to be an ordinary man for the past fortnight. She didn't know who he was, and it had enabled them to become friends.

He wanted to do something for her, to share with her some way of admitting what this respite had meant to him. And since it was Christmas, it seemed an opportune time.

"We only have a few days left before I go," he reminded her. "Franklin and my staff will arrive soon."

Her mood dimmed, and she predicted, "You want me to try walking outside again, don't you?"

It wasn't quite what he'd intended, but it was one way of distracting her from the sewing. Jonathan stretched out his hand to her, setting the walking stick aside. "I want to try walking on my own. We could go together."

She appeared wary of his suggestion. "And what if you fall?"

He made no reply, but beckoned to her. She released a sigh and took his hand. Jonathan guided her palm around his waist, placing his arm across her shoulders. "You'll help me keep my balance."

Though she appeared worried at their closeness, neither did she pull away. Instead, she guided him forward, allowing him to lean against her as he needed to. With her body pressed close, he caught the soft floral scent of her hair. The wayward strands curled across her throat, but he kept his arm around her shoulders, trying to ignore the urge to act upon his instincts.

"You've already touched the door once," he said. "Walk with me again. Just to the door."

Her steps slowed the closer they came. Jonathan tightened his arm around her, offering, "I'll be with you, every step."

"Don't be angry with me if I fail."

"I'll just kiss you, if you do." He tossed the threat lightly, not really meaning it. But the color rising in her cheeks made him aware that she *wasn't* impervious to his attentions. "Unless you want to fail." He stopped walking, waiting to see her response.

She didn't look back at him. "I'll do the best that I can." Her mouth tightened in a line, as if she were trying to muster the courage.

He squeezed her fingertips in silent reassurance. "Remember, you've done this before."

She nodded and took one step forward. There was hesitation in her gait, and he saw the fear beginning to slip under her skin. To distract her, he said, "Tell me about your other designs. Besides the unmentionables."

Victoria gripped his hand and looked into his eyes. "The last gown I made was white with blue stripes. It was for my sister." Another step forward, and he allowed her to set the pace, not forcing her to move any sooner than she was ready.

"Do your sisters sew?"

She shook her head. "Margaret can do some sewing, but it's not really her favorite pastime. She prefers to order us around." There was a glint of humor in her eyes. "Although I'm the eldest, she likes to inform everyone of how a proper lady should behave. I believe she's memorized some etiquette books."

"And the others?"

She took another step, but her tension seemed to ease as she talked of her family. "Juliette is nineteen, and she's very good with numbers. She's the one who slipped into Mother's study and saw how dangerous the finances were. Mother likes to pretend everything is all right, but Juliette told us that we're several thousand pounds in debt." She sobered a little. "If my sewing can help remedy that, then it doesn't matter what we sell."

He offered no argument, though he had already decided to quietly settle their debts. The money meant nothing to him, and it was the least he could do for their family after Victoria had saved his life.

She faltered as they grew closer to the door, and he asked another question to distract her. "What of your youngest sister? There are four of you, am I right?"

"Yes. Amelia is sixteen, and she's quite good at cajoling others into doing whatever she wants them to. She could sell wool to a sheep," Victoria remarked.

They were standing at the door, and Jonathan continued to hold her hand. She had gone pale, her gaze fixed upon the floor. From the stiffness of her demeanor, he predicted, "You're not ready to step beyond the door, are you?"

"No." Her voice came out emotionless, as if she were trying to hold back an immense fear. In every facet of her bearing, she looked ready to run.

He relaxed his grip on her hand, only to realize that she was holding tightly to him, as if he were giving her the strength to stand there. As if she needed him.

The knowledge slid over him, past the years of loneliness. His hand closed over hers, guarding her. For the past few years, he'd done everything he could to become the richest man in England. And the more wealth he'd amassed, the emptier his life had seemed.

Until now. This woman knew only the man, not the duke. And the more he came to know her, the more he understood how rare she was. Whether or not she could overcome her fears, he couldn't say. But he felt the need to help her, to do something in his life for another person. It was Christmas, after all.

"One day soon, you'll have to visit the crofters," he reminded her. "To inspect their work."

She shook her head. "I'd prefer that they come back to the house."

He guided her hand to the doorknob, and her fingers had

turned to ice. "How do you know they won't sew unmentionables only suitable for courtesans?"

Victoria drew her hand back from the doorknob. "Just because we make undergarments that are . . . different does not mean we're designing for ladies of that nature. Some of the garments are—" Her voice broke off, and her face transformed, as if an idea had suddenly struck her. Inhaling sharply, she stared at him. "You're right. I never thought of it that way, but we simply must."

"Must what?"

Victoria let go of his hand and tore away from him, racing up the stairs. "I need paper and ink."

He stared at her, wondering what thoughts had suddenly taken possession of her. When one minute passed, then five, he realized she wasn't planning to return. It struck him that he'd effectively been dismissed.

Making his way toward the stairs, Jonathan debated on whether or not to wait longer. In the end, he decided to satisfy his curiosity. He leaned on the banister, struggling to climb the stairs. He reached the first landing and called out, "Miss Andrews?"

No answer.

He muttered a curse beneath his breath and managed to drag his useless leg up the remainder of the stairs. One of the doors in the hall was slightly ajar, and he hobbled his way toward it. When he knocked, he heard her answer, "I'm not finished yet."

Peering inside, he saw that she was seated at a desk, writing furiously. Jonathan opened the door a little wider. "What are you writing?"

"I'm sketching." She dipped her pen in ink and scribbled faster. "More designs." She turned back to look at him, and there was excitement in her eyes. "You were right, you see. There are many different women. Some will prefer a more modest design. Others . . . well, they may want a more—" She stopped, as if unable to choose the right word.

"Seductive?" he offered.

"I was going to say a more 'daring' garment. But they should have the choice, don't you see? If they want a beautiful chemise made of silk and ribbons, then they should have it."

He leaned against the doorframe, torn between wanting to dissuade her from these ideas . . . and wanting to see precisely what her imagination had come up with.

"And what sort of 'daring' garment did you envision?" he asked, crossing his arms as he stared at her.

She blushed, not answering the question. Instead, her pen continued moving over the paper, though the lines were slower. He watched her for a moment before offering his own suggestion.

"If you use a sheer material, the woman's lover will be tantalized by the sight of her naked skin."

The pen fell from her fingertips, and she looked appalled by his words. "I should not be having this conversation with you. You shouldn't even be in my bedchamber."

"To be precise, I am not in your bedchamber. I am in the hall." He was beginning to enjoy her discomfiture.

"Please," she begged. "Just go away and let me finish. I can't think properly when you're here."

"Do you want me to look at the drawings and offer my opinion?" he asked. He doubted if any of her designs would be daring enough for her intentions.

She was aghast. "No, you will not."

"I've seen unmentionables before, Victoria. In fact, I have a particular preference for—"

"You needn't say it." She buried her face in her hands, too embarrassed to even meet his gaze.

"But you'll wonder about it, won't you?"

He felt no remorse for teasing her. A woman like Victoria Andrews, innocent and unknowing of the ways between men and women, shouldn't even consider designing intimate undergarments. He hoped she would abandon the idea and return to sewing gowns. Or better, if she didn't have to sew at all.

She was bent over her work, her brow furrowed as she sketched. If he did nothing to stop her, he feared she'd remain in her room for the rest of the night, caught up in the drawings.

Before he left, he said, "Come downstairs in an hour, won't you?"

She sighed. "Why? So you can tease me further?"

"Because it's Christmas." He had no desire to remain alone downstairs, not when he had other plans for them.

She tilted her head back to look at him, her expression softening. "All right. In an hour."

It was well past the hour when she finally set her drawings aside. Victoria studied each of them. She'd created a chemise and corset designed for a woman like herself, modest and feminine. Then she'd designed a different set of garments meant for a married woman. The cut was more daring, with bolder colors designed to attract a husband's notice. The last drawing made her blush simply to look at it. It was a garment that could only be worn by a courtesan.

She was ashamed to admit it, but Jonathan's advice had been accurate. Her earlier drawings had been far too demure. His suggestion, that she use a sheer fabric, had inspired a corset and chemise reminiscent of a sultan's harem. The design was almost entirely transparent, one that would reveal a woman's breasts instead of cloaking them. A layer of padded silk beneath would lift up the curves, offering light support. The garment was sinful, baring everything.

It was scandalous. She couldn't imagine any woman wanting to buy it. But then, the crofters' wives had suggested it earlier, laughing that it would encourage a man. Victoria touched her hands to her cheeks, not truly understanding what they meant.

Inside, she grew apprehensive about joining Mr. Nottoway downstairs. She'd given the servants their holiday, without truly thinking of what that meant—being by herself in the house with a man who had kissed her. It was dangerous, not at all proper.

And yet, she was grateful not to be alone on Christmas.

She folded up the drawings and put them inside the drawer of her desk before she rose to go downstairs. She searched the parlor first, then the dining room, before she finally found Jonathan seated before the fire.

He'd discarded his tailcoat and his cravat was loose. In the warm light, his sun-darkened hair gleamed and he stared into the fire as if searching for answers. At his feet rested a pile of packages, wrapped in brown paper.

"What are these?" she asked, interrupting him as she moved closer.

"Gifts for you," he said. "It wouldn't be right to celebrate Christmas without them."

A startled warmth stole through her heart at the sight of the presents. "But how? You couldn't possibly go out with your leg."

"Some were borrowed," he admitted.

She sent him a chiding look. "You *stole* my belongings and wrapped them up?"

"It isn't stealing when you haven't removed them from the house," he pointed out. "But if you don't want them, I'll put them back."

In spite of herself, she was eager to see what he'd selected. "There seem to be quite a few of them."

"Oh, I took the liberty of wrapping gifts for myself, as well." He gestured toward the dining room. "Go and fetch a chair. We'll open them together."

She turned from him, unable to stop her smile. She'd never

imagined that anyone would go to such trouble for her. As she pulled the heavy chair across the room, an inner voice reminded her to guard her feelings. She couldn't allow her heart to soften, not when he was leaving. He might have shown her a kindness, but in the end, he would go, just as he'd said he would.

"Open this one first," he instructed, handing her a slender object.

She untied the string and slid off the paper, revealing a spoon. Mystified, she asked, "What is this for?"

"It's for the cup of hot tea I'll make for you later this evening."

His matter-of-fact tone made it seem as if the gift was of little importance. But it touched her that he'd thought of it. She held the spoon, studying his face. He'd taken some time to shave, and she wondered what it would be like to touch his smooth face.

"Now choose one for me to open." He pointed to three misshapen packages that were set aside from the others.

Victoria selected a package slightly smaller than her hand and passed it to him. When he unwrapped the ivory queen from her father's chess set, he sent her a wide smile. "An excellent gift, Miss Andrews. I would enjoy playing another game of chess with you."

She suppressed a groan, for she disliked the game thoroughly. "I don't know if I would have given you that gift, had I known what it was." But she accepted the next gift he passed to her. Inside the brown paper, she found a piece of currant cake that Mrs. Larson had baked only yesterday. "To go with my tea?" she predicted.

"Yes. And if you'd like to share it with me, I wouldn't complain. It is the last piece, after all."

"You are most generous," she teased, breaking off a piece and passing it to him. Instead of taking it from her, he guided her hand to his mouth, his lips brushing over her skin as he took the cake.

The touch of his lips made her smile fade. He was playing a

game with her, one she couldn't hope to win. In his eyes, she saw a shadowed desire, a hunger that made her long for far more.

To distract them both, she reached for the second, larger package. "I suppose this is for you."

Jonathan tore off the paper and revealed his own shoe. She hadn't even noticed he'd taken it off. At her confused expression, he explained, "It will be quite useful. Especially when I'm dancing with you."

She shook her head. "I haven't danced in years." She didn't even know if she would remember how.

"It's a gift for both of us," he offered. "You'll be in my arms."

She stared at him. "You're making fun of me."

He leaned forward, his wrists upon his knees. There was a flare of intensity in his green eyes, of a man who saw far more than she wanted him to. Without responding to her accusation, he demanded, "Open the last gift."

Victoria reached for the small packet he gave her and found a pair of her own gloves inside. "What are these for?"

"They're to keep you warm, when you step outside for the first time."

She clutched the gloves, glancing over at the window. Flakes of more snow fluttered against the glass, outlined by the glow of the candle upon the sill. She still didn't believe it could possibly happen. Though she'd made it as far as the front door, she'd gone no farther.

"I don't know what to say."

"Just thank me." He reached for the last package and shook it slightly. It was small, barely the size of her palm. "I wonder what this could be."

At first, she didn't recognize the piece of greenery. But when she spied the telltale white berries, she went still.

"Now this," he said in a deep voice, "is what I wanted most."

"Mistletoe," she whispered. She didn't know where he'd found it, but she knew what it meant.

It was dangerous to kiss him again, for with each gift he'd given, he'd broken down another barrier to her heart. When he left, she would be more lonely than ever before. It hurt even to imagine it.

Jonathan reached out to her hand. "Our time grows short." Holding up the mistletoe, he added, "There's no one to see us. No one to criticize or tell us it's improper." He stood up, pulling her close as he tucked it into her hair. "The question is, do you have the courage?"

Fear rose in her eyes as she stood staring at him. "I don't know that it's a matter of courage anymore."

He rested his hands upon her shoulders. "You don't want to kiss me again?"

She lowered her face, resting the top of her head against his chin. "You're going to leave Scotland. If I kiss you again, it will only make me dream of things I'll never have."

He sobered, for he'd not thought of it that way. With her standing so near to him, he moved back to look into her gray eyes. He glimpsed the brokenness in her expression and her fears.

Jonathan cupped her face, moving his hands up through her hair. He couldn't explain what it was about Victoria Andrews that attracted him. But he'd glimpsed the unfulfilled longings in her, desires echoed within himself.

"Tell me you don't want this," he murmured, his mouth barely above hers.

Her hands covered his, her eyes closing. "I don't want you to break my heart."

"That isn't what I want either," he confessed. Her warning pierced through him, even as he lowered his mouth to hers. Whether or not she knew it, she'd captivated him. He wanted her to feel something, to care.

In his mind, he imagined her soft skin beneath him, her hair spread out upon the sheets as he touched her. Her mouth surrendered to his, and in her kiss, he tasted the sorrow of a woman locked away from the world. A woman who held dreams but not the courage to reach for them.

Her hands threaded into his hair, pulling him closer as if she needed him. As if she craved him as badly as he wanted her. Her kiss was like water, slowly washing over the stone of his heart.

And God help him, he couldn't stop himself from touching her. His fingers moved down the back of her gown, opening the buttons, one by one. As he bared her back, he warmed the cool skin with his palms, traveling lower until he reached the tightly laced stays.

He slid his tongue into her mouth and Victoria gave a quiet moan, as if startled by the intrusion. But as she grew accustomed, she tentatively touched his tongue with her own.

Her arms wound around his neck as she succumbed to the mindless pleasure that took both of them. Jonathan went rigid, hissing as her hips pressed close against him, reminding him of how badly he wanted her.

He dragged his mouth away from hers, nibbling at her earlobe, kissing the soft part of her neck. "Tell me to stop," he ordered. "Tell me that I should leave you alone and this isn't the kind of woman you are."

"I don't want you to stop." Her hands gripped his head, arching back, while he kissed the bared skin above her square neckline. "Not yet."

"You deserve better than a man like me," he murmured against her skin. "And I think you know it."

Warnings roared through his mind, but he ignored them, savoring the warmth of her skin and the soft catch in her breath. He could imagine laying her back upon her bed, kissing her breasts while sliding inside her wetness. He wanted to be the man to take her, to teach her the pleasures of becoming lovers.

Victoria took his face between her hands and guided him back to her mouth, kissing him as if it were the last time. He gloried in the roughness of the kiss, and knew that her mouth would be swollen red after this. His hands were moving down her shoulders, edging the unbuttoned gown to expose the breasts he wanted to touch.

And when he revealed her corset, her breathing was hitched, her hands frozen upon his arms. In the flickering firelight, her skin was golden, the tops of her breasts covered by a layer of white lace.

He drifted his knuckles over the soft mounds, waiting to see if she would pull away.

Victoria didn't move. With a stricken face, she watched him as if uncertain what was happening between them.

He touched the back of the corset, sliding his hands lower, until he reached the laces. His fingers rested upon the ties, while he kissed her throat.

"I know you think I'm trying to seduce you," he murmured upon her skin. "And though I would welcome you in my bed, that isn't my intent this night."

Her hands froze as he lowered his mouth, unlacing her corset as he kissed the soft swell of her breasts.

"If you say the word, I'll stop," he told her. But her eyes closed and her face grew taut with unspoken needs.

"I want to lower this gown right now," he said against her throat. "If I could, I'd free your breasts and take them into my mouth."

She shivered, as if imagining it. He wanted to draw out her arousal, tormenting her with words. "But this corset won't allow it."

He continued freeing her from the laces, talking against her skin. "But imagine another garment. One where your breasts would rest upon a bed of satin, barely covered by a sheer lace. I could see your nipples through the fabric, watching them tighten while I touched them. I could taste them through the lace, stroking them with my tongue."

She forced herself to pull away, though he could see the flush of arousal upon her face. "Is that what men desire?"

"No," he said, loosening the corset until he could slide it lower, baring her breasts. "This is what I desire."

And with that, his mouth closed over her nipple. She let out a shuddering gasp, her hands moving through his hair as he tasted the soft flesh. Her breasts were smaller than he'd thought, but the intensity of her reaction made him grow harder. She was moaning with every flick of his tongue, her body trembling.

He was aching for her, wanting so badly to take her into his bed. Instead, he moved toward the wingback chair, sitting down as he pulled her to sit on his uninjured leg.

"Take it off," he commanded, raising her arms above her head. She didn't protest, but let him free her from the whalebone cage, granting him full access to her naked skin.

He didn't ask why she'd allowed this, but he suspected it had everything to do with his impending departure.

Once more, he took her mouth, kissing her hard as he caressed her breasts with his fingertips. "Imagine a man and a woman, slipping away from a ballroom," he said in a low voice. "In the garden, with her gown the same as yours." He bent lower, taking her breast in his mouth again, laving the tip. "With one of your new corsets, he could pleasure her . . . and no one would ever know."

His hand moved down her skirts, lifting beneath the petticoat, until his hand touched her leg.

"What are you doing?" she asked, fear guiding her voice.

"Should I stop?" He trailed his bare hand against her thigh, and she went motionless, as if unable to speak. He moved his palm higher, and against the back of his hand, he could feel the silk of her intimate hair.

Her head fell back, and he took her breasts into his mouth again, using his tongue to torment her. A flush covered her skin, and he could feel her body heat rising. Though it was another form of torture to him, he didn't want to stop.

She was wet at her slit, and he teased her with his fingers.

"Ohh," she breathed as he slid one finger into her moist entrance. Her fingers dug into his shoulders, her body shaking at the intrusion.

Jonathan was lost in his own haze of need. The touch of her body, the taste of her skin, was driving him beyond the ability to stop. He used his hands to touch her, to caress the hooded flesh that guided her pleasure.

She arched against his hand, convulsing as he entered her with a second finger. No longer were either of them thinking, but he was determined to take her into her own ecstasy. He wanted to be the man to watch her shatter, to see the languid pleasure take her.

"Victoria, open your eyes," he demanded.

She did, and in the clouded depths, he saw a woman of passion awakening. She bit her lip as he plunged and withdrew, her wetness coating his fingers.

"If I could, I'd be inside you right now," he said, using his thumb against her swollen flesh. "I'd lift you on top, and I'd feel your wetness surrounding me."

He quickened his strokes, kissing her hard as he guided her closer to release. "I'd thrust inside you, over and over."

She leaned into his touch in a counterpressure, her breath gasping until he deepened the touch of his thumb in throbbing circles until she began to sob, her fists clenching as she bucked against him.

An agonized moan broke forth when at last she seized her release, crying out as he took her past the brink. Her hips pressed against his hand as she trembled, and he caught her in a kiss, cutting off his own groan as his own release struck without warning. She kissed him with the full intensity of a woman well-pleasured, and he cupped her warm breast, rewarded when she let out another shudder.

Jonathan cradled her in his arms, reaching for the mistletoe in her hair. Slowly, he lowered the sprig of berries down her face, over her throat, to the swollen breasts bared before him. He circled one nipple, then the other, before it fell to the carpet when she pulled him into another dark kiss.

In that moment, he realized that he would allow no other man to have her. The fierce possessiveness was undeniable. He wanted Victoria Andrews in his bed, to spend each night touching her in this way.

To awaken with her beside him.

He held her in his arms, his hands passing over her back as he breathed in the scent of her hair. All too well, he understood how impossible this was. Victoria didn't belong with a man like him, caught in an aristocracy where only money had saved him from becoming an outcast. She knew nothing of his world, and he couldn't imagine subjecting her to it.

She deserved better than to become his mistress.

He needed a wife, but not one who secluded herself from the rest of the world. He required a woman who understood the intricacies of London society, who could fulfill her duties as a hostess and provide the requisite heir and the spare. There were dozens of ladies who could easily assume that role.

And yet, when Victoria's hand moved to touch his heart, he wished that wife could somehow be her.

Chapter Eleven

L ATER THAT NIGHT, Victoria lay in her nightgown within her own bed. Though Jonathan had kissed her once more, bidding her goodnight, her thoughts lay in chaos. She didn't know what had possessed her to let him touch her so intimately. What he must think of her now.

She buried her head in the pillow, her cheeks burning. Every part of her body felt alive, as if his touch had transformed her.

But even more, she now understood what he meant about the unmentionables. The early designs were flawed, suited to a maiden—not a lover. Her mind was caught up in transforming the designs, while her heart bemoaned the liberties she'd allowed him to take.

Though she tried to console herself with the fact that no one would know what she'd done, she couldn't avoid her own shame. She'd behaved like a wanton, surrendering to the tremulous feelings and reveling in the pleasure he'd given.

The guilt plagued her, as she worried over how this had changed their friendship. She doubted if they could go back to what it was. If it had ever been anything at all.

Closing her eyes, she clenched her legs together, almost wishing she could erase the moment they'd shared. And yet, she didn't regret it. He'd given her a gift, a glimpse of carnal knowledge that she never would have had otherwise.

Inside, the bleak truth remained. He was leaving. These moments with Jonathan would become memories, stolen fragments of a dream.

Unable to sleep, she pushed back the covers and lit one of the lamps. Her room was freezing cold, but she needed to occupy her hands. Anything to escape the tumultuous thoughts racing through her mind.

Victoria reached for the purple corset she'd been constructing earlier. The color was a rich amethyst, and the matching chemise had a drawstring to adjust for a woman's bust. Staring at it now, she realized it was entirely too prim.

She seized a pair of scissors and began tearing out the seams, changing the construction while her mind drifted back to the moment Jonathan had touched her. Her hands reshaped the fabric, as she envisioned his hands upon her nipples, how he'd taken her into his mouth.

She worked through the night, sewing up the seams until her eyes blurred. When at last the first rays of dawn slipped across the horizon, she set the sewing aside. It was, by far, the most scandalous garment she'd ever created. Likely, it wouldn't sell.

But she'd poured her own desires and needs into every stitch, remembering the swift pleasure that had consumed her. There were pieces of herself in this corset, dreams of another life.

She packed it away in brown paper, her feelings bruised and hurting. When it was done, she stared outside at the sunlight as it pierced through her window.

It would be today, she vowed. No matter how long it took, she would take her first step outside.

It shouldn't be this difficult to brew a cup of tea. Jonathan had searched everywhere for Mrs. Larson's hidden container of tea leaves but had come up with nothing at all. A cup of boiling water wasn't precisely what he'd wanted to bring to Victoria.

The tea was a distraction, a means of speaking with her. He didn't doubt she would be embarrassed by what had happened between them. But he held no regrets. Instead, her passionate response had flared up the desire to touch her again. To sheathe himself within her body and pleasure her until she grew pliant in his arms.

One night would never be enough. And he didn't know what to do or say now.

Quiet footsteps intruded, and he looked up to see Victoria standing before him. She wore a light blue morning dress with gloves and a bonnet.

"I want to try again to go outside," she said. Not a word did she say about their intimacy last night, but he saw the restlessness in her eyes, as if she hadn't slept well.

"Are you ready?" he asked. Thus far, she'd been nowhere near venturing beyond the door.

When he studied her, he caught a glimpse of iron resolve. As if she were somehow trying to punish herself for the way she'd allowed him to touch her. He set down the kettle and saw that her face was pale, her gloved hands clenched together.

"Why now?"

"Because you're leaving soon." She revealed nothing of her feelings, merely stated the fact. "After you're gone, I might not have the courage again."

She spoke as if he were leaving tomorrow. As if there would not be another chance for her.

"Do you want me to go, after what happened between us last night?" He couldn't read whether it was her anger speaking or shame.

Vulnerability passed over her face, and she lowered her gaze. "I don't fault you for it. I could have told you to stop."

Jonathan closed the distance, until she was backed against the kitchen table. "There's no shame in what we did, Victoria." He didn't want her believing that there was any reason to feel guilt. He rested both hands on either side of her. "Unless I hurt you."

She shook her head slowly, admitting, "You made me forget everything else. And I believe . . . with your help, I can forget about my fear."

"All right." He offered her his arm, and she took it, looking as if she were walking toward her own beheading instead of the front door. They went up the stairs, toward the main floor. Her steps grew slower, until she stood an arm's length from the door. For a moment, she stared at it, as if gathering her courage.

"It can wait until tomorrow," Jonathan offered.

"No, it can't." She closed her eyes. "Go on and open it."

Her face had gone white, the terror locked inside. Jonathan moved to her side, his own gait unsteady without the walking stick. With his arm around her, he felt her frigid skin. "Are you certain?"

She nodded, still keeping her eyes tightly screwed shut. Jonathan opened the door slowly and felt the instant transformation in her posture. She started to bolt, but he used his strength to hold her in place.

"Don't," he warned. With both arms around her, he held her trapped. "Open your eyes."

"I can't."

"Yes, you can. You don't have to move at all, but you must look around you."

Her arms came around him in a tight embrace, clinging to him as if he were the ledge above a precipice. Jonathan leaned in, kissing the side of her face and moving down to her throat. Against his mouth he felt the tremor of her rapid pulse, but she didn't let go of him.

"You're with me, Victoria. I won't let any harm come to you."

He stood motionless, heedless of the wind blowing powdery snow toward them. "Look at me," he commanded.

Her eyes fluttered open, her panicked gray eyes staring into his. "I'm here," he reminded her. "And I won't let go."

Her arms locked around his neck, but she nodded.

"Would you care for that dance now?" he teased.

A faint crease touched her mouth, but she shook her head. "It's freezing out here."

"I could warm you afterward."

Her cheeks flushed at his wickedness, and he adjusted his grip around her waist, moving her slightly to the right. "What are you doing, Jonathan?"

"We're going to take one step beyond the threshold. Nothing more," he promised. "If you think you can manage it."

Her eyes never left his. In them, he saw her growing doubts and the fear that shadowed all else. "I don't know," she whispered.

"Will you try?"

Victoria tightened her grip around his neck and gave a single nod. Her eyes closed again, and he held her against him as he took one step beyond the door. The snow had drifted up to their knees, and she gave a slight shiver when they were within it.

"Perhaps it wasn't such a good idea. Our feet are getting wet," he noted. "Shall we go back inside?"

She shook her head. "No, not yet." A minute crept onward while she stood still, the snow blowing against her bonnet. Snowflakes caught on her lashes, her mouth slowly relaxing from its tightness.

And then she opened her eyes to look around her. The fear was still there, but beneath it, a note of triumph. Though she never let go of him, a soft smile spread over her face.

The trip from London to Scotland had taken far longer than Beatrice had ever imagined. After the snow had grown too deep to continue by coach, she'd hired a driver to take her the remaining distance by sleigh. She huddled within the conveyance, hot bricks at her feet, while she shivered. With every mile homeward, she worried over the revelation that Victoria was stranded alone with a stranger.

She'd wanted to confront Mr. Sinclair, to demand what he knew about the wounded man. But he'd left a day earlier, and might be there already.

Her mind turned over the conundrum, not knowing what to do. Why had Mr. Sinclair left? Did he believe Victoria was safe, so long as the man was unable to harm her? Troubled thoughts brewed inside, for she didn't know what to do. She wished Henry were here to help her through this mess.

But then, he hadn't been here for several years. She'd had to solve every muddle on her own. If this man had indeed ruined Victoria, he must be made to wed her.

Her gaze slipped down to the handkerchief Sir Alfred had left behind in the coach. It had contained half a dozen sugar biscuits with the note: *For your journey.*

She'd eaten them over the course of several days, unable to stop the flutter that arose in her heart at the gesture. When was the last time her husband had done anything like this?

Or when had she done the same for him? The truth sank within her, for she was just as guilty for being thoughtless. She'd stopped bothering with her appearance, giving all of her attention to the girls.

She reached for the handkerchief and shook out the crumbs, folding it neatly. Though Sir Alfred claimed he wanted only friendship, she suspected that he was only waiting for a hint of returned interest.

Beatrice twisted her wedding band. Henry had given her garnets for faithfulness. And although she *had* been faithful to him all these years, perhaps it was time to put more effort into their marriage. To try and resurrect what they'd lost.

He was a baron now, with the responsibilities that accompanied the title. Most men sold their commissions and ended their military service. Why, then, had he returned to the battlefield? Was he avoiding them? Sobering at the thought, she promised herself that she would write a proper letter, one that would remind him that he had a wife and family waiting at home for him. Perhaps he might return if she asked him to come.

The coach followed the jarring road north, while all around her the green Highlands rose. Trees nestled against the hills, their branches coated with snow, while a silvery loch gleamed in the distance.

When she saw the gathering of tents, her heart sank a little. The Scottish refugees were still here, camped upon their land. A few of them came out to stare at the coach, and when she saw a mother holding the hand of a young girl, it reminded her that only a few thousand pounds separated their fates.

She'd met with the solicitor and learned that their situation was dire indeed. Perhaps it was a blessing that she'd been forced to leave London immediately. At least she hadn't had to see her daughters' faces at the meager Christmas presents she'd left with Charlotte. After sending most of the dress money they'd earned to the land steward at Norfolk, she had nothing but stockings and a pair of gloves for each of them.

The coach pulled up to the driveway, and she stopped short at the sight before her. Victoria stood embracing a man Beatrice had never seen before. The two of them were leaning in to each other, the man watching her daughter with the eyes of someone who desired her.

But more than that, Victoria was standing outside, for the first time in years. It was nothing short of a miracle. Her daughter wasn't pushing the man away, either. Her arms were wrapped around the man's waist, and there was a light in her expression, as if she were . . . happy.

Beatrice didn't know what to think of that.

When the driver opened the door, she took his hand and stood in the middle of the snowdrifts, staring.

"Lady Lanfordshire, shall I bring in your bags?" he was asking.

She shook her head, hurrying forward. The only thing that concerned her at this moment was finding out precisely who this man was and what his intentions toward Victoria were.

"Victoria!" came her mother's voice.

Jerking backward, Victoria was shocked to see Beatrice hurrying through the snow. She tried to go back inside the house, but Jonathan tightened his grip on her hand. "Don't run," he warned. "We've done nothing wrong."

Oh, yes, they had, but she didn't want her mother to find out about any of it.

"We'll stand and you can introduce me to her," he said.

When her mother reached the steps, her gaze shot from Jonathan and back to her. There were a thousand questions bubbling within Beatrice, Victoria had no doubt, but her mother voiced only one.

"Are you all right, my dear?"

Victoria managed a nod. "This is Mr. Jonathan Nottoway, Mother."

She introduced Beatrice in turn, and Jonathan gave a respectful bow. "Lady Lanfordshire."

At a loss on how to explain herself, Victoria offered, "We should go inside and I-I'll make some tea."

"Where is Mrs. Larson?" Beatrice asked, in a voice lined with steel. There was no mistaking her disapproval, but there was nothing she could say to make this any easier.

"She went to visit her family for the holiday," Victoria managed, as her mother came inside the house. "Where are my sisters?"

"Still in London." Beatrice removed her bonnet, shaking the snow from her skirts. To the driver she called out instructions to bring her belongings inside.

She moved inside and turned to Jonathan. "Wait for me inside the parlor. I know you'll understand that I must speak with my daughter alone."

There was no mistaking the reproach in her tone. There was no way to know what her mother was plotting, but Victoria gave a nod to Jonathan.

"You did well," he said, in parting. The compliment slid past her defenses, warming her. Despite the tongue-lashing she knew her mother was about to impart, she *had* overcome her fears and taken that first step. Jonathan had given her that, and she was eternally grateful for it. It offered hope that she might take a second step soon, and then a third. By the summer, she might be able to visit the crofters.

Before she could entertain that daydream any further, Beatrice took her hand and half-dragged her toward the kitchen. When they were alone, she stared at her, as if not knowing where to begin.

Truthfully, Victoria didn't know either. "Mr. Nottoway was shot by one of the crofters," she said at last. "I saved his life with Dr. Fraser's help. He's been convalescing here."

"I'd say he's been doing a sight more than that," her mother retorted. "He had his *arms* around you, Victoria. Or were my eyes deceiving me?"

"No." Color blazed in her cheeks as she recalled what else she'd allowed Jonathan to do. The intimacies she'd shared with him went far beyond the boundaries of proper behavior.

"Are you in love with him?" her mother asked, softening her voice. "Has he . . . been kind to you?"

In love? Bewildered at the thought, she faced her mother, uncertain of what to say. She'd grown accustomed to having

Jonathan around, and in his arms, he'd made her feel safe. Because of him, she'd managed to take the first step outside.

"I've only known him for a fortnight," she said, avoiding a direct answer, "but he has been kind to me."

"I ask this, because I am going to demand that he marry you."

"Marry!" She gaped at her mother, already shaking her head. "But I cannot marry him. I couldn't leave—"

—*this house,* she'd been about to say. But he'd changed that. If he held her, guiding her outdoors, it was possible that she *could* leave. She tried to imagine herself as Jonathan's wife, but could not envision herself as mistress of a household. The very thought terrified her.

Although he'd said little of his wealth, she was well aware of it. The cut of his clothing, the breeding in his voice . . . everything spoke of money. Whereas their family was struggling to survive their debts.

She simply couldn't imagine him offering for someone like her.

"He has compromised your name," Beatrice argued. "You were with him for weeks, alone and unchaperoned." She frowned, adding, "And what happened to Cousin Pauline and her husband? Surely they would have come by now."

"The letter you sent must have been lost," Victoria said absently. "They never arrived."

Her mother's mouth tightened and the darkness in her gaze held suspicion. Even so, Victoria wasn't about to reveal the truth.

"And why would Mrs. Larson leave you here? I shall speak to her about this. Such irresponsibility."

"I sent her away," Victoria said. "She wanted to visit with her family members for Boxing Day, as did Mr. MacKinloch. It was only right."

"You are an unmarried lady," her mother emphasized. "I cannot agree with you. You should never have been alone with this man."

"He's returning home as soon as his staff arrives," she felt compelled to point out. "And I see no reason to force an unwanted marriage on him. He was shot, and I took care of him. That's all."

She kept her tone firm, hoping her mother wouldn't see through her. Turning toward the large oak kitchen table, she rested her palms upon the wood, shielding her feelings.

"Even so, I shall speak with him." Beatrice removed her bonnet and the expression on her face resembled a judge about to sentence a prisoner to death.

"I won't do it," Victoria interrupted. "If you demand that he marry me, I'll say no."

She knew what she was—a fearful coward of a woman who would only draw resentment from Jonathan if he were forced to wed her. And though the past few weeks had reawakened her dreams, she couldn't bear to have him despise her.

"And what of us?" her mother countered. "Don't you care what others will say about you, and the shame it will bring upon your father?"

Considering the ladies' undergarments she was making, Victoria doubted if her compromised position was even worth noting. "Let Mr. Nottoway leave," she insisted. "And none of us will say anything more about it. All will go on as it did before."

"I don't understand you," Beatrice said quietly. "Today was the first time I've ever seen you set foot outside that door. Surely, he means something to you."

He means enough to me that I will set him free, Victoria thought. The idea of forcing Jonathan to wed her was impossible.

"I won't marry him," she insisted again. "So put it from your mind."

With that, she left the kitchen, retreating to her room. On the way past the stairs, she saw Jonathan leaning against the doorframe of the parlor. His dark blond hair was rumpled, and his green eyes met hers with the look of a man who wanted to follow her up those stairs.

Victoria's hands curled against the banister, feeling as if he could see right through her veiled emotions.

"It will be all right," she said quietly. "I've told her that nothing happened between us."

The dark look in his eyes flared. "Really." Then she saw his expression transform from annoyance to a look of ruthless determination she hadn't seen before. As if he had his own intentions and she would have no say in them.

Startled by his sudden change, she walked up the staircase, fully aware of his eyes watching. And she had no idea what he planned to do now.

Jonathan had no doubt that Lady Lanfordshire would demand marriage to her daughter. He was prepared for her arguments, but it was Victoria's calm response that dug into his mood. She'd promised to smooth matters over, to behave as if nothing had happened.

Something *had* happened. And he didn't want to walk away from her, leaving her behind. The moment they'd shared last night had played over and over in his mind, splintering his conscience. He'd taken advantage of her innocence, touching her in a way only a husband should.

But worse was the dark sense of possession. He wanted no one else to share Victoria's bed, and the thought of another man taking her intimately sent a haze of anger through him.

He needed a wife and heirs. It was a fact he couldn't avoid, and though he already knew the sort of woman he was supposed to wed, he'd shied away from those matrimonial chains for years. He didn't want a wife who would lie on her back and think of ways to spend all of his money.

He wanted Victoria.

He wanted a woman who would hold tightly to him, knowing

he would keep her safe. He wanted to see her smile, to walk beside her until she was able to overcome her fear.

She wouldn't want the life he led; he knew that. But there were other ways. He had amassed enough wealth now that he was nearly the richest man in England. If he wanted to keep his duchess to himself, isolating her from the others, then by God, he could do so. The more he thought of it, the more his mind pulled together possibilities. He had endless estates throughout England and abroad. When the war ended, she might enjoy living in Italy or somewhere on the Mediterranean where she could enjoy the sunlight and the sea.

He rather liked the idea of an isolated home where no one could hurt her. Where he could put aside his rank and responsibilities and simply be himself.

She would refuse the marriage, if he asked. Especially if she learned he was a duke. But he hadn't acquired wealth by kindness or softhearted ways. He knew how to get what he wanted, by any means necessary. And though it might require forcing her hand, he didn't care. He would do what was necessary to have her.

When Lady Lanfordshire entered the parlor, he cut off her opening argument. "I intend to marry her."

The relief in her eyes was immediate. "Do you?"

He gestured for her to sit down, taking command of the situation. Keeping his voice low, he began with his trump card. "I am Jonathan Nottoway, the Duke of Worthingstone."

Although he saw the surprise pass over her face, to her credit, Victoria's mother kept her composure. "And what brings you to Scotland, Your Grace?"

"A land acquisition. One that went badly, I'm afraid." He outlined the events of the past few weeks, ending with the revelation "Your daughter does not know of my title. I thought it best to keep it from her. Even so, I am in need of a wife, and it was"— Jonathan paused, trying to find the right words—"a welcome change to become acquainted with a woman who thought I was an ordinary man."

The matron's face softened. "You must be accustomed to women admiring you for your rank instead of your person."

No, they'd admired him for his money.

"Quite so." He cast another glance toward the hallway. "I have become friends with Miss Andrews, and I believe she and I would get along well enough. Though I'd rather keep my rank from her until after we are wed, given her fears."

Lady Lanfordshire nodded, folding her gloved hands in her lap. "Your instincts are correct. While it is a great honor, Victoria would be overwhelmed at the prospect of becoming a duchess." Raising her chin, she added, "But I believe she would make a very good wife. And in time, she would adapt to her new circumstances."

From her willingness to accept him, either Lady Lanfordshire knew nothing of the scandal surrounding his parents, or she didn't care. He suspected the former, and decided there was no reason to enlighten her. They were his father's sins, after all.

"Like you, I believe Miss Andrews would eventually settle in." He regarded her directly. "I do not require a dowry from her. I ask only that she conduct herself as a proper wife."

He didn't believe there would ever come a time when Victoria would want to be a duchess.

"You should know that Victoria's father is a peer," Lady Lanfordshire added. "My husband inherited the title of baron when his elder brother passed on. He is now Colonel Lord Lanfordshire."

It would indeed make matters easier, though as the daughter of a lesser peer, others might still cast aspersions on her upbringing. "Lady Lanfordshire," he offered, "as I cannot ask Lord Lanfordshire for his daughter's hand, I would ask your permission to wed her."

"You have it." She gave a nod. "So long as you do not mistreat her or make her unhappy." A furtive smile crossed her face. "I want what is best for her."

He appreciated the woman's candor, particularly her willingness to carry on his deception a little longer. "I will wed her here, in Scotland," he said. "It would be best if we return to London or one of my other estates only after we are already married."

Beatrice sobered. "Do you think you can convince her to marry you?" She sent him an apologetic look. "I fear she might refuse."

There was little doubt of that. But he shrugged and said, "I believe I know of a way. It is not particularly kind, but it will work." He gave her the details of the arrangement, and Lady Lanfordshire laughed.

"You are correct, Your Grace. She may not like your methods, but I believe she will indeed agree to your proposal."

Chapter Twelve

"WHY WOULD you do this?" Victoria demanded, ripping out a seam in a short length of silk.

"Because the crofters need a more permanent place to live," Jonathan answered. "Don't you agree?"

"This isn't right, and you know it." She threaded her needle, wishing she could take a pair of scissors and release her anger upon the fabric. Instead, she was forced to be careful with the delicate panel.

"Marry me, and I will grant them permission to return to Eiloch Hill," he said. "They may rebuild their homes with wood from my forests or stone, as they prefer. It's a beneficial solution."

She tossed aside the needle and stood up, unable to keep up the pretense of sewing. "Beneficial to whom? Not I."

With long strides, she crossed over to the window on the far side of the dining room. With her hands pressed to the glass, she fought against the choking anger. He was manipulating her to yield to his whims, as if the past few weeks had meant nothing at all.

"I will respect your wishes, of course." His voice was cool and calculating. "But what do you suppose will happen to the refugees when your father learns they are here?"

She already knew the answer. The Colonel would force them to go.

"I am offering them a place to stay, for your sake," Jonathan continued. "All I ask in return is that you become my wife."

"But why me? We hardly know each other."

From behind her, quiet footsteps approached. She felt his presence before he spoke, and the heat of his body made her yearn to lean back against him. His hands came up to her shoulders, and she felt his mouth near her ear. Shivers erupted against her skin when he spoke.

"I need heirs," he admitted. "And I'd rather have a wife who would welcome my attentions in her bed."

A rush of heat poured through her. She stood with her back to him, and he pulled her into a closer embrace, his arms crossed over her breasts. She already knew what it was to be touched by this man, and she *did* want more.

To stall from giving him an answer, she asked, "Heirs to what?"

He hesitated for a brief moment. "To my lands and estates."

She'd never questioned him about his lands, though she'd guessed he was likely a lesser peer, like her father. "Even if I did agree to wed you, for the sake of the crofters," she whispered, "I can't leave this place. You know that."

"You walked outside, just this morning."

"Only because I was holding on to you." She couldn't see it as a triumph, for she'd barely made it past the door. "You ought to have a wife who's not such a coward."

"Another wife would have let me bleed to death. She wouldn't have stitched me up when I was shot."

Victoria stepped free of his embrace and turned to face him. "You aren't marrying me for the right reasons. And I don't believe you'll turn your back on those people just because I refuse you."

His expression turned as cold as the frost outside. "I have dozens of estates, Miss Andrews, from here to Italy. Their fate is of no concern to me—only to you."

He moved back from her, limping slightly on his bad leg. "I've given you a choice. You may refuse to wed me, if that's your wish, but I won't make the offer again. The crofters can go live anywhere else in Scotland, and I'll lose no sleep over their fate." Giving her a slight bow, he turned his back and left her alone.

Victoria returned to the table, reaching for her needle and thimble. Normally the act of sewing brought her peace, but today it did nothing at all. In frustration, she gathered up the pieces and returned them to her basket.

How could he make such a demand? Yes, she wanted the life of a normal woman. Yes, she wanted a husband and children of her own. But it had always been a daydream, never something within her reach.

It was fear that held her back. Fear that if she dared to reach for the dream, he would be disappointed in her. She couldn't wed a man like Jonathan and remain behind closed doors.

Then, too, she'd watched her parents grow further apart over the years until they seemed hardly more than acquaintances. Her father was kind to her mother, but she knew he'd stopped writing letters. Time had frayed the edges of their marriage, and though Beatrice had tried to hide her feelings from her daughters, Victoria had seen it weigh upon her mother's spirits.

She didn't want the same thing to happen to her, nor did she want Jonathan to look upon her with regret or disappointment.

But you care about him, her heart insisted. *You want to live with him and share his life.*

God help her, it was true. But he was also keeping secrets from her. She'd never pried, never asked more about who he was or how much wealth he possessed. And yet, she sensed he had something to hide.

She walked away from the dining room, the house growing brighter in the afternoon sun. Her mother had gone to fetch Mrs. Larson and Mr. MacKinloch, believing that Victoria was settling her own betrothal in her absence.

Anger rose up within her that Jonathan would dare to put other people's lives in jeopardy over this. She strode over to the door, letting the frustration well up inside her until she was ready to strike out at the wooden panel out of rage.

She sensed Jonathan watching her from the parlor door. His presence was palpable from the shadows, as if he didn't believe she was capable of walking outside alone. Yes, she'd taken her first step beyond the door this morning. In his arms, she'd managed to look upon the face of her nightmare.

With her palms against the wood, she heard him take a few steps toward her. "Do you want me to walk out with you?"

"No." She was so angry with him right now, she wanted him nowhere near her. The urge to prove to him that she did possess the strength to face her fear was gaining a foothold. She didn't need him to hold her hands like a small child. She reached for the doorknob, her heart pounding so fast, she no longer knew if it was fury or fear.

"Are you certain?" There was no judgment in his voice, only a quiet offer.

In an act of defiance, she flung the door open, heedless of the freezing air. Snow swirled around her, but she held back the terror and took the step alone.

It was so cold, her lungs burned from the frigid air. The hem of her dress grew sodden in the snow, but she took a second step, then another.

With a glance behind her, she saw Jonathan watching. There was a slight smile on his face, but she wasn't at all pleased by it.

"You see? I knew you had it in you." There was pride in his voice, but it irritated her. The anger grew hotter, rising within her skin with a force she'd never imagined. She wasn't an object to be collected like another piece of property. He couldn't simply buy her, use her for his heirs, and discard her.

His marriage offer had shown her a darker side to him, one that she didn't like at all. Did he honestly believe she would *want* to wed him after he'd made such a condition? The Scottish refugees were suffering in such cold, and if she'd had any control over their fates, she'd have allowed them to build houses immediately. It was wrong for children to be sleeping inside a barn, regardless of the circumstances.

"You should come inside," he said. "It's getting colder outside."

"And what about the people living in weather like this?" she demanded. "Huddled in tents, trying to keep a fire going?"

"You hold the power to change their fate," he reminded her.

His answer was like a match, flaring the oil of her anger into a fiery blaze. Victoria marched into the nearest drift, plunging her hand within it. Balling up the snow tightly in her palms, she flung it at his face. The snowball exploded against his cheek. "Don't you *ever* demand that I marry you to keep other people from suffering."

His amusement vanished. For a horrified moment, she couldn't believe what she'd just done.

Jonathan stared at her, slowly brushing off the snow from his cheek. Gone was the proud gentleman and in his place stood a man with vengeance on his mind. He reached down and picked up a handful of snow, molding it in his palms.

"Don't you dare," she warned.

"You started it." He advanced upon her, and she grasped her skirts, trying to get away. The deep snow caught at her until she nearly lost a shoe in the drifts. Though she struggled to escape, he was upon her in seconds.

"Now, then." His voice turned dangerous, his expression predatory. "What shall I do with this?" He held up the snowball, catching her around the waist.

"I can think of a good place for it," she shot back.

In response, he took the snow and crushed it against the back of her neck, the freezing droplets sliding down her gown. She let out a shriek, trying to push his hands away.

But then his warm mouth was upon her neck, replacing the

cold snow with his heated kiss. The freezing flakes melted against her skin, and her body reacted violently to the sensuality of his tongue licking away the droplets of water.

His strong arms held her captive while he leaned in. The shock of hot and cold made her gasp. He pulled her hips against his, and she could feel his arousal against the juncture of her thighs.

"Was this what you wanted to start?" he demanded. He kissed her hard, his hands pushing past the pins of her hair, fusing their mouths together. She was drowning against him, helpless to do anything except kiss him back. His tongue entered her mouth while he gripped her hips, sending a ripple of sensation between her legs.

It was both a surrender and an empowerment. Her mouth was upon his, her tongue mingling with the heat of him, while he rocked against her.

"I want you," he whispered harshly. "I want to take you upstairs and see every inch of your bare skin. And when I pleasure you, I want to feel you clenching me inside you."

His erotic words spun a vision she could hardly imagine. But a part of her was broken, for not once had he mentioned love.

"What is your answer?" he demanded. "Are you going to marry me?"

She said nothing, burying her face against his chest as he helped her out of the snow. There was no choice in this. He held the power to give the crofters a permanent place to live, a shelter where the Earl of Strathland couldn't harm them. She only had to sell herself.

"Yes," she whispered. But she couldn't help feeling as if she'd given away a part of her soul.

"They haven't left Ballaloch, my lord."

Brandon Carlisle, the Earl of Strathland, stared at John

Melford, his factor. "What do you mean, they haven't left? The crofters were evicted weeks ago. Surely, they've gone by now." Their leases had ended in winter, which he'd thought would force them to move west quickly, in order to gain shelter.

Strathland moved to stare out the window. His manor house stood atop the hill, overlooking thousands of acres of land. The sheep nearly blended in with the snow, the herds milling close together.

The older man cleared his throat, casting a glance toward the door. "They took refuge with Lady Lanfordshire and her daughters. So far as we've seen, the crofters have kept our sheep from grazing on that land, ever since the first snows fell. They've also kept them off the property belonging to the Duke of Worthingstone."

"You needn't worry about Worthingstone," Strathland remarked. "He travels frequently, and I highly doubt a man like His Grace would set foot in Scotland. Our sheep can continue grazing on his property next spring, and he'll never know about it."

"I'm afraid that's no longer true, my lord. It seems that the duke was here to inspect his land. One of the crofter boys shot him."

God help them. He'd heard nothing of the duke's arrival, and he demanded of his factor, "Is he alive?"

Melford nodded, and Strathland exhaled with relief. "Arrange a trial and hang the boy who shot him, as a lesson to the others."

His factor made no argument, but inclined his head. Strathland didn't care that a boy had done it. There needed to be a clear understanding that violence would not be tolerated, particularly against the English nobility.

"Where is the duke now?" the earl asked.

"He was taken in by the eldest Andrews daughter and Dr. Fraser saved his life."

Paul Fraser was a thorn in his side, one Strathland wanted to be rid of. But the man was like a wraith, here one moment, disappearing the next. Because of Fraser, hundreds of Highlanders were refusing to leave. They were faithful to Fraser, never disclosing where the man had gone.

"There's more, my lord," Melford continued. "I've heard that the duke plans to marry one of the daughters."

"Not Juliette," Strathland ventured. The memory of the beautiful young woman slid through him, like a faint dream. She'd eluded him for months now, but he intended for that to change.

"No, my lord. The eldest daughter, Miss Victoria Andrews."

The earl relaxed his grip upon the armrests. Interesting. He couldn't imagine why the duke would even consider lowering himself for a baron's daughter. It was a complication he hadn't expected, but one that could be easily managed. Once the pair of them had gone to London, he could regain the grazing land.

In the next year, he wanted full command of this region. He intended to triple his herds of sheep, if all went according to plan. The price of wool had quadrupled, and these lands were perfect for the herds. With any luck, he could use the profits to free himself from the vast debts his wife had accumulated while she was living. Though he ought to have mourned her death, he wasn't at all disappointed she was gone. She'd done nothing but bleed his profits dry, and he was well rid of her.

"Has the wedding taken place yet?"

"No. Lady Lanfordshire is awaiting the arrival of her other daughters, and the wedding will commence then, before His Grace returns to London."

The earl rubbed his chin, thinking to himself. He'd never wanted to grant the land to Worthingstone, but he'd had little choice after the gambling losses. He'd mistakenly believed that luck was with him that night, after he'd won the first few hands of cards. But gradually he'd sunk deeper into debt until he'd had nothing to offer except the land. At the time, he'd believed there was no harm in losing Eiloch Hill, for the house upon the land was hardly more than a farm dwelling, not at all appropriate for a duke. He'd never imagined Worthingstone would journey so far to inspect the land himself.

Clearly, he'd been wrong.

Brandon had to find a means of encouraging both families to leave. Though he'd offered to buy the land from Lady Lanfordshire, she was powerless in her husband's absence.

"My lord, if I may, the only way to send the crofters to the coast is to take away their refuge." Melford glanced outside, where the snow was drifting against the window. "Without the Andrews family to grant them shelter and food, they would have no reason to stay."

"What do you suggest?"

Melford shrugged. "Accidents happen, from time to time. A candle or a lantern might tip over and start a fire. With no house, they'd have to return to London, wouldn't they?"

"And the duke would certainly take them there." He nodded, liking the simplicity of the idea.

"After the wedding would be the best time," Melford advised. "I have someone in mind who could set the fire. He could ensure that the house is destroyed."

The earl nodded. "I'll leave it to you to manage, so long as I am not involved." He sat back in his chair, reaching for the crystal wineglass. "If you find Fraser, see to it that he's no longer our problem."

"As you wish, my lord." Melford bowed. "And I presume you do not wish the Andrews ladies to be harmed in the attack."

"I would prefer that they leave when the fire begins," Strathland said. "A little fear wouldn't be amiss."

"I shall see it done," Melford promised.

As he swallowed his wine, Strathland sat back in the chair, envisioning the vast acres of land stretching across the Highlands. The wool profits would increase in the coming years, and the evictions had only aided him in making more room for sheep.

He'd amassed most of northwest Scotland now. Rather like the ruler of his own kingdom.

He lifted his glass in a silent toast to himself.

"Are you certain this is what you want, Victoria?" Margaret held a pair of elbow-length ivory gloves while Juliette laced up the back of her gown. "You hardly know this man. Even if it was highly improper for him to be here—"

"She saved his life," Amelia interrupted. "It was terribly romantic, and he's desperately in love with you. Isn't he?"

Victoria had no idea what to say to that, and she sent Margaret a silent plea for help. But it was Juliette who came to her rescue.

"If he doesn't already love her, he soon will," her sister pronounced. With a tentative smile, Juliette squeezed her hands. "There aren't any flowers right now, but I have some dried heather you could carry."

Victoria managed a helpless smile, trying not to think of her impending wedding. Her mother had refused to let her see Jonathan beforehand, and supposedly his staff had arrived from London and had taken him back to his house to get dressed. She hoped he had also begun arrangements to bring the crofters there, but thus far, she had seen none of them leaving.

She smoothed a wrinkle from Juliette's green muslin gown. Her sister's dark hair was braided and coiled atop her head, while she wore a single ostrich feather within the arrangement.

Amelia stood back to look at her, and her face held nothing but adolescent excitement. Her eyes sparkled, and she lowered her voice. "I'm wearing one of the new chemises with my corset, and it's absolutely divine."

Margaret gaped. "You are *not* wearing something so inappropriate, Amelia. You should take it off, this instant."

"But who would even know?" Her sister sent her a sly look. "I imagine you're wearing one, too, aren't you, Victoria?"

She didn't speak a single word, but her blush revealed the truth.

"There is nothing at all wrong with your undergarments," Juliette interrupted. "And Margaret, if you'd care to look at the recent sales, you would know that this is just the beginning. By the time we've sold the rest of Aphrodite's Unmentionables, even princes will be falling at your feet for a chance at the dowry you'll have."

That news shut her sister up, though Margaret still appeared anxious. Victoria adjusted the shoulders of her gown, feeling unsettled as she stood before the mirror. With the help of the padded corset, her breasts were pressed against the scooped neckline. Her dress was a long-sleeved ice blue muslin, trimmed with lace. The color reminded her of the frost upon the window and the chill inside her heart. She'd debated for hours on what sort of unmentionables to wear. Her mind demanded that she choose a virginal garment, tightly laced, covering every part of her bodice.

But instead, she'd chosen an ivory chemise that was sheer, with a low-cut corset. The garment was delicate, with white embroidery that resembled swan feathers. Something beautiful, and yet, it would tempt her husband.

The thought of Jonathan's hands upon her sent a silent thrill inside. Though she was not pleased by the way he'd coerced her into this wedding, another part of her was looking forward to the night ahead. He'd promised they would spend their wedding night at his house, where there would be no one to intrude upon them.

She hadn't yet decided how she would manage the short journey to Eiloch Hill, but she'd put it out of her mind. If she had to cling to Jonathan every mile of the trip with her eyes shut, she would do what she must.

Last, she put on a blue silk bonnet trimmed with silver embroidery and ribbons. Her gloves did nothing to keep her hands warm, and inside, the anxiety heightened.

Amelia and Margaret hurried off to finish their own preparations, leaving her sister Juliette behind.

"Are you afraid?" her sister whispered.

"A little." Victoria hadn't told any of them the true reasons for the marriage, particularly the fate of the crofters.

"I know you were . . . stranded with him for a long time," Juliette said, staring at the carpet. "He didn't hurt you, did he?"

"No. Not at all." Victoria understood her sister's worry, but took her hand in reassurance. "He never tried to . . ." *Seduce me,* she almost said. But that wasn't precisely true. He'd awakened her to temptation, touching her in wicked ways.

"You don't have to speak of it," Juliette said, squeezing her hand. "Did Mother tell you what to expect tonight?"

"Whether or not she did, it's not something I'm going to tell you." Her cheeks were burning with embarrassment and a hint of curiosity. The truth was, her mother had said very little. Just that she should submit to her husband and, with any luck, she might become pregnant quickly.

A quiet knock sounded at the door, and Beatrice Andrews entered. At the sight of Victoria, her mother's eyes glistened with tears. "You look beautiful, my dear. Your father would be so proud of you."

She crossed the room to embrace her, and Victoria clung to her for a moment longer. Her mother had grown terribly thin, but the love in her arms was undeniable.

"I'm so happy for you," Beatrice whispered. "And this will be just the beginning. You can't even imagine the life ahead of you."

Something in her mother's voice made her draw back. "Why would you say that? I'll be living only a few miles away."

A flush came over Beatrice's face. "Forgive me, you're right. Of course you'll be nearby." But the overbright tone sounded false, planting seeds of suspicion within Victoria.

Her mother glanced over at the sewing basket, clearing her throat. "But I am grateful you've managed to make a successful marriage. At least it means none of you girls will be making dresses anymore." She sent Victoria a pointed look. "Margaret told me about what you've been doing. Although the money was welcome, none of you should have lowered yourselves to engage in selling goods. This will be the end of that, won't it?"

It was a statement, not a question. Victoria was saved from an answer when the clock chimed. A bright smile spread over her mother's face, and she opened the door. "It's time, my dear. His G—" Her words cut off immediately, amending, "That is, Mr. Nottoway is downstairs waiting for you."

Victoria followed her mother, holding the small sprig of dried heather that Juliette had given her as a bouquet. Her heartbeat quickened as she descended the stairs toward the parlor.

She could hardly believe she was about to marry. It didn't seem possible, not within so short of a time. But when she followed her mother into the parlor, she saw Jonathan standing in formal attire worthy of a prince.

His tailcoat was dark blue, trimmed with gold embroidery, while his cravat was a stark snowy white. A blue matching waist-coat was revealed beneath the tailcoat, and his buff breeches were snug against his thighs.

The cut of his clothes and the fabric itself held the promise of wealth. She had nothing at all to bring to this marriage. Her mother had offered a modest dowry, which Jonathan had refused. He wanted only one thing from her—an heir.

A shiver broke through her at the thought of him touching her this night. He'd combed back his dark blond hair and his cheeks were clean-shaven. As he took in her appearance, the expression on his face revealed his satisfaction with her appearance. For a moment, she imagined them alone, and she remembered the Christmas gifts he'd given to her.

That gentleman had been kind and teasing, a man she liked. He'd been patient . . . and he'd made her smile.

But then, there was the ruthless man who had demanded marriage. He'd put her in an impossible position, one where she had no option to refuse. He'd said he didn't care what happened to the refugees, and she could almost believe that.

Before she entered the parlor, Mrs. Larson interrupted her mother. "Forgive me, Lady Lanfordshire, but the crofters have asked if they might witness the wedding. They've also brought gifts." Her face blushed, but she said, "It would mean a great deal to them if they could show their appreciation to Mr. Nottoway."

Beatrice turned to Victoria. "It's your decision, my dear. If you wish for me to keep them out, I will."

"No." She shook her head, despite the nervousness of being surrounded by people. "If they will just . . . stay back toward the hall, so it's not so crowded."

Mrs. Larson beamed. "I'll keep them back. I fear Mr. MacKinloch's sister isn't well at the moment, and he's gone tae take care of her. But I can manage these folk, same as he would. Most are kin to me and mine." She went to the doorway and opened it.

Outside, Victoria spied dozens of men in full Highland attire. They wore short jackets and belted plaids in a pattern of brown, red, and green with sporrans hanging from their waists. One by one, they bowed to her, entering the house, with the ladies following behind. They, too, had worn the plaid colors, some of the younger married women wearing a *kertch* over their hair, while the children fidgeted with excitement. Some carried instruments—fiddles, pipes, and drums, while she saw others carrying barrels of what could only be ale or mead from her father's cellar.

The vast number of people sent her apprehensions even higher. They filled the hallway and even the dining room. Victoria ap-

proached her husband-to-be, who raised an eyebrow at their presence, but he didn't refuse them.

Jonathan took her hands, and the clergyman greeted them,
beginning the short ceremony. Victoria never heard a word the
minister said, for she was caught up in her own anxieties. The
very presence of these people made it impossible to change her
mind. She no longer had a choice in this marriage, and it hurt to
know that her bridegroom's reasons for wedding her had nothing
to do with affection.

It was time for the vows, and Jonathan held her hands, speaking them clearly. When it came time for hers, Victoria faltered a
moment. She studied his green eyes, wondering if they would
ever have a marriage based upon love. Or whether she could
break past her shyness to be a real wife to him.

"It will be all right," he murmured, beneath his breath. She
could only hope so, as she dutifully repeated her own vows.

When the brief ceremony was finished, Jonathan brushed a
light kiss upon her cheek. A loud cheer came from the dining
room, and one of the Scots bellowed, "That's no' a proper kiss,
Sassenach! Try again, or we'll show you how 'tis done!"

Her face went crimson, but Jonathan sent her a wicked look as
he bent and took her mouth in a more thorough kiss. Victoria
was so startled, she could hardly kiss him back. The crofters
applauded, some playing the round drums in celebration. One by
one, they lined up to congratulate them, and Victoria was startled to see one man hold out a simple clay dish. A fiddler began
playing a lively tune, and as each of the Highlanders came forth
to extend their good wishes, they dropped a penny into the dish.
Their gesture touched her deeply.

These people, who had nothing at all, couldn't afford to give
money away. And yet, they had, out of thanks. Her eyes blurred
with tears as the dish filled with pennies. Moving to Jonathan's
side, she murmured, "We can't accept these."

But he took her gloved hand and whispered against her ear,

"Give them their pride, sweet. If we take that from them, then they've nothing left."

She squeezed his hand in understanding.

Before long, the men and women pushed the dining room table against one wall, loading it up with food gifts they had brought to share. Mrs. Larson had prepared a luncheon of roasted hen and salmon, but Victoria saw the others adding cheese, butter, oatcakes, and eggs, as well as small portions of beef, duck, muir-fowl, and milk.

"Where did they get all of this?" she whispered to her new husband.

"My footman Franklin arranged to bring a great deal of food when he returned from London. It was distributed among the crofters, but it seems they've decided to share it with us."

The music filled up the house, and men and women began to dance. Jonathan took Victoria's hand and led her to the side as the women whirled in the arms of their men. "I'm afraid I can't dance with you yet," he confessed. "Not with my leg."

Mrs. Larson moved toward her, scolding her gently. "Now why is it your laces are done up so tightly, Miss Andrews?" She moved behind Victoria and loosened them, before she also loosened the ribbons on her bonnet and shoes. "Now, then. It's unlucky to have your wedding dinner in the house—it's supposed to be in your father's barn, but given your circumstances, I've asked the men and women to have it inside."

"It's unlucky not to have it in the barn?" Jonathan questioned. "You'd rather the food smelled like horses?"

Mrs. Larson's hands clenched into fists upon her barrel-shaped waist. "Now, don't ye be tossing your nose at things ye canna understand, lad. Our Miss Andrews has waited long enough to be a bride. I'll not have her wedding be tainted with bad fortune." To emphasize her point, she removed Victoria's bonnet.

"Why are you taking my bonnet?" she asked.

Without answering, Mrs. Larson snatched the top hat that Jonathan was carrying in one hand. "I'll be needing that, too."

"For what?" Jonathan tried to retrieve it, but the housekeeper was adamant.

"Why, the two who catch them will be the next to marry. Come now, you can throw them from atop the stairs." She gestured for them to follow, and Jonathan exchanged a look with Victoria.

"I suppose we must," she acceded. It was beginning to wear upon her, having everyone's attention upon them. She eyed the stairs, feeling uncomfortable at the thought of all the people staring.

But then, Jonathan took her hand. Almost as if to prevent her from fleeing, she mused. As he guided her up the stairs, he never took his eyes from her. Beneath his strong gaze, she suppressed a shiver, for she could read his thoughts. He wanted her, and now that they were married, he had the right to touch her as he desired. The thought of his body upon hers was both startling . . . and irresistible.

Renewed fear welled up inside her when she saw the crowds gathered below. Jonathan turned her away from them and Mrs. Larson passed them the bonnet and hat. Before Victoria could accept hers, the housekeeper lowered her voice. "I knew that ye were meant to marry him from the first moment ye stood at his left."

Victoria frowned, not understanding. But the housekeeper's face held a mysterious smile. "He was brought here, tae be your husband, lass."

Then she hurried down the stairs, leaving Victoria to stand beside Jonathan. He said nothing about the housekeeper's superstitions but offered, "You can go first. The ladies are waiting."

She threw her bonnet over the railing and was surprised to see her sister catch it. Juliette's face bloomed with color, but she accepted the teasing with good nature.

Jonathan threw his hat over the railing, and it started to fall into the hands of one of the Highlanders. Before the man could grasp it, another man jumped for it, seizing the hat. A roar of approval sounded from the men when they saw it was Dr. Paul Fraser. The man lifted the hat in triumph and started to approach Juliette.

As soon as she saw him, the young woman passed the bonnet to Amelia and fled.

Jonathan leaned in to Victoria, murmuring, "I gather she doesn't like the doctor?"

"No, they've been friends for years. But ever since last year, she's avoided him." She'd wondered if somehow the doctor had offended her sister, but Juliette would say nothing.

Yet, she didn't miss the way Paul Fraser slipped away from the crowd to follow.

Jonathan led her down the stairs where the dancing had continued. The ale flowed freely, and men and women were feasting, dancing, and enjoying the celebration. But although this was her wedding day, it overwhelmed her. There were so many people, and everything had happened so fast. The urge to leave was irresistible, along with the desire to disappear into one of the rooms and gather up her thoughts.

"A toast!" cried out one of the MacKinlochs. "To the bride!"

The men raised their glasses, cheering once again, and Victoria caught a name she didn't recognize in the midst of the celebration. Jonathan handed her a cup of ale, but though she raised it, she didn't drink. "Did they just call you Worthingstone?"

She'd paid so little attention to the ceremony, she hadn't recognized the name.

"It's . . . one of my titles," Jonathan said.

It meant he was an English peer, as she'd suspected. Worthingstone. She'd not heard the name before, but her mother likely had. She frowned, not understanding. "Then what is your—"

He cut off her question, capturing her mouth in another kiss.

All around her, Victoria heard the encouraging merriment, but she recognized his gesture for what it was: a means of not telling her his rank.

She didn't know whether he was a viscount or an earl, but her heart beat faster at the thought. Her mother's words now took on a new meaning: *You can't even imagine the life ahead of you.* What had she meant by that?

The kiss ended, and Victoria confronted him. "Take me away from them. I want to talk with you alone."

He didn't argue but caught her hand, leading her away from the others. Some of the guests teased them as he guided her through the house and down toward the kitchen. It was hot inside the small room from the heat of the stove.

It only took one pointed look from him, and the crofters who were busy cooking the food departed in haste, giving them privacy.

"Do you want to remain in here, or shall I open the door for some fresh air?"

She ignored the question and confronted him. "Who are you? I want the full truth."

"Does it matter?" His voice grew guarded, and she didn't know what to think of that. "It's not as if I'm the Prince of Wales."

"You have a title."

"So do you," he said. "You're now my wife." He pressed her slowly against the door, his arms on either side of her.

"What is your title?" she demanded. "Am I now Lady Worthingstone instead of Mrs. Nottoway?"

When he didn't answer, she rested her palms between them, to hold him at a slight distance. "You owe me the truth."

"Jonathan Nottoway is my name," he said quietly. "I didn't lie to you about that. You were the one who made up the name Smith."

"And what about Worthingstone?"

His hands moved to her waist, drawing her close. In the

suffocating heat, she felt a bead of perspiration moving down her skin. He held her in such a tight embrace, she could feel the length of his arousal pressing close.

"I am Jonathan Nottoway," he murmured against her throat. Thousands of shivers broke over her as his mouth drifted lower, his hands moving up her bodice to cup her breasts. "And after my father died over a year ago, I became His Grace, the Duke of Worthingstone."

Chapter Thirteen

H E SENSED the change in her from the moment he let the truth fall. Victoria's body tensed, and her hands came up to push him away.

"Nothing's changed," he said. "It's just a name."

"Everything's changed." Shock filled up her expression, as if he'd physically struck her. "You're a duke."

"Yes." He didn't bother denying it.

She leaned back against the kitchen door, her gaze turned from him. "Why would a man in your position ever marry a woman like me? A woman who can't even walk outside!"

"Because she saw the *man*, not the duke," he countered. His hands moved into her hair, pulling the pins free as he seized her mouth in another kiss. By God, he wasn't a man of words. He couldn't tell her what the past fortnight had been like, but he could show her. He kissed her hard, tasting her anger mingled with sorrow.

He wouldn't apologize for what he'd done. Victoria Andrews was a woman who deserved a better life than this. He could help her family through their financial crisis until their father returned home.

But more than that, he didn't want to leave her behind. It wasn't safe here, and he wanted to protect her.

She broke free of the kiss, her eyes glimmering with unshed tears. "I can't be a duchess, and you know it. I don't have it in me."

"I won't ask that of you," he swore. "I have dozens of estates, all over England and Europe. You can live wherever you choose." He drew her in a closer embrace, her head resting beneath his chin. "I have all the money you would ever need."

"It's not about the money," she whispered. "It's about bringing shame upon you."

He didn't know how to respond. He didn't give a damn what people said, and if they dared to gossip about her, he wouldn't hesitate to use his power against them.

"I know what's expected of me," she continued. "I'm supposed to command dozens of servants and host lavish parties on your behalf." Her voice held a weariness, as if she never wanted such a life.

"You don't have to do any of that," he said. "As a duchess, you can do as you please."

"No. You have duties, and it would be my place to support you in them." Raising her gray eyes to his, she added, "Any other woman would be thrilled beyond words. I know Margaret would be." She took a deep breath, before reaching out for his hand. "With your wealth and position, you can help my family and the crofters . . . but I can't help but wish you were an ordinary man."

A hollow feeling centered inside him, for he could do nothing about his birthright. But knowing that she preferred *him* instead of the duke made him wish he could throw it all away.

"Behind closed doors, I am an ordinary man." He drew his hands around her waist, rubbing circles against her spine. "Only now, I can give you jewels and silks instead of spoons and gloves."

He was trying to help, but from the look on her face, he was getting nowhere. "And there are other advantages to being a duchess," he said. "You'll never have to touch a needle again."

Her eyes turned sad. "I enjoy sewing, Your Grace. And I *want* to continue the work I've done."

Once again, he'd chosen the wrong thing to say. Gently, he reminded her, "Duchesses don't make their own clothing, Victoria. There's no need for it."

"Of course they don't." She folded her hands and stared at him. "How am I to spend my time, then?"

He was baffled by her sudden change in mood. "If you wish to embroider, I won't stop you, but you can pay others to make your gowns. And think of your sisters," he reminded her. "You can give each of them a Season, and I'll offer my full support."

She rested her cheek against his chest, her palms upon his ribs. "That would please Margaret and Amelia."

He embraced her, hoping that she was softening toward the idea. In time, she would grow accustomed to her new life, he felt certain.

"What about the crofters?" she asked, drawing back.

He didn't understand her concern. "What about them? I've told you, I'll allow them to build homes upon my land. They can pay rent, or we'll work out an agreement of labor in return for their living arrangements." It was more than reasonable, even generous.

"They've been sewing unmentionables for me," she reminded him. "They will receive a portion of income from it."

"And once those garments are sold, you won't have to sew any more. Their services won't be needed."

"Then how are they to support themselves? They can't farm here; the land is too poor."

"The same way they did before," he insisted. In her eyes he read the doubts. For some unknown reason, she'd taken responsibility for these people. She might not believe they could survive without the sewing income, but he would find work for them. The idea of his wife, a duchess, continuing a business that sold seductive unmentionables to ladies of the ton was impossible. He couldn't allow it.

But if he told her so, it would cast yet another shadow upon their wedding day. He held out his palms to her. "Will you trust me in this, Victoria? I won't let anyone suffer because of our marriage. Not your family. Not them."

She didn't move, but let her hands remain at her sides. There was such pain in her eyes, as if she deeply regretted marrying him. "Why did you lie to me about who you were?"

"I believed it was necessary at the time. You would never have married me if you knew I was a duke."

She held herself around the waist as if trying to keep herself away from him. "My mother knew, didn't she?"

He gave a single nod. "I was truthful with her."

"You knew she would be delighted with the marriage."

He let his hands fall back to his sides, refusing to beg for Victoria's affection. "Like any mother, she was glad to see her daughter wed to a duke."

"And neither of you cared about what I thought."

He wasn't going to allow her to blame this on him. "You had the chance to say no. I offered for you because I thought we could make a good marriage. That you would want children and a different life than this one."

"You should have told me the truth."

"If I had, I wouldn't be married to you right now." He walked away from her, standing before the kitchen hearth. Above them drifted the sounds of merrymaking and laughter. A true celebration that belied the growing distance between them.

She gave no answer, and he wasn't about to ask for forgiveness. "We should return to the others." He didn't doubt the guests would believe he and Victoria were behaving like lovers at the moment, though nothing could have been further from the truth. Jonathan started up the stairs, waiting for her to follow. When she didn't, he debated returning alone. But instead, something drew him back to her side. She was facing the door, and when he reached her, he saw the silent tears on her face.

The sight of her devastation caught him like a fist to the stomach. He'd never expected to make her cry.

"Would you rather end this now?" he demanded. "Should I send them away and make arrangements for an annulment?"

She shook her head. For a moment, she leaned her head against the door. "I'm afraid," she admitted.

"Don't be." Jonathan took slow steps toward her, standing behind her. Though he wanted to touch her, to pull her back into his arms, he sensed if he made a single move, it would drive her further away. "I'll help you. Or I'll take you somewhere no one will bother you. You won't have to face society, if that's what you're afraid of."

"No." She let out a soft sigh and turned to face him. Her gray eyes were wet with tears, but she seemed to gather her emotions back under control. "I'm not afraid of them. I'm afraid you'll grow to hate me." She reached out and took his hands in hers. "I can hardly walk out that door, much less go to London. I'm afraid that one day, you'll look back on this as the greatest mistake you ever made."

He tightened his hold upon her fingers. "There were dozens of women I could have married," he said quietly. "Daughters of marquesses, even other dukes. Women who were born to lead a life of privilege, who could be the perfect duchess." He raised her hands to his mouth. "But I can't fathom spending an hour in their company. That, and they would never bother to play chess with me."

That earned him a slight smile. "I don't want to play chess with you, either."

With his fingers, he brushed aside her tears, leaning his forehead against hers. "I'll likely disappoint you as a husband, Victoria. I can't help that. But I can honestly say that I wanted to marry you." His hands moved down her neck to her shoulders. She didn't pull away from him and it renewed his hope. "I want to take you into my bed and give you children." His hands trailed down her back, pulling her hips to his. Her breath caught when he held her close, inhaling the scent of her hair.

"Will you try to be my wife for a while?" he asked.

Her hands came up to touch his hair, moving over his cheeks. The softness of her touch sent a thrum of need rising inside. He wanted to be with her, skin upon skin.

"I will try being your wife," she agreed at last, "but not your duchess."

It was the best he could hope for, under the circumstances.

⚜

Victoria lifted her mouth to Jonathan's and though her mind was roiling with confusion and hurt, she kissed him back. He was relentless, capturing her mouth as if he intended to seduce her this very moment. She clung to him for balance, dimly aware of his hands moving over her, stroking the area covering her breasts.

"I know your corset won't let you feel my hands," he breathed against her cheek. "But imagine me touching you again, the way I did the other night."

She closed her eyes, not revealing the truth—that she could feel everything. The corset she'd worn did indeed keep her waist and hips small, but though it supported her breasts, the thin layer of satin made it possible to feel the warmth of his hands. She gave a cry when he seemed to guess where her nipples were, lightly stroking them. "I want my mouth on your skin," he told her. "And I want to be inside you."

His words overwhelmed her, shocking her with the intimacy. What would it feel like to be joined with this man, to feel the weight of his body upon hers?

She couldn't voice a response, and he didn't allow her to speak. Her lips were numb from being kissed by him, but other needs were aroused within her. She wanted these layers of clothing to be gone, to understand this madness in the secrecy of his bed.

A loud pounding noise came from the kitchen door behind them, a knocking that made Jonathan curse. "Whoever it is can go away."

Victoria tried to pin up a stray lock of hair, feeling self-conscious as her husband watched her. "You may as well answer it," she said. "They don't sound as if they plan to leave. And the sooner they do . . ."

Her answer was enough to make him jerk the door open. "What is it?" he demanded. Then a moment later, he took a step back, his face transformed with anger. He crossed his arms and glared at the young man standing there.

The boy couldn't have been more than twelve or thirteen, Victoria guessed. His face appeared familiar, though she couldn't place where she'd seen him before. From the white look upon his face, he looked as if he wanted to flee on the spot. She started to come forward, but Jonathan held her back with a hand. "Did you come to finish me off, then? Since the first bullet didn't complete your task?"

And she understood then, although the boy had no weapon in his hands. "He's the one who shot you?"

At Jonathan's nod, she now recognized the boy's fear. After what he'd done, his life could be the penalty.

"I'm sorry for what I did," the boy muttered, looking as if he wanted nothing more than to run away. "Dr. Fraser said . . . I could be finding ye both here. I came with a warning."

"Warn us about what?" There was no trace of mercy in the duke's voice. He pressed Victoria back a little further.

"Lord Strathland," he admitted. "I thought ye were him, because I'd ne'er seen him afore. Not too many Sassenach here." He gave a light shrug and took a step backward into the snow. "I was spying on his factor, Melford. He said he was sending someone to set fire to this house."

"Why?"

The boy stared back at him, and in the child's eyes, Victoria saw hopelessness. "He doesna want any of us here. If the Andrews family is gone, he can claim all o' this land for his sheep."

He pulled his ragged coat tighter, adjusting his cap. "I was wrong to pull the trigger, your lordship. And after all that, ye helped me mam when she was dying. Gave her something to take away her pain." His brown eyes held a lifetime of regret. "I just thought . . . I could warn ye. That's all." He stole a glance behind him. "Best hurry afore they get here."

Victoria moved to Jonathan's side. "Thank you for warning us," she said to the boy. On the kitchen table, she spied a bit of left-over bread and tossed it to him. He caught it and nodded his thanks before he left them.

"Do you think he's telling the truth?"

Her husband's expression had gone cold and hard. "I wouldn't doubt it. I'll talk with Dr. Fraser and gather up a group of men to search. If there are others bent on attacking us, we'll see them before they arrive."

"Send some of the crofters," she said. "You don't need to go with them." Although his leg had mostly healed, he couldn't run. The last thing she wanted was for him to be in danger.

But Jonathan wasn't listening at all as he moved toward the stairs. "I don't intend to be shot a second time, Victoria. I'm not as helpless as you might believe."

She hadn't meant to imply that. But the thought of him venturing out into the snow, to face a group of armed men, didn't sit well with her.

"And what am I supposed to do here?" she demanded. "Gather the women together and wait for our house to be set on fire?"

He stopped walking and turned to face her. In his green eyes, she saw an unyielding resolve. "My footman Franklin has returned with a small staff. He's awaiting us at Eiloch Hill, and it would be easy enough to send servants to fetch you."

She started to protest. "I can't leave. Not so soon."

But he ignored her, touching her cheek. "And later, my men will take you, as well as your mother and sisters, to travel back to London. It's too dangerous here."

"And what about you?" Not only was it impossible for her to leave, but she didn't want to imagine him at the whims of these men.

"I'll stay with the others and put a stop to this fire, if that's what they're planning."

She didn't speak a word, for the idea of fleeing was beyond impossible. She'd only made it a few feet beyond the door and he didn't know . . . God help her, he didn't know what she'd endured the last time she'd traveled. But she said nothing about it, only met his gaze.

"I'll follow your trail and catch up to you as soon as I can," he promised. He reached out to her, kissing her swiftly. "With any luck, the boy is wrong and there's no threat at all."

"You don't believe that." Deep within, she sensed the danger rising around them.

He shook his head. "These men and women were already driven off their land once before. The earl never wanted me to gain that land, but he was in my debt and had no choice."

Victoria gripped his hand in hers. "Be safe," she pleaded. "Promise me."

"I do." His mouth curved in a faint smile. "Besides, I have a wedding night to claim."

꙰

It was dusk when they rode out. Jonathan had loaded dueling pistols inside his topcoat, while several of the Highlanders carried torches. His leg ached mercilessly as he followed Cain Sinclair and Paul Fraser, but he made no complaint. All were grimly aware that the boy's warning carried weight.

For the next hour, they split off into four groups, each

searching the regions surrounding the Andrews land. Jonathan traveled north, along with Dr. Fraser who knew the land well.

"Do you think the boy was telling the truth?" he asked Fraser.

The doctor drew his horse to a stop, staring at the land surrounding them. "Aye, I don't doubt it. Even after the crofters were driven off the earl's land, he wanted them to move away to the coast. He thought they'd become fishermen."

"But you don't believe that's an option."

Fraser turned to look at him, and the man's dark eyes held such veiled anger, Jonathan was startled to see it.

"I don't, no," he said abruptly. "Strathland treats these men like sheep to be herded away, as he wills it. It doesna matter that these families have been here for generations," he said. "All that matters is profit." He drew his horse closer to Jonathan's, nodding for them to change directions. "They've said you offered them a place on your land. In exchange for Miss Andrews as your wife."

He stiffened. "It wasn't quite that mercenary. I asked her to wed me, and she agreed. I'll take care of her and her family until Baron Lanfordshire returns."

A rueful smile crossed the doctor's face. "And leave the crofters to do as they will?"

It reminded him of the conversation he'd had with Victoria. It angered him that they expected him to act as caretaker for these men and women. "I've given them a place to build their homes. It's enough."

Fraser stared out at the clouded horizon while the wind swept across the fallen snow. "Is it?" Without waiting for an answer, he spurred his horse onward, turning back toward the house.

Jonathan rode behind the man, searching for any sign of people gathering. As they drew nearer to the house, the scent of the air shifted.

Smoke.

"Son of a bitch," Fraser grumbled, urging his horse faster. "They waited. The goddamned bastards waited until we went searching."

The sound of chaos and screaming filled the air as they neared the Andrews house. Jonathan rode past the men and women, ignoring the flames that had taken hold of the house. Dimly he was aware of Sinclair and Fraser gathering the men and women away from the conflagration, but he saw no sign of Victoria.

Damn them all, had they left her inside? He dismounted and hurried toward the house, wincing against the pain of his leg.

"We can't find her." Lady Lanfordshire ran to Jonathan's side, her eyes filled with tears. "We've been searching everywhere, but there's no sign of Victoria. She won't leave the house." Sobbing, the woman said, "Please, you must help her."

Jonathan was already taking off his coat. He untied his cravat and wound it around his nose and mouth, ducking into the smoke-filled house. Though the house shouldn't be burning so hot with all the snow, the reason became clear soon enough. Someone had broken a window and tossed a torch into the parlor. The drapes and furniture were on fire, the heavy smoke filling up the room.

"Victoria!" he called out. "Where are you?"

There was no answer. He listened hard for any answer at all, but she didn't call out to him. One by one, he searched the rooms, shouting her name. But still, there was nothing.

He didn't know if she'd tried to leave the house, but time was running out. The crofters were trying to extinguish the flames, but to no avail. He had to find her before there was no escape.

The smoke thickened, making it more difficult to breathe. His heartbeat raced, for the last thing he wanted was to become a widower this night. If he had to bodily drag her out, he would save his wife from burning.

Quickly, he climbed the stairs, repeating his shouts, searching for her. Her room was empty, but he spied a bundle of fabric.

Without really knowing why, he forced the window open and tossed the fabric outside. It might be her raw materials or possibly some sewing, but he doubted if she would want to lose it.

It was then that he heard a slight noise coming from the wardrobe. Throwing the door open, he found her wedged inside, her knees drawn up. Her face blanched when she saw him, and she was trembling violently.

"I-I tried," she whispered. "But my legs wouldn't work. The smoke—"

He didn't waste time arguing with her but lifted her into his arms. "Close your eyes," he demanded. "Hold tightly to me, and don't open your eyes. No matter what happens."

She did, and her grip around his neck was so hard, she clung as if he were the only person who could save her. With his arm under her knees, he was unsteady on his feet. His leg had healed slightly, but carrying his wife was another matter entirely. Though he tried to take her down the stairs, excruciating pain radiated through his thigh.

Jonathan gripped the banister hard and slowly lowered her to her feet. "My injured leg isn't quite stable. I thought I could carry you out, but I'm afraid it won't allow me to." Her eyes remained closed, and he put his arm around her waist. "I will help you to get out of this house," he promised. "But I'll need you to walk with me."

She held him tightly, keeping her face against his chest.

"You can do this," he promised. "I won't let go."

She nodded, and he kept both arms around her. Around them, the smoke had grown thicker, the flames stretching toward them. "We're almost there. Keep walking."

She was coughing hard, and his eyes burned through the haze of smoke as he led her out the door. The icy weather contrasted sharply with the heat of the fire, and he saw her flinch when she stepped into a snowdrift.

"Remember when you threw that snowball at me?" he asked,

guiding her away from the house and into the snowdrifts. "I never imagined you would do such a thing."

"You made me angry," she managed.

"I deserved it." The snow was making it more difficult to walk, and Victoria's pace had slowed. Ahead, he spied a coach, with her sisters climbing inside. Beatrice wept at the sight of them, and only then did she join her other daughters in the coach.

Cain Sinclair and Paul Fraser were ushering the crofters toward Jonathan's land. Both were mounted on horseback and heavily armed. Though no one knew who had started the fires, it might have been one of the men disguised among the crofters.

Jonathan started to guide Victoria toward the waiting coach but realized there was not enough room for both of them. "Do you want to go with your family or stay with me?"

"I w-want to be inside," she whispered. "Anywhere but here."

"I could send you with the others in the coach," he suggested. "I'd find you later." It was evident that she would have difficulty traveling this night. Though she hadn't gone into hysterics, he could see the panic tensing her features.

"Stay with me," she pleaded. Her grip tightened around his waist, as if she couldn't bring herself to let go.

Behind him, the fire raged. Although the crofters had tried to put it out, the interior continued to burn. Black smoke billowed into the air, and he had no doubt that within another few hours only the stone exterior would remain.

"Please," Victoria begged. "Just take me somewhere close by." Her body was trembling, and he gripped her tight.

"I'll find something." He called out to Cain Sinclair, waving until the man hurried forward.

"Is there another shelter nearby?" Jonathan asked. "Someplace closer than Eiloch Hill, where I could bring Victoria until morning?"

Sinclair's gaze met his, and then passed over Victoria. "Aye. If she canna make it as far as your house." His somber look revealed that he was well aware of Victoria's difficulties. "You can take shelter at my house," Sinclair offered, pointing up into the wooded hillside. "It's half a mile from here, up the hillside." He reached into his pocket and withdrew an iron key. An ironic smile crossed his face. "It's not what you'd be wanting for a wedding night, but you can build a fire and stay warm. I'll send the coach back for you, come the morning."

Jonathan took the key and nodded his thanks. To Victoria, he whispered in her ear, "Can you make it to Sinclair's house?"

She didn't answer, but he saw no choice for them. "Is there another horse?"

Sinclair shrugged. "There's a mule, but she's a stubborn lass and won't do much of anything."

"I need to get Victoria out of this snow, and I'd rather not have her walk any farther than she has to." Truthfully, his own leg was plaguing him. Half a mile seemed like an endless distance, but he doubted if the mule could carry both of them.

The man stared for a moment, as if assessing whether or not it would work. Then he shouted in Gaelic to his younger brother. Within moments, the boy was coaxing a brown mule toward them. Jonathan lifted Victoria upon the animal and took the reins. He uttered his thanks to Sinclair and the man passed him a torch to light the way.

"Follow the path up the hill and through the woods. Ye shouldna have any trouble findin' it."

Jonathan nodded to Sinclair as he returned to the others. "Come on, then." He lightly patted the mule's flanks. Victoria was stiff, her body so rigid, he knew how terrified she was.

"I said, let's be off," he told the mule, urging her forward again. The wind was picking up speed, blowing through his coat, and he realized that his wife barely had anything to cover her gown. Jonathan took off his coat, trying to put it over her.

"I'll be all right," she protested, but her shoulders were still trembling. He ignored her, knowing she needed the warmth.

Once again, he took the reins and tried to drag the mule forward. When she didn't cooperate, he asked Victoria, "What is the animal's name?"

"I don't actually know. She's not used to anyone riding her. I think Mr. MacKinloch used her to help plow the garden." She shivered and gripped the edges of the coat.

"Move along then, damn you." He tugged at the animal's bridle and was encouraged when the mule took a step forward. "It appears I've discovered her name."

There was a trace of a smile on his wife's face, and he used the animal for support, as they trudged toward the hillside.

"I don't think that's truly her name."

"She responded to it." He sent Victoria a wry look. "Are you all right?"

Her smile faded away as she seemed to remember her surroundings. "Not really. I'll be glad when we're inside. You must be freezing."

"We'll build a fire once we've reached Sinclair's house."

She gave a nod, but as he led the mule up the hillside, Victoria glanced back at the house. The fire had died down, and although the stone structure remained, the roof and interior were ruined.

"I don't understand why someone would do this. We've done nothing wrong at all." Tears rose up in her eyes, and she let them fall, her arms wrapped around the mule's neck. She shut her eyes, and at a closer glimpse, he saw that her body was trembling again.

"Hold on," he ordered. "We'll have shelter soon enough, and when we do, we'll talk about it." But her desolation went deeper than sorrow about the house. From the look on her face, it was as if a part of her had gone up in flames.

"H-hurry," she begged, keeping her eyes tightly shut. Her face was so pale against the firelight of the torch, he wondered if she was struggling not to faint. Even her breathing had quickened, as if she were fighting against panic.

He didn't speak throughout the rest of the journey, but led the mule through the woods, hoping the house would be easy enough to find.

Within another few minutes, he spied it. The mule kept stopping, but when she caught sight of the wooden house, the animal's pace quickened as if she was also eager to be out of the cold.

Jonathan helped Victoria to dismount and unlocked the door, handing her the torch. There was an immediate relief in her demeanor, and she eagerly went inside while he saw to the mule. He guided the animal into the lean-to and settled it down for the night with water and feed.

When he returned to his wife, she stood within the interior of the modest dwelling. It was dark and cool, except for the torch that she'd set upon the hearth.

"We'll need a fire," he said. She helped him gather tinder while he stacked the peat. His hands were numb from the cold, but he managed to light the fire with the torch, feeding more tinder and bricks of peat until there was a small blaze.

Victoria had gone quiet, staring into the light. She took off his coat and settled it over his shoulders, sitting beside him. Her mood grew pensive and quiet. He couldn't guess what thoughts were going through her mind at the moment, but he didn't press for answers. Instead, he warmed his freezing hands and feet before the fire, simply taking comfort from her presence.

"It's gone now, isn't it?" she whispered. "The house, I mean."

He nodded. "In the spring, we'll try to rebuild."

She drew up her knees, and stared into the flames, her breath forming mist. "I always . . . thought I would live in that house until the day I died. I couldn't imagine leaving it." She stretched out her hands to warm them but didn't look at him. "I feel lost right now." Glancing around her, she studied the interior of Sinclair's home. "This is the first time I've been in anyone else's house in over five years."

It was small, with only one bed and a trundle beneath it. One iron pot rested near the hearth, and although the dwelling was clean, it held an austerity, as if no one had bothered to make it into a true home.

"I knew Mr. Sinclair was poor, but I didn't realize it was this bad," she whispered. "He has hardly anything at all. We should have paid him more. He has a younger brother to take care of."

In answer, Jonathan reached into his waistcoat pocket and withdrew a handful of coins. Silently, he placed them upon a wooden stool near the hearth.

"Why didn't you leave with your mother and sisters when the house caught fire?" he asked Victoria.

Her gray eyes met his. "I wanted to, but I couldn't bring myself to go. Perhaps a part of me wanted to die with it."

The thought disturbed him deeply. He reached out and pulled a pin from her hair, freeing a long lock of burnished gold hair. Then another. One by one, he loosened all the pins until her hair fell below her shoulders. "You'd rather die than be my duchess?"

"That isn't what I said." She knelt beside the fire, staring into the flames. "But without you with me, I couldn't bring myself to go. The smoke was so terrible and the fire so hot . . ." She lowered her gaze, shivering at the memory. "It was impossible."

"This isn't the wedding night I had planned for us," he said quietly. "But I'm glad we're both alive."

She nodded, lifting her eyes to his. Her face turned crimson, but she seemed to gather her courage. "Will you help me undress? There's something I-I want to show you."

Chapter Fourteen

HIS HANDS moved to the buttons on the back of her gown. One by one, he opened them, while his mouth descended upon the back of her neck. Victoria was unprepared for the violent shivers that poured through her or the way her body responded to him.

"Satin," he breathed, running his hands along the laces of her corset. She supposed she could have worn nothing at all beneath the gown, but . . . she'd wanted to wear one of her own creations. To see if it pleased him.

But instead of turning her around, he let the gown fall against her waist. From behind her, she heard the soft sounds of his own clothing being removed. When she turned to sneak a glimpse, she saw him remove his wedding tailcoat, laying it upon a chair. Then he lifted his shirt over his head.

The sight of his bare chest fascinated her. His golden skin was lean, with a light down of hair between his pectoral muscles. There was not a trace of softness upon him, and when he saw her watching him, his hands reached for the top button of his breeches.

"Wait," she pleaded, not at all ready for what was to come next. She didn't know what to expect from him, but she was unprepared for the sight of his body. "You—you might get cold."

It was a ridiculous thing to say, but she'd blurted it out without thinking. Jonathan's hand caught hers, and he guided it to touch his chest. Beneath her fingertips, she felt the rapid beating of his heart. The firm muscles reminded her of smooth marble, and without meaning to, she traced the outline of his body, moving lower to his ribs.

"Do I feel cold to you?" he demanded.

She couldn't answer, for his skin was quite warm. Only when she felt the heat of his mouth against her throat did she admit, "No. You're not cold at all. But—"

"Don't be afraid of me." He reached behind her, lifting away her gown, leaving her to stand in only the satin corset. "Turn around."

Her breathing was unsteady, but she managed to obey him. In the dim light of the room, she turned slowly, revealing her chemise and corset. His sharp intake of breath was audible. His green eyes centered upon her, drinking in the sight of her bared skin and the creamy wisps of embroidered satin.

"You took my advice, I see." There was a hunger in his voice as he reached out to the sheer lace that covered her breasts. The touch of his knuckles upon her erect nipples sent a wave of aching between her legs. "I like this very much."

His hands moved to her back, finding the ties of her corset. "Do you remember what it was like the first night I touched you?"

She couldn't breathe when he untied the stays, loosening the panels. Yes, she did remember. Such wickedness was a taste of sin itself. But as he caught her mouth with his, she found herself helpless to protest. His mouth was unraveling her senses, pulling her into dark temptation.

"Look at me," he demanded, framing her face with his hands. She felt so exposed in the firelight, and yet he held her spellbound. "I will never hurt you. Not this night, or beyond it."

He removed the corset, his green eyes burning into hers as he studied the chemise. With his hands, he cupped her breasts through the lace. But instead of baring her skin, he bent and took one nipple in his mouth.

The sensation of his tongue and the light abrasion of the lace sent a shock of heat through her. His mouth suckled gently, his tongue swirling over the erect tip she could not hide.

"You're perfect, Victoria," he breathed. She could do nothing except clutch his head as he bent to the other breast, laving it with his tongue. The contrast of the cold air and the heat of his mouth was deeply erotic, sending a thrill of wetness between her legs. Though her mind was frightened of the raw sensations, her body wanted more.

He lowered the chemise, and this time his hands moved to cup her bare breasts, stroking them until she could not stop the moan that broke from her. "I wanted to touch you like this, from the first time I kissed you. And this time, I don't intend to stop."

She dared to touch his chest, her body aching with need. "Are you certain you want to remain wedded to a woman like me?" The words needed to be said, though a thickness rose up in her throat. "You might as well be a prince, and I, a washerwoman."

"There's nothing I want more," he murmured. In the cool air, her skin prickled with gooseflesh. "If I hadn't come for you, would you have stayed in your room while the house burned?"

She took a breath and regarded him. "Probably." Though he likely believed that she was mad to risk burning alive rather than go outside, she wanted him to hear the truth. Taking one of his hands in hers, she turned back to face the fire, drawing his arms around her from behind. "I almost died five years ago when we first traveled here."

Just mentioning that time sent a cool chill over her body. She shivered, and Jonathan drew both arms around her. "You don't have to talk about it."

Victoria knew that, and yet, she needed him to understand why she'd retreated from the outside world. Perhaps then, he would realize why she was utterly unprepared to be his duchess.

She leaned against him, and the heat of his body seemed to shelter her. "We were traveling here, from England," she said. "I was seventeen, and I hated the thought of leaving London. My father wanted us to live here, in Scotland. He never liked the city, and he wanted to be away from his brother. They were always quarreling."

Especially after their uncle kept falling further into debt. Although her father had been careful with his own funds, his brother had squandered most of the inheritance.

"Since it was doubtful my sisters and I would ever have a Season, I suppose he wanted us to be away from society," Victoria finished.

Her skin grew icy, as she admitted, "We traveled in two coaches. On each night of the journey, we changed coaches, sometimes to be with my mother and father. We stayed in different inns along the way, and one afternoon, Juliette begged my father to stop. The land around us was beautiful, and she wanted to walk around for a while. He indulged her, and we ate our luncheon outdoors that day."

Though Jonathan's arms were around her as she spoke, he never interrupted or asked questions. "It was a beautiful day," she whispered. "I went walking on my own and somehow, I must have fallen asleep in the sunshine. When I awoke, the coaches were gone. My parents and sisters both thought I was with the other."

Her skin had turned to ice, but she forced herself to continue speaking of that day. "I was outside for the rest of the day and through the night. I tried to follow the tracks of the coach, hoping they would turn around and find me. But somehow, I went the wrong way. I-I got lost and there were endless green hills and forests around me."

She closed her eyes, drawing his arms as tightly around her as she could manage it. "I don't remember when they found me. It must have been several days." Even now, she couldn't forget the aching in her stomach and the stale taste of the water she'd drunk. She'd survived the ordeal, but only just.

"And you never went outside again," he finished.

"No. I couldn't." She turned slightly in his embrace, feeling even more awkward with her chemise around her hips, her upper body bared. "Every time I tried, I remembered how cold and frightened I was. How the days passed until I believed they weren't ever going to find me."

"But they did." He leaned his face against hers. "And I swear to you, I'll keep you safe. Nothing like that will ever happen to you again."

She wanted to believe it. The duke was a strong man, demanding and steadfast in his pride. Because of his confidence, she'd made it this far. But would she have the strength to enter his world and assume all the responsibilities and duties of a duchess? She didn't know, for the very thought overwhelmed her.

"You've forgotten something," he said. "I won our wager. You did go outside within the fortnight. And you traveled far more than a few steps."

Though the urge came over her to deny it, she managed to say, "I was afraid I never could."

He framed her face, forcing her to look at him. "The courage was always there, Victoria."

She couldn't quite bring herself to smile, though he was right. She *had* taken the first steps to free herself from this prison.

"What reward will you claim?" she asked. In answer, he guided the remainder of her clothing off until it pooled upon the floor.

"I'm claiming you, Victoria."

Tangled thoughts clouded her mind, but Jonathan guided her to lie upon his wool topcoat. His bare chest pressed against her, and she shifted beneath him. The hard length of his arousal pressed against her, as if to remind her that she was now his wife.

"You're still afraid of me, aren't you?" He was poised above her, still wearing his breeches.

"No," she whispered. "But I wish my life could be the way it was. I fear it will never be the same again."

"You're angry at me for not telling you the truth."

"Yes." By keeping it from her, he'd made her feel like a fool. Her cheeks burned to think of the conversation they'd had when she'd guessed he was nothing more than a baronet. Oh, she'd known he had wealth—but not this.

It was like a fairy tale, with the prince wedding the servant girl and expecting her to somehow transform into a princess. But her fears weren't going to disappear now that she was a duchess. It might take years before she was comfortable leaving his house, attending a ball where everyone would stare at her. God help her, she didn't want her weakness to humiliate him.

"I can't change my title," Jonathan said, his hands resting on either side of her. "But I'm still the same man who spent those weeks with you." His hand slid over her bare shoulder, moving over her breast and down to her ribs. As he began to unbutton his trousers, a shiver of anxiety crossed over her. "Try to forget that I'm a duke."

His hand slid through her hair, drawing it over one shoulder. He traced down the length of it, drawing a silky lock over her breasts.

"I'm going to spend the rest of this night pleasuring you. Until you beg to have me inside you." His promise, to evoke those feelings of delicious release, sent a wave of warmth flooding through her.

"You belong to me, Victoria. And have, ever since you dared to sew me up with pink thread."

⚜

The sight of her slim body took his breath away. Though he'd coerced her into marriage and they'd had a rough beginning to their life together, Jonathan wasn't about to let her retreat into herself. He wanted her to kiss him back, damn it all. He wanted her arms around him, their bodies skin to skin.

He kissed her, testing her response. If she truly didn't want him, she would push him back. Her lips held firm for a moment, before she began to yield. She was returning the kiss, her hands coming up to his face. It pleased him to know that he was the one causing her to arch, to break out in gooseflesh as she surrendered her body to him.

The night he'd touched her so intimately was branded within his mind. Jonathan sensed that there was no way he would ever get enough of touching her. For she had known him as a man, not a duke. She'd revealed her deepest fears to him, and he now fully understood her hatred of the outdoors. It wasn't about the cold air or the physical environment. It was her fear of being lost and abandoned.

He drew back to study her, while he moved his hand over her ribs to her narrow waist. She averted her eyes, but shifted her legs when he pressed against her.

God above, he wanted to be naked, to feel the soft triangle of hair pressing against his arousal.

In the firelight, her hair held a darker cast. Her breasts were small, less than a handful, but her nipples were a pale pink, inviting him to taste them again. And taste them he would.

She'd closed her eyes again, as if to shut him out. "Look at me," he demanded. He didn't want her pretending he wasn't there, remaining still as if to endure his touch instead of reveling in it. "I want to see what you're feeling when I touch you."

Her gray eyes fluttered open, but there was apprehension within them. Even so, he intended to win this challenge. By the time this night was over, he wanted her mindless with ecstasy, her body writhing with need.

He slid his hand down her hip, moving between her legs. Gently, he parted them, though she hesitated to obey. His hand moved to her womanhood, and he cupped her, pressing the heel of his hand against her flesh.

A broken breath caught in her throat, and he moved his hand again, changing the slight friction. He could feel the dampness of her own reaction, though she might protest. As he took one nipple in his mouth, he stroked and caressed her intimately. Her fingers dug into his hair as she shuddered.

"I don't care what title I might have inherited," he swore. "The only title that matters right now is husband."

He slid two fingers into her wetness, asserting his domination. He wanted her slick and hot, needing him desperately. She leaned in to his touch, moving in counterpoint to the thrusts of his hand.

Then, without any warning at all, he withdrew. He let her lie there, her breasts taut and rosy from the way he'd suckled them. She was wet, while she struggled to catch her breath.

She raised up, slowly letting her legs fall open for him. It pleased him to see her this way, but he wanted far more. He rested on his stomach, lifting her bottom with his hands until he guided his tongue to the place where he wanted to penetrate her.

She jolted at his sudden move, crying out as he used his tongue and mouth to arouse her more. Her breathing came in quick gasps, her body straining against him. He increased the pressure against the hooded flesh above her center, and she arched harder. She was so close, he slowed the pace, gently nibbling at her.

"You want me inside you," he murmured against her slit. "You want to feel me stretching you, until I've filled you."

She gave no answer, her face twisted away. He saw her wild shiver, the glistening arousal upon her sex. She wanted him as badly as he wanted her. And yet, she would not speak the word.

His erection was so hard, he didn't doubt it would be a brutal night unless he could finish inside her.

"I can't even put my thoughts together," she pleaded.

He drew back again, waiting for her to grant him permission, to let him join with her.

"Say it," he ordered.

Instead, she reached for his hand, guiding it back between her legs. She used him to touch her more roughly, and she let out a cry as the release rushed through her. Against his hand, he felt the moisture of her, and he cursed as she shuddered, rubbing his hand against her.

When she had finished, he guided her hand to his breeches, forcing her to touch him. Her expression was languid, but she stroked him through the fabric. He increased the pressure of her hand, and when her hands curled around his length, fisting him in a rhythm, he lost his own control. His body seized up, a growl emitting from his throat as his own release struck.

She tried to move her hand away, but he trapped it in place. When it was over, he stared at the fire, feeling so angry with himself. This wasn't at all the sort of night he'd wanted.

"Go and use the bed," he ordered. "I'll sleep here on the floor."

"There's room for both of us," she offered. "If you don't mind sharing." She was on her knees, trying to put on her chemise. At the sight of her rosy breasts, he suppressed a groan.

"You need your rest tonight. And if I come anywhere near you, I won't stop touching you." He didn't mention that he intended to bring her out of Scotland and back to London in the morning. It would only give her nightmares.

In the end, she walked toward him and drew him down for a single kiss. The gesture undid him, and it took the greatest act of control not to follow her into that bed.

⚡

"You'll be safe here for the night." Paul Fraser took the reins of the horses, leading them away while Lady Lanfordshire and her daughters entered the duke's house. He lowered his head against the cold, his brain infuriated by what had happened. But which of the crofters had a reason to start the fire? Why would they risk harming the family who had granted them sanctuary? He didn't doubt that the Earl of Strathland was somehow involved.

Near the house, he saw Mr. MacKinloch ushering the ladies inside. Though perhaps none of the others had seen, he stared at the man. He'd been gone from the wedding, looking after his sister who was supposedly ill. But since then, he'd heard other talk about the girl.

Before the door closed, he hurried forward and caught up to the man. "We need to talk."

"I must look after Lady Lanfordshire and her daughters," Mr. MacKinloch protested. He paled, trying to free himself from Paul's grasp. It made his guilt even more transparent.

"Now." He shut the door and hauled the footman toward the stables.

Panic turned the man's face white, but he stopped struggling. "Wh-what are you wanting, Fraser?"

"Why'd you do it?" Paul gripped the man's coat, pinning him against the stable wall. "Why would you be setting their house afire, after all they've done for you?"

"I-I didn't—"

"Don't lie." He wrenched the man's cuffs up and revealed the traces of oil on his hands. "You weren't at the wedding, were you? You said your sister was ill, and you had to take care of her. Instead you were pouring oil so that none could put the fire out. For God's sake, why?"

The footman tried to run, but Paul tightened his grip. "So help me, I'll drag you out and let the crofters judge you. Do you think they'll be showin' you mercy, when you've destroyed the only home they have?"

"Melford took my sister," Mr. MacKinloch confessed, his voice ragged with fear. "She's only seventeen." Anguish spilled out as he admitted, "He gave Colleen to his men and said they'd each . . . take turns with her if I didna set the fire. What was I to do?"

"Ask us for help," Paul insisted.

But the footman lowered his head. "It's nae use. They have guns, and they're stronger." The utter defeat in his voice spoke of a man who'd lost all hope. "I did it to save Colleen."

There was nothing Paul could say, for words wouldn't change what had happened. He didn't tell Mr. MacKinloch that likely Strathland's men had already raped his sister. The footman had succumbed to desperation, and there was nothing to be done about it.

"Please don't be telling Lady Lanfordshire," Mr. MacKinloch begged. "I'll take Colleen and go to the coast. I willna show my face here again."

It wasn't right to let the man go when he ought to stand justice for what he'd done. Paul said nothing, unable to make any promises. But he released the footman, unsure of what to do now.

The man hurried out, straightening his coat as he left. True to his word, he didn't return to the house, but pulled his coat tighter and disappeared among the crofters. Paul remained in the stable, his thoughts torn up.

"Thank you for trying to put out the fire," came a woman's voice. He looked up from the horses and saw Juliette Andrews approaching the stable. Her voice was calm and quiet, though the pallor of her face spoke of a woman uncertain of what to do now.

"I was glad to help." Paul turned back to the horses, not wanting to stare at her. For the past five years, Juliette Andrews had caught him firmly within her spell. With her soft green eyes and darker hair, she held the mysterious beauty of the forests where she wandered. The first time he'd seen her, he'd wondered if she was a nymph or fey born.

But it was her ever-present sadness that haunted him. She was hardly more than nineteen, a girl really. But she carried the weight of the world upon her shoulders. In her, he saw the reflection of himself—someone who'd put childhood behind far too soon.

"You stopped answering my letters last year," he said, walking closer. "You haven't written me in months. Not even when I asked you to marry me. "

Her expression grew bleak, her eyes miserable. "It didn't seem right."

He wanted to pull her into his arms, to hold her close and reassure her that nothing had changed between them. That she held his heart, as she'd always done.

"I'll wait until you give me the answer I want to hear" was all he could say, knowing he would not get a response to his marriage proposal. Something was holding her back, and he couldn't say what it was.

"Who do you think set the fire?" she asked, changing the subject.

He didn't answer at first, though he now knew who it was. Instead, he gave the one truth he could. "I'm certain Strathland had a hand in it."

There was a flash of hatred in her expression before she suppressed it. "Then there's no reason to ask why, is there? He wants us gone from Scotland so he can control the land."

"I believe so, aye."

She kept her emotions shielded but nodded in acknowledgment. "I don't know what we'll do now. Our debts are rising, and we've only just started to earn money with Victoria's sewing."

"She'll no' be able to sew anymore as a duchess," Paul pointed out. "But it may be that the Duke of Worthingstone will help your family."

"I hope so." She stared off into the darkness, a softness stealing over her face. "It was a lovely wedding. I never thought Victoria would be the first of us to wed. But I'm glad for her."

"What of you? Did you enjoy your Christmas in London?" A sudden flare of jealousy caught him, with the fear that she'd found a husband better suited than a man like him.

"I enjoyed visiting with my aunt and her son," she confessed. A fleeting smile shadowed her before she shrugged. "My sister Margaret loved every moment of it. She made lists of every eligible bachelor and ranked them all." Juliette met his gaze, adding, "Though I know she's happy for Victoria, I imagine Margaret was quite chagrined that our sister found a better match than she did, without having a single Season."

"And was there a gentleman you fancied?" The words escaped him before he could stop himself.

Juliette stiffened at the question. "I don't think that's any of your business."

Inwardly, he cursed himself for even voicing the question. He hung up the saddle and went to work unfastening the bridle. Without looking at her, he said, "I embarrassed you earlier today when I caught Worthingstone's hat."

Her face flushed, and she nodded. "It wasn't your fault. But you did embarrass me, yes, with the way you were watching me." Her face tightened and she clasped her hands together. "You shouldn't. Others might think that—"

"That I'm in love with you?" He dared to voice the words. "And I'll wager I wasna the only man looking upon your bonny face." It was one he wanted to see every morning for the rest of his life.

"I'm not the woman for you, Paul," she whispered. She was dangerously close to refusing him, but he forced himself not to interrupt. "You should turn your eyes elsewhere. I don't intend to marry anyone at all."

"Especially a Scottish rebel?" he dared.

She lifted her shoulders in a helpless shrug. "It's dangerous, the way you ride out with the others."

"I'm a doctor. I ride many places." He took her hand in his, locking their fingers together. "And I'm no' the only one who was watching you. Ever since I returned from Edinburgh, I've seen Strathland riding near the borders of your land."

"Don't speak of him." Her face had gone utterly white and she clenched her middle. "I don't want to even think of that man."

"He wouldna hesitate to take advantage of a young lass like yourself." Paul drew so close, there was less than an arm's length between them. "I followed you, when I could. So you had someone to watch over you."

Although he made no move to touch her, he saw her withdrawing as if she didn't want to acknowledge his interest. Like a wounded creature, she took a step back from him.

He released a slow breath. "I would ne'er ask for more than you're able to give, Juliette. I'll do naught except be a silent guard, when you've the need of one."

The pain in her eyes didn't waver. "I appreciate your friendship, Dr. Fraser. But find someone else for your attentions. I'm not the one for you."

And with those words, she disappeared into the night.

One week later

The trip to London had rivaled all of her worst nightmares. Though, true to his word, her husband had never left her side, Victoria had spent most of the journey with her eyes shut tightly. By the time they reached his town house, every ounce of blood seemed to have drained away from her body. Her hands were freezing, and she couldn't assemble a single rational thought.

The red-brick town house stretched three stories high with arches above the white stone window frames. She could not tell how many rooms were inside, but before she could wager a guess, the footman opened the door to the coach. Jonathan took her hand and leaned in close.

"One step at a time," he whispered in her ear. "We're almost there."

If she didn't faint by the time she reached the top of the stairs.

Victoria gripped his hand, wishing that she had a better gown and bonnet to wear. While these clothes were perfectly suited to rural Scotland, she didn't doubt that they were four or five years out of fashion.

When the footman led them inside, she found all of the servants lined up and waiting. She counted at least fourteen, and Jonathan introduced her to her lady's maid. Her name was Mary, and the young woman had dark brown hair tucked beneath a neat white cap.

"I'll be glad to order a bath and show you to your room, Your Grace." Mary bobbed a curtsy and smiled. Victoria sent a look to the duke, but he only nodded and lifted a hand in dismissal.

"Your Grace, might I speak with you in private a moment?" Victoria asked. Inside, she was a twisted mass of nerves and she needed a moment to steady herself.

Jonathan guided her into his library, where polished mahogany shelves supported row upon row of leather-bound books. After he closed the door, she released a slow sigh.

"What is it?"

"I can't quite catch my breath with all that's happened. I just need a moment." First, leaving the house in Ballaloch. Then journeying south for a week, until at last they reached his town house in Mayfair. Her husband had been endlessly patient, not even demanding that she share his bed. It was as if he sensed how much the journey had drained her spirits.

She moved to stand with her hands on either side of his desk, trying to assemble the churning thoughts. Upon the desk, she saw a mountain of calling cards and invitations, neatly stacked into five different piles. One invitation was open, and she saw the date of November 1809, more than a year ago. Had no one answered them?

"It looks as if you have many admirers," she ventured, curious about all the cards. "Are all of these invitations?"

He shrugged. "Likely. But we won't attend any of the assemblies or balls. We'll remain here at home."

She frowned, for as a duke, he had a responsibility to attend some of them. "You needn't stay behind on my behalf. If you want to go—"

"I don't." To emphasize his point, he picked up one of the stacks and tossed it into the hearth. "The last thing I want is to be surrounded by idle gossips who only want to whisper behind our backs."

She couldn't find any words to answer that. Though she wasn't eager to attend a ball, she understood that eventually she would have to. It wasn't possible to remain behind doors, or her husband would resent her.

But also, she *wanted* to attend a ball again. Once, she had loved watching the people but had been too young to attend. In her mind, she envisioned dancing with her husband, while other ladies spun in their colorful gowns.

From behind her, Jonathan reached over to untie the ribbons of her bonnet. He lifted it away, and leaned against her ear. "Pretend that we're alone, like we were at Christmas."

"And you're a man, not a duke," she finished in a whisper.

There was a sudden flare of interest in his eyes, and his hand moved down to her waist. "We won't travel for a while," he said. "You can grow accustomed to your new home."

It didn't feel possible that this place could ever feel like home. Without her mother or sisters, she was lost. They had stayed behind at Eiloch Hill, but she hoped they would return to London soon.

Her gaze moved across the library, where she began to see more than she had before. There was a thin layer of dust upon the bookshelf, and a cobweb hung from a silver sconce. Neglect hovered within the air, and she wondered why his servants hadn't bothered to clean this room. A premonition pressed at her that not all was well in this house. She sensed a darkness, as if her husband had been deeply unhappy.

"How is your leg?" she asked, trying to change the subject. Though it was mostly healed, he still walked with a slight limp.

"Well enough."

There was an air of restlessness about him, and his hand palmed her ribs, drawing her closer. It was as if he craved her touch, his control tightly caged. His gaze was taut, his mouth a thin line. When she reached up to touch his shoulder, her hand grazed his neck, and she felt the rapid pulse there. Every muscle, every part of him, was strained to a breaking point.

"Will I meet any of your family?" she asked, unsure of what else to say. She knew his father was no longer living, but he'd never spoken of his mother or anyone else.

"Not yet."

She silently wished she'd said nothing at all. Gently, she reached out to him, trying to bridge the distance. "Why are you so angry with me?"

"I'm not."

But she could see the frustration, the raw needs. Softly, she raised up to her tiptoes, wondering if a kiss would calm the storm within him. The moment her lips touched his, his mouth claimed hers in a rough embrace.

It was as if he were starving for her, and he pressed her against the bookcase, devouring her mouth while his hands moved everywhere. Down her shoulders, over her sensitive breasts, to her hips. He pulled her flush against himself, and she couldn't stop the gasp when she felt his arousal against her.

His hands fumbled with her skirts, and she was terrified that if she didn't stop him, he would take her right here in the library.

"Jonathan," she breathed against his mouth, trying to hold him back. "Wait."

Abruptly, he jerked away, his hands gripping either side of the bookcase, his head lowered. "I'm sorry. I lost sight of where we were." There was more to it than that, but she couldn't read the thoughts behind his shielded expression. His anger hadn't diminished, but it was not toward her. It was self-disgust, and his knuckles curled across one of the shelves.

"Should we go upstairs?" she ventured, uncertain if it was the right thing to offer.

He let her go, stepping back as he gathered his control. "No. I won't do that again, I swear it."

"I didn't mind." Though her mouth was swollen and her hair losing its pins, she rather liked the thought that he'd lost control of his desire.

"I could have hurt you. And I swore I would never do that."

The frustration behind his words made her aware that his dark mood was her fault. And though she was frightened of sharing the duke's bed, she knew it was her duty.

"I am fine," she insisted. Yet, he was uneasy around her, as though something else weighed upon him. She studied the remaining piles of invitations, noting the one dated 1810. Had he attended any gatherings at all in the past year?

"I'll let you retire to your room," he said, leading her back out to the hall where her maid awaited her.

"Your Grace, if you'll just follow me," Mary offered. The young woman smiled warmly, but when Jonathan took his leave, Victoria felt the nerves catch hold again.

This place, his home, was more magnificent than she ever could have dreamed. As they ascended the stairs, she admired the marble balustrade and the oil paintings on the walls. Some were portraits, while others depicted hunting scenes. It seemed that nearly every inch of space contained frames, but instead of making her feel overwhelmed, the effect charmed her. It was as if an elderly gentleman had decorated the walls with the intent of showing off every painting he owned.

At last, Mary opened the door to her room. Inside, there was a thick Aubusson rug, gilded French chairs, and royal blue draperies.

Not unlike a queen's dressing room, Victoria thought to herself.

"When your trunks are brought in, Your Grace, I'd be glad to help you into a fresh gown." Although Mary kept her reaction hidden, Victoria knew the maid was well aware of her outdated attire.

"My belongings were burned in a fire," she explained. "I'll need some new clothing. Perhaps I could—" She was about to suggest that they bring her a length of muslin, only to remember that duchesses weren't meant to sew their own clothing.

"Oh, I'm terribly sorry," the maid apologized. "How dreadful for you. If you wish it, I could send a servant to Madame Benedict's with your measurements. She's one of the best modistes in all of London."

At the mention of Madame Benedict, a knot tightened within Victoria's stomach with a hint of guilt. There had been so many orders for more corsets and chemises . . . and now she didn't know if she could fulfill them. Nor did she know what had become of her fabrics or the pieces the crofters had already cut. She was dismayed to think of it.

"I know she could have a gown for you before tonight, and then, in the morning, I would be glad to accompany you shopping," Mary finished.

The idea of venturing out into town wasn't at all appealing, but she didn't say so. "Something simple, for now," she agreed. "And I'll sketch out another gown that she can make and have delivered to the house."

While she searched for ink and paper in the writing desk, she asked, "Does His Grace have a secretary to manage his correspondence? I saw a stack of unopened invitations in the library . . ."

Mary turned red, but she admitted, "Yes, he does have a secretary. The invitations weren't answered because they belonged to His Grace's mother. He did not want anyone in the library, nor were we permitted to touch anything." Her lips tightened, and Victoria realized how uncomfortable she'd made the young woman.

"It's all right," she said. "I won't tell His Grace that you confided in me." The maid looked visibly relieved, and Victoria busied herself with writing down her measurements. Then, she took a second piece of paper and began to draw a high-necked muslin gown with long sleeves. She kept the design demure but then added a decorative trim and some ribbons. Although Mary kept a short distance away, she could tell the girl was watching.

"Why, that's lovely, Your Grace."

"It's not too out of fashion?" She hadn't seen the latest gowns and couldn't be certain.

"No, with the right material, it will be perfect. I'll see to it, straightaway." Before the maid could leave, the duke appeared in the doorway.

"I need some new clothes, if you wouldn't mind," Victoria explained to her husband. "Mary has offered to procure them for me."

"The duchess will need a complete wardrobe as befits her station," Jonathan informed the maid. "Send the dressmaker here in the morning, with samples of her fabrics and trims."

"Here, Your Grace?" Mary risked a glance at Victoria, and she nodded in agreement.

"That would be best." She sent her husband a silent look of thanks, and he waved a hand to dismiss the maid. Closing the door behind him, he regarded her.

"Does this room suit you?"

"It's . . . very fine." Almost too fine, truthfully, but she didn't want to offend him. "I'll feel like a princess sleeping in here."

He crossed the room and took her hand. Leading her to the window, he opened the drapes to let her look outside at the people. With his hands on her shoulders, he said, "I know you must be tired from the long journey."

She nodded, and his arms came around her waist. "You'll have everything you want or need," he promised. "Just ring for it, and the servants are instructed to obey your orders."

Turning in his arms, she faced him, feeling the winter chill beneath her skin. "I knew you were wealthy, but I could never have imagined all this . . ." She tightened her grip around his waist, but he held her at a slight distance, as though not wanting to get too close.

"You'll grow accustomed to it." He extricated himself, and added, "I'll leave you in peace, so you can rest before we dine together this evening." It was then that she realized that none of his belongings were here, and he apparently had no intention of sharing her bed.

"Where are you sleeping? I thought this was your room, too."

"My room is at the end of the hallway," he explained. "You'll be comfortable enough here."

Alone, she realized. He would sleep far away from her, except on those nights when he chose to visit her. She was beginning to wonder if he would ever do so. Something had changed today. From the moment he'd entered this house, she'd noticed a tension about him, a discomfort as though there were bad memories here.

"I'm sending men back to Ballaloch," he informed her. "They will rebuild your father's house and by the summer, your mother and sisters can live there once more."

Though he spoke as if it were nothing, his thoughtfulness touched her. The house held memories for her, some better than others, but she had never wanted it to be burned. "Thank you. It's the kindest wedding gift you could have given to me."

"Your family can return to London in the meantime," he continued. "Though we haven't discovered who set the fire, most of the crofters believe Strathland was responsible. I don't want your family there."

"He wanted my mother to sell the land," Victoria said. "Perhaps he thought a fire would get rid of us."

"He and I have a score to settle." A darkness clung to his voice, as if he considered the fire a personal threat. "This isn't over; I promise you that."

Squeezing her hands, he released them and started to walk toward the door. "In the meantime, I have to meet with my solicitor this afternoon. After you rest, you may explore the house and meet with the housekeeper to plan the menus. I will see you tonight."

Already he had resumed the role of duke, keeping his careful distance. She studied Jonathan, wondering what had happened to the man who had played chess with her or the man who had touched her intimately. He was almost a stranger now, surrounded by servants who were paid to obey his every bidding.

In parting, he added, "I have no doubt that you'll adjust to your new role quite easily." He gave a slight bow to her and left the room, not even waiting for a reply.

For a long moment, she stared at the closed door. Her life had been upended and scattered into pieces. She'd married this man with the knowledge that she'd protected dozens of families by doing so. He'd given her a home, enough money to do as she pleased, and there was the promise of future children.

This was what she'd always wanted, wasn't it? Why, then, did she feel so abandoned and alone?

Chapter Fifteen

BEATRICE ANDREWS stared at the letter before her with blurred eyes. Her greatest moment of joy, to see her eldest daughter wedded to a duke, had been overshadowed by the devastating loss of their home.

And now she had to tell Henry about the fire. A tear slid down her cheek as she tried to find the will to get past this tragedy. Her daughters were unharmed; that much was a blessing. They had not yet learned who was responsible for setting the fire, but even if they found the person, it wouldn't rebuild the stones or salvage the furnishings.

Dear Henry, she'd written. And then she'd set down the pen, unwilling to burden him with more. What could he do, after all? He was in Spain fighting, and she shouldn't send him news that would only cause more worry.

But keeping the truth from him was worse. Better to be honest and try to rebuild before he returned.

She dried her eyes, staring at the bundle of fabric that Margaret had found near the house. It contained silks, satins, and all manner of fabrics that Cain Sinclair had purchased and delivered to her eldest daughters. And although she believed she could ask the duke to help them, pride kept her silent.

Within this bundle of fabric lay a great deal of hope. Victoria's needle and skill had brought them twenty pounds, and from Margaret's secrecy, she suspected there was more than that. If all of them worked together, it was possible they could earn the money needed to hire builders. Beatrice wasn't particularly skilled at dressmaking, but she could sew straight seams.

Her sister would die of mortification if she even suspected Beatrice was considering this. Ladies did not become merchants. Especially the wife and daughters of a baron.

Then again, she was so weary of being told what to do and how to do it. Obedience had not gotten her far, and she still suspected the land steward was bleeding them dry. Year after year, she'd allowed herself to fail, making poor decisions and worrying over what Henry would think.

It was time to change that. Time to stand on her own feet and dig her way out of the pit of financial ruin she'd created.

The Duke of Worthingstone had given them a place to live at Eiloch Hill, but she didn't want to rely on his generosity for too much longer. And if that meant wielding her needle, she would set aside her inhibitions and do so.

"Mother?" came the voice of her daughter Amelia. "Are you all right?"

Beatrice set down her pen and took a deep breath. Yes, she was going to be all right. She'd done everything wrong, but that was going to change. Starting tomorrow, when she returned to Ballaloch to hire men to rebuild her house.

"I will be," she answered, opening her arms for a hug. Her daughter balanced on the arm of the wingback chair and held tight.

"We'll help you," Amelia promised. "I've spoken to Margaret and Juliette, and we're going to do more sewing. With your permission," she added. Her face turned crimson, as if she were apprehensive of Beatrice's answer.

Beatrice gave a nod. "So long as you are discreet, I won't protest."

"Thank you." Her daughter's face still held a flush, but likely, it was only excitement. "I'll go and tell Juliette."

After Amelia had gone, Beatrice picked up her pen again. The words didn't come easily, but she wrote to Henry, telling him about Victoria's marriage and the fire. She confessed their financial hardships, admitting her faults.

But she couldn't bring herself to speak of the broken feelings, or the years of regret. In so many ways, it was like writing to a stranger. Her husband had loved her once, but the distance was so vast, she couldn't quite reveal the hurt or fears inside.

If she wanted her life to change, then she had to begin with herself. She had to simply keep faith that hard work and courage would grant her the strength she needed.

✾

When he opened the door to his wife's room, Jonathan found Victoria sewing. "You didn't come down for supper."

"No," she admitted. Her writing desk was filled with pieces of fabric and he saw a half-finished chemise hanging over the back of a second chair. This one was more demure than the others, but he'd spied many different colors of silk, satin, and lace.

"Where did you get these?" he asked.

She set down her needle and shrugged. "Mary brought me a gown from Madame Benedict's, but it did not suit. I've cut pieces from my wedding gown and the new gown. I'm making a new garment from both."

It was then that he saw the ice blue gown she'd worn at the ceremony. Though parts of the gown had been ruined by smoke and the snow, she'd salvaged large portions of it. The new gown was ivory, trimmed with pearls and lace. It was suited to a young girl, not a newly married duchess.

He saw that Victoria had begun combining the two fabrics,

creating ice blue sleeves and an ivory bodice. Though the gown was unfinished, it was far more striking than he'd guessed.

She was wearing her dove-colored traveling gown while a small bath of water stood in the corner. It appeared that she'd gotten caught up in her work and forgotten it.

"Duchesses do not sew," he reminded her. "There's no need for it."

Her gray eyes flashed with anger. "Why must I give up something I enjoy?"

He sensed he was treading on dangerous ground, but better for her to learn the truth from him than for the servants to begin whispering. "Because it simply isn't done. It's too common."

She picked up a panel and threaded her needle. "Other duchesses might not, but *this* duchess does. Sewing is what I do. It's who I am, and I'll not give it up." Beneath her cool words, he detected a simmering anger, mingled with resentment.

He decided to drop the subject, for there had been many changes for her this day. "Are you hungry?"

She shrugged, her needle flashing in even stitches. "A little."

"Where is your maid?"

"I sent her away. I wanted to be alone when I sew."

Jonathan let out a sigh and pulled the bell cord to ring for a tray. Without asking what she wanted, he requested an assortment of food, and the footman disappeared to obey his orders.

Despite the long meeting with his solicitor, he'd never stopped thinking of Victoria. Like an obsession, she was burned into his mind. He'd wanted to leave behind the reports of all the estate profits and losses, spending time with his wife. Truthfully, he hated London and wished he didn't have to live in this house. Every time he set foot within it, he was reminded of his father.

If the property weren't entailed, he'd sell it tomorrow. As it was, when he did come to town, he preferred to remain behind closed doors. He was determined to protect Victoria from all the malicious talk against his family.

The food arrived, and Victoria thanked the footman, tasting the soup he'd brought. It reminded him of the night they'd shared a meal in Scotland and the first time he'd kissed her. She sipped at the spoon, drawing his attention to her mouth.

A curling strand of blond hair hung upon her bosom, and his mind conjured up the image of the strands tangled against her bare skin. He wanted to watch her come undone, to join their bodies until he could lose himself in her. But his earlier loss of control made him hesitant.

"Will you come with me for a moment?" He extended his hand, and she set aside the sewing, rising from her chair. With her palm in his, he led her toward the window. She'd closed the drapes, but he pushed them back. Outside it was dark, with only the slight glow of lanterns to reveal the streets and passersby. The noise of carriages rumbled past, while a low fog drifted across the amber lights.

"There's far more to the world than you've seen, Victoria. I want to show it to you one day." He held her in his arms, forcing her to look outside. The scent of her skin held traces of flowers, and he breathed against her neck, tightening his hold. "We'll leave London and go back to the way it was in Scotland. Alone."

"I would like that," she whispered. "But first I need to face London."

"No." He would never expose her to their scrutiny. "Put it from your mind." He rubbed her shoulders, turning her to face him. She'd grown thinner over the past week of traveling, and shadows hung beneath her eyes. But she was no less beautiful to him.

"Are you ashamed of me? Is that why you don't want me to leave your house?" Her gray eyes regarded him with a quiet solemnity.

"Not at all. But I don't want them to upset you. And they will

not curb their tongues merely because you became my duchess."
He leaned in to steal a kiss, wanting to reassure her. At first, she
remained still, accepting his kiss, but not returning it.

Against his mouth, she murmured, "I don't want you to regret
this marriage."

"There's only one thing I regret," he murmured against her jaw.
Nipping at the sensitive skin, he kissed her again, his mouth trying to force a response from her. It was tentative, but when he
pulled her closer, her arms came around him, her head leaning
back. "I mean to remedy that now."

Her eyes widened as she caught his meaning. "Don't be afraid,"
he ordered. "Kiss me back." If it took every ounce of control he
had, he was determined not to frighten her.

He sensed the moment she started to lose herself in the kiss.
He slid his tongue within her mouth, and when she imitated the
gesture, desire tightened inside him. His hands moved down to
her bottom, pulling her close.

"I'll give you the life you've dreamed of, Victoria," he swore. "If
you're willing to reach for it."

From the crimson cast to her skin, he could tell that he'd flus-
tered her. She knew, full well, that he desired her. But he didn't
know if she would refuse him or not. Her shoulders were tight
with tension, and he massaged them slowly.

"Wh-what are you doing, Jonathan?"

"I like the way you use my name, instead of my title," he
replied, ignoring her question. He continued rubbing her shoulders, before he unfastened the first button of her gown. A second
followed, and her posture stiffened.

"What color is your chemise, I wonder?" His mouth lowered to
the soft part of her neck, his tongue flicking against her skin.
"Blue, this time? Or perhaps a pure white, like you wore on our
wedding night?" He reached for the laces that bound back her
traveling gown and loosened it further. "You might think you're

hiding yourself beneath these colorless gowns, Victoria. But I know your secrets." After he'd unfastened the back of her gown, he revealed a bright red corset and chemise.

God in heaven.

The vivid color contrasted against her skin, making him want to tear it off. "Where did you get this?"

"Madame Benedict sent it with the gown."

He leaned in and spoke against the back of her neck. "I like it." Slowly, he drew his hand down her spine, watching as the goose-flesh rose upon her shoulders. "Take off your gown," he ordered.

"I'd rather you undressed me," she answered.

Jonathan reached for the hem of her gown, lifting it up. His hands passed over her rib cage and breasts until he beheld her in only the red chemise and corset. "I'm beginning to understand why you and your sisters earned a small fortune selling these."

She gasped as he moved before her, loosening the corset even more until he could lift it away. He lowered the chemise and bent to taste the erect tips of her breasts.

Her hands threaded into his hair, and she looked into his eyes. "I want the wedding night we should have had, Victoria." He drew his hand beneath her petticoat, grazing her inner thigh until he cupped her damp curls.

A ragged gasp emitted from her throat when he slid a finger inside her, his thumb brushing against her hooded flesh.

"Wait."

He stopped touching her immediately. Victoria closed her eyes, wishing she could stop the violent upheaval inside of her. Even his words were arousing, and she knew what he wanted from her.

"All of this is overwhelming to me," she whispered. "I am willing . . . but a little frightened."

In the firelight, his chest was firm, the muscles rigid. She remembered what it was like to have his body pressed to hers, to feel the sensual touch of his hands upon her.

Jonathan turned toward her, his expression shielded. "You're afraid of me."

She nodded, not knowing how else to explain it. The air was cool, and she tried in vain to hide herself from his gaze. Every part of him was taut, as though he were holding back a storm. There would be pain when he joined with her, but she also remembered the intense pleasure he'd given her.

Her answer seemed to concern him, for he brought his hands to her waist. "Then we should slow down."

She breathed a little easier, thankful that she hadn't offended him. His hand remained at her waist, and he took her other hand. "I promised you a dance on Christmas. Will you grant it to me now?"

Her cheeks warmed at the idea. "What about your leg?"

"Believe me. I'm not thinking about my leg at all." There was irony in his voice as he held her closer. "Follow my lead."

He stepped forward, guiding her backward. Her feet stumbled, but he showed her the simple steps of a waltz. Though she had been taught to dance years ago, it had been so long, she could hardly remember her footing. When Jonathan tried to turn her, she tripped again, but he steadied her. "Count with me. One, two, three."

She was terrible at it, but the more she tripped over her own feet, the easier it was to laugh at herself. Never once did he let go, simply correcting her until she managed to find the pattern and follow him.

The look in his green eyes held a hunger she was beginning to understand. She let herself be guided by him, losing herself. And she knew that this was a prelude to another kind of dance.

When she stumbled again, he lifted her up, his arms beneath her bottom. He held her body against his, and she caught her breath at the sensation of his hard flesh against her own yielding skin. Though he did nothing but hold her up, she saw the question in his eyes. He wanted her, and although he had a husband's claim to her innocence, he would give her the choice.

This time, she chose not to be afraid.

When he lowered her against his heated length, she found herself opening against him. She wrapped her legs around his waist, while he supported her bottom.

In silent answer, she lowered her mouth to his in a kiss. He kissed her hard, his tongue threading with hers. She shuddered as his body rubbed against her, and Jonathan took her back to the bed, letting her down.

He undressed, and she averted her gaze, not yet ready to see him. The bed lowered with his weight, and his wide hands caressed her as he took off the undergarments, baring her to his touch.

"Don't be afraid of me," he murmured against her shoulder.

Victoria took a breath, trying to slow the harsh beating of her heart. She faced the wall, shocked when he guided her beneath the covers and moved behind her. His hard shaft was nestled against her bottom, and his hands came around to stroke her breasts.

"I enjoyed dancing with you."

"I was terrible." But even so, she had enjoyed the moment with him. She turned to her side to face him, and the complete intimacy of being naked started to evoke her fears again.

He was kissing her, his hands moving over her body as if to memorize every inch of her skin. The chill of fear mingled with the flush of desire, and when he bent to her breast, she felt the intrusion of his hands between her legs. Her body reacted instantly, growing slick with the movement of his fingers.

He guided her hand to his swollen erection, and her thoughts scattered apart. He was hard and warm to the touch, his body responding to her tentative stroke. She caressed the length of him, both fascinated and afraid of his size.

"Careful," he warned. "If you keep touching me like that, I won't last." He pushed her hand away and moved atop her. Though his body weight wasn't too heavy, she felt his chest pressing against her breasts. Below the waist, his shaft nudged between her legs.

"Victoria," he breathed, and she tensed as he eased against her. She closed her eyes, and though he continued to touch her, her fears began suffocating the desire. The intensity of the feelings took command of her, and she couldn't say what had caused her to shy away.

His dark eyes held back a maelstrom of emotion, as if he were bent upon possessing her. As if, by joining with her, she would be fused with him, losing herself.

She tightened against him, faltering when she felt his intrusion. Although her body was wet, she felt trapped beneath him. He wasn't going to let her move, and when she gasped against the pain, he thrust forward.

Instinctively, she tried to push at the weight of him. He withdrew, only to sheathe himself inside her again.

She couldn't catch her breath, and the sudden rush of regret spilled over her. It was too intimate, too close. With every movement, she felt herself merging with him. Her body was reshaping, accepting his invasion, and when she dared to look at him, she saw the reflection of herself in his eyes.

He'd refused invitations for over a year, becoming a recluse, like herself. And she began to wonder if his avoidance of society had anything to do with her at all . . . or whether it was born of his own demons.

He'd given her so much, teaching her not to be afraid. With every moment she'd spent with him, he'd given her the courage she needed. She'd become a stronger woman at his side.

And despite his desire to protect her, she wanted to face every last fear, becoming the wife he needed her to be.

She began touching him, running her hands down his spine,

meeting his thrusts with a counterpoint of her hips. And when she raised her knees, he shuddered, plunging within her. The rhythm changed, and he palmed her bottom, until he was fully sheathed. She couldn't move, but he was so hard, she grew breathless at the feeling of him probing her so deep.

He never stopped, and she grew weak at his penetrations, her body trembling as he quickened the tempo. A blissful release slid over her, and she couldn't stop the tears. They were tears of happiness, but the moment he saw them, he stopped.

"I'm sorry," he said, withdrawing from her body. "I didn't mean to be rough with you." He moved away from her to the edge of the bed, his hands at his sides, his head lowered.

"No, you weren't." She tried to reach for him, but he wouldn't look at her. "You didn't hurt me, Jonathan."

Yet, he didn't seem to hear her. He continued to stare at the wall, and she couldn't understand what had come between them. He wouldn't admit what was haunting him now.

Already he'd reached for his fallen clothing, and she could see that he was rigid with self-loathing. Despite her protests, he dressed quietly and left her room, closing the door behind him.

She pulled a pillow against her bare skin, trying to understand him. Before he'd touched her, he'd reassured her that he would never hurt her. Despite her protests to the contrary, he believed that he had.

Victoria cursed herself for daring to cry, but the night had been so wonderful, she hadn't been able to stop herself. She pulled on a nightgown and curled up beneath the sheet. Something was troubling Jonathan deeply, secrets he'd never confided.

And for the first time, she began to realize that she was not the only one with something to hide.

Chapter Sixteen

JONATHAN REPLACED the stopper on his inkwell. He'd spent most of the night going over his accounts in the hopes that it would somehow distract him from the vicious sexual frustration. He'd made his wife cry without intending to. And though she'd claimed that she was all right, nothing could have extinguished his arousal faster. He never wanted to see her weep, least of all in his bed.

Over and over, he'd tried to think of what he could have done to make it easier on Victoria. He'd thought she was ready for him, but he should have waited. Once he'd been inside her, he'd lost all sense of control.

Just like your father, his conscience mocked. The thought was appalling.

His parents had loved each other once, until his father's jealousy had turned brutal. He never wanted to even imagine himself in the same way. But his feelings for Victoria were far too uncontrollable, and he hardly knew himself when he touched her.

She hadn't come downstairs this morning and likely wouldn't. The guilt nagged at him, and he decided a better tactic would be to enlist help. He'd sent his secretary to buy a suitable gift of apology to Victoria. Then, to his footman, he ordered, "Send an invitation to my aunt Melanie to pay a call upon the duchess this afternoon."

He started to order his coat and hat, when he spied Victoria standing at the top of the stairs. It was the first time he'd seen her leave her room, and he remained where he was, hoping she would come down.

He could not tell whether she was angry with him, but he could think of nothing to say. *I'm sorry* wasn't nearly enough.

"Your Grace," she called out.

A few of the servants were startled that she had not come down to speak to him, but he suspected the reason why. He waited to see if she might approach, but she only clung to the banister.

"I-I thought we might talk . . ."

Upon her face, he spied uncertainty, and he didn't doubt that this conversation would end badly. Better to avoid it until she'd had a chance to forgive him. Quietly, he ordered the footman to make arrangements for his landau. Without being asked, another servant went and fetched his topcoat and hat.

"This evening, perhaps." Jonathan sent her a light bow and allowed the footman to help him with his coat. By tonight, she would have received his gift and that might mend their differences. "My apologies."

Lifting his hat in a silent farewell, he walked to the front door, even though his carriage could not possibly be ready. For now, he simply wanted to escape the house and the look of sadness on his wife's face.

After spending her morning hours with Madame Benedict, Victoria had ordered a full wardrobe with gowns for every occasion. She'd been measured from head to toe, and the modiste had showed her an assortment of gloves, bonnets, and stockings. She had even suggested that Victoria should consider ordering more luxurious undergarments from Aphrodite's Unmentionables.

Though it was hard to hold back her smile, Victoria obeyed, ordering a selection of corsets and chemises in every color. It was good for the crofters' wives, after all.

Then she'd spent the rest of her time navigating her way through the house. Though outwardly it had appeared to be the same size as the neighboring dwellings, she'd underestimated how much deeper it was. There were endless drawing rooms, a music room, the servants' quarters, and even a garden outside.

When she reached the drawing room on the second floor, large windows lined the walls. Clouded morning light filtered into the room, and the windowpanes were lined with snow. Victoria went to sit near the window and touched the cool glass. The sight of the crystalline drifts reminded her of the day she and Margaret had slipped outside into her uncle's garden, throwing snow at each other when they were young girls.

"Victoria, don't!" her sister protested. "You're getting my pelisse wet."

In answer, she scooped another ball of snow into her gloved hands, moving closer to Margaret. "Then you'd better run."

"If you throw that, I'll tell Mother!" Her sister squealed and darted away.

Victoria raced after her, her skirts covered to the knees in snow while she took aim at Margaret. A moment later, her sister turned around and plastered her in the face with her own snowball. Neither of them had been able to stop laughing, even when Beatrice caught them, scolding them for such unladylike behavior.

A pang caught at Victoria's heart, for she missed her sisters dreadfully. There had been a time when she and Margaret had been best friends, allied against Juliette and Amelia. They had spent endless hours together, playing games and talking about their future husbands.

But now, all of that had changed.

Margaret would have reveled in this new life, particularly in the pearl and diamond necklace the duke had sent. Victoria had stared at it in disbelief, not understanding why Jonathan would send her such a gift. Was it an apology? Or was it meant as a wedding gift?

She'd tucked it away, certain that the duke was avoiding her. But he couldn't do so forever. She could only hope that her plan to reconcile them would work.

A quiet knock sounded at the door, and when Victoria called out her permission to enter, her maid Mary dropped a curtsy. "Your Grace, you have a caller. It is His Grace's aunt, Lady Rumford."

Victoria's stomach twisted with worry. Jonathan hadn't wanted her to meet any of his relatives, and she wasn't certain what the lady would think of her. "Send for tea and refreshments," she ordered. "I will greet her in the blue drawing room."

Mary took a moment to help her tuck away a few wayward strands of hair, likely bemoaning Victoria's lack of a suitable wardrobe. But it would take time before Madame Benedict could sew more gowns. Once she was presentable, she went downstairs to greet Lady Rumford.

The plump, dark-haired woman was standing near the window. She was dressed in a high-necked blue jaconet gown with long sleeves and a fluted ruff. She smiled warmly and extended both hands in greeting. "I am Lady Rumford," she said, squeezing Victoria's hands and smiling. "But you may call me Aunt Melanie, if you wish."

"I am Victoria Andr— I mean, Nottoway."

Melanie let out a sigh. "He told me you lived in Scotland for many years. I was afraid you might not be accustomed to our ways." Releasing her hands, she added, "What you meant to say was that you are Her Grace, the Duchess of Worthingstone."

The woman behaved as if Victoria had been brought up in a barn among cattle. Of course she knew the proper form of address. Yet, she suppressed the urge to defend herself, not wanting to offend the woman. "I did not feel the title was necessary among family."

"It is always best to begin with the title and be more familiar later. Titles do grow complicated, but as the wife of a peer, you must adapt to this."

She took a seat across from Lady Rumford, and a footman arrived with the refreshments.

"I must say, you are a pretty thing," Melanie admitted, while Victoria poured her a cup of tea. "His Grace does have good taste, and his mother would have been quite pleased with you, if she were here." A hint of sadness clung to her words.

"Was Jon—I mean His Grace—close to his mother?"

Lady Rumford nodded. "My sister Catherine was sweet and gentle, always wanting to please others. I still miss her." Her eyes held back tears, and she reached for a handkerchief.

"I'm sorry," Victoria murmured. "I can't imagine how terrible it would be to lose a sister." Though she wondered what had happened to Jonathan's mother, she didn't ask.

Lady Rumford's mouth tightened. "I shouldn't have spoken of it. Catherine's death was a great tragedy, and the scandal still lingers. You must be prepared for it. When you attend dinner parties and balls, there will be talk."

Victoria didn't know how to respond to that, for she didn't feel quite ready to attend social functions. Simply leaving the house to get into a carriage was difficult enough. But her lack of a reply didn't seem to dishearten Lady Rumford at all.

"I do believe the best way to introduce you as the new duchess would be to host an intimate gathering of the duke's closest friends and our immediate family. Next week, I think. I can help you with the guest list, and then—"

Next week? Victoria bit her lip to keep from blurting out no. "Lady Rumford, I do appreciate your desire to help me, but really, there's no need—"

"Oh, fiddle. Of course you'll need help, and I would be glad to lend my knowledge and assistance." She poured a cup of tea for both of them, passing one to Victoria.

It was time to be honest with her husband's aunt. "I have never been presented at court, nor have I ever made my debut in society," she began. "Until a year ago, my father did not even have a title. I need a little more time to . . . prepare for such an event."

Six months at the very least, she thought.

Several expressions passed over Lady Rumford's face. Surprise, curiosity, and a hint of frustration appeared before she finally veiled her emotions. "Your Grace, I can understand why you might feel awkward and ill-prepared to be the wife of a duke. But all of this can be *learned,* don't you see? His Grace has been through the most terrible circumstances during the past year and a half. It's little wonder he traveled so frequently. But now that you're here, you can do wonders to soothe his troubles."

Her attention sharpened at the mention of his "troubles" and "terrible circumstances." Victoria desperately wanted to ask, but she held her tongue. She took one of the ginger and currant cakes, hoping Lady Rumford would elaborate.

"Since no one knows anything about you, they are all eager to understand why the duke eloped. This secret marriage is terribly romantic, don't you see? Already the ladies are wondering how you managed to ensnare the man every woman wanted to marry."

Because I sewed up his leg with pink thread, she thought drily.

"Well?" Lady Rumford prompted. "How did you manage it? Did you"—she lowered her voice into a whisper—"let him compromise you?"

"No!" Victoria gaped at the idea and took another bite of cake to distract herself from the woman's implications. "I only . . . saved his life after he was shot."

A wide smile spread over the matron's face. "Why, then, you nursed him back to health and he fell in love with you. Isn't that right?"

"That's right," came a male voice from the doorway. Jonathan removed his hat and entered the parlor, leaning down to kiss his aunt hello. "I see you've come to torment my wife."

"Nonsense, my boy." Lady Rumford reached up to pat his cheek. "I'm trying to convince Her Grace that she should host a ball or a dinner party here next Friday. We'll show her off to everyone."

His smile tightened. "No, I don't think so."

Though Victoria knew he'd said it to give her an escape, she didn't want to hurt the older woman's feelings. "Perhaps another time, Lady Rumford."

Disappointment creased the older woman's face, but she accepted defeat. "Well, if I cannot host a party, then I should like to take your wife out shopping in the morning. We shall spend all of your money, if that is agreeable, Worthingstone."

Victoria discreetly shook her head, and when his aunt reached out her hand, Jonathan took it. "Not too early, Aunt." His voice held the hint of sin and Victoria felt her face flood with color.

"Oh, you devil. Such wickedness." But she laughed as he helped her stand from the chair. To Victoria, she added, "Send word to me when you wish to go, Your Grace. It would be my pleasure."

Victoria returned to her chair while Jonathan escorted his aunt out. The tea had gone cold, and she had no doubt that the pair of them were talking about her reluctance to host or attend a gathering. *But you will,* her mind insisted. *You must.*

She wasn't about to let this house become her new prison, regardless of her discomfort. Taking a breath, she steeled herself for what lay ahead. When her husband returned, he closed the door to the drawing room behind him. "She means well."

"I know she does," Victoria answered. Jonathan moved to stand by the window, staring at the streets below them. For long minutes, he said nothing and only the soft ticking of the wall clock resounded in the silence.

This was her chance to speak with him, and she rose from her seat, walking behind him.

"I never meant to hurt you last night," he said. His voice was quiet, and he admitted, "I don't want you feeling threatened by me."

She stared at him, trying to make sense of it all. "I wasn't threatened at all. It might not have ended the way I wanted it to, but you didn't have to go."

"Yes, I did. But I hope the necklace will atone for my actions."

She was at a loss for words. A necklace—truly? She wanted *him,* not cold jewels. "You don't need to give me jewels. I'd much rather have—"

"Thimbles and thread?" he interrupted. "Or perhaps a length of muslin?" The tone of his voice spoke of a man who believed she disliked his gift. It wasn't that at all. But she didn't ever want him to believe that he had to apologize by spending vast amounts of money on her. A kiss would have been enough.

"I was going to say I'd rather have you," she answered quietly. "But a thimble isn't a bad idea." She tried to muster a smile, for such a gift held more value to her. She loved sewing, loved watching lengths of material transform into beautiful garments. It was such an intrinsic part of her, she couldn't ever imagine giving it up.

Rising from her chair, she turned to face him. "I married you to save the crofters, not for your wealth."

"I suppose you wish you hadn't," he responded.

"Stop putting words in my mouth that aren't true." She held on to her waist, trying to hold back the feelings inside her. Though she hadn't wanted to wed him, now that it was done, she was determined to make the best of this marriage. Even if it meant transforming herself.

Jonathan moved in closer, his hand reaching for hers. He removed the glove she was wearing, then lifted her palm to his lips. A light shiver fluttered through her at the touch of his mouth. "We haven't begun well, have we?"

"We haven't even been married a fortnight," she said. "A quarrel was inevitable." Searching for an excuse to distract him, Victoria spied a small game table in the corner. "Would you care to play chess?"

His eyes narrowed. "You must not be feeling well."

"Likely not." But it was the only thing she could think of to soothe his mood. Without allowing him to refuse, she moved toward the game table and set up the ivory pieces while he took the black. They played for several minutes, and she surprised herself by taking several of his pieces.

"Little thief," he muttered. "Taking what's rightfully mine."

She only smiled and moved her knight into position. "Isn't that what wives are supposed to do?"

She was rewarded with a dark laugh. "*Touché.*"

He moved his bishop and while she was distracted with the board, his foot moved against hers. "We've been invited to a ball next week. Your aunt Charlotte is hosting it for your sisters."

Her hand froze upon the chess piece. "They've returned from Scotland?"

"Not yet, but soon."

Joy filled her up inside at the idea. She wanted to see them so badly, but a moment later, she realized what he'd said. Charlotte was hosting the ball, which meant she would have to face her fears again, venturing out of this house.

But Jonathan continued, not allowing her to speak. "My secretary will decline the invitation, and you won't have to go."

She stared at the white pieces, not at all pleased by that. Yes, it would be difficult, but she couldn't simply stay at home and hide away from the world. She had to try to attend, no matter how much she might cling to her husband's side.

"This is my aunt," she reminded him. "We should be there."

Charlotte was her family. Her aunt would never permit anyone to speak ill of her. Was it possible to transform herself for one night, to become another person? Madame Benedict had promised to finish an evening gown within a few days. And then she had the diamond necklace. Perhaps . . .

"She would understand if you didn't attend." From the duke's expression, he had no intention of going.

"I want to be there for my sisters," she said. "And I want you to go with me." If Jonathan stayed at her side, she believed she could face the fear. She took a deep breath, praying he would agree.

Jonathan took another chess piece and regarded her. "I think it would be best if you didn't. Not so soon." He rested his hand upon the table, as if he didn't believe she could manage it.

She said nothing, though a twinge of annoyance pricked at her that he had assumed she would not know how to conduct herself. This wouldn't be the first time she'd been a guest at a party. She'd watched enough young ladies to know what to expect.

The idea of standing in front of society, baring her insecurities, was frightening. And yet . . . Lady Rumford had offered to help her. The matron would likely be delighted with the idea.

It burned within her, the wish to stand at Jonathan's side as his duchess. To prove to him that she *could* assume this role and be his wife.

She had to try.

🦌

The snows had melted, and Beatrice had spent the past week watching the rebuilding efforts. Though it hurt to see the charred interior, at least the stone exterior had not suffered too badly. The Duke of Worthingstone had sent a dozen men to work on the house, and though she'd asked about paying the men, they claimed that His Grace had already done so. She was so grateful for the help, she'd decided to put aside her pride. The duke would not permit his wife's family to endure hardship, not when he had the means to provide for them.

She'd remained at his house on Eiloch Hill with his staff, while her daughters had gone to London to stay with Charlotte. Although the duke's home was in need of its own repairs, at least she had a roof over her head and a bed in which to sleep. She was determined that her own house would be finished before Henry returned.

"Lady Lanfordshire, there's a letter come for you."

Beatrice turned and saw Mrs. Larson holding out the letter on a silver tray. The moment she saw her husband's handwriting, her spirits sank. Henry hadn't written her in so long, she worried what it might say. When she read the contents, dread filled her up inside.

"Are ye all right, my lady?" Mrs. Larson asked, wiping her hands upon her apron. "It's no' bad news, is it?"

She forced a smile on her face. "The Colonel was wounded in the last battle, but he's recovering. It seems that they will be sending him home early to convalesce."

The housekeeper murmured words in Gaelic beneath her breath in prayer. "He's no' too badly hurt, is he?"

Beatrice shrugged. If they were sending him back, it had to be serious enough that he could no longer fight. But she worried over what he would say about the house. The men could only work so fast in the midst of snow and rain. And in this part of Scotland, the weather was merciless.

"When will he be arriving?" the housekeeper asked. "Could the men be finished with the house by then?"

Beatrice shook her head. "I don't know. The men are working as fast as they can. And the crofters are too busy building their own homes on the duke's land, so they can't help."

Mrs. Larson nodded. "Well, if it isna finished by the time he returns, at least you've a place here, thanks be."

Beatrice nodded her thanks. "I still don't understand why the fire was started. We've done nothing at all to hurt anyone." She rested a hand against the doorframe as she watched the workers. "Margaret said Victoria brought work to the crofters' wives. They were paid for their sewing."

"'Tisn't money they need, but rather food," Mrs. Larson said.

"You're right. But it makes me uneasy living here, knowing that one of them started the fire." A shiver ran through her. "And then Mr. MacKinloch disappeared. You don't think that he—"

The housekeeper paled. "I canna be saying. But if he were to betray ye like that, he'll get what's comin' to him, I can promise ye that."

"I'm glad the girls returned to London," she admitted. "It's safer." Had it not been for the house, she'd rather be there herself.

Beatrice picked up Henry's letter again, searching for some hint that he might have missed her or the girls. There was nothing except the terse announcement that he would be home by the early spring, if not sooner.

She walked outside, heedless of the melting snow. For the past few years, she'd been alone. Would her husband ignore her, as he always had? Or had he thought of her at all during those years?

Regardless, she did not intend to make excuses for the fire, nor allow him to blame her for it. With any luck, the house would be finished before he arrived.

And when Henry returned from Spain, she would discover what hope, if any, was left for her own marriage.

Chapter Seventeen

JONATHAN STOOD at the foot of the wooden stairs, resting his hand upon the railing. Slowly, he walked up the stairs, a heaviness centering within him. His mother had died here, and his father had taken his own life. For a moment, he stared at the floor below the railing, wondering if Catherine had known she was going to die. Even now, he expected to see her hurrying down the stairs, a bright smile on her face and a warm embrace for him.

As for his father, he hoped the bastard was burning in hell.

Although Jonathan had done what he could to silence the gossip, he'd hated the way everyone had looked at him. The duchess had been murdered, and some questioned whether his father's harsh temper ran within his own blood.

It didn't. He told himself that, time and again. And yet, when he was with Victoria, she conjured a side of him he'd never known existed. It was as if she'd transformed his stony existence into a man of flesh and blood—a man who desperately wanted her.

I won't be like my father, he swore to himself. He would maintain his control, no matter how much she tempted him. He didn't like the reckless infatuation that simmered inside him with the need to possess her. The need for distance, to calm the unrest, was heightening with every moment he spent in this house.

He had to return to Scotland. Already, he'd sent investigators to question the Earl of Strathland about the fire. Jonathan strongly suspected that the man had played a part in it, though he hadn't set it himself. Lady Lanfordshire had admitted that the earl's men had pressured her to sell their land on several occasions.

As a duke, Jonathan held far more power than the earl. It was possible he could use his influence to protect Lady Lanfordshire and the crofters. But he questioned the wisdom of returning to a place of such unrest and violence.

Strathland had made many enemies among the Highlanders, and although he had been within his rights to evict the tenants once their lease was ended, there was no need to burn their homes. The crofters' resentment at being homeless was an open, festering wound. Eventually, it would result in bloodshed, and Jonathan didn't want Victoria's family in danger.

Remaining here, in London, was akin to turning a blind eye, believing that nothing terrible would happen. And he instinctively knew that if Lady Lanfordshire were caught between two feuding sides, she would suffer for it.

He stood outside his wife's bedroom door at the end of the hall, resting his hand upon the wood. This time, he could not stand by and do nothing while others suffered. Even if it meant facing down the earl himself, Jonathan refused to hide from the danger.

"This is the most beautiful room I've ever seen." Amelia walked through Victoria's bedchamber, admiring the furnishings and moving straight toward her wardrobe. After exclaiming over the new gowns, her sister closed her eyes and leaned back against the wardrobe door. "It's truly the most unfair twist of fate. You stayed at home while we tried to find husbands. And yet, you were the one to catch the richest husband of all."

Victoria sent her a sympathetic smile. "It wasn't my intention to wed a duke."

"With my misfortune, I'll never marry." Amelia crossed the room and sat beside Juliette. "That would be the most wretched luck. And I truly was trying to find someone, just before Christmas."

"Juliette and I tried to find husbands, not you," Margaret corrected. "You're only sixteen."

"I can look, can't I?" Amelia countered. "Some of the men won't be married in two more years . . . and there was this exquisite viscount." She sighed, flopping down upon a settee. "I would let him compromise me whenever he wanted to."

Margaret glared at her and turned back to Victoria. "We should lock her away for the next two years. She shouldn't be speaking of such things."

Victoria hid her smile, knowing her youngest sister's propensity for drama. To change the subject, she asked, "How many of the unmentionables did we sell?"

Juliette reached inside her reticule and pulled out a folded piece of paper. "Our mother has the bundle of fabric that Worthingstone saved from the fire. With the help of the crofters, we finished most of the orders. Although Mother still thinks they were sewing gowns," she noted. "I've tallied up the amounts here. Sixteen corsets, fourteen chemises, and we have orders for thirty more."

"And the money?" Victoria couldn't help asking. Though she didn't need it anymore, she was curious about their profit. "Did you earn very much?"

Juliette smiled and passed her the paper. "More than enough. Over a thousand pounds."

Victoria sank into a chair, her heart pounding. Her own stays felt so tight, she couldn't catch her breath. It was more money that she'd ever expected to see. "A thousand? But it can't be."

"It can, and it is." Juliette sat across from her. "Mr. Sinclair escorted us back to Aunt Charlotte's, and he delivered the garments to Madame Benedict's shop. He sold all of them."

"This will change the crofters' lives," Victoria said. "They won't have to struggle so much to survive." She imagined the joy on the women's faces when Mr. Sinclair delivered their share of the profits.

"It can't continue," Margaret admitted. "If anyone found out we are behind it, Father would be humiliated. Not to mention what all of society would think of us. You might be married, Victoria, but the rest of us aren't. The men would believe we're harboring sordid thoughts." She sat down, her back ramrod straight. "It's not at all appropriate, and it's a bad influence upon Amelia. We should cease this immediately."

"Does the duke know?" Juliette asked quietly.

Victoria nodded. "He knew about it before Christmas. But he doesn't want me to sew anymore."

"He's right. Duchesses do not sew," Margaret agreed. "They embroider. And even then, not very often."

Her sister's insistence on propriety was grating upon Victoria's patience. "If I want to sew, then I will. What I do in the privacy of my room is no one's concern."

"I'm only trying to help," Margaret said. "You should be aware of your social position."

Amelia sent her a sly look. "Don't believe her at all, Victoria. She may try to be proper, but she's wondering about what goes on during a wedding night, as much as the rest of us. Was it as exciting as I think it would be? Did he tear off your unmentionables?"

Victoria gaped, and Margaret put up a hand in protest. "She is *not* going to share such details with you."

"No, she'll only share them with the pair of you, later." Amelia sighed with dismay. "It's so unfair."

"I, for one, believe that Victoria's wedding night can remain her own private information," Juliette said. She took back the slip of paper and asked, "Will you send any new designs back to Scotland? At the very least, the crofters' wives can sew them for you."

Grateful for her sister's intervention, Victoria replied, "I have a few sketches. But I'll need to make the patterns for the women. Did the families return to Eiloch Hill, as the duke promised?"

"Yes. Dr. Fraser sent a letter that they are building their homes. The old ones were burned, so they have to start anew." A blush came over Juliette's face at the mention of Dr. Fraser. Whatever disagreement they'd had before seemed to have dissipated.

While her sister continued describing the duke's efforts to help them reconstruct their home in Ballaloch, Victoria retrieved the sketches she'd done. These were more modest undergarments, based upon comfort rather than seduction. She showed the sketches to Margaret, who approved of them wholeheartedly. But Juliette shook her head. "These don't sell as well, I'm afraid. They may be beautiful, but the women want more revealing unmentionables."

Victoria's face turned crimson, for she knew exactly what they wanted. "We should still make a few garments that are meant for younger women." She didn't want to dwell upon the material that reminded her of the way her husband had touched her. He'd enjoyed the sheer fabric, and the memory of his wicked mouth sent a secret flare through her.

She wanted him to share her bed tonight, despite the way he'd avoided her these past few days. Every moment leading up to their joining had been decadent, her body reacting strongly to his touch. Now that he'd withdrawn from her, it had only reignited her interest in him. As if he were forbidden.

"It's getting late," Margaret said, reaching for her bonnet. "We should return, for Aunt Charlotte will be expecting us."

While her sisters donned their gloves and bonnets, Victoria rang for a footman and gave orders for a brougham to be brought for them. Each of her sisters hugged her in farewell, but it was Margaret who lingered a moment.

"You look pale, Toria," she murmured, using their pet name for her. "Are you feeling all right?" She lowered her voice to a whisper and asked, "Has the duke been kind to you?"

"Yes, very." She tried to muster a smile, but she felt the shadow of apprehension. In the past few days, she had done nothing at all to prepare for Aunt Charlotte's ball, nor had she sent word to Melanie for help in etiquette. Right now, she felt as if she were teetering on the brink of her decision, but fear held her back.

"I understand Aunt Charlotte is hosting a soiree," she said, trying to brighten her tone.

Margaret smiled. "Yes. She also has arranged to present Juliette and me at court. His Grace has made his support known, and already we've begun fittings for our court dresses." Her eyes sparkled with excitement. "You must tell him how grateful we are."

"I will," Victoria promised.

"We'll come the next morning, after the ball, and tell you all about it," Margaret promised, squeezing her hands.

Not once did her sister ask if Victoria would be at the soiree. The idea had never entered Margaret's mind, and it chafed to realize it. Her own sisters were so accustomed to her absence, they would be shocked if she were to attend.

"We'll come pay another call soon," Margaret promised.

After her sister departed, Victoria stood staring at the piles of fabric all over the room. These represented her work, her life.

No one believed her capable of leaving this house, of becoming a duchess. Even though Jonathan had wed her with the intention of getting an heir, he, too, expected her to remain a recluse. All of them wanted to make excuses for her, instead of helping her to change.

She didn't like it.

Yes, she was afraid. Yes, she knew others would speak unkindly of her if she tried to go. But was she supposed to remain behind closed doors for the rest of her life?

I don't want to, she realized. She was weary of secluding herself. Worse, she recognized that her husband would have to attend events like this one, whether he wanted to or not. She didn't want to be left behind, for it wasn't right.

Before she lost her courage, she walked over to the writing desk, pushing aside the pile of silk. Seizing a pen, she dipped it in the inkwell and began to write to Lady Rumford.

If she was to attend her aunt's ball in the next few days, she would need every last piece of advice the woman could offer.

Once she had sealed up the letter, she walked downstairs and gave it to a footman to deliver. Slowly, she walked to the back of the house, toward the door that led outside to the garden.

With each step forward, her hands shook, but she managed to touch the knob, opening it. Outside, it was raining, the droplets spattering against the stone fountain. The walled garden held no blooms of spring, for it was too early. But she forced herself to place one foot in front of the other, steeling herself against the rain.

The wetness washed over her hair and cheeks, sliding down to dampen her skin. One step. Then another. She raised her face upward, forcing herself to welcome the rain. To accept the coldness and recognize it for what it was—the freedom she'd been too afraid to seize.

She rested her palms upon the stone fountain, never minding that her knees were shaking and she should have brought a pelisse to wear over her gown.

I will do this, she vowed. She would force herself to walk outside each day and spend more and more time in the garden until she defeated the enemy of her fear.

When she glanced behind her at the house, she saw her husband standing at an upstairs window, silently watching.

Victoria stared down at her dinner plate, her stomach in so many knots, it might as well have knitted itself into a scarf. "Am I doing the right thing?"

"Of *course* you are," Lady Rumford said. The matron stood, waiting for Victoria to join her. "Now we must see to your attire. Mary has prepared your gown, and we'll make you so beautiful, London will be agog at its newest duchess."

Victoria followed Melanie above stairs, feeling wretched that she'd ever agreed to this. Although Lady Rumford had drilled every etiquette lesson possible into her brain, she couldn't remember all of them.

But it's Aunt Charlotte's ball, she reminded herself. It was family, and . . . likely it wouldn't be so bad. Her aunt would smooth over any mistakes she made.

Over the next hour, Mary and Lady Rumford dressed her in a short-sleeved emerald gown of India muslin, trimmed with gold. It draped in folds over her shoulders and down her back, leading to a demi-train. White gloves encased her arms, and she wore a lace tippet around her shoulders. The diamond and pearl necklace hung at her throat, and the largest teardrop pearl nestled just above the square neckline. Mary had threaded green ribbon into her hair, and she'd parted Victoria's hair in the center, snipping curls on either side of her forehead in the latest fashion.

"You look exquisite." Lady Rumford sighed. "And your late entrance will be so dramatic."

"I'm scared," she confessed. "I've never done anything like this before." Though she'd kept the promise to herself, spending more and more time in the garden, attending this ball was something else entirely.

"I shall accompany you," Lady Rumford promised. "I've known Charlotte for years, and I, too, was invited to this soiree."

"What about the duke?" she ventured. Her husband had not agreed to go with her, and she questioned the wisdom of going alone. Though he would not deny her the right to see her sisters, she suspected he would not attend either.

"His Grace has not attended any public gatherings since my sister—" Lady Rumford took a breath and amended, "That is, he hasn't attended anything in a long time."

Victoria recalled the pile of unanswered invitations and Jonathan's insistence that they would not go to any balls or assemblies. "Will he go with us tonight, do you think?"

Lady Rumford's expression turned sympathetic. "It doesn't matter, Your Grace. We will go together, and enjoy ourselves whether he does or not."

Victoria wanted to believe it, but she had no way of knowing how the evening would go. Although she'd attended parties with her parents as a young girl, she'd never worn a dress as beautiful as this one, nor diamonds. She managed a weak smile as Mary helped her into her pelisse. "Thank you for helping me prepare for this."

"It was no trouble." Lady Rumford smiled. "I hope you have a wonderful time. But regardless, I trust you will succeed magnificently."

Her confidence was shaky, and as she accompanied Lady Rumford to the front door, fear struck hard. For a moment, she stood on the stairs of the house, the terror of the past sinking into her veins.

You can't control your fear, Jonathan had said. *But you can control how you respond to it.*

"Are you all right?" Melanie asked, her face concerned.

Victoria took a deep breath, forcing herself to walk outside the door, toward the waiting carriage. She wouldn't allow herself to falter or run away. Not when she'd come this far. Each step was like climbing a steep mountain, but when at last she was inside the landau, she questioned whether this was a good idea.

Lady Rumford filled the silence with conversation, reminding Victoria of how she would be announced, of the various rules of introduction, and how she was to remain aloof. Rather like a princess.

The clenching in her stomach spread a chill throughout her body, the icy nerves possessing her. Beneath her skirts, her knees were trembling, and God in heaven, why had she ever thought she could do this? She wasn't at all ready.

"Your sisters will be glad to see you," Lady Rumford reminded her kindly. The matron reached out and took her hand. "And I know your mother would be proud of you."

They were the words she'd needed to hear. She took a deep breath, realizing that this night was not about proving anything to Jonathan. Nor to anyone else. It was about seizing control of her own doubts, stifling the insecurities that held her back.

It was for herself.

And though her knees were shaking beneath the India muslin gown, as she trudged up the stairs, she promised herself that she would succeed in this. Somehow.

🏃

"Why, Victoria, what a wonderful surprise." Her aunt Charlotte's face broke into a smile as she came into the hall to greet them. "Forgive me. I meant *Your Grace*." She smiled and embraced her. Victoria wondered if Aunt Charlotte could sense the rapid pounding of her heart. "I'm so glad you decided to attend."

Her anxieties trebled, and she gripped her hands together, wondering if Jonathan would come. He'd gone out earlier this evening, and she wasn't certain if he had any intention of accompanying her.

"And Lady Rumford, so good to see you." Charlotte welcomed the older matron while the footman closed the door behind them, taking their pelisses.

The two older women exchanged pleasantries, and Charlotte explained, "The dancing has begun, if you'd like to join us."

"Go on without me," Victoria directed Lady Rumford. "I would like to speak to my aunt for a moment."

When they were alone, Charlotte eyed her with curiosity. "I haven't seen you since you were seventeen," she remarked. "You've grown into a lovely young woman."

Victoria murmured her thanks. Though she desperately wanted to be a part of the family gathering, she needed a moment to collect herself before facing them. "It-It's been a long time since I've attended a soiree, Aunt. Might I watch from the doorway for a short while? Just to remember what it's like, before I go in?"

Understanding came over Charlotte's face. "Of course you may. Your sisters will be so pleased to see you." She guided her toward the large drawing room, where the sound of a string quartet filled the air with music. There was conversation and light laughter, and her aunt brought her to the edge of the doorway. "I'll wait with you here, for as long as you like. And when you're ready, I'll have the footman announce you."

"If you please," she begged, "I'd rather not be announced. And you mustn't neglect your guests on my behalf." She preferred to join in quietly, with no one staring at her. Though she knew she was supposed to allow her aunt to introduce her to the other guests, shyness held her back.

Charlotte hesitated. "You shouldn't be standing out here alone, my dear. It's not proper."

Victoria sent her aunt a rueful smile and rested her back against the wall. "I'll only be a moment, I promise."

But instead of leaving her behind, Charlotte moved beside her and offered a gloved hand. "I know your mother could not be here tonight, so I'll stand in for my sister." She squeezed Victoria's hand. "All of this is more than you are used to, I know."

"I feel as if everyone will stare at me, seeing only my faults."

Charlotte continued to hold her hand. "I won't allow anyone to speak a word against you. And I think His Grace would be proud of you."

"Is he here?" she asked, hoping that her husband had arrived.

But her aunt only shook her head. "None of us expected him to come." With a wry smile, she added, "He rarely does."

The observation bothered her, and now Victoria was having second thoughts about being here. She took a deep breath, risking a glance inside at the dozens of people. "Perhaps I shouldn't have come, if he won't be here."

Her aunt chose her words carefully. "If you don't mind my asking, why did you?"

The question startled her, and Victoria wasn't certain how to answer. She'd wanted to change herself, to stop hiding away. But there was another reason, one easier to speak of to her aunt. "For my sisters."

It was partly the truth, but not all. She'd also wanted to prove to her husband that she could conquer her fears. Because of him, she'd had a reason to venture past the closed doors of her life. And if she ever wanted them to have a true marriage, she needed to meet him halfway. "I also came for my husband, the duke."

"Being a duchess isn't only about wearing expensive gowns and hosting parties," Charlotte continued. "It's about loving your husband enough to get through them. Heaven knows, my husband Nelson would rather be flayed alive than attend all the balls he's escorted me to. But he knows I enjoy dancing, and he endures it for my sake."

Her aunt reached out and touched Victoria's cheek. "Whether or not His Grace decides to come, try to enjoy yourself. Don't be afraid of what others will think. Simply be here for Margaret and Juliette."

"I wish I weren't so terrified of what's beyond that door," she confessed.

"There is no woman in that ballroom better than you, my dear." Charlotte stood from the stairs and reached out her hand. "Come, now."

"Go in without me," Victoria urged. "I'll follow in a moment, I promise."

Her aunt gave her hand a squeeze and smiled in acknowledgment. "If you don't, I'll come back to fetch you."

Victoria peered into the room, watching the colorful gowns swirl as the men and women began an English country dance. Her sister Margaret appeared delighted to be among the women, and from her skill in dancing, it was clear that she had practiced the steps. Juliette faltered somewhat, and Amelia stood against one wall with another matron, as if wishing she could join in.

One step, then another.

Victoria entered the room, but her attempt to remain unnoticed utterly failed. The moment she stepped inside, several heads turned. She searched the room for her sisters, but as she made her way toward them, the women stared at her, murmuring behind their fans.

Blood rushed to her face, and she focused her attention on the floor. Fainting would do her no good. She had to get through this, no matter how uncomfortable she was.

It took endless minutes to make her way across the room. She was conscious of her appearance, but she raised her chin and tried to behave as if she belonged here. Aunt Charlotte joined her and began introducing her to the guests. Once the people learned who she was, she heard the word *Duchess* spread across the room like a wildfire.

"Your Grace, I was just telling my friends all about your elopement with Worthingstone. It was terribly romantic, was it not?"

Victoria managed a nod and a forced smile, but other women started to approach for an introduction. Her sisters had caught sight of her, and the look of joy on Amelia's face gave Victoria a renewed strength. She would *not* embarrass herself or her husband. A smile and proper manners were all she needed to survive this night.

She spoke to each of the people, though she doubted if she would remember any of their names in an hour. After a few more introductions, she saw a woman staring at her. Though she did not approach Victoria, her eyes held a shadow of anger. Without looking away, the woman murmured to the person beside her, and it was clear that Victoria was the subject of their conversation.

She squared her shoulders, refusing to let it bother her. Charlotte continued to bring her closer to Margaret and Juliette, but before she could reach her sisters, a hand came down on her shoulder.

"Your Grace," came her husband's voice. When she turned and saw Jonathan, the sight of him stole her breath. His black tailcoat outlined his tall form, the snowy white cravat bringing her attention to his face. He wore dark breeches and his gaze fastened upon her as if she weren't quite real.

"You were not at home when I returned."

"No. I needed to be here for my sisters."

He took her hand in his and led her away from the others, not caring that it might seem rude. "Are you all right?"

"I can't quite breathe," she admitted. "I never thought I would make it this far."

He moved to stand beside her. "You're beautiful, Duchess." She felt the warmth of his hand upon the clasp of her necklace, before his palm slid down her back. "It's rather like walking outside for the first time, isn't it?"

She nodded. "I'm afraid of what they think of me," she admitted. "But I wanted to be here."

His hand tightened upon her shoulder. "They won't dare to say a word." His voice grew soft, almost menacing in tone. "My fortune is ten times that of nearly everyone in this room. If they speak out against you, they will regret doing so."

She tilted her head to face him. "Money won't change the way people think or feel, Your Grace."

"You're wrong." He nodded toward the crowd. "It's all they care about." His voice grew hollow when he admitted, "Even you wouldn't have married me, were it not for my ability to support the crofters."

The bitterness in his tone shocked her, for she'd never realized how he'd come to believe that. It wasn't at all true and never had been. She reached out to take his hand, choosing her words carefully.

"That isn't true. I was afraid to marry you." All her life she'd wanted to meet someone like him, but she'd never believed it would happen. She tightened her hold upon his hand.

"Money is all that matters. It's power, Victoria. And without it, no one cares who you are."

❧

Jonathan led his wife toward her sisters, knowing the young women would help put Victoria at ease. He still couldn't believe she had left the house. Gone was the quiet, reticent woman who'd never ventured out of her room. In her place was a stunning creature, clad in an emerald gown, her hair curled and bedecked with matching green ribbon. She was easily the most beautiful woman there, and her shyness only added to her mysterious allure.

Victoria held his hand tightly, and Jonathan led her to stand on the far side of the drawing room. He sensed her panic building, and he demanded, "Breathe, Victoria. It's going to be all right. We'll pay our respects and then go."

She took a breath and eyed him. "Promise you won't ask me to dance." The terror in her face was the same he'd seen when she'd approached the front door.

"Pretend you're walking with me outside in the snow," he said. "There's no one here but me."

"That isn't helping," she insisted. But he squeezed her hand and leaned in against her ear.

"I'm imagining what color your unmentionables are, at this moment. And whether or not you'll let me take them off of you when we get home."

Her face turned scarlet, but she was saved from a response when he brought her to her sisters. Seeing Amelia and Juliette brightened his wife's face. As they chattered, her youngest sister exclaiming her excitement, relief transformed Victoria's expression. She warmed at the sight of them, and there was love in her eyes.

When she turned to him, she sent him a quiet smile of thanks. The smile caught him without warning, and in her gray eyes, he caught a glimpse of warmth. As if she were glad to have him at her side. He sent her a nod, but beyond all else, he wanted her to feel safe with him. To know that he would protect her from anyone who might make her uncomfortable.

From the outskirts of the room, he was distracted by the other guests. Most were staring at Victoria with a blend of curiosity and some of the ladies eyed her with resentment. He knew several of the matrons had wanted their daughters to wed him, but he'd not expected them to view Victoria with such open hostility.

He met their gossiping whispers with his own dark stare. *Offend her, and you offend me.*

To their credit, most retreated to their own devices, some joining in the next dance set.

It was then that he spied Lady Meredith Baldwin approaching. His former fiancée ventured a quiet smile, but his suspicions sharpened. For a woman who had abandoned him when she'd believed him penniless, he wanted little to do with her.

"Your Grace," Lady Meredith greeted him. "I was quite surprised to hear of your marriage." She dropped into a curtsy before turning toward Victoria. "This must be your new duchess."

Though her words were courteous, he didn't miss the ice beneath them. Her gaze centered upon the diamond and pearl necklace around Victoria's throat as if she envied it. It was clear that she'd never cared about him a whit. She had wanted control of his fortune, a fortune she'd mistakenly believed was lost. Jonathan took Victoria's hand, sensing that Lady Meredith intended to cause trouble.

His wife murmured a polite greeting, but her face held a strain, almost as if she knew who the young woman was. Lady Meredith added, "It must be so different for you, having lived in Scotland for so long. London must be positively overwhelming."

"We lived in London when I was a girl," Victoria responded. "It's quite the way I remember it."

Jonathan resisted a smile. Good. She'd recognized the woman's intent and parried it with her own response.

"As the daughter of a baron, I'm certain you must be feeling intimidated in your new station," Lady Meredith continued. "Especially enduring the scandal of what happened to His Grace's parents. Everyone here is still talking about it." With a trill of false laughter, she added, "Perhaps your house is haunted by their ghosts, Your Grace."

Jonathan made no effort to hide his anger. "You've overstepped your bounds, Lady Meredith."

The young woman paid him no heed. In her eyes, he saw the desire for vengeance, and she saw no reason to sheathe her claws.

"I'm merely trying to warn Her Grace that it will take some time for people to stop talking of the scandal. She should be prepared for it."

Victoria studied the woman and remarked, "I would think that after a year, most *polite* ladies would no longer speak of something that causes pain to others."

Lady Meredith's expression hardened. To Victoria she said, "I was betrothed to Worthingstone once." Her mouth curved in a dark smile. "After what happened to his family, I suppose it's best that our engagement ended. Who knows if that sort of thing passes down from father to son?"

A smug look spread over her face as she left. Jonathan took Victoria's arm and guided her away. "We're leaving."

"She's upset you." Victoria stopped walking, her face concerned. "I've not seen you this way before."

Meredith's barb, suggesting that he was just like his father, had hit too close to his darker fears. The rage he'd felt toward her was an inhuman anger, barely held in check.

Jonathan gathered his control, not letting his wife glimpse any emotion at all. "I don't want to speak of it." His tone was harsher than he'd intended, but Victoria thankfully didn't ask again. Instead, she fell silent and watched the women dancing. As time passed, he sensed her growing discomfort, but he'd fought hard to silence the talk over his mother's death. He wasn't about to enlighten her on things best forgotten.

His aunt Melanie interrupted at that moment and smiled at Victoria, greeting them both. "Have you told your wife how well she looks this evening, Worthingstone?"

He bowed to his aunt and nodded. "Of course."

To Victoria, the older woman asked, "Forgive me, Your Grace, but I should like to steal my nephew away for a moment, if that would be all right?"

Jonathan started to protest, but Melanie wasn't at all listening. "She'll be just fine, won't you, Your Grace?" She took both of his hands in hers, adding, "There, now, you see? Her sister Margaret is coming to speak with her."

Before Jonathan realized what she was about, his aunt had

guided him into the next dancing set. "My leg isn't fully healed," he pointed out, not wanting to leave Victoria.

"I'm twice your age," she countered. "I think you can survive one dance with your aunt. Your wife is safe with her sister; you needn't worry."

He took his place across from her in the line, and Melanie sent him a discerning smile. "Her Grace is lovely, isn't she? Everyone is talking about her and wondering how you came to marry her. But she's so terribly shy."

Jonathan pressed his palm against his aunt's as they turned in the opposite direction, walking side by side. "She's been very isolated for the past few years."

"But she came here for *you*," the older woman insisted. "Because she wanted to be your duchess."

He took her hand in the promenade, not really believing that was the reason. But Melanie pressed further, "Sometimes, Worthingstone, you can be quite blind. That young woman cares a great deal for you."

"I've provided well for her. Neither she nor her family will want for anything." And within another few days, he would ensure their safety in Scotland.

"She doesn't want your money, my dear boy. And I suspect you know that."

He did. But neither did he want Victoria to look upon him with revulsion when she learned of his past. Nor did he ever want her to be afraid. He wanted to keep her shielded in his house where no one could bother her.

"She has a soft heart," Melanie told him. "And if you love her, you'll—"

"She didn't marry me for love, Aunt." Victoria had sacrificed herself on the marriage altar because he'd forced her into it.

"Whether or not she did, you have only to look upon her face to see her feelings. And if you're wise, you'll do everything in your power to protect them."

The dance ended, and Jonathan bowed, taking his leave from her. He searched the room for a glimpse of Victoria.

She stood beside the door, waiting.

⚜

Jonathan stared into the embers of the fire, hours after they'd left the soiree together. Victoria had held her own as the duchess. Her quiet nature had made her appear timid to the others, but she had done nothing at all to warrant their disapproval.

He loosened his cravat and rested his head against one hand. Inside, his frustration was brewing. He should have known that the stories surrounding his parents' death would not be silenced, even after more than a year.

After a quiet knock, the door to his room opened, and he saw his wife still wearing the emerald gown. "I thought you had gone to bed already."

"Not yet." Crossing the room, she came to stand before him. He could see from her posture that she was tired, but he didn't know why she hadn't called her maid to help her get undressed.

"Do you want me to ring for Mary?" he asked.

She shook her head and took his hands in hers. For a moment, she stood before him, as if trying to decide whether or not to stay.

"Will you tell me what happened to your parents?" she asked at last.

"No." He had no desire to see disgust in her eyes, not when he could shelter her from it. "They died, and that's all I'll say."

She came to stand behind his chair, her hands resting upon his shoulders. "It hurts you still."

"Yes." He stared into the burning coals, feeling as if the burden of the past year still weighed upon him. He'd journeyed from estate to estate, consoling his grief by escaping from his responsibilities. And the last thing he wanted was for his wife to look upon him with pity.

Her hands moved to his neck, caressing his skin. Every part of him went rigid as she bent and touched her mouth to his throat.

"I don't want your pity," he said, jerking away from her.

Victoria stared at him as if he'd struck her, and he took a breath to calm the edge within him. She didn't understand how the lightest touch weakened his control. He didn't trust himself with her right now. After the last time he'd hurt her, he wasn't about to frighten her again.

"I'm sorry," she whispered. "I'll go."

But that made him feel like even more of a bastard. She'd come here to talk with him, and his bad temper wasn't making it any easier.

"No, you don't have to. I'm not angry with you," he said. Her hand stilled upon the doorknob and she returned to stand before him.

"Will you help me?" she asked, turning her back to expose the fastenings of her gown. She began pulling pins from her hair, and the honey length slid over one shoulder, entrancing him.

Jonathan unfastened the back of the gown before she raised her arms for him to lift it off. Her chemise was a pure, virginal white . . . but the corset was a deep green silk. It lifted her small breasts up, giving him a glimpse of curves. One of her creations, he guessed.

"Why did you come to my room, Victoria?" he asked. If she'd only wanted to talk, he was a dead man.

In answer, she guided his hands to the laces of her corset. "Because I wanted you."

Jonathan didn't trust himself not to take her this very moment, for as soon as he touched her, he suspected he would lose sight of everything.

"Are you sure?" he murmured, his hands clenched at his sides.

Her gray eyes regarded his with a simple trust. "You taught me not to be afraid in Scotland. I don't want to be afraid of sharing your bed, either."

He freed the laces, pushing the loathsome corset and the chemise away until she stood before him naked from the waist up. Her breasts were soft, tempting him to lean in and take her nipples into his mouth.

He grazed his knuckles across her breasts, watching the nipples tighten. She let out a low breath, then guided both of his hands to cup her flesh.

Chapter Eighteen

NEVER BEFORE had her heart beat this rapidly. Victoria stood in front of Jonathan, his hands tracing the outline of her small breasts. In the firelight, his face revealed tension, as if he were struggling to keep control.

She did care about this man. He'd given her the priceless gift of freedom, and although his world was foreign to her, she was glad she'd broken out of her fear.

For a time, she simply stood with her hands upon his shoulders, letting him touch her however he wanted to.

"You remind me of my mother," he said quietly. "She was small, like you. A softhearted woman who never would have hurt anyone in her life."

He removed his waistcoat and cravat, before lifting his shirt away. Then he drew her to stand between his legs, moving her hands to his heart. Beneath her fingertips, she felt his rapid pulse.

"And your father?" she asked.

"He was the most evil bastard I've ever known. He didn't deserve a woman like my mother."

She drew her hands over his chest, caressing his skin. His pain ran deep, mingled with guilt.

"It's my fault she's dead," he confessed, his gaze empty. Victoria moved to sit on his knee and pulled him into an embrace. His head rested beneath her chin, his arms around her bare skin. "She told me to go away, not to interfere, for it would make him even more angry."

His muscles were taut with tension, his mouth heated against her throat. The warmth of his body against hers was a comfort she hadn't expected. And it was as if she were granting him absolution for his sins.

"He imagined all sorts of crimes against her, believing she had committed adultery."

Victoria stroked his hair, letting him speak. Even though she didn't truly want to hear it, she knew that he needed to let it out.

He drew back, his eyes gleaming with pain. "He used to beat her sometimes. She stopped going to parties and balls because others would have seen the bruises and scars. I remember watching her cry when I was eight years old and hating myself because I wasn't strong enough to stop him."

"And when you were older?" she asked.

"I went after him one night. I warned him never to touch her again, and I broke a few of his ribs." His expression turned bitter. "He did the same to my mother the next day. I realized that the only way to keep her safe was to take her away, somewhere he wouldn't find her.

"I gained the property in Scotland from the Earl of Strathland when he owed me a gambling debt. It was so isolated, I hoped she would leave him. But she swore she'd never abandon my father, that he loved her." A grim expression settled over his face. "How could she love a man who treated her like that?"

Victoria touched his cheek, and he captured her hand with his. "She's dead now, because of him." The fierce hatred spilled forth, and a horrifying thought occurred to her, one she'd never before considered.

"Did you kill your father?" she whispered.

His features hardened, and he stared into her eyes. "I wanted to. Does that shock you?"

She shook her head, letting out a slow breath. She hadn't believed he could do such a thing, but then, she understood his protective nature.

Jonathan released her, his gaze fixed upon the wall. "He lost his temper one night. The servants told me he struck her so hard, she fell down the stairs and broke her neck. After my father killed her, he put a pistol to his head and pulled the trigger."

The hollow timbre of his voice held a weariness of a man who didn't want to relive such a moment. She understood the burden he'd carried within him, and the pain of losing someone he loved so much. Her heart was filled with the need to make him whole again, to heal his grief.

"And you locked yourself away from the world."

He nodded. "I didn't want to see or speak to anyone. I heard the whispers, and I wanted to escape it all."

"It's not your fault," she whispered. "You tried to save her."

"It is. I should have taken her from him, no matter how much she protested. If I had, she'd still be alive."

"It's not your fault," she repeated. "You gave her the choice, and she refused." He needed to hear it, to overcome the guilt he carried.

Victoria took his face between her hands and pulled him down into a kiss. At the first touch of her mouth upon his, he grew impatient, forcing her to open. When she did, his tongue slid inside, sending a shock of sensation that echoed between her legs. His hands were upon her everywhere, spinning her own feelings into a storm of sensation and need.

"Jonathan," she whispered, holding him close as he swept her up and brought her to the bed.

He stripped off the remainder of her clothing, before removing his own. At the sight of his naked body, she thought of the first time he'd tried to make love to her. Inside, she felt tremulous, her body rousing to his touch.

"I left London afterward because I didn't want to face anyone for a time." He pressed her against the cool sheets, touching her hair as he moved her to her side. "I wanted to forget how they died."

"It will get easier. In time," she murmured, reaching out to touch his chest. He captured her hand and held it there, and he covered her legs with one thigh.

He stretched over her, his body pressing against hers. She could feel the thickness of his arousal upon her stomach, and she reached out to touch it, cupping him in her palm. He inhaled sharply as she caressed his length, her thumb touching the blunt head of him. A bead of moisture coated her thumb, and he pinned her wrists to the bed. "No, Victoria. Not yet."

He held her prisoner while his mouth began a slow descent over her body, nudging her legs apart with his knee. She was shocked to feel his shaft sliding against her folds, and her body grew wet. When he drew his tongue over her nipple, she struggled against his hands. Below her waist, she strained against him and was rewarded when he slowly drew his erection against her intimate flesh.

He swirled his tongue across one breast while he guided her hand to the other nipple. "Touch yourself," he ordered.

Embarrassment flooded through her, and she protested, "I've never—"

"Do it," came his command. "You know what you like to feel. I want to watch you."

Her cheeks burned, but when she touched her own erect nipple, a burgeoning sensation pressed downward, creating an answering ache within her swollen folds. Jonathan surged against her, and she felt herself grow even more aroused.

Emboldened by the forbidden nature of touching herself, she

rolled the nipple between her fingertips. Jonathan moved her hand and licked at the delicate flesh, replacing her fingers there until the arousal grew more intense. She closed her eyes, and he guided her other hand to the other breast, murmuring words of encouragement as she touched herself. Both nipples were wet from his mouth, and she couldn't stop her shuddering breath, a moan catching in her throat. There was a thrumming within her skin, a rise to the call he'd evoked.

His mouth moved lower, his hands spreading apart her legs. When she felt his breath against the warmth of her womanhood, she arched her back in instinctive response. His fingers found her wet, and he rubbed the hooded flesh that made her grow even more swollen. While his fingers moved upon her, she felt the warmth of his tongue licking her intimately. It was soft and wet, as if he were afraid of hurting her.

The light sensation became a slow torture as he intensified the pressure, building it higher. She needed him inside her, needed his touch to push her over the edge.

Her breath came in gasps, and his tongue drew its own rhythm over her body. She didn't want this slow burn, not when it was driving her past the brink of sanity.

Tell him what you want, her mind ordered, though she faltered at the fear of what he would think of her. The longer he tormented her, the more frantic her body became.

"Please, I need—" Her words broke off, as she reached for his face. He stopped instantly, brushing a kiss against her thigh.

"What do you need?"

She tried to guide him higher, and he balanced his weight upon his forearms, his face still resting against her stomach. There was wariness in his eyes, and she had no idea how to ask for what she wanted.

"Show me." His voice was gruff, and she took his hand and guided it between her legs. He found the rhythm immediately, and she arched against him, her body throbbing as she grew closer to release. Without knowing why, she began to touch her own breasts, and it only intensified the movement of his hand.

The aching unfolded inside her as he kept up the rhythmic stroking. She felt herself reaching harder, needing more.

"Take it, Victoria," he breathed against her skin. "Let me give this to you."

The fiery release struck her in a shuddering eruption, and she couldn't stop the cry that she released. Jonathan covered her mouth with his, and guided himself to her slick center.

When he hesitated, she eased herself against him, pulling his hips forward. His rigid erection slid within her wetness with a friction that made her gasp. Although it took a moment for her body to adjust, there was no pain this time.

He remained inside her, watching. "Are you all right?"

She nodded, opening her eyes. "Don't stop."

This time, he moved slowly. He withdrew and penetrated again, making her gasp at the wave of pleasure that struck. "Again?"

"Again." The rhythm of his thrusts was both a surrender and a conquest. She took him into her body, lifting her knees to grant him deeper access. And when she kissed him hard, sliding her tongue into his mouth, he let go of his control.

He took her mouth like a ruthless warrior, echoing the plunge of his body with his tongue. She felt the barriers crack apart as he joined with her, his pace relentless. Another fist of pleasure struck her hard, and she moaned when he pumped inside her. He never ceased his tempo, pressing harder, and her hands came up between them, helpless to do anything except drown in the fierce pleasure that filled every part of her body.

Jonathan withdrew and changed her position. He pulled her to the edge of the bed, rolling her onto her stomach. She lay upon the sheets, her backside facing him, while her legs touched the carpet. His hands came up beneath her pelvis, cantilevering her hips up until he plunged inside her wet depths. Having him enter her from the new position was staggering, and his hands filled with her breasts as he quickened his pace. Her fists dug into the covers as he took her roughly, his hot length penetrating over and over.

Victoria couldn't stop the cry that released from her as he took his pleasure, and when at last he was spent inside her, she shuddered with aftershocks.

She had never experienced such madness in all her life. Her body was deliciously used, and he pulled her to him, his heartbeat pulsing fast as he lay atop her. Without speaking, she sensed the thoughts that tormented him. Softly, she kissed his mouth, touching his hair.

It's not your fault.

His body was tense, his head lowered. But he wouldn't look at her, nor would he speak.

✿

Jonathan left in the middle of the night. He dressed quietly and walked downstairs, the darkness encompassing his mood. He felt exposed by the way Victoria made him feel. Touching her had become an addiction, and he doubted if he'd ever be able to stop.

With every moment he spent at her side, he felt his control slipping away. The carnal needs had superseded his sense of reason, and he was afraid of what was happening to him. Victoria was ripping apart his expectations, weakening his willpower.

He stood by the window of the library, staring out into the midnight darkness. He'd wanted his marriage with Victoria to be based upon mutual respect and his ability to provide for her. But instead, his mind was consumed with images of this night, of being so close to her, their bodies were merged into one. Her yielding flesh had accepted his, and her shudders of ecstasy haunted him with the desire to return to her at this moment. He wanted to spend his nights watching her arch her back and sigh with pleasure.

He wanted to love her. And he wanted her to love him back. But when he was with Victoria, he lost command of himself. His lovemaking tonight had held a violent edge, a possessive need that he didn't understand. The feelings he held for his wife were too strong, too unpredictable.

He lit a taper and sat at his desk. His footman had brought the post earlier, and he'd ignored most of it. But when he eyed it again, he saw a letter from the Earl of Strathland. In it, the man denied any involvement in the fire, and he promised to question the crofters to learn who was responsible and sentence the guilty parties.

It wasn't Strathland's place to do so. The clans had been invited to lease the land at Eiloch Hill, and the earl had no authority there. If he brought his factor there, he was blatantly trespassing. And Victoria's parents would be caught in the middle of it.

The last time he'd ignored danger, his family had died. And though he didn't want to leave his wife, he owed it to her to protect her mother.

And that meant returning to Scotland.

Colonel Henry Andrews, Baron Lanfordshire, trudged through the snow and stared at the half-built house before him. He'd traveled hundreds of miles to come home, hoping for a glimpse of his wife and daughters. Instead, it appeared that a fire had ravaged the structure.

Cold fear iced through him at the thought of his family suffering. He hastened his pace, and a slight note of relief eased him when he saw his wife, Beatrice, carrying a pile of charred wood outside one of the doors.

Her blond hair held glints of gray, and she was more slender than he'd ever seen her. But God above, he wished he could run across the yard and take her in his arms. He wanted to hold tightly to the woman who had stood by him all these years, to breathe in the warm scent of her and forget about the harsh memories of war.

But he wasn't a young man of twenty, and he'd sensed a coldness in her letters. He didn't know what she felt for him, if anything. Although he wanted to mend the breach, he'd never been a man who could say the right things at the right moment.

He watched her for a moment, taking in the sight of her profile. Still beautiful, after all these years. He took another step, waiting for her to see him. She turned at the slight sound, and the burned wood in her hands went crashing to the ground. Her hands flew to her mouth in shock, but she didn't move.

Henry waited for some sign that she was glad to see him, but there was nothing except the flush of surprise upon her face. He shuttered his own disappointment and closed the distance between them. Though he wanted to embrace her, his arm was bandaged in a sling.

Would she show some sign of joy that he'd returned? His heart beat faster, waiting for something . . . anything.

"Beatrice," he said, nodding to her. It was the only word he could manage, but it didn't capture any of the words inside him. *It's been so long. I've missed you.*

"Henry." She nodded in return and wiped her hands upon the apron she was wearing. It surprised him to see her dressed almost like a servant. Once, she had prided herself in wearing lovely gowns of all different colors. But despite the serviceable dark blue wool, it didn't diminish her looks. "It's been a long time."

He kept waiting for some sign that she wanted him to embrace her, but she kept her hands at her sides as if she weren't truly glad to see him. "It has" was all he could manage.

Glancing up at the charred roof and the stone walls, he asked, "What happened to our home?"

"Someone set fire to it a few weeks ago." She lifted her chin and nodded at the crofters, who were carrying out the debris from inside. "I wrote to you, but I suppose you never got the letter. We're still in the process of rebuilding."

"And the girls?"

She softened at his mention of them. "They're fine, and all of them are staying in London. Victoria got married a few weeks ago, to the Duke of Worthingstone."

Had his wife told him that Victoria had sprouted wings and flown, he'd not have been more surprised. "A duke? For our Victoria?" Ever since his daughter had been lost, he'd seen her retreat within the four walls, no longer the quietly mischievous girl she'd been. So much had changed.

A genuine smile spread over Beatrice's face. "It was a shock to me, too. I never dreamed she would ever find a husband at all, much less a duke."

He wanted to tell her how good it was to see her smile, that he didn't care anything about the house, so long as his family was safe. But the words wouldn't come, trapped beneath years of his own awkwardness.

"I've missed a great deal, it seems." And though he'd written a handful of letters, there had been little time to write more than a few words. The fighting in Spain had occupied most of his time, and when he'd had a spare moment to write, he'd never known quite what to say.

There was a sheen of brightness in his wife's eyes, and she was holding back tears. "You have, yes." She touched the front door as if she wanted to leave his presence, and the harsh ache of loneliness swelled within him.

"There's a lot of damage inside," she admitted. "I've been living at Eiloch Hill for the past fortnight, but I believe the roof is sound now." She opened the door, continuing to talk about who they believed might have started the fire and how long it would take to restore the rooms and the furnishings.

He didn't hear a word of it. All he could do was stare at his wife, memorizing her features.

"Henry?" she asked, pausing at the doorway to the parlor. "Are you all right? Does your arm pain you?"

He wanted to say so much to her, to ask a thousand questions and somehow make her realize that he did still love her, even after so many years apart. But in the end, his reticence made it impossible to do anything except shake his head. "It's nothing."

He reached out to take her hand, but at the same moment, she turned away to lead him to another part of the house. For a moment, he kept his hand motionless, frozen in midair. But she didn't turn around.

In the end, he lowered his hand, swallowing back the regrets and vowing that he would somehow make things right between them.

"Your Grace." Brandon Carlisle, the Earl of Strathland, entered the drawing room at Eiloch Hill where the Duke of Worthingstone awaited him with his other guests. "Colonel Lord Lanfordshire," he greeted, "and Lady Lanfordshire." He bowed to them in greeting, before sitting across from them.

Though he kept a friendly smile on his face, he knew the purpose for this gathering—to confront him. He didn't delude himself into imagining it was for social reasons.

"I was flattered to receive this invitation," Brandon said, thanking the maid who poured him a cup of tea. "It's kind of you to think of a neighbor."

Lady Lanfordshire's face was strained. "We have some matters to discuss."

"Some of your men tried to question the crofters," the duke began. "But trespassers are not welcome on my property."

"The Scots were my tenants for years. I know them better than anyone, and I thought it best to investigate the fire. You would not want a criminal dwelling among you."

"I will do my own investigation," the duke finished.

Brandon sipped at his tea and changed tactics. "Have you thought about my offer, Lady Lanfordshire?"

At Colonel Lord Lanfordshire's frown, he elaborated. "I've offered to buy your land on several occasions."

"It's not for sale," the Colonel responded.

Brandon had expected that and was ready with his proposal. "I've increased the herds of sheep, and they need more land for grazing. I'm sure you know how much the cost of wool has risen in the past few years. But I've thought of another alternative that might serve as a way of keeping the land within your family."

He set his teacup down, adding, "You have three unmarried daughters. I am widowed, and I could easily provide for any one of them. Your grandchildren could inherit this land, thereby combining our holdings. Both of you could relocate to your house in London or another estate."

From the shocked expression on Lady Lanfordshire's face, she hadn't anticipated the offer. "But the girls—"

"The girls will marry men of their choosing," the Duke of Worthingstone interrupted. "I will sponsor each of them for a Season. They deserve better than to be traded for sheep."

Strathland bit back a laugh. "I was not implying that, not in the least. But I have developed an affection for your younger daughter, Miss Juliette Andrews. Perhaps I could come to London and court her, along with her other suitors. She would have the choice of whether or not to accept me, of course. But it would be a solution for all of us."

"No." The duke's answer was final, and he sent Brandon a look of his own. "I invited you here to be sure you understand my point. The lands at Eiloch Hill and at Ballaloch are not yours. Nor will you send your factor or any of your men to threaten our families or the crofters who have been granted permission to build their homes here."

His autocratic airs irritated Brandon. Though outwardly he inclined his head in silent acquiescence, he wasn't about to abandon his goal to achieve control over the western Highlands.

"Keep to your own lands, and our families can live in peace," Worthingstone said, "or you will not like the financial consequences."

In other words, *Submit to my authority and do not dare to rise against me*, Strathland thought. He understood the duke's point perfectly, but it didn't mean he intended to obey.

Every man had a price. Even Worthingstone.

Chapter Nineteen

Spring 1811

"**Y**OU CANNOT keep refusing invitations," Lady Rumford remarked at luncheon. "Just because the duke is away doesn't mean you shouldn't go out and enjoy yourself. I would be glad to help you, should you desire to try it."

Though Victoria appreciated the offer, the idea wasn't at all appealing. "I accept my aunt Charlotte's invitations, and it's enough for me. But thank you, Lady Rumford."

"I'm certain it pleases Charlotte. And because you've become so mysterious, *everyone* wants an invitation to her parties."

"Which benefits my sisters," Victoria pointed out. "The rest doesn't matter."

"Well, of *course* it matters." Melanie straightened and slid her fork into an oyster. The strong scent made Victoria's stomach wrench, and she swallowed hard. "With your husband gone, it's your duty to be the duchess in his absence. Not to hide away in your rooms."

Victoria couldn't reply, for a wave of nausea passed over her. She hadn't intentionally stayed away, but she'd grown so tired as of late. Though she'd managed to avoid most of the parties, since there were fewer of them in winter, now that it was spring, it was all changing. Already her sisters Margaret and Juliette had been presented at Court and would make their official debut.

But now, she had another reason to remain in seclusion.

"Has your husband written to you at all?" Melanie asked gently.

Victoria shook her head. He'd left her the night after he'd made love to her, and in the morning he was gone. There was only a note explaining that he'd gone to supervise the rebuilding of her mother's house. She didn't know when he would return or why he'd left.

You should go back, her heart warned. But the thought of journeying alone to Scotland was overwhelming. She forced herself to walk outside each day, and though it was easier, the fear was still there. The only reason she'd made it to London was because she'd never let go of Jonathan.

Lady Rumford took another bite of oysters, and the scent was enough to send Victoria running. It was a sickening odor, cloying until she felt the bile rise in her throat. When she reached the stairs, the room spun, and she had to sit down to fight the dizziness.

"My dear, you look frightful." Lady Rumford had hurried after her, the worry evident on her face. "Are you unwell?"

Victoria kept her head down, trying to keep herself from fainting. "I will be all right in a moment." There was a roaring in her ears, and she added, "It was the smell of the oysters."

Her husband's aunt suddenly gasped. "Oh my. Oh my, oh my. You're going to have a baby, aren't you?"

"I think so, yes." She'd missed her monthly ever since Jonathan's departure, and all the symptoms were there. Though she hadn't consulted a doctor, she felt certain it was true.

"Why, that's such wonderful news!" Lady Rumford came to sit beside her on the stairs, patting her hair. "And so soon after your marriage bodes well for many children. I'd say this one will be born in the autumn, don't you think?"

If I survive that long. Victoria swallowed back the sickness and managed to lift her head. "I hope the duke returns before then."

Though she was both terrified and thrilled to be having a child, the months without Jonathan had been miserable. Her only consolation had been burying herself in designs for the undergarments. She'd sent the sketches to Mr. Sinclair, who had taken them to the crofters and brought her vision into reality.

Aphrodite's Unmentionables had become a wondrous success, and Victoria was more careful than ever to maintain secrecy. It was enough that the crofters' wives had work, and they were slowly earning their own fortunes.

She needed nothing for herself, but through the duke's generosity, she'd begun a charity project of her own. Although the Poor Laws had provided aid to those who could not take care of their children, she'd made arrangements with a local parish to provide special assistance to women—particularly those whose husbands were cruel to them.

She'd created a sanctuary for them, a small haven within the city where they were protected from husbands who beat them or their children. And she'd made arrangements for a more permanent building, a shelter named after Jonathan's mother. It had given her a purpose, another means of filling the endless days without her husband.

She took a deep breath, willing away the dizziness, though the nausea remained.

"Do you feel well enough to return to the dining room?" Lady Rumford asked, holding out her hands.

Victoria shook her head. "I'd rather not. I can't bear the scent of the oysters, if you don't mind."

"I remember those days well." The matron shuddered. "Thank the good Lord, the sickness passes. Else none of us would have more than one child."

Victoria rose from the stairs, taking Lady Rumford's hand, and excused herself. She pushed open the door leading outside and went to sit in the garden. The morning sunlight warmed her face, and Victoria sat upon a stone bench beside clusters of budding crocus and tulips. No longer did it feel quite so threatening to be outside, though she had not yet managed to pay calls upon her sisters.

Each day brought her closer to overcoming her fears, and she believed that she would eventually have the freedom her sisters took for granted. Closing her eyes, she lifted her face up, breathing in the scent of spring and of thankfulness.

The sound of a man clearing his throat interrupted her reverie.

"Your Grace, forgive me, but there's a caller for you," the footman said. "Mr. John Melford is here on behalf of the Earl of Strathland. He says he has a letter from your mother. I've left him waiting in the drawing room, but I can show him out if you are not receiving."

At the mention of Strathland, Victoria's heart quickened. Although no one had been able to prove that the earl had been implicated in the house fire, she had no doubt that he'd been responsible. The instinct to refuse Mr. Melford was strong, but she wanted the letter more.

"Can you ask him to give you the letter and I will see him another day?" She had no desire to speak with a stranger, much less a man involved with Strathland.

The footman shook his head. "He refused to leave it with me. But I have seen it, and it was indeed from Lady Lanfordshire."

Her nerves tightened at that. "Then I will receive him. But only if you and another footman are present in the room." She could have asked Lady Rumford to stay as well, but she suspected the contents of the letter would not be welcome news.

Steeling herself, she rose from the stone bench and followed the footman to the drawing room. The man sat on the edge of a chair, his hat in his hands. He wore a tattered gray tailcoat, and the cuffs were worn and frayed. His gaze slid over the room, as if taking note of her husband's wealth.

"Your Grace, I am John Melford, the Earl of Strathland's

factor," he said, rising at the sight of her, and inclining his head. "Thank you for receiving me." From within his coat pocket, he withdrew the letter. But he held it in his palm, instead of offering it to her. Victoria glanced behind her to ensure that the footmen were still present.

"Why have you come?" she asked.

He glanced behind him for a moment, then turned back to her. "Lord Strathland is aware that your family is rebuilding their house with help from His Grace's men."

"After the fire, yes." A prickling sensation crossed her spine, but she forced herself to gather courage. Already she knew the answer to the question she hadn't yet voiced. "The earl's men started it, didn't they?"

"Your footman, Mr. MacKinloch, started it," he corrected. "For reasons unknown to us. By now, he's on the other side of Scotland. It's unfortunate that the *accidents* continue." His brown eyes held a warning, and at last he held out the letter. "It would be better if your family sold off the land and returned to London. Ballaloch is a dangerous place."

The unveiled threat lingered between them, and Victoria took the letter. At the familiar sight of her mother's handwriting, a chill flooded through her. She'd believed Beatrice would be safe enough among the crofters, but now she wondered.

A wave of homesickness rushed over her, and she tore open the letter, skimming the contents. Her mother had written that both Jonathan and Victoria's father had returned to Ballaloch. Though her mother had never questioned why the duke had come alone, it was as if Beatrice had sensed their estrangement.

The duke might return to London if Victoria mentioned her pregnancy, but she'd only just become aware of it. Then, too, she wanted him to return of his own free will—not because it was expected of him.

The loneliness of being here without him left an aching emptiness inside her. If she were a stronger woman, she would return to Ballaloch and confront him. But the idea of making that journey again was unthinkable.

"I can bring your reply with me when I return," Mr. Melford said. "It would be no trouble."

"And what did you want me to write in the letter?" she demanded. Clearly, Melford had not come merely to deliver the message. His presence was here for another reason entirely.

"Ask your family to return to England," Melford said. "Sell the land and leave the crofters to us. Lord Strathland will offer an excellent price for the property, and you needn't finish building the house."

In other words, he wanted them to relinquish all control of the Highlands to the Earl of Strathland. That was the purpose for his visit—to threaten them unless they left. She could hardly believe he'd suggested it.

"I thought the earl lost part of his land in a gambling debt to my husband," Victoria pointed out, but Melford ignored her.

"The Scots can relocate along the coast and find new homes there," he finished.

"And if my family refuses?" Her skin had gone cold, just thinking of the fire. In her mind, she could remember the choking smoke and the wretched fear that she would die. Not only were her mother and father in danger, but so was Jonathan. It was entirely possible that he could be killed, and the thought was an anguish that rippled through her. She rested her hand upon her unborn child, as if to protect the baby.

Immediately, Victoria wished she hadn't done so. Melford hadn't missed the gesture, and his knowing look made her even more afraid.

"It's possible that your family would refuse the offer," he acknowledged. "But you remember what happened to your husband the last time he went to Scotland." His eyes drifted down to her womb. "It would be safer for all of you if you remained here."

Victoria tightened her grip upon the letter. He was trying to intimidate them, and she needed to warn her husband. "I will write to them," she agreed. "But I'll send my reply with my own messenger." That way, she could be assured that Melford wouldn't alter the contents of her letter. Cain Sinclair was in London, and she intended to consult with him. He, of all people, would know what to do.

As Melford departed, she closed her eyes, afraid for her family. But most of all, she feared for her husband.

⚘

"Victoria won't come," Margaret insisted. "She rarely leaves the house."

"You'd best hope she comes," John Melford insisted. The dull tone in his voice revealed a man who held no qualms about killing.

The air within her coach seemed suffocating, and Margaret eyed the door, wishing she were close enough to get out. They had pulled to a stop in front of the Duke of Worthingstone's town house. Rain spattered against the roof of the coach, a drenching downpour that made it impossible to see. She heard the driver dismount and suspected he'd gone to knock at the door.

Her thoughts spun out in a thousand directions as she prayed her sister's fears would keep her firmly ensconced in the house. But what if Victoria agreed? What if her sister defied her fears and ventured into the harsh weather? This man might kill them both.

Margaret steeled herself. She couldn't let that happen, especially now, when her sister was expecting her first child. She eyed the door, wondering if she should attempt to flee.

"We'll wait here," Melford said. "She'll come out to the coach as soon as she reads the note."

But Margaret shook her head. "Victoria won't leave the house. She's too—" *Afraid,* she almost said. Then again, she'd seen a change in her sister since she'd married the duke. Several times Margaret had come to call, only to find Victoria sitting in the garden or cutting flowers. It was as if her sister was determined to overcome her fears.

"When she reads my note, she'll come," Melford insisted. "If she values your life at all." To emphasize his words, he nicked the back of her neck with his blade. The warmth of blood dripped against her skin, the sting of the blade a harsh reminder of what was to come.

Margaret's pulse was pounding, and she wondered if the man would kill her when Victoria didn't arrive. She could only hope that her maid would know that she was missing and fetch help. Yet, doubt overshadowed her hope. Even if her maid *did* discover the truth, how would she know where Melford had taken her?

"Are you going to kill me if she doesn't come?" she asked, fearful of the answer.

Melford shrugged. "There may be other uses for you."

She didn't even want to think of what those uses might be. Margaret gritted her teeth, staring outside at the rain.

Don't come, don't come, don't come, she pleaded. Or if anyone came, let it be Cain Sinclair. The Highlander might be ill-mannered and rough, but he could save her easily.

The minutes ticked onward, and when nearly an hour had passed, the door to the coach opened. Outside stood Victoria, holding an umbrella over her head with a footman behind her. The moment she saw Margaret with the blade across her throat, she blanched.

"Get in the coach, and I'll let her go," Melford said.

"Run," Margaret begged. But Victoria stood frozen in shock, the umbrella falling from her hand. The expression of terror on her face meant she wasn't going to move and she might even faint.

The footman saw what was happening and tried to pull her back. "Your Grace, no!"

Melford met Victoria's stare with his own. "Tell your footman to get back, or I slit her throat." He pressed the knife harder, and more blood welled up on her skin. Margaret remained motionless, a tear rolling down her cheek. She didn't know what to do, but she believed this man would kill her.

"Please," she whispered.

Victoria turned to the footman. "Stay back."

"I decided that a visit to Ballaloch would suit better than a note," Melford said. "You'll come with me and convince your husband to leave."

At that moment, the footman lunged inside the coach to protect them both. In that moment of distraction, Margaret wrenched herself away from Melford.

"Go back!" she shouted to her sister. "Hurry!"

Victoria hadn't moved. Her face was stricken while rain poured over her, dripping from her bonnet as the two men struggled. Margaret grasped her skirts and tried to push her way out, but Melford caught her. In a last, desperate urge to escape, she threw herself from the coach. The world tipped, and a searing pain cracked against her skull as she struck the cobbled stones. She faded out for a moment, her head ringing.

When she opened her eyes, the last thing she saw was Melford forcing her sister inside the coach. The footman lay slumped upon the ground, a pool of blood widening beneath him.

Chapter Twenty

THE JOURNEY to Scotland was grueling, a teeth-rattling journey that numbed Victoria's mind and body. Melford had
changed drivers and coaches several times, never bothering to
stop for the night. The food he'd given her was stale and taste-
less, but she could have dined on the finest cuisine and never
tasted a bite, for all the fear within her.

She was his hostage now. After he'd killed her footman, she
didn't doubt that he would do anything necessary to achieve
Strathland's wishes. But at least Margaret was free. She prayed
her sister could go and get help.

Every mile was a torment, the world closing in on her. The last
time she'd traveled, she'd been with Jonathan, holding tightly to
him the entire time. It had terrified her, but she'd managed to
endure it. This time, she pressed her hand to the glass window,
uncertain she could bear it. Every mile brought back memories
she couldn't face.

Deep inside, she felt a slight pressure within her womb. The
barest flicker of movement, like a tiny hand reaching out. Victoria closed her eyes, pressing her hand to the small bump. Her
throat tightened, and she pushed back the terror. The movement
was a calming touch that gave her hope and the courage to continue. No longer was this about her own fears—it was about

protecting her loved ones. She would not sit back and become this man's victim. His act was of desperation, and that spoke of his own fear.

Though she didn't know what she could do to stop him, she was determined to make her escape when possible. Her unborn baby's life depended on it.

The snows had melted in the Highlands, but the roads were muddy and difficult to travel upon. When they reached the stretch of land near Glencoe, the driver abruptly stopped. Melford opened the door and the driver called out, "Someone's following us."

"Then go faster. We'll outrun him," her captor countered.

"It's too dangerous," the driver answered. "The mud's getting deeper, and the horses are having trouble."

"If they catch up to us, there will be more trouble for both of us. Do it," Melford ordered. He slammed the door shut and regarded Victoria. "I suppose your sister thought to send help."

She met his gaze. "She did. I'm certain of it."

The driver urged the horses faster, and the vehicle slid against the mud, veering sideways before they corrected their course. Victoria gripped the seat, fully aware that they were miles from Ballaloch. The rider would catch up to them, and she would seize her chance to get away. If only they were closer to home, the crofters might help.

Without warning, the coach slid sideways. She heard the horses rear up, and a harsh cracking noise resounded. A scream caught in her throat as the coach slid further and broke free of the horses. Instinctively, Victoria shielded her stomach, her body colliding against the coach as it turned upside down and rolled down the steep hillside. Pain lashed through her, and she heard Melford call out to the driver. When at last the coach went motionless on its side, he forced open the door and climbed out, closing it behind him.

Victoria's back ached, and she prayed that her child was unharmed. Dizziness swept through her, and she took a moment to gather herself before she attempted to stand up. The moment she did, a harsh cramp seized her.

Dear God, no. Please. Her hand moved downward to the baby, and she prayed she wouldn't miscarry.

The air inside the coach was suffocating, while outside the rain poured. She tried again to reach for the door handle, but she wasn't strong enough to force it open.

After minutes of pounding against the door and shouting, no one came. Victoria struggled against the handle, fighting back tears.

It's just like before, her mind warned. *You'll be left here to die.*

She closed her eyes, forcing back the memories of being outside in the cold, with no food or shelter. The terrifying isolation, of not knowing if anyone would find her, had paralyzed her with fear.

But she couldn't remain stranded here. Not again. She'd been lost the last time, wandering off the road in search of her family. This time, she knew better. If she could get out of the coach, she could follow the road, using the tracks of the horses that had gone before her. If she had to walk every last mile to Ballaloch, she would. Her hand closed over the handle, but just as she tried to push it open again, she heard gunshots.

Then silence.

Minutes later, the door opened and a shadowed face stared down at her.

☙

"It's an ill wind that blows," Mrs. Larson claimed, nodding to Jonathan as she barreled inside with her basket. "I saw two crows circling the house in this rain."

"Do come in," he said drily. The housekeeper came to visit the crofters on a regular basis and felt it her God-given duty to report to him about their welfare.

She eyed the footman Franklin and instructed, "Ye had best open all the windows."

"The windows?" The footman sent her a blank look, and protested, "But the rain will come in."

"I presume you wish to let out the evil spirits?" Jonathan asked.

The housekeeper shrugged. "It's your business if you're wanting tae keep the bad spirits lingering. The omens are there, and ye must pay heed."

"Go and open them, if you wish," he offered, gesturing for her to come in.

"I'll leave that to your man. He's your servant, not I." Mrs. Larson held out the basket to him. "Lady Lanfordshire sent these."

Jonathan lifted the cloth and saw hot currant buns inside. "You made them, I suppose."

"I did, though I don't know why she thought I should bring some to you. Leaving your lady wife in a town like London." She let out a frustrated sigh and lifted her hands up in surrender. "The poor wee lamb is surrounded by wolves. What kind of a husband do ye call yourself?"

"She's safer there than here," he pointed out. "Or are you forgetting the fire?"

"It's not right, a husband and wife apart. How are ye expecting to get any bairns on her?" She wagged a finger at him. "If ye were my lad, I'd—"

Her voice broke off when a crow suddenly struck a glass window. "Dear Lord, preserve us." Mrs. Larson glared at the footman. "Evil spirits indeed."

She lifted her shawl over her head against the rain and opened the door. At that moment, Jonathan saw a man hurrying across the glen, the rain pounding against him. Though he could not see the man's face, Mrs. Larson's prediction made him wonder why he was hell-bent on reaching the house.

When he saw the face of Cain Sinclair, a frigid tension gripped him. From his bedraggled appearance, it seemed as if he'd been running for hours.

Sinclair was out of breath, his clothing soaked from the rain. "Your wife . . . coach accident" was all he could say.

God above. The air left his lungs with the thought of Victoria hurt or dying. He couldn't bear to think of it. He could hardly speak but managed to ask, "Is she alive?"

Sinclair nodded, pointing back on the road. "About ten miles through the mountains. We need horses."

Jonathan's shoulders sagged with relief, though inwardly, he was shaking. He knew how terrified she was of the outdoors, and every minute she spent alone was nothing short of agony. "Why did you *leave her there?*"

"Melford took her hostage," Sinclair countered. "The bastard shot my horse, and the other two couldna make it this far. Looked like they went lame after the accident. Else I'd have brought her with me, long before."

"Where is Melford now?" Jonathan demanded, even as he ordered Franklin to prepare his horse.

"He had an accident," Sinclair answered quietly. From the glint in his eyes, Jonathan suspected there was no accident at all. "Follow me."

"I'll get some of the crofters tae help," Mrs. Larson said. She hurried out into the rain, drawing her *kertch* over her hair.

"Get the midwife, too," Sinclair ordered. "Just in case." His voice grew quieter, and the revelation left Jonathan speechless.

A midwife. The man's implication was quite clear, and a desperate fear roared through him. Not only had he abandoned her in London . . . but he'd made her pregnant.

He never should have left. He'd been angry with himself, confused by the emotions Victoria had provoked. The months he'd spent away from her had done nothing to diminish the feelings. Instead, her absence had only heightened how much he needed her.

When Jonathan's horse was brought by the groom, he mounted and rode hard, not waiting for Sinclair to take the lead. With every mile that passed, his fear multiplied. She was out there alone, and after such an accident, it was quite possible she'd lose their child.

What if he never saw her again? What if she not only miscarried their child but lost her own life, too? What if she died, never knowing how much he needed her?

The harsh rain needled his skin, transforming into ice crystals. He followed the endless road, wishing to God he could go back and undo his mistakes. He'd thought that he could bring her out of her fear of the outdoors, but the truth was, she'd led him out of his own hellish memories. The weeks he'd spent with her in Scotland had given him moments of light to heal his broken past.

She was his reason for being, his reason to breathe. He couldn't imagine returning to a life without her seated in a chair, stitching a seam. Or watching the frustration on her face when he won a game of chess.

He loved her, and no amount of gold would ever replace her in his life. He'd give every last pound to know that she was safe.

When he saw the remains of the coach on the bottom of the hillside, his heart stopped. The bodies of Melford and the driver lay upon the ground, and the awkward position of the factor's neck revealed the reason for his death. The coach lay upon its side, one door thrown open at the top. Jonathan guided his horse carefully down the hill, and when he reached the shattered vehicle, he climbed atop it, calling out, "Victoria!"

Strong arms held her close, the rain dampening her face. Though her body ached with pain, someone had found her.

"Thank God," she heard a man say. His deep baritone voice was familiar, though she kept her eyes closed. It sounded like Jonathan, though she couldn't bear to think of opening her eyes and finding out it was only her imagination.

"You came for me," she whispered to the husband in her dreams. She'd hoped he would. After Cain Sinclair had found her, she'd tried to get out of the coach. But the harsh pain had struck again, making her worry that if she tried to walk, she might lose the baby.

"I came as quickly as I could," he answered. He held her in his arms, carrying her until she felt herself being lifted onto a horse. "Are you in pain? Is the baby—" His words broke off as if he couldn't voice his worst fears.

Slowly, Victoria dared to open her eyes. At the sight of the duke, she couldn't stop herself from crying. It was a blend of joy from seeing him again and fear for their baby.

"It hurts," she admitted. "I don't know if I'll keep this child or not."

"I'm sorry," he murmured, brushing a kiss against her temple. "I was wrong to leave you for so long." He embraced her tight, and against her ear, he whispered, "You're everything to me."

"Take me home," she begged, burying her face against his neck. "Please."

He cradled her across his lap to keep her from being bumped by the horse too much. "Melford was going to use me to threaten you," she murmured. "The earl wants to control all of this land— my parents' and yours."

"I won't allow that." He held her close, and she embraced him as he urged the horse back. She dared to open her eyes, forcing herself to look at the road ahead. The mountains sheltered the valley between them, the green hills sodden with melted snow. Though it was freezing outside, she didn't feel the cold at all.

Jonathan had wrapped his coat around her, as if she were his most precious possession. She was too aware of her husband's arms around her and the words of endearment he whispered in her ear.

When they reached his lands at Eiloch Hill, she saw that his former house had been enlarged, with a new wing added. Surrounding it were dozens of thatched cottages, and one by one, the MacKinloch crofters emerged to ensure that she was all right. The men raised their hands in welcome, the women hurrying forward as Jonathan carried her from the horse.

The midwife, Bridget Fraser, awaited them. "We'll tend to her now, lad," Mrs. Fraser promised. "With God's grace, we'll save the wee bairn."

But as Jonathan carried her upstairs, his eyes stared into hers. He laid her down upon the bed and sat beside her. "I love you, Victoria." The dark torment in his eyes made her reach for his hand. "And I shouldn't have left."

She was about to reassure him, to answer his feelings, but he continued on. "If you never want to go back to London, if you want to stay here for the rest of your days, I don't care," he confessed. "You don't have to be a duchess. Just be my wife."

Seeing his fear made her long to put his worries to rest. "I love you, Jonathan. And wherever you go, my place is with you." She pulled him down into a kiss. "Just promise me one thing."

"Anything."

"Promise I'll never have to play chess with you, for as long as I live."

An abrupt laugh escaped him, as he embraced her. "Never again. I promise."

The days grew warmer and Victoria grew rounder. Though the midwife had confirmed that she'd only suffered bruises and the baby was fine, her husband had not once shared her bed. It seemed that he was terrified of hurting either of them. Even at night, when she'd leaned over to kiss him, he'd been overly protective, gently turning down her unspoken invitation to make love.

It was making her even more frustrated. As the pregnancy transformed her body, she'd grown more sensitive to touch. And frankly, she wanted her husband. She'd reimagined the last time he'd made love to her, many times, until she cuddled against him at night, wishing he would forget himself. Though she didn't understand why he wouldn't touch her, she'd decided she was tired of waiting.

The morning sun had barely creased the horizon when she awakened. Carefully, she lifted away the nightgown she'd worn and leaned over to Jonathan. He hadn't worn a nightshirt, and was naked except for a pair of cotton drawers. She moved toward him, pressing her bare breasts against his warm back. They were more swollen than usual, and she rather liked the way pregnancy had given her curves she'd lacked before.

Her husband was still asleep, and she reached around to the ties of his drawers. When she reached inside them, she found his manhood was thick and hard. A smile came over her as she squeezed it lightly, caressing him with her palm and fingers.

"Victoria," he whispered, his words filled with sleep.

"Shh." She touched him, delighting in the way his erection responded to her. He was hard, and with every stroke, she felt her own body growing moist.

"We can't," he gritted out, and she answered his words by moving her hand up and down in a rhythm. "God above, that feels good."

"Take off your drawers," she ordered, reaching to his waist. But he caught her wrists and held them steady.

"I would never forgive myself if I hurt you," he said. "If you lost the baby because I took selfish pleasure from you—"

"You haven't touched me in so long," she responded. "It makes me feel as if I'm nothing but a cow, as if you don't want me anymore." Her voice broke, and she fought back frustrated anger.

"I'm dying with wanting you," he answered. "Do you know how long it's been?"

"Almost five months," she said.

"Four months, three weeks, and five days," he responded. He rolled her to her back and his mouth came to kiss her throat. "Twelve hours and thirty-two minutes."

She smiled in the dark at that. "You don't know that for certain."

"And forty-five seconds," he finished, his mouth kissing a path lower. "Every night we were apart, I worried about how I'd hurt you."

"You didn't hurt me at all," she said. "But I couldn't understand why you left me—" Victoria closed her eyes, fighting against the bitterness that rose up.

"I was afraid," he admitted. "Not just of hurting you . . . but of the way you made me feel. It was the most powerful thing I'd ever known. I thought if I stayed away for a time, I could go back to being the man I was. I was wrong."

She shivered when his hand moved to touch her sensitive breasts. His tongue flicked across one, and she reacted strongly, her body needing him.

"I loved you, and I knew how badly I'd disrupted your life. I took you away from your home and tried to give you a world you didn't want."

"You should have been truthful with me." Her hands moved within his hair, arching when his mouth closed over the other nipple. She tried to reach for his body, to guide him atop her, but he withheld himself. "I would have gone willingly, if you'd given me time to adjust."

"Aunt Melanie wrote to me about what you did for the widows and orphans. About the shelter you built for them."

"It was a better use of your money than jewels or gowns," she said, guiding his hands down lower. He cradled the bump of her womb, and the light flutter within it made her smile. "I hope you don't mind."

"You gave sanctuary to women who had none. It's what I wished I could have done for my mother." He kissed her womb, and then brushed his hand over her mound of curls. Before he could move away, she guided his hand between her legs, revealing how badly she wanted him.

He let out a low breath, cursing when he touched her wetness. "God above, you don't know how badly I want to be inside you right now." He teased the hooded flesh above her entrance, and though she tried not to make a sound, the ecstasy of his touch was making her more swollen.

"I want you there, too."

But he ignored her, stroking her in a gentle rhythm that built up higher until she trembled. The sweet surrender broke through her in a shimmer of wondrous pleasure. A pleasure meant to be shared with the man she loved.

He lay back upon the bed, lying so still, she wondered what he was thinking. She reached out to touch him, and he was so hard, he let out a gasp as she closed her fingers over him.

"Victoria, no."

But she ignored him and lifted his hands above his head. "Don't move your hands from this position. Be assured that I won't let you hurt me at all."

He was rigid, almost groaning as she straddled him. "I've been thinking about you for so many weeks, wishing for another chance to be with you." She lifted his shaft, guiding him inside her, and he slid within her wetness as if he'd been made to fill her.

The exquisite sensation made her breathing shudder, and she gently lifted her hips and sank upon him again. Her husband's arms were taut, his body tense as she moved.

"You're killing me," he groaned. "You're so tight and wet."

"I want you to feel the same joy I felt a moment ago," she said. She wanted to bring him that rush of need, the torment and rise of ecstasy, until he found his release. But the more she rode him, the more her own body responded. Her breathing quickened as she took him inside as she transformed the pace.

Her husband was moving in counterpoint, thrusting as she took him deep inside. He ignored her demand to keep his hands where they were and instead reached up to touch her breasts.

"Again," he demanded. "I want to watch you shatter again. This time with me inside you." His fingers caressed her nipples, his thumbs pressing the sensitive tips as she ground herself against him. She took him faster, the wildness consuming her until she convulsed against him, the white heat spreading through every part of her body.

Jonathan grasped her hips and when she shuddered upon him, he took his own pleasure, a growl tearing from his throat as he filled her with his essence. "I love you," he murmured, still buried inside her as he gently guided her to rest on her side.

Victoria kept one leg over his hip, holding his head against her heart. Every part of her was satisfied, and she reveled in the love they shared. It didn't matter whether he was a duke or a servant. He was the man she adored, the man she wanted to share the rest of her life with.

"If you never want to set foot outside again, it would be all right with me," he teased, stealing a kiss. His hands moved up her spine, capturing her hair. "We could spend the rest of our lives in this bed."

She held him close, smiling as the sun filled their bedroom with light. "There will be time enough for that," she agreed. "But I won't live in fear again. Not with you at my side."

Epilogue

THE GARDENS bloomed with hyacinths. Jonathan stood on the stone pathway, watching his wife. She sat upon a wooden bench and cradled their infant son in her arms. Her rose muslin gown was adorned with ribbons that swayed in the light breeze, making her resemble a rare blossom. The ties of her bonnet had come loose, and he was thankful she'd remembered to wear a pelisse. Many days, Victoria was so eager to be outside, she forgot one.

Though it was early spring and slightly cold outside, she lifted her face to the sun and smiled. Little Christopher was bundled up in warm clothing, his blanket made of soft fleece.

The sight of them constricted his throat. Both his wife and son were the greatest gifts he'd ever received, and he marveled that they were his family.

When she saw him standing, Victoria smiled. "We've had a letter from Margaret. She's getting married in London and has asked us to attend."

"And you want to make the journey?"

She nodded. "I've already asked Mary to begin packing our belongings." Jonathan moved to sit beside her, reaching out for his son's hand. The small fingers closed around his knuckle, and he marveled that such a small being could have an enormous grasp upon his heart. But it was his wife who had become the other half of himself. He couldn't imagine living without her.

"Have you created any new designs for Aphrodite's Unmentionables?" he asked, his hand sliding around her waist.

"Perhaps," she said, enigmatically. "I may need your guidance. Some of the newer designs might be too scandalous."

The blush on her cheeks made him laugh. "I hope they are."

Turning serious, she said, "I thought you believed my sewing wasn't appropriate for a duchess."

"It is a risk, keeping this secret," he told her. "But if it pleases you to continue, I won't stand in your way. You should consider allowing your sisters to take command of the business, however, and send them the designs as it suits you." He leaned in to kiss the curve of her neck.

"Then we don't have to stop?"

"I see no reason to deprive the crofters' wives of an income. So long as no one finds out . . ."

"It will remain a secret," Victoria promised. She sobered a moment and asked, "You don't think the Earl of Strathland will cause any more trouble, do you?"

He shook his head. "I spoke with the wool buyers and made an arrangement. If he does not stay within his boundaries, they will not buy from him. His income depends upon his willingness to leave us in peace." Since the death of his factor Melford, the earl had kept to himself. It was enough.

Jonathan stood, offering his arm to lead them back inside. After kissing their son and giving him over to his nursemaid, Victoria took his hand in hers and guided him up the stairs.

With a wicked smile, she turned over her shoulder. "I'm wearing your favorite color this time."

His imagination conjured up the vision of his wife in a scarlet chemise and nothing else. She laughed as she ran up the stairs, knowing he would catch her. Jonathan took the steps two at a time and lifted her into his arms. Nuzzling her throat, he opened the door to his bedchamber and brought her inside.

He reached for the buttons of her gown and when he bared her skin, he found the crimson silk she'd promised. As he lifted the gown away, he saw her staring outside at the sunlight. And for a moment, he held her, sensing the wistfulness within her.

"I never thought I would be grateful for a gunshot wound," he murmured against her nape.

"You set me free." Victoria turned in his arms, raising her gray eyes to his. "For that, I will always be grateful."

He framed her face with his hands, and she stood on her tiptoes to kiss him. Against her mouth, he tasted the sweetness of their future together.

And it was a gift beyond price.

EXCERPT FROM *UNRAVELED BY THE REBEL*, BOOK TWO IN THE SECRETS IN SILK QUARTET

SCOTLAND, 1811

"YOU'LL BE the next to marry!" The housekeeper beamed. "Isn't that wonderful, lass?"

Dr. Paul Fraser never took his eyes off Juliette Andrews, though she was staring at the blue silk bonnet as if it were a poisonous snake. She'd caught her sister's wedding bonnet by accident, and the cheers were deafening.

Before he realized what was happening, the bridegroom had tossed his hat over the top of the railing. It was about to fall into the hands of one of the Highlanders, and Paul seized it before the man could lay claim to it.

He knew what the token meant, and he wasn't about to let another man court the woman he was determined to marry. Ever since he'd laid eyes upon her five years ago, when he was hardly more than an adolescent boy, he'd developed an obsession with Juliette. They had been friends for years, though she had grown more distant in the past year. He couldn't understand what had happened, but he was determined to win her affections.

She was an enigma to him, with her sad green eyes and the brown hair that often escaped from its topknot. Like her eldest sister, Juliette kept apart from the others. But she wasn't softspoken or a coward. No, there was an undeniable strength, and she never hesitated to speak her mind.

She shoved the bonnet into her younger sister Amelia's hands and started for the door. Paul couldn't have stopped himself from following if he'd wanted to. One of his friends, Rory MacKinloch, caught his arm.

"She's a bonny lass, but with a tender heart, Doctor. Mind yourself." Rory tightened his grip upon Paul, as if he considered himself Juliette's adopted big brother.

Paul shrugged the man's hand away. "I've known her e'er since the day she set foot in Scotland. I'd kill any man who threatened her."

A knowing smile spread over the man's face. "She doesna seem to be loving you back, Fraser. You might set your sights on another."

"She's the one for me. Always has been." He crossed through the crowd of wedding guests, knowing Juliette had slipped away outside. When he reached the front door, he opened it and saw that the clouded sky held the promise of rain. Juliette had grasped her skirts and was running toward the barn.

Paul fingered the hat in his hands and set it upon the doorstep. He trudged through the soft mud, ignoring the wind that buffeted his clothing. When he reached the barn, he stood at the entrance. Juliette had retreated farther inside, her hands resting against one of the stalls as if to steady her thoughts.

"You followed me." She glanced at him, her face frowning. "I was afraid you would."

She tucked a strand of fallen brown hair behind one ear. "Why won't you leave me alone, Dr. Fraser?"

"I'm watching over you," he said. "To be certain you're safe." It was partly the truth. But even more than that, he suspected that Juliette wasn't entirely angry with him. She crossed the distance and folded her arms across her chest, staring at him.

"I'm safe. Now you can go back with the others."

Her eyes blazed with frustration, and she pointed outside. Instead of obeying, Paul took a step closer. She didn't retreat, but instead stood her ground. "I said you should go."

"So you did." He reached out to take her hands, bringing them to rest upon his chest. Her gloved fingers were small, but when he released them, she didn't pull away. Instead, she glared at him.

"Why me? There are dozens of women back there who would fall down at your feet, if you would but look at them."

"They know it wouldna make a difference. There is only one woman I want."

"Not me."

But he remained silent at her insistence. He knew she was not indifferent to him, by the very fact that her hands were upon him still. He liked the soft pressure of her touch and the way she lifted her chin to defy him.

"We're meant," he told her. "Our fates have been tied together for years. Ever since the day I first saw you."

Her hands pushed back against him, but she only stumbled herself. "I've told you a thousand times. I won't marry any man, least of all you."

He moved behind her, his mouth against her ear. "Because I'm poor?"

"Poverty has nothing to do with it." She leaned her head back against him. "I know the sort of life you want. And it's not for me."

"I want the life every man wants. I want a wife and bairns. I want to spend my days making you happy." He leaned his face against her temple, but at his words, she jerked away as if he'd struck her.

"Leave me alone, Paul Fraser."

He took a step backward. "Is it all men? Or just me?"

She turned around, her eyes piercing. "All men. And if it's a wife and children you want, you should look elsewhere."

He said nothing, knowing that words would never wear her down. Someone had hurt her, he was certain. But like a stream that could wear down any mountain, he intended to quietly smooth away her reluctance.

"Why did you run?" he demanded. Though he kept his distance, she wrapped her arms around her waist, as if to ward him off. "Have I done something to make you afraid?"

"I don't want you to be led down the wrong path," she admitted. "I can't give you the life you want. It's not fair to let you believe in us."

"Tell me this. Why did you write to me, all those years whilst I was in Edinburgh?"

She lifted her shoulders in a shrug. "I was being polite."

"If you had wanted to forget me, you would ne'er have accepted any of my letters. But you answered every one." He kept her palm in his, watching the play of emotions over her face. "Something happened in the last year, didn't it?"

She went utterly pale at his words, and he saw that he'd stumbled upon the truth. "M-my father became a baron."

"No. That isna the reason. You're no' the sort of woman who cares about a title."

She flushed and pulled away from him. In her green eyes, he caught a glimpse of heartache, as if she'd lost the best part of herself.

"What happened to you, Juliette?" He deliberately used her first name, wanting to remind her of the days when they'd been close friends, hardly more than adolescents. "Did someone hurt you?"

She closed her eyes, crossing her hands around her waist. "You're a good man, Dr. Fraser. And you deserve so much more than a woman like me." Juliette braved a smile before she returned outside, leaving him to wonder about the secrets she held.

ACKNOWLEDGMENTS

First, I want to thank my agent, Helen Breitwieser, for believing in this book from the very beginning. You saw the potential and were an unfailing support every day of this journey. I'm so grateful to you for your faith in this story and in me.

Special thanks to Larissa Ione for being a true friend and for suggesting that I make the story slightly naughtier.

And thanks to Kelli Martin for giving this series a home.

About the Author

Frank Willingham, 2010

Rita® Award Finalist Michelle Willingham has published more than twenty books and novellas. Currently, she lives in southeastern Virginia with her husband and children and is working on more historical romance novels. When she's not writing, Michelle enjoys baking, playing piano, and avoiding exercise at all costs.

Visit her at www.michellewillingham.com or interact with her on Facebook: www.facebook.com/michellewillinghamfans.